ASYLUM CITY

Also by Liad Shoham

LINEUP

ASYLUM CITY

A NOVEL

LIAD SHOHAM

Translated from the Hebrew by Sara Kitai

HARPER

An Imprint of HarperCollinsPublishers

HarperCollins books may be purchased for educational, business, or sales promotional use. For information, please e-mail the Special Markets Department at SPsales@harpercollins.com.

Originally published as *Ir Miklat* in a different form in Israel in 2013 by Kinneret Zmora-Bitan.

FIRST EDITION

Library of Congress Cataloging-in-Publication Data has been applied for.

ISBN: 978-0-06-223753-8

14 15 16 17 18   OV/RRD   10 9 8 7 6 5 4 3 2 1

TO MY PARENTS, HAYA AND AVI

ASYLUM
CITY

Chapter 1

A blast of cold air struck Michal Poleg in the face when she stepped out of the bus in north Tel Aviv. She pulled her windbreaker tighter around her. She hadn't dressed warmly enough, as usual, and as usual, she hadn't taken an umbrella. At least there was a break in the "storm" the weatherman had predicted in dramatic tones. For the time being, it wasn't raining. That's how it always is around here, she thought. Two drops of rain and they call it a storm. But the real storms, the things that actually matter, get ignored. Typical. A white car pulled up in front of the bus she'd just exited and a man in a black leather jacket got out, glancing in her direction.

She started walking quickly, making her way from Milano Square to Yehudah Hamaccabi Street. In five minutes she'd be home. It had been a long day. She'd been working as a volunteer at OMA for just over a year. They usually closed at five on Friday, but on days like this, when it was cold and wet out, they were busier than normal so they stayed open late. The Organization for Migrant Aid couldn't keep regular business hours. They had to do what they could to find a solution for all the refugees who didn't have a roof over their head, and there were too many like that. But whatever they did, it was never enough.

Michal wasn't in a good place these days. She was sensing a regression, as if she was back where she was when she first came to work at OMA. Her rough exterior, the defenses she'd built up around herself, were starting to crumble. In the early days she'd sit openmouthed, listening in disbelief to the stories she heard, not knowing how to respond. She'd go home and lie on the couch with a bag of frozen vegetables on her head, staring at the ceiling. She couldn't take it in. She felt she was fumbling in the dark, that she'd landed in a strange place, on a different planet where she didn't know the rules. In time, she learned what to say, what she could and couldn't do to help, and mainly, how to listen in silence. It was all down to Hagos, their interpreter. He taught her that there was strength in silence, that sometimes just listening to people did more good than shouting to the high heavens. But shouting to the high heavens was exactly what she felt like doing now, because despite his strength and his silence, Hagos had been deported back to the infernal country he'd fled, and they'd murdered him there, just like she'd feared. She'd had enough. She was sick of feeling helpless, of being powerless to make a difference. She wanted to do something more than listen; she wanted to make a real change, not just put out fires.

That's why she filed a complaint with the Bar Association a few days ago against Assistant State Attorney Yariv Ninio. The lying weasel had concealed from the court the legal opinion of the Foreign Ministry that could have saved Hagos. Itai didn't want her to do it, but she felt compelled to take action. She couldn't sit back and do nothing.

As she crossed the square, Michal noticed that the tall man in the leather jacket was right behind her. His footsteps echoed through the open space, now deserted due to the "storm" and the late hour.

The refugees she worked with needed her to be focused and dedicated. They could sense when she was on edge. Without Hagos, she had no one to talk to. Itai was too busy, and lately every conversation with him ended in an argument. She found it hard to talk to Arami, the other—now the only—interpreter. She knew how devoted he was to the men and women who came to them for help, and she always felt guilty around him, as if she were responsible for their hardships. She had the feeling he regarded her as a government agent: rich, white, complacent.

Michal glanced behind her. The man was less than two yards back. He looked her directly in the eye, his face expressionless. Here she was in the old north of Tel Aviv, presumably one of the safest sections of the city, and she was frightened. She regularly wandered the slums around the old bus station that were home to the refugees without sensing any fear. People just didn't understand. Racism and prejudice were so deeply embedded that it was very hard to uproot them, especially when the government and that loathsome Member of Knesset Ehud Regev were conducting a relentless campaign against the refugees, labeling them "dangerous," "drunken," "violent," and "disease carriers." Try to explain that they were human beings just like us who wanted nothing more than to live a normal, quiet life, that one of the main reasons they left their homes and their homelands was to escape the violence.

She kept up a quick pace, attempting to put more distance between herself and the man behind her. I'm probably paranoid, she tried to convince herself. She turned right into a side street just to be sure. Across the street from her was a clinic, its windows dark. She passed a small playground, filled with toddlers and their nannies in the morning, but empty at this hour of the evening. The swings were swaying back and forth in the wind. She realized she hadn't imagined it. The man was following her. She heard his footsteps coming closer.

In Michal's world, there were two types of Israelis: the ones who tried to help, to do the right thing, and the ones who wanted to hurt or exploit. It was a polarized world with no middle ground. You were either a devil or an angel. She had no doubt which category the man stalking her belonged to.

She started walking faster. Despite the cold, she was soaked in perspiration, her blouse sticking to her skin. What the hell was she supposed to do now? It was a mistake to turn into this quiet little street. What was she thinking?

She'd never seen the man in the leather jacket before, but she was sure he was sent by the people she'd confronted near the office a couple of days ago. Hagos had told her explicitly to steer clear of them, but she couldn't hold back. Her mother was right. "My little Michal has a knack for getting into trouble," she liked to say with a sigh.

Two months had elapsed since she went to the Police Department's Economic Crime Unit. That was the first thing she did when Hagos was deported. She reported what Hagos had told her about the "Banker." She'd even managed to snap a picture of him coming out of a restaurant on Fein Street, and she handed that over, too.

But meanwhile, nothing had changed. The "Banker," whose name she still didn't know, continued to walk free around the old bus station. When she saw him there again the day before yesterday, she couldn't control herself. She was just coming from a shift at the women's shelter on Neveh Sha'anan Street, an experience that invariably left her feeling depressed, when she saw him mingling with a group of refugees, strutting around cockily in his fancy suit as if all was right with the world. She accosted him in the street, screaming that he was an extortionist bastard, a filthy crook whose money funded rape, smuggling, torture, and slavery. She didn't give a second thought to the women peeking out in fear from behind the curtains. He looked at her with a mixture of shock and bewilderment. It seemed like he was about to say something, but before he did, two goons, obviously his bodyguards, grabbed her by the arms and dragged her away, and none too gently, either. The "Banker" vanished into an alley, fleeing like the chicken he was. His goons released her and walked away. But she wasn't finished. She followed them up the street, yelling, "Scumbags, maniacs, gangsters." Passersby stared at her in astonishment. "Who do you work for? Who gets the money?" she screamed at them. She was positive the "Banker" and his goons were only a link in a bigger chain, that someone more powerful was calling the shots, most likely a large crime syndicate that spread its tentacles out in all directions, destroying, devastating, exploiting, crushing. They ignored her. As soon as they reached the corner, a car pulled up beside them and they disappeared inside.

That's what happens, she thought. When the government doesn't provide basic services, a vacuum is created, and that vacuum is filled by all sorts of scum. When people don't have work, they drink and shoot up; when they don't have doctors, they go to back-alley abortionists; when they can't use a proper bank, they turn to the "Banker," whose organization rakes in millions. The refugees had no choice. They couldn't walk around all day with everything they owned on their back. They needed loans to survive and a way to transfer their earnings to their families back in Africa. The government turned a blind eye, it didn't want to know, creating an opportunity for ruthless thugs to take advantage of the weak and impoverished.

She knew all too well that her screaming wouldn't make any difference. The "Banker" would continue to demand money and the refugees would continue to pay exorbitant interest. But at least now they'd know they were being watched, that they couldn't just blithely go about their business, because despite what they might think, somebody cared. Michal also wanted to give meaning to Hagos's death, maybe even make up in some small way for the fact that she wasn't able to prevent his deportation. Hagos wouldn't have been happy about her attempt to get at the "Banker," but that would just be fear talking, the result of the defenselessness imposed on people like him by the establishment.

She turned her head again. The man was still following her, gazing straight at her. She realized he didn't care that she could see his face. In fact, it seemed as if he wanted her to. She started running, slowly at first and then faster. She could hear his steps quickening until he was running behind her. The sound of his footsteps hitting the sidewalk reverberated through her body.

She couldn't let herself feel scared, and more to the point, she couldn't let them see she was scared.

"What do you want?" she said, stopping suddenly and turning around. She was breathing heavily.

He stood and stared at her in silence, his eyes trained on hers. There was no one else around. A cat wailed, making her jump.

"Why are you following me?" she asked. Her mouth was dry.

He didn't move, just kept looking at her with a blank expression on his face.

"Who do you work for?" she persisted. Her breathing was still not steady. His silence was threatening.

Hearing footsteps approaching from the other end of the street, Michal swung her head around. A second man in a black leather jacket was walking toward her. He could have been a twin of the first one. She stood caught between them, not knowing which way to turn. Her heart was pounding. She had to do something—now! "What do you want from me?" she asked, not managing to keep the tremor out of her voice. She was willing to sacrifice her life for something meaningful, but not like this, not without accomplishing something first, not when she was just getting started.

The first man advanced toward her. She wanted to scream, but she was paralyzed by fear, unable to move a muscle or force any sound out. Why had she come down this street? She'd played into their hands.

He stopped no more than a yard away and she thought she saw his right arm move. He was going to hit her. She threw her arm up to shield her face, but his hand shot out, grabbed her raised arm, and twisted it behind her. A kick to her knee made her drop to the ground. The pain was agonizing. She struggled, but they didn't let up. Her face was slammed into the cold asphalt by a blow to the nape of her neck. Her nose and mouth filled with blood. One of the men flipped her over, sat on top of her, and gripped her throat with one hand, bringing his face close to hers. She got a strong whiff of inexpensive cologne that made her stomach turn. She tried kicking at him to free herself, but it was useless. She didn't want to die. Not here. Not now. Not like this.

Chapter 2

ITAI Fisher returned the bicycle to the docking station outside Habima Theater. "Leave it a few blocks from her apartment," Ronny had instructed him on the phone yesterday, "so when you get there you're not sweaty and out of breath. In fact," he explained, "it's better if you don't let on right away that you use rental bikes, that you don't have a car. If she asks how you got there, where you parked, try to change the subject or say something vague about how you don't live so far away. And remember, don't start going on about pollution, living green, saving the environment." Itai didn't manage to get a word in before Ronny added, "At least not until you get laid."

Ronny's advice was getting on his nerves. He wasn't a sixteen-year-old virgin about to go on his first date. He didn't need someone to tell him what to do. It wasn't cool. The stock jokes at his expense were also getting tired. But no matter how much he felt like slamming the phone down in Ronny's face, he didn't. Ronny was his best friend, maybe even his only friend. They'd grown up together in the same apartment building in Holon, gone to the same schools, served in the same army unit. He knew Ronny loved him like a brother, and he knew he meant well. Besides, like his mother always said, if something irritates you, it's probably true. It irritated him whenever she said that.

Since Miri dumped him six months ago, he hadn't had any serious relationships, just casual sex now and then with some volunteer who was more interested in emotional release than she was in him. He had no explanation for it. Maybe it was the job. He worked too hard in an occupation that was too draining, and he was physically and mentally exhausted when he got home. Yeah, it was easy to blame the job.

Itai started up the street, gradually getting his breath back. He loved riding a bike, and he loved the feel of the wind on his face as he pedaled nimbly, especially now in the winter when the air was clear and bracing. Besides, it was the only quiet time in his day when he could think in peace.

He pulled the cell phone from his pocket. It was Saturday, but still, in just the twenty minutes it had taken him to get here, he'd gotten three messages: one was from a Sudanese man who hadn't been paid his wages, one from a man from Eritrea who'd been evicted, and one from his mother wishing him luck on his date. He knew he should be mad at Ronny for telling her, but he just laughed. The truth is, he figured his mother was in on it as soon as Ronny started saying things like "We're not getting any younger," and "People shouldn't be alone." It wasn't the first time he realized they talked about him behind his back. Whenever Ronny came to visit his folks, Itai's mother would come down from her apartment two floors above—"I just happened to drop in," she'd tell him—to pump him for information about her son. Quite a few years had passed since he left home, but she still hadn't gotten over the fact that she couldn't simply walk into his room to "tidy up" and search for clues to his private affairs. When he complained to Ronny about colluding with her, his friend just grinned and said, "You know your mother's unstoppable." Since he *did* know she was unstoppable, that she always got what she wanted in the end, he decided to take it in stride. Let them talk. As for the two Africans, he'd get back to them after the date or tomorrow morning. There was nothing he could do on a Saturday night at this hour anyway.

The one person he was hoping to hear from hadn't called. He was disappointed not to see a message from Gabriel. He'd bought watercolors and brushes for him yesterday and was curious to know whether he'd used them. Although he tried to treat all the asylum seekers the same, he felt closer to some than to others. Gabriel's shyness and modesty drew him in. And it didn't hurt that he spoke very good English. It was easier to forge a connection with someone when you didn't have to go through an interpreter to talk to them. He didn't discover Gabriel's artistic abilities until the young man began to trust him and open up to him. He was extraordinarily talented and sensitive. "I guess we know what our grandkids are going to look like one day, Dov," his mother said under her breath to his father when he told his parents about the African's drawings at one of their family dinners.

HIS phone rang as he was turning right into Sheinkin Street from Rothschild Boulevard. Michal. He breathed a deep sigh. He liked her, even though she was what his mother would call a "difficult lady." Michal was the ultimate volunteer. She didn't miss a day. She was a hard worker who gave her all for the asylum seekers who came to them for help, one of what Ronny called his "suicide bomber types." But they'd been butting heads lately. She wanted them to take a more aggressive approach, to take action against the cause of the disease and not just the symptoms. He disagreed. In his opinion, it was better to concentrate their efforts in one area and not go off in all directions. A small group like OMA couldn't fight the big battles. Their job was to help people with problems that were critical to them, no matter how small and mundane they might seem. He could barely raise enough money to keep the organization going, and now that MK Ehud Regev had started accusing agencies like OMA of being traitors to their country, it was even harder to find donors. The politician's words were beginning to have an impact. It's easy to scare people, especially when there was no obvious solution, when the reality of the situation was so complex and had so many implications. Mounting big campaigns, filing lawsuits, or appealing to the High Court of Justice would eat up all of their resources and leave them with nothing to offer the asylum seekers who needed their help so badly.

They argued about it again yesterday. Michal told him that despite his objections, she'd filed a complaint against Yariv Ninio with the Bar Association, accusing him of being a racist who was responsible for the murder of Hagos and others, and demanding his disbarment. She maintained that the Foreign Ministry had determined that deporting migrants to Ethiopia on the grounds that they were illegal aliens from Ethiopia, and not refugees from Eritrea as they claimed, put their lives at risk, and that Ninio was aware of that opinion and had not only concealed it, but had argued repeatedly in court that the deportees were in no imminent danger.

Itai was livid when he heard what she'd done. Despite his contempt for people like Ninio and everything they represented, and despite the fact that, like Michal, he'd been very fond of Hagos and was deeply affected by his death, he didn't believe OMA should go to war against the State Attorney. Especially not when Michal didn't even have any proof that the ministry's legal opinion really existed. And they definitely shouldn't make accusations of a personal nature. During the hearing on the appeal against Hagos's deportation order, he'd been very much aware of the tension between Michal and Ninio, and he didn't think it had been in Hagos's best interest.

Itai thought he'd convinced her it would be a mistake to file the complaint, and now it turned out she'd gone and done it behind his back. He was furious with himself for not keeping a closer eye on her. He should have anticipated that she'd go ahead with her plan.

ITAI declined the call. Michal had tried to reach him last night and several times today. He was screening her calls. He didn't have the energy to fight with her again. They couldn't even agree on Gabriel, their joint project. He thought he should be allowed to go on drawing and painting freely, to express himself however he wanted, and when the time came and he was ready, they'd help him take his art to the next level. But Michal wasn't willing to wait. She was never willing to wait for anything. She wanted things to happen now. A few days ago she'd reamed him out for not using his connections at the Bezalel Academy of Art (his uncle was a professor there) to arrange a scholarship for Gabriel.

He stood still for a minute and looked around him at the busy street. The cafés were crowded. The skies had cleared, ending a string of rainy days and drawing hundreds of Tel Avivians outside. He spent most of his time in a different part of the city. It was equally crowded there, but much less pleasant. So near and yet so far.

The girl he was going to meet—Ayelet—worked in the architects' office with Ronny's wife. "She's a great girl and she's hot, so don't screw up," Ronny had said, sending him to check her out on Facebook. He liked what he saw. Ronny had always had good taste in women. She seemed nice when he spoke to her on the phone, too.

"BESIDES the business with the bike, do you have any other advice for me?" he asked Ronny after taking a deep breath and counting to ten.

It turned out his friend had a whole litany of advice, including a list of subjects he shouldn't bring up: foreign workers, migrants, social protest, cartels, crooked politicians, affordable housing. "I swear I don't get you," Ronny went on. "So many women ripe for the picking. If I were in your shoes . . . I've got to say you're an embarrassment to men everywhere. Instead of going out and having fun, you spend all your time dealing with the problems of people whose lives are so deep in shit there's nothing you can do for them. What about it, Itai? Can you have a conversation without mentioning the women who are raped in Sinai? Think of it as a favor to me."

"How about the weather? Is that okay?" He had to give a little after such a histrionic speech.

"Well, I don't trust you to talk about anything else, so the weather sounds like an excellent way to go," Ronny shot back.

"So I can tell her how cold it is in Levinsky Park, how the asylum seekers stand around all day in the rain, shivering and hungry, and no one gives a damn?"

"No worries. You keep joking about it and I can promise you one thing: you're not getting laid."

"Okay, fine. I've got it. I can only talk about how the weather affects people in north Tel Aviv."

"And take her someplace normal, a café or a pub," Ronny went on, ignoring his last remark. "Not to a demonstration or some restaurant run by refugees. Can you do that?"

"Café. Cappuccino. White sugar, not brown. I ought to write this down," he said, smiling.

"Asshole." Itai could imagine the smile on Ronny's face at the other end of the line, too. "And if, heaven forbid, she orders chicken breast, don't make a face. Just take a deep breath and think about the breasts on her, okay, bro?"

HE walked to the end of the block and turned left into Melchett Street. Again his phone started ringing. Michal again. He resisted the urge to pick up. It's just her way to trigger my sense of guilt, he reminded himself, to make me feel I'm not doing enough. He knew that tomorrow she'd find some reason to read him the riot act in any case.

Ronny was right. He deserved a night off every now and then. If he picked up, they'd just argue and it would ruin his mood.

Deep in thought, he didn't notice the woman approaching.

"Hi," she said, extending her hand. "Ayelet." Her skin was warm and smooth. He felt his body respond to the scent of her delicate perfume and her tight black dress.

"Hi. I'm Itai," he answered. "I heard there's a great pub around the corner."

Yes, tonight he was going to take a little time off from himself. The phone in his pocket was still ringing. He ignored it.

Chapter 3

THE winter sunlight streaming in through the window was making Yariv Ninio's eyes sting. He reached out automatically to the other side of the bed. It was empty. His bladder was full. He started to get up, but a stabbing pain in his head forced him back down.

He wanted to call out for Inbar, but his mouth was too dry. His tongue felt like rubber.

He lay in bed, weary from a night of restless sleep. His temples were throbbing. Suddenly he remembered that Inbar had left on Thursday to spend a few days in Eilat with her girlfriends. An early bachelorette party. He didn't get it. The wedding was two months away but she was already frantic. He didn't have the strength to deal with all the drama.

Again he tried to sit up but was hit by a wave of nausea. Last night he'd gone out to a bar with Kobi. He shouldn't drink so much. He always regretted it the next morning.

The pressure in his bladder became intense. Yariv pushed himself up into a sitting position. Dizzy and headachy or not, he had to get to the bathroom before he burst.

When he was finally on his feet, he found it hard to breathe. He realized he had a stuffy nose. He looked down and a shiver ran through his body: he was fully dressed. He'd slept in his clothes, his shoes still on his feet and ugly brown stains on his shirt.

A fragment of memory from last night suddenly flashed through Yariv's mind: he's standing outside Michal's building shouting profanities at her. Then he's knocking on her door, calling out to her, waiting to tell her to her face what he thinks of her complaint, what he thinks of her in general.

He made his way as quickly as possible to the bathroom, struggling for breath.

"Go away, Yariv. Go home. You're drunk." Michal's voice resounded in his head.

He gaped in surprise when he saw his face in the mirror. His nose was swollen and his nostrils were clogged with dried blood. Under his eyes were dark blue bruises that were already turning black. What the hell had happened to him? More to the point, what the hell had he done?

Chapter 4

WITH a few quick strokes of his pencil, Gabriel Takela was trying to capture the arc of the pigeon's wing as it perched on a power line looking down at the street below. He was getting soaked by the rain, but he ignored it, just as he ignored the stench from the large green Dumpsters filling the space behind the restaurant. When he was drawing, he was totally absorbed in the emerging picture, even if it was no more than a pencil sketch in a small pad. It helped him escape. At such times he didn't think about the present, the future, or the fact that nothing was likely to happen anytime soon that would change his life for the better.

He sketched trees, animals, buildings, children, occasionally adults—Israelis he saw in the street. He felt compelled to. Forms and colors accosted him everywhere, begging to be captured on paper. But he never drew anything from home. Or women. It aroused too much emotion and longing.

Yesterday Itai had brought him watercolors and brushes. Gabriel could barely contain his excitement. He desperately missed painting in color, breathing life into his black-and-white drawings, yellowing the leaves and greening the grass and attempting to capture the colors of a white man. He was so overwhelmed, he hadn't even opened his present yet.

He knew he was good, that he had a keen eye and a quick hand. Even Michal had asked him to draw her. Despite his reluctance, he eventually gave in. Michal and Itai were like family, the big brother and sister he never had. He didn't have anyone else. There used to be Hagos, but Hagos was dead. Before that there was Liddie, but she was dead, too.

Amir, the restaurant owner, allowed them a fifteen-minute break every three hours. They also got a free lunch and could take home any food that was left over at the end of the day. Amir was a good man. He paid them a decent wage, and he paid on time, too. John told him the law said they should get more, but it was enough for him. Before Gabriel found this job he'd worked for people who paid much less and never let him take a break.

Not far away, three other Eritrean boys who worked in the restaurant were sheltering from the rain under an awning. Gabriel kept his distance, not joining in their animated chatter. He didn't used to be like this. Back home he'd had lots of friends and loved to be the center of attention. But that was a long time ago. Now he was a different person.

Just as he began on the pigeon's feet, it spread its wings and he watched it fly away. He was bringing his eyes back down to the pad when his cell phone rang.

"Gabriel?" He recognized the speaker immediately. Her voice was shaking.

His body responded with a shudder to what his head still hadn't grasped. Was it possible? He was afraid to hope. He dreamt so often of hearing her voice. He could imagine the moment, the instant he would get a sign of life from her. He agonized constantly over what had happened.

"Gabriel?" she asked again, and his eyes filled with tears. He heard a hacking cough in his ear.

HE thought she was dead. The others urged him to accept it. At the border, just before Rafik released them, he asked where she was. Rafik moved his finger across his throat and grinned. Gabriel's body was weakened and exhausted, but nevertheless he felt the blood rushing to his head. He wanted to kill him right then and there. He didn't care about the consequences or how close he was to Israel and freedom. Rafik raised his rifle and cocked it. Gabriel saw him place his finger on the trigger, the same finger he'd gestured with. If the others hadn't pulled him out of the way, the Bedouin would have shot him without flinching, like he once saw someone shoot a rabid dog in his village back home.

"LIDDIE?" he asked hesitantly, still afraid to believe it. His voice was trembling with emotion.

THE last time he'd seen her was in Sinai. Rafik had his eye on her from the beginning. It frightened them both the way he looked at her. There'd been rumors in the refugee camp in Sudan about the things the Bedouins do to women. Gabriel put his hand on her shoulder to indicate that she belonged to him, that she was a married woman, although in actuality she was his little sister. Liddie hid her face as best she could, trying to make herself invisible. Rafik didn't make a move on her the first two days. Just stared. Gabriel allowed himself a sigh of relief. But the third night, everything changed. The Bedouin woke Liddie up and dragged her out of the tent by her hair. Gabriel raced to her defense, throwing himself at Rafik. But Rafik wasn't alone. Two of his henchmen grabbed Gabriel and held him down. No matter how hard he struggled, he couldn't free himself. Rafik dragged Liddie away, screaming and pleading. Like him, she resisted, and like him, she could do nothing to save herself. Michael, one of the other men in their group, tried to come to their aid, but a third Bedouin struck him in the face with the butt of his rifle, drawing blood. After that, no one else moved.

"LIDDIE, is that you?" he asked again.

He heard a bloodcurdling scream at the other end, followed by more coughing.

"Liddie?" He was shouting, causing his three workmates to turn and look.

"Help me, Gabriel . . . help me," he heard between tears and coughing.

WHEN Rafik disappeared with Liddie, the Bedouins holding Gabriel started in on him, kicking him in the head, the abdomen, the ribs. Their feet kept coming, as if he were the ball of rags they used to kick around in their schoolyard soccer games. At some point he lost consciousness. When he came to he found himself chained to the rest of the men in their group. Michael offered him some water. The long cut on his face was infected. For several days he burned up with fever. He owed his life to the Israeli doctors who treated him.

"THEY beat me, Gabriel . . . help me," Liddie begged.

"Where are you? Tell me where you are," he shouted frantically.

More coughing.

"Liddie?"

"Gabriel?" The voice was male.

"Give me back my sister. What are you doing to her?" He was crying now, too.

"Listen up, you son-of-a-bitch. If you want to see your sister again, it'll cost you twenty-five thousand shekels. You got one week. Be in Levinsky by the slides on Thursday. We'll find you. You don't bring the money and we kill your sister, understand?"

Gabriel didn't know what to say. The excitement of hearing Liddie's voice, of learning that she was alive, had been replaced by anxiety and horror. Where would he get that kind of money in a week? The little he earned he sent back to their mother who had stayed behind.

"Understand?" the man repeated.

"Help me, Gabriel, help me," he heard Liddie crying out in the background, pleading as she had done the last time, in Sinai. He hadn't been able to save her then, but he wasn't going to let her down again.

"I understand, don't hurt her!" he yelled.

The call was disconnected.

Gabriel stood there motionless for a few moments, gripping the phone tightly in his hand. He'd heard about calls like this. The Bedouins in Sinai set a price for the passage to Israel, and then in the middle of the desert they demanded more. If you didn't pay you were tortured. People called their family, their friends, anyone who could raise the money. Meanwhile, they were held hostage.

But the man on the phone wasn't a Bedouin. He was speaking in Gabriel's mother tongue, Tigrinya. Had Liddie crossed the border? Was she here in Israel?

A chill went down his spine as he recalled how he himself had been tortured. He reached out and touched the scar on his left cheek. Like the burn marks on his hands and feet, it was a memento that Rafik's Bedouins had left on him for the rest of his life.

Where had Liddie been all this time? What were they doing to her?

GABRIEL was standing at the bus stop, his drawing pad clutched to his chest. He'd asked Amir to let him off early. Time was running out. If he couldn't come up with twenty-five thousand shekels in a week, his little sister would die. Those people had no conscience. He knew that.

He had to find a way. He'd promised his mother before they left that he'd take care of Liddie. Now, every time he sat down to write her a letter, he felt too ashamed, too guilty, to tell her that his sister wasn't with him.

Where would he get the money? He lived with fifteen other Eritreans in an apartment near the old Tel Aviv bus station, five to a room. He and John shared a mattress. It had taken a long time before he could afford the luxury of a mattress and a roof over his head.

Gabriel had heard about a man who went to the Israeli police when he got a call like this. His son was murdered.

He had to talk to Michal and Itai. He had to tell them. They were good people, and smart, too. Maybe they could tell him what to do. He called Itai's cell phone several times but got no answer. When he called OMA, Naomi told him Itai hadn't come in yet. He was at a meeting in Jerusalem. He called Michal at home, but the line was busy. She was probably still there. She didn't arrive at the office before two o'clock on Sundays. He couldn't wait. He had to talk to her right now. She wouldn't get mad, she'd understand. She said he could get in touch with her at any hour of the day or night if he needed help.

Gabriel got on the bus and found an empty seat. He didn't look the other passengers in the face. They didn't look at him, either. He'd already learned that Africans were invisible to Israelis. They could stand right next to you and not notice you. Just don't look them in the eye or make any trouble. Then they noticed you and got scared. And only bad things ever happened when they were scared.

Chapter 5

YARIV listened with half an ear as attorney Shlomo Lankry argued before the court. He had no patience this morning for the self-righteous homilies of a man whose eloquent orations about social justice and morals didn't prevent him from fleecing his clients.

The slightest movement of his head was painful. Yariv had managed to clean the clotted blood from his nose, but it was still sore and swollen. The two aspirin he'd taken hadn't done much good, either. He would have gone to the doctor if he didn't have to be in court, even though there wasn't much point. As an army medic, he'd seen quite a few broken noses in his time, and he knew there wasn't a lot you could do.

He also had another reason for preferring to be in court this morning. It kept him from thinking about last night. It was too daunting, particularly the fact that he couldn't remember how he'd gotten his injuries and what exactly had gone down with Michal.

But he was getting antsy. He wanted to go back to his empty apartment, close the blinds, and go to sleep. He didn't have the strength for anything else, including Inbar, who'd called from Eilat. As if he cared where Sivan stood on the question of a sit-down dinner versus a buffet. He could tell from her tone that she was offended when he brushed her off, but he didn't care. He had more urgent things to worry about.

There was no doubt in Yariv's mind that Michal would use whatever happened last night to get back at him. After all, she'd already filed a formal complaint with the Bar Association.

THEY'D dated for a couple of months about three years ago when he was a criminal prosecutor handling rape cases and she was a volunteer at one of those women's organizations that ran a hot line. She was all right, no more than that. Cute face, reasonable body, big ass. Some-where between a six and a seven. He hit on her because he thought it would be good for his career, that he'd get bigger cases if she con-vinced the poor women she worked with to ask for him by name. It never happened. At least not like he was hoping. He broke up with her after a while when he got tired of her and her holier-than-thou attitude. If there was one thing he couldn't stand it was self-righteous jerks, and Michal was the mother of all self-righteous jerks.

They ran into each other on a regular basis ever since, not only be-cause of their work. They lived in the same neighborhood, just a few blocks apart. He was over her, with Inbar now, but he still couldn't get out of his head the things she used to do in bed. He'd never had sex like that with anyone else. He was pretty sure she was having the same thoughts whenever they bumped into each other. Yet despite the sexual tension between them, they always remained civil.

All that changed a year ago. That's when he got moved to the State Attorney's Office and was assigned to handle the petitions filed by illegal aliens against deportation orders. Meanwhile, Michal had found time among all her rape victims and battered women and the rest of the wretched of the world to volunteer at some aid organiza-tion. She began to treat him like the enemy. He figured she still resented him for dumping her.

Every time they ran into each other in the street, she took the opportunity to lecture him in raised tones. It pissed him off the way she berated him. And he was sure she was sleeping with that African of hers, Hagos. The thought disgusted him. There was no line the girl wouldn't cross when it came to sex. He could testify to that himself.

"MR. Ninio?" The judge's shrill voice interrupted his musings. He'd appeared before her dozens of times and didn't have a very high opin-ion of her. Today he actually hated her. Her voice was drilling a hole in his head.

He rose and threw her an irritated look for intruding on his thoughts. Before leaving the house, he'd used Inbar's makeup to try to hide the bruises under his eyes. He hadn't done a very good job. Inbar's complexion was paler than his, and he didn't know what to do with all the creams, tubes, powders, and the rest of her junk. When he went by the office to get the file, Eran in the next room asked him what happened to him. "I fell off my bike," he said shortly, disappearing into his office. At the start of this morning's proceedings, the judge asked him the same question and he gave her the same answer. It was none of their business.

"How does the State stand in respect to the petition?" she asked with obvious impatience. He realized his mind had been wandering again and he was standing there looking like an idiot with makeup on his face. There was nothing he hated more than being caught off guard.

"The State objects," he answered firmly, although he had no idea what they were talking about. Objecting was a conditioned reflex for lawyers. "If you don't have anything to say—object," he remembered being told by his mentor when he was an intern.

"Would our learned friend like to share with us the grounds for the objection?" She wasn't going to let up.

"My colleague's petition is irrelevant. It is nothing but an attempt to divert the proceedings from their true purpose, which is to determine whether the State's determination that the petitioner is not from Eritrea but from Ethiopia is unreasonable," he reeled off, sitting down demonstratively. Why did she have to badger him?

The judge gazed at him for a moment and then reiterated his objection for the record.

He didn't even have to glance at the file to phrase the objection. He'd argued against enough of Lankry's petitions. The man filed them by the armful, and the wording was always sloppy. Illegal aliens had enough problems, they didn't need another one in the form of a hack who demanded huge fees to file a worthless petition.

Lankry specialized in them. He promised his clients they had nothing to worry about, collected his fee in advance, and then wrote a
petition virtually identical to the ones he'd filed in the past for other
illegals, and which had previously been denied by the court. When
the judge rendered the decision, his client was being held pending
deportation and couldn't do anything about it. Of course, he'd already taken his money.

AS the hearing continued, Yariv allowed his mind to wander again.
He was incensed by the complaint Michal had filed against him. She
claimed he knowingly presented the court with false information and
was guilty of deception, fraud, and falsification. Because of Assistant
State Attorney Yariv Ninio, and he alone, her African boyfriend had
been murdered.

He didn't give a damn what she claimed. What bothered him
was that the complaint revealed the existence of the report prepared
by what Ehud Regev called "the bleeding hearts in the Foreign Ministry," which stated that aliens deported to Ethiopia faced a concrete
threat to life. Michal argued that concealing the document was tan-
tamount to holding a gun to the deportee's head. She demanded his
disbarment on the grounds of conduct unbecoming a member of the
bar. The complaint made his blood boil, especially when he read her
repeated reference to him as an "unenlightened racist" and a "serial
killer in legal disguise."

LAST night he'd caught sight of Michal from the bar on Ibn Gvirol
Street where he was having a drink with Kobi. She was right across
the street. From that moment on, he hadn't been able to think of
anything else. He knew he'd have to justify himself, defend himself
against her allegations, maybe even reveal their history, and it drove
him around the bend. He was sure there were plenty of well-meaning
souls who'd use the complaint as an excuse to deny him permanent
status in the State Attorney's Office as he'd been promised. He had

some friends in high places, but those people had enemies, too, and he was an easier target.

"YOU'RE up, Mr. Ninio," the judge prodded.

The minute he started talking, she'd attack him. She'd say she was uncomfortable with the State's position and threaten to grant the petition. He'd have to submit to her tirade and take her abuse. Out of the corner of his eye he would see Lankry's client smiling, convinced the judge was on her side, that she was going to win. But the judge and Lankry knew as well as he did that it was just for show. It was always the same in the end. She'd rule in favor of the State and sanction the woman's deportation.

Over ninety-five percent of the petitions filed on behalf of illegal aliens were denied. Yariv himself had a near-perfect record. Like everyone else in the office, he wanted to advance and land high-profile cases. And who gets them? The prosecutors with the most wins to their credit.

Ehud Regev had promised him he had his back. Now Yariv had to pressure him to make good on that promise. He was sick and tired of this garbage, of all the migrants and their lawyers. That wasn't why he'd decided to become a prosecutor. What kind of private practice could he start later on with a specialty in illegal alien cases? He had to move on, and the sooner the better.

THE judge glanced at her watch.

"I suggest we adjourn for thirty minutes. We'll reconvene at twelve o'clock," she declared, rising.

Grudgingly, Yariv packed up his things. What a waste of time, and just when my head is about to explode, he muttered to himself.

"If I were you, I'd give up now. You're going to lose," Lankry said, speaking in English for the benefit of his client.

"Yeah, right, like always. You're so used to beating me," Yariv answered derisively.

"You look like you've already taken a beating this morning. What happened? You rub somebody the wrong way?"

Unable to hold back, Yariv stuck his face in Lankry's and grabbed him by the lapel. "Don't mess with me, Lankry. It's not a good idea," he said menacingly before letting go. The other lawyer took off without responding.

Yariv exhaled. This really wasn't his day. He tossed two more aspirin in his mouth, found a quiet corner, and pulled out his cell phone. It was the last thing he felt like doing, but he knew he had no choice. He needed to apologize to Michal, even if he couldn't remember what he was apologizing for. If he could persuade her he'd done it because he was still in love with her, because he was jealous or something, she might cut him some slack, maybe even withdraw her complaint. He couldn't afford to let her ruin his career over something stupid. She wasn't worth it.

It had been a long time, but he still had her number in his phone. He tapped his foot nervously while he waited for her to pick up. The fact that he couldn't remember what happened last night was doing his head in.

Chapter 6

WHEN Itai turned his cell phone back on at the bus stop, he suddenly remembered Michal. He'd been screening her calls all weekend, planning to get back to her on the way to Jerusalem this morning. But he got home so late from his date with Ayelet last night that he fell asleep on the bus.

His spirits were high. The meeting at the hotel with the potential donor from Florida had gone well. No promises were made and no check was handed over, but he was optimistic. Itai wasn't a novice at this. The meeting had lasted an hour and a half, not the typical ten minutes. And unlike most people, Abe hadn't sat there sighing, "How awful." To Itai's mind, there was nothing more sanctimonious and predictable than that "how awful." He knew by now that "how awful" people didn't really want to know. They didn't want the details. They didn't care, and he wouldn't get any support from them. They just said what was expected of them and moved on. Abe was different. He didn't cluck his tongue and he didn't cite his family history and his "moral duty to help refugees." He asked about the specifics of their work and the costs involved.

Itai still had a good taste in his mouth from his date, too. He'd followed Ronny's advice not to be Itai Fisher and just go with the flow. Surprisingly, it worked. It turned out he was capable of going a whole evening without Supreme Court petitions and human rights violations. Ayelet laughed at his stories about Ronny (that was his friend's idea, to make sure he didn't talk about his work), he laughed at her stories (and she had lots of them), and they kissed at the door to her building. Determined to take "not being Itai Fisher" as far as it would go, he asked if she'd like him to come upstairs with her for a coffee. He had to confess he felt relieved when she said, "Maybe next time." There were still limits to how much change he could tolerate in a single evening. He decided to walk home. His head was completely clear of concerns about candidates for deportation, unpaid wages, and temporary visas, and he reveled in the moratorium he'd imposed on himself.

So he was just now listening to his messages. "Itai, it's me again." He heard Michal's voice. "Why haven't you gotten back to me? I've been trying to reach you for two days. I don't get it. Why are you ignoring me? Is this some kind of game? I'm always there for you when you need something from me."

Her schoolmarm tone was irritating.

"I'm not just nagging you for no good reason. I need to talk to you. It's urgent," the message went on, eliciting a sigh from Itai. Everything was always urgent with Michal. Her world was black-and-white. Asylum seekers were saintly martyrs, the government (particularly the Immigration Police) was evil incarnate, Regev was the Devil, and Ninio was his apostle. You were either good or bad, and you had to choose. It was a childish attitude, he thought. Reality was more complicated. A life of poverty and hardship didn't automatically produce good people. And like it or not, Israel couldn't, and shouldn't, be the solution to Africa's problems. So even though he knew it didn't fit the public image of liberals like him, he believed firmly in the need for a border fence. That was another bone of contention between Michal and him.

"I wanted to tell you in person, but since you're not talking to me, I'll have to do it this way. It might interest you to know that I was assaulted last night on my way home. Two men. They roughed me up. . . ."

Itai stood frozen in place as the bus pulled up and the doors opened.

"I'm all right, more or less. Mostly, the idiots just wanted to scare me. But they don't know who they're dealing with," she said with a trace of bravado in her voice.

Shaken, he sat down on the bench at the bus stop. He hadn't

been expecting this. Michal assaulted? By whom? The bus went on its way, leaving him there.

"That's not the only reason I'm calling. I found out something today and I'm in shock." He could hear Michal's breathing quicken. "We've been blind the whole time. I have to talk to you. Please, please, call me back. I don't care what time it is. It's extremely urgent."

Chapter 7

GABRIEL was sweating despite the cold. He was running as fast as he could, fleeing Michal's apartment before her neighbor could catch him and call the police.

He crossed one unfamiliar street after another until he didn't know where he was. He was gasping for breath and his body was cramping. The injera he'd eaten before leaving for work rose in his throat. When he couldn't go any farther, he stopped at a corner where there was no one around. Panting and frightened, he retched violently.

HE didn't plan on going into her apartment. Not even when he knocked on the door and saw it slide open slightly. He just stood where he was and called out to her. When he got no answer, he started to turn around and leave. He'd see her in a couple of hours at the OMA office, he consoled himself. Besides, he thought, he'd been in such a rush to find her and tell her about Liddie that he hadn't given himself time to think about what to say. Then he heard her neighbor coming up the stairs and a dog barking. He didn't want any trouble. Michal had told him about her crazy neighbor who yelled at her all the time and hated Africans. Gabriel was a little scared of the dog, too. It barked at him whenever he came here. That was the only reason he went inside.

WITH halting steps, he made his way back to the main street. His shirt was stained with vomit. His eyes burned. The city had become a threatening place again, like when he first arrived in Tel Aviv. He'd never seen so many people before, so many cars and buses. He came from a small village in Eritrea near Keren where everybody knew everybody and everybody knew him. He was put off by the unpleasant smells coming from the stores around the old bus station, bewildered by all the strange food inside. People walked too fast, talked too fast, and it made him dizzy. And he felt anxious all the time because he didn't know the rules in this new place, didn't know what to say, what he was allowed to say.

People were staring at him as he continued unsteadily down the street. He felt like shouting, screaming, letting out the pain filling every inch of his body. But he didn't utter a sound. His brain told him there were certain things he must not do. If he wanted to survive, he had to remain faceless, invisible.

RIGHT away he could see that Michal was dead. The bruises on her face and her vacant eyes said it all. He'd seen dead people before, in his village, in the refugee camp, on the way to Israel. He wanted to go to her and cover her face, close her eyes, say good-bye, but his feet carried him backward step by step, pulling him out of the apartment. Unaware that her neighbor was standing behind him in the doorway, he bumped into him as he retreated. The dog started barking wildly and the neighbor spat something that sounded like a profanity. Michal lying there, white and lifeless on the red carpet. . . . He couldn't deal with it. His head was pounding. He ran. The sight of Michal's body on the floor continued to haunt him.

WHEN Gabriel reached the old bus station, he collapsed onto a bench in Levinsky Park and burst into tears. He cried for Liddie, for Hagos, for Michal, and for himself and his miserable life. People passed by, barely glancing his way. Everyone here carried the burden of their own sad story on their back.

At the restaurant he saw Israelis laughing because they had a happy life. They threw food away without thinking twice. And his life? Nothing but sorrow, pain, and hardship. Why? Where was the justice in it? Hagos and Michal were such good people. They helped migrants like him find their way through the confusion and fear.

Without them, he might never have gotten out of this park. Now they were both dead and he was back here.

And what about Liddie? What had his little sister ever done wrong? What was he going to do now?

Itai! Gabriel got up and started in the direction of OMA. Suddenly, he stood still. What would Itai say when he told him? He knew Itai was fond of him, but would he still feel the same way when he heard how he'd fled from Michal's apartment like the coward he was?

No. This wasn't the time to talk to Israelis. He needed someone like him, someone who would understand. But who? His mother was far away, and he hadn't made any real friends in the few months he'd been in Israel.

Arami. He could go to Arami, the interpreter at OMA. He'd heard good things about him. They'd even spoken a couple of times. People said that Arami was very sensible, that he offered practical advice, not just idle words. The Israelis liked him, too. He'd helped them out once in the detention camp when he first arrived, and he spoke English very well. That's why they offered him work as an interpreter. He translated for the police and sometimes in court. Arami would help him. He needed someone like him to tell him what to do.

Chapter 8

ANAT Nachmias realized she'd walked into a trap the moment she entered the restaurant. She didn't even need to call on her training as a police officer and deputy chief of the Special Investigations Unit. The evidence was right in front of her eyes: her parents were already there. In all her sixty years, her mother had never gotten anywhere on time.

Her folks had an unchanging ritual. Wherever they went, they arrived at least half an hour late with her mom, out of breath as if she'd just run a marathon, exclaiming, "I'm so sorry, but I had to finish . . ." Then came a story about some chore that, if left undone, would have resulted in a terrible tragedy.

That was her dad's cue to jump in, complaining, "She's going to kill me one day the way she's always late. I almost had a heart attack." Turning to Anat, he'd say, "Your mother is planning the perfect murder. Show me a jury that would convict her. They ought to teach her tactics in the police academy."

Her parents were not only there on time, they were holding hands. Okay, now she knew something was going on, and it wasn't good.

"Who's sick?" Anat decided to cut to the chase.

They looked at her, baffled.

"Well, your father's cholesterol is high, and me, I've got high blood pressure, you know, because of the circumstances. But all in all, thank God . . . ," her mom said.

"Why do you think someone's sick?" her dad asked.

"No reason. My mistake. Forget it," Anat said with relief. Still, there was something fishy about this lunch. She didn't buy her mother's story that they'd simply decided to take a day off from work and happened to be near her office.

"To tell the truth," her mom began hesitantly, "Dad and I want to talk to you about something important."

Up to a few years ago, whenever her parents wanted to talk to her, it was always about the same subject: her job. They couldn't get it into their heads that their bright delicate little girl had decided to become a cop. They regularly joked about cops going around in pairs, one who knows how to read and one who knows how to write. They were contemptuous of the police, claiming they were incapable of solving crimes, and they still held a grudge against every cop who ever wrote them a ticket. And then all of a sudden they discovered they'd raised a policewoman. There was a weed in their garden. It was years before her mother was able to utter the words, "My daughter is a police officer." Before that, she'd always say she was a civil servant. Even now she invariably added, "But she also has a law degree. She graduated first in her class."

It took Anat a long time to convince her folks that their nagging wouldn't do any good. Their daughter was a cop, and that wasn't going to change.

When the "why don't you quit your job and we can be a normal family again" phase was over, her parents (her mom, to be exact) found a new subject to harp on: she was over thirty (thirty-two, to be exact) and still single. Her mom didn't care that she'd put herself out there but hadn't managed to find the right man. She took the fact that she wasn't married as a personal affront. Every Friday night at the family dinner she was forced to listen to her mother's lengthy philosophical musings over how the Goldsteins' daughter Dikla, with her crooked teeth, was already married, and the Zilberbergers' daughter Efrat, with her big nose, already had a baby, while their lovely daughter didn't have anyone.

Although Anat kept her opinions to herself and answered her mom's laments by assuring her, "It'll all work out. Sooner or later someone will want me," she, too, was upset that she had no one. There were days when she got home from another bad date or scanned the dating sites on the Internet in vain that she began to harbor the fear that she'd be stuck like this, alone, for the rest of her life. She ridiculed her married friends whose lives were a monotonous routine and who were run ragged by their kids, but she also felt a twinge of envy.

Not surprisingly, her mom drew a direct line between her single status and her work. After all, what normal man would want to marry a woman who had such a masculine job, a woman who spent her days dealing with rapists and murderers? There was no chance she'd find a husband at work, of course. Who would her well-educated daughter, the girl who graduated at the head of her class in law school, choose to go out with—the cop who could read or the one who could write?

A waitress in a black uniform took their order. When her mother said she'd just like a glass of water, she wasn't hungry, Anat became even more anxious. Her mom didn't need to put on a whole production for the "do you know what it's doing to your poor mother to see that you're still single" speech. Normally, she just picked up the phone.

"So what is it this time, Mom?" she asked impatiently when the waitress left.

"Listen, Anat honey," her mother said, pausing to heighten the drama. She'd always had a well-honed sense of the theatrical.

"Yes?" she urged.

"It's not easy for Dad and me . . . ," her mother began, pausing again.

"What isn't easy?"

"First of all, I want to tell you that we love you, and whatever you say, we'll understand," she said, glancing at her husband who nodded in agreement.

"What are you talking about?"

"Listen, honey," she repeated, hesitating once more before going on.

"Spit it out, Mom. The suspense is getting on my nerves."

"Your mother thinks," her dad intervened, "that maybe, and it's fine, sweetheart, I mean . . . we'll understand. . . . In any case, your mother thinks that maybe you like girls more than boys."

"What?" Anat spluttered, her astonishment making her voice louder than necessary, causing several heads in the restaurant to turn in their direction.

"It's the way you dress," her father explained, nodding at her baggy ripped jeans. "Mom read on the Internet that it's the style favored by . . ."

"It was a very good article. It made everything very clear," her mother cut in. "What girl would decide to become a cop if she didn't . . ."

Anat's parents looked at her expectantly.

"You think I'm a lesbian?" she said, breaking the silence. She was still stunned. "First of all, you can both relax. I'm not. Second of all, if I were, I wouldn't be ashamed to tell you, believe me. And about being a cop, come on. That's so absurd, it isn't even worth wasting my breath."

"So explain to me why you told Ohad, the Blausteins' boy, that you don't want to go out with him."

She knew she should be mad, but she couldn't keep from laughing.

"Well done, Mom, very well done," she said, clapping her hands.

"Anat, sweetheart, what's wrong with you?" her father asked.

"I've said it before, Dad. The fact that Mom isn't an interrogator is a huge loss to the police force. When it comes to mind games, nobody . . ."

"Enough, Anat," her dad said firmly. "We're very glad you're not . . . and even if you were we'd support you, because we love you and there's nothing wrong with it. But that's no reason to insult your mother."

"I'm not insulting her. Look, I'll spell it out for you," she answered, trying to catch her mother's eye. The older woman was looking down at the table. "Mom knows I'm not gay. All this nonsense about what she saw on the Internet is a diversion. She's just mad that I wouldn't go out with Ohad Blaustein after she worked so hard to persuade his mom to get him to call me. That's the whole story. Your role here is . . ."

"So why wouldn't you? Do you know how embarrassing it was for me to face Bilha?" Her mother broke in before she could explain to her dad that he was merely a pawn in his wife's game.

"He's nice enough, but what can I say? He doesn't do it for me. I wasn't trying to embarrass you or offend him. It happens. Like I told you on the phone, I appreciate the effort."

"I just can't understand it, honey," her mother replied, placing her hand over Anat's. "If you keep on like this . . . what are you waiting for? Prince Charming? You know, when I met your father . . ."

To Anat's relief, her phone started ringing and the beeper in her bag came to life. It was like a gift from heaven.

"Hold on a second. It's work," she said, interrupting her mother who was about to tell her how her dad courted her and she rejected his advances because he was chubby and she didn't find him attractive, but in the end she gave in and it hadn't turned out so bad.

"Nachmias?" It was Amnon, the duty officer. "Female body at 122 Stricker Street. Possible homicide."

"On my way," she said, disconnecting.

"I have to go. Something came up," she said to her parents as she gathered her things together. "We'll continue this engrossing conversation later, I promise," she added, seeing the disappointment on her mother's face.

"What happened?" her dad asked.

"Could be a murder." The turning point in her dad's attitude to her job came when he started to see her name in the paper.

"And you'll be involved in the investigation?" he asked, still surprised by the kind of work his daughter did.

"I doubt it," Anat was forced to admit. "My boss is at a seminar in Austria. They'll probably hand it over to Major Crimes."

"You can't go out dressed like that, honey. It's freezing outside," her mom scolded.

She glanced at her reflection in one of the many mirrors in the restaurant. The figure she saw didn't look like a police detective worthy of respect. She took out a rubber band and used it to pull her hair back in a bun. That was the most that a skinny five-foot-two woman with freckles could do to make herself look older and more professional.

Her phone rang again. The heavy coughing on the other end told her it was her boss, David, the head of the Tel Aviv District Special Investigations Unit. She'd never met anyone who smoked so much, and there were a lot of smokers on the force.

"Nachmias, I spoke with the District Commander," he began before being stopped by another bout of coughing. "I want this case. I'll be back in three days. You're in charge till then. The DC will talk to the Chief. I told him I trust you two hundred percent and he has nothing to worry about until I get back."

"Do you think they'll play along?" she asked, stealing another glance in the mirror. She'd been too lazy to wash her hair last night and now it was frizzy. Who would hand a case to someone whose hair was sticking out in all directions?

"I'm working on it, doing everything I can from this end," he said with another cough. "You just do your job."

As usual, he didn't wait for a reply before hanging up.

Chapter 9

GABRIEL gazed at Arami expectantly, waiting for him to say something, to offer him some consolation after the horrifying experience he'd just told him about. They were standing in an alley not far from Arami's house. The rain was beating down on the plastic awning above their heads. Garbage bags were piled on the sidewalk.

Arami's continued silence unnerved Gabriel even more.

"You believe me, don't you?" he asked, pleading. "You believe I had nothing to do with it?"

"Of course I believe you, Gabriel," Arami said finally. "I know you didn't kill her."

Gabriel felt a little calmer. At least he wasn't alone. He raised his eyes for the first time since he'd finished telling his story. The expression on Arami's face seemed wise and sad at the same time.

"What should I do?" The fear filling his chest felt icy.

"I'm thinking, Gabriel, I'm thinking," Arami said, moving deeper into the alley.

Gabriel followed, his heart racing. It felt like his head was going to burst.

"Maybe I should go to the police and tell them what happened," he muttered.

Arami said nothing, just kept looking around nervously.

"I've heard you say they don't really care about us. We're like bugs, it doesn't matter if we live or die," Gabriel went on. "But still . . . maybe . . . I mean, if I tell them how it happened . . . that Michal was already dead when I got there . . . maybe . . ."

"It's not that simple," Arami said with a sigh, taking a seat on an upside-down vegetable crate.

"But you know people there," Gabriel said. "Maybe if you tell them you believe me. . . ." He'd heard the story of how Arami came to work for the police many times. There weren't a lot of success stories like his among the refugees. When Arami arrived in Israel, they threw him in the detention camp like everyone else. Then one Friday night, a pregnant Sudanese woman started screaming that her baby was coming. The handful of soldiers left on weekend duty didn't know what to do. Arami took charge. After assuring the young soldiers, in very good English, that he knew what he was doing, he delivered the baby. In gratitude, the Israelis gave him a job interpreting for the police. Michal explained that Arami sat in the interrogation room and told the Eritreans what the cops were saying and vice versa. Sometimes they even asked him to translate in court. Gabriel said he could do that, too. He also knew English. His father was a minister, he taught him. But Michal didn't think it was a good idea. They had no interest in helping the cops, she said. An older man like Arami had no choice. He needed steady work because he had to send money back to his wife and children in Eritrea. But that wasn't the case with Gabriel.

"We have to think, not rush into anything," Arami said, interrupting his gloomy thoughts.

"Do you think I should talk to Itai? He's a good man," Gabriel suggested reluctantly. He knew how hard it would be for him to tell Itai what he'd seen.

"No, absolutely not. You can't trust any Israelis," Arami said firmly. The rain had picked up. Water was streaming down the flimsy awning. Gabriel's teeth were chattering from the cold.

"I can't go back to my apartment," he said, stating the obvious.

Arami nodded in agreement.

"So what do you think I should do?" he asked to break the silence. He was beginning to wonder if Arami really believed him.

"For the time being, the best thing for you is to hide out in the park," Arami said finally.

Levinsky Park is the first stop for all the migrants who arrive in

Tel Aviv. During his first two and a half months in Israel, Gabriel had stayed there, too, sleeping on two cardboard boxes he found in the market and covering himself with one of the thin blankets handed out by the aid workers. When it rained, he took shelter under the awning of a butcher shop, shivering in the cold. It would be easy to hide among the hundreds of anonymous faces in the park.

"I'll do what I can to help you. They don't think we're human beings. They can go on believing we just came down off the trees, but we know we're good people. I'll help you. We Eritreans have to stick together," Arami said, putting a hand on his shoulder.

Gabriel couldn't resist hugging Arami before he took off. He couldn't remember the last time he'd embraced anyone.

It was still raining heavily as he walked down the street. He was soaking wet, but he had to find a place to hide. The police were probably looking for him already. Michal's neighbor had seen him. Even if all Africans looked the same to them, he was sure to remember the scar on his cheek.

Chapter 10

ANAT wasn't surprised to see Eyal Ben-Tuvim from Major Crimes pulling up at the crime scene. On her way here, David had called again to warn her that Eyal was trying to snatch the case away from the DC. "Lean on the gas and get there fast," he'd bellowed. David might be in Austria, but he was still trying to run the show as if he were right here in Tel Aviv. Grabbing the case for his unit wasn't just a matter of pride or ego. It was personal. David and Eyal had been rivals ever since the academy. And the fact that they'd both been in the running for David's current job didn't help.

"What's up, Nachmias? Since when does David let you out on your own?" Eyal asked nastily.

"I'd rather be on my own than with you guys from Major Crimes," she retorted with a saccharine smile.

"We're catching this case. Call David and tell him he can light another cigarette and go on eating Wiener schnitzel in Vienna," he shot back as they both strode quickly toward the building. A homicide in a peaceful neighborhood like north Tel Aviv could be a godsend in the race for promotion to superintendent. It would get a lot of press and the brass would be keeping a close eye on the investigation. It was also a refreshing change not to have to deal with the murder of another junkie, wino, or hardened criminal taken out by one of his kind.

They passed the two patrolmen posted at the entrance to the building and started up the stairs. The first minutes were critical. They had to seal off the area as hermetically as possible and try to freeze the crime scene so they could get a picture of it just as the perp had left it. It wouldn't be long before the place was mobbed with the ambulance crew, the CSI team, the medical examiner, and, of course, the higher-ups: the chiefs of Major Crimes and Intelligence, the DC, the Region Commander. In the academy they taught you to leave the scene undisturbed, not to let anyone in, not even the Chief of Police himself. But in the real world? Well, that was something else entirely.

Amnon, the officer in charge, was waiting for them at the door to the apartment. Anat guessed that one of the patrolmen downstairs had responded to the call.

"CSI, the medical examiner, and the mobile lab are on their way," he informed them. "And an ambulance. But you can see for yourself the paramedics won't have much to do here."

A woman in her late twenties or early thirties was lying on the living-room floor. Her blue eyes were wide open. There was a large bruise—dark blue and swollen—under her left eye, and a long scratch on her right cheek. Four small blue marks showed on the left side of her neck, with a larger one on the right. Anat didn't need the medical examiner to tell her that the victim had been strangled, that whoever did it used only one hand, and he was right-handed. The woman's head was twisted backward at an awkward angle. Anat could see bruises on her arm through the sleeves of her thin white sweater.

"Allow me to introduce you," Amnon said. "Michal Poleg, thirty-two. She's single like you, Nachmias. No record."

As usual, when Anat arrived on the scene the male officers became more interested in examining her than in examining the body. They were just waiting to see a twitch of revulsion or, even better, a tear. When she first made detective, she spent hours practicing her poker face in front of the mirror. She knew that the sights she'd be exposed to would turn a man's stomach, too, but as a woman, she didn't have the privilege of letting it show. By now she'd seen enough bodies in all sorts of disgusting conditions that she didn't have to make an effort to keep her composure. She sometimes wondered what her family and friends would think if they could see how coolheaded she was around a corpse.

"Imagine that," Eyal said, "someone else your size."

Anat was used to the jokes about her height, too. She didn't rise to the bait.

The two detectives pulled on gloves and crouched down next to the body almost simultaneously. Just at that moment, the CSI team made their entrance.

"Make sure to take pictures of everything and go over the room with a fine-tooth comb," Anat said. They threw her a look of disdain. To be honest, she sounded ludicrous even to herself. David had impressed on her the importance of marking their territory by barking orders in all directions. "You have to piss in every corner so they know it's your turf," he'd instructed her over the phone in typically graphic language.

"So what're you thinking, Nachmias?" Eyal asked in a condescending tone.

If it was anyone else, she would have said, "I don't think there's any point in questioning her," but she held her tongue. Eyal had no sense of humor.

"The marks on her neck indicate she was strangled. We have to find out if she was raped first, but I doubt it. It doesn't look like her jeans were disturbed."

In an almost synchronous movement, they both felt the body to check for rigidity.

"Less than twenty-four hours," Anat said quickly before Eyal could ask her again what she thought.

They rose and began surveying the scene. The room was filled with heavy, dark wood furniture. An elaborate chandelier hung from the ceiling. Anat opened one of the dresser drawers and was hit by the strong smell of moth balls. Inside were ironed white sheets with flowers embroidered around the edges, the sort of thing her grandmother would have.

If she had to guess, she'd say Michal had inherited the apartment and everything in it. It didn't seem to reflect the taste of a woman her age.

One picture stood out among the framed tapestries on the walls: a delicate pencil sketch of the victim gazing into the horizon. Moving closer, Anat saw it was signed with the letter "G" alone. Books and newspapers were strewn on the floor and an empty beer bottle stood on a small side table next to the sofa. The coffee table was broken, the glass shattered. Wondering if Michal was the sort to sit on her couch drinking beer on her own, she looked around for another bottle or a glass, but she didn't see any.

"There was a struggle." For some reason, Eyal felt the need to state the obvious.

Anat strode to the door to check for signs of forced entry. There weren't any. Michal Poleg knew her murderer.

Something caught Anat's eye. She brought her face close to the dark metal door. She missed it before when she came in and went straight for the body, but now she saw there were bloodstains on the outer side of the door.

She gestured for one of the CSIs to take a sample. Eyal was watching her every move.

"Find something?" he asked skeptically.

"Blood," Anat answered, taking care to sound as impassive as if she was talking about the weather.

"Take a sample and send it to the lab," Eyal directed the CSI, who nodded obediently. Anat wondered how he would have reacted if she'd said that.

"You should talk to her next-door neighbor," Amnon advised.

Both detectives turned to him in surprise. Canvassing the neighbors wasn't usually top priority, especially not in an area like this where it was less than likely that any of them would do a runner.

"He witnessed the murder," Amnon explained. "The patrolman told me."

"Okay. Make sure nobody messes with the scene and check every surface for prints," Eyal commanded, making a quick exit. He seemed to be in a race with Anat to get to the apartment next door. The door was open. When they walked in they found a man in his seventies. His thinning hair was disheveled and the tail of his plaid shirt was sticking out of corduroy pants. He was standing in the middle of a living room very similar to the one they had just left, the same sort of dark heavy furniture, shouting at a patrolman who looked very happy to see them. A woman, presumably his wife, was sitting on a sofa covered in plastic, wiping her eyes and petting a brown-and-white Amstaff.

"She ruined the neighborhood," the man screamed. "I don't have anything against them, but people should stay where they belong. It's no good to mix with them. All you get is a lethal cocktail. I told her so, but did she listen? She didn't give a damn, and now she got what she deserved."

"Don't say that, Shmuel. She was a nice girl," his wife cut in.

"Nice? Her grandmother was a nice woman. This one? I don't like to speak ill of the dead . . ." The expression on his face clearly said just the opposite.

"Shmuel and Dvora Gonen," the patrolmen informed them.

The Amstaff jumped off the woman's lap and padded to Anat. Automatically, she reached out to pet it. She loved dogs, especially big ones. If Eyal hadn't been there, she would have asked the dog's name. It helped people open up, made them feel more comfortable. But he would undoubtedly regard the question as unprofessional.

"Chief Inspector Eyal Ben-Tuvim. This is Inspector Anat Nachmias," Eyal said by way of introduction, stressing the difference in their ranks to make it clear who was in charge.

Shmuel Gonen looked at her in surprise. When civilians envision a detective, they generally picture a man, certainly not a short, skinny woman with frizzy hair, freckles, and a wrinkled jacket.

"Are you the one who called the police?" she asked in a businesslike tone, removing her hand from the dog. It's best to start with short, informative questions.

"Of course. With my own eyes, I saw the African . . ." Anat

could tell he was revving up for another barrage, but Eyal nipped it in the bud.

"Amnon," he shouted into the hallway.

"I put out an APB, but there's nothing yet. Looks like he got away," Amnon yelled back.

"Shit," Eyal spat. Something in his expression changed. It was barely detectible, but Anat knew him well enough to notice it.

"Okay, let's start from the beginning and take it one step at a time," she said to Shmuel Gonen in an effort to get things back on track.

"I'll be right back," Eyal said, heading for the door.

Anat wasn't surprised.

"Go on, I'm listening," she said, looking directly at Shmuel Gonen to show him he had her undivided attention.

"You sure? Shouldn't we wait for your boss?"

"Go ahead, I'll fill him in," she said encouragingly.

"So like I told the officer here, I was coming up the stairs when I heard shouting from her apartment," Shmuel recited reluctantly.

"Who was shouting? Did you recognize Michal's voice?"

"Yes, that's what I said," he snapped.

"It's very important, sir. You actually heard her shouting?" She repeated the question.

He looked at her as if she were too slow to understand a simple sentence.

"Go on, sir, I'm listening," she said, calling on all her patience.

"He was on top of her, the black guy," he continued.

Dvora Gonen let out a wail. The dog curled up at her feet.

"What do you mean 'on top of her'?" Anat knew she needed a precise account. You don't solve cases with vague statements.

"His hands were around her neck. He was strangling her," Shmuel said, thrusting out his two hands to demonstrate.

Anat was thankful for all the hours she'd spent practicing her poker face. What the neighbor was describing did not match what the body told them. "I realize it all happened very quickly, and this must be very hard for you, but it's important that you try to tell me what you saw as precisely as possible," she said, giving him a chance to change his story.

"That's what I saw," he insisted, raising both arms to demonstrate again.

"Okay, then." There was no point in getting hung up on this detail, she decided. They'd check with the medical examiner first. "What happened next?"

"I yelled at him to leave her alone. He was shocked to see me there. Right away he jumped up and came toward me. I thought he was going to kill me. But I screamed as loud as I could. 'Help, murder,' I screamed, and he got scared and ran away. Her body could have lain here . . . the guy was crazy." Shmuel's face was flushed with agitation.

That was the cue for another sigh from Dvora. "God help us," she moaned.

"Did you ever see him here before?" Anat asked them both.

"Yes, he was here," Shmuel answered quickly. "It's not nice to speak ill of the dead, but she had a fondness for the black ones. All those illegals from Africa. She started her own absorption office right here in the building. I was afraid to leave my apartment. The guy who murdered her was here, too. I'm not a racist or anything, and just between us, they all look alike so it's hard to tell them apart. But I recognized him because of the scar on his face."

"Where was the scar?" Anat hoped his memory of this detail was clearer.

"Like this, here," he said drawing a jagged line down his cheek with his finger. "I could see right away that he was a thug."

Anat glanced at her watch. It was a quarter to three in the afternoon.

"When did this happen?"

"Two and a half hours ago, more or less."

That was also problematic. Of course, she'd have to wait for the autopsy, but in her estimation Michal Poleg had been dead for more than two and a half hours. Five or six was more like it, maybe even longer.

"Do you happen to know where she worked?" she asked.

"Where? At some aid organization for Africans, where else? She was one of those idiots who want to turn our country into a national home for the blacks, as if we don't have enough troubles of our own. The guy must have attacked her before she left for work."

Eyal came back and gestured for her to follow him out into the hallway.

She had a feeling she knew what was coming.

"You can call David and tell him he won. I just spoke to my boss. The case is staying in the district," he announced smugly.

"Really? What a surprise," is what she wanted to say, but she just smiled politely and said, "I'll let him know."

"Good luck," Eyal called over his shoulder as he scampered down the stairs and fled the scene. She stood there watching him leave. The minute Shmuel Gonen uttered the word "African," she knew Eyal would be out of here. There'd be a lot of press, all right, but not the good kind. There'd be pressure from the public, and the brass would demand results, and fast. And she'd have that slimy politician, Ehud Regev, on her back. Lately he was on television all the time, wagging his finger and warning against the illegal aliens and all the diseases and violence they brought with them. In every interview she'd seen, as soon as he got through ranting about the Africans, he started in on the cops. He held them accountable for the whole situation.

Everyone would want to know why it was taking them so long to catch the perp when they had an eye witness. Try explaining that if an African decides to disappear, it's almost impossible to find him.

Chapter 11

YARIV was sitting in his office staring at the e-mail he'd gotten from State Attorney Doron Aloni summoning him to a meeting on a private matter the day after tomorrow. It wasn't unusual for him to be called into Aloni's office, but it was generally to discuss a case, not a personal issue.

Ever since he'd been transferred to the illegal alien division, he'd been in Aloni's bad books. His boss didn't like his association with Ehud Regev. He'd tried to talk him around, but Aloni kept saying he had to choose sides. It wasn't a tough decision to make. Aloni was finished. He'd be gone within six months. Regev, on the other hand, was very well positioned in the Knesset. With his connections, he was on his way up.

What did Aloni want from him? Was it the fucking complaint Michal filed? Not likely. If that's what it was, he would have asked for his written response, not summoned him to a private meeting. He wasn't the first attorney to have a complaint filed against him. There were procedures for dealing with it.

No, something else was going on. Michal probably reported how he'd showed up at her house last night shouting drunken obscenities at her. She'd milk it for all it was worth just to get back at him.

What could he tell Aloni? What kind of excuse could he offer? After what he did, even Regev would have a hard time defending him. He might not even want to. Regev was obsessed with the illegals. He saw it as his mission in life. However much respect the politician might have for him, he could very well decide to withdraw his support from a man who couldn't control himself, a man who got plastered and then went and banged on a woman's door in the middle of the night, even if the woman in question was Michal Poleg. Ever since she'd demonstrated outside Regev's office, the mere mention of her name made him see red. But that might not be enough to save him.

WHEN he got the legal opinion written by Dr. Yigal Shemesh from the Foreign Ministry, Yariv thought long and hard about what to do with it. If he took it to Aloni, he would tell him it was their duty as officers of the court to reveal its existence. But that would mean he'd lose all his cases. They could no longer employ the tactic of deporting Eritreans on the grounds that they were actually from Ethiopia. Yariv himself had come up with that idea, and he'd gotten a lot of pats on the back for it. So he took it to Regev, who told him to make it disappear. They couldn't listen to the bleeding hearts in the Foreign Ministry, he said. The future of the State of Israel was at stake. Yariv still hesitated. He wasn't driven by Regev's ideological convictions. Sometimes he got caught up in the politician's missionary zeal, but it never lasted long. He wasn't particularly fond of the migrants, but he didn't hate them, either. Mostly, he was just sick of them. He was grossed out by their wretched conditions, their despair aroused his contempt, and he didn't like the way they smelled. He wanted to move on and get away from these garbage cases as soon as possible so he could deal with things that really mattered.

In the end, he decided to keep Dr. Shemesh's legal opinion to himself. Michal was right. He not only hid it from the court, but he even continued to argue that the deportees were not in any danger.

The first time he saw Michal's complaint, he panicked. Was he wrong to put all his eggs in Regev's basket? Did he back the wrong horse when he hid the opinion? He knew Regev was a seasoned politician, the kind who made empty promises and told people what they wanted to hear. But when he thought about it calmly, he realized he didn't have anything to worry about. First of all, Michal didn't actually have the legal opinion. Somebody must have told her about it, but she hadn't gotten her hands on it. If she had, she would have attached it to her complaint. Without that piece of paper, what evidence did she have?

Secondly, Regev was right. Yariv wasn't obligated to make use of every opinion he was handed. The Foreign Ministry said one thing and the Ministry of the Interior said another. As a prosecutor, he was entitled to use his judgment. And don't forget that the illegals' petitions were filed against the Ministry of the Interior, not the Foreign Ministry. Michal treated the document like the Holy Grail. She was convinced it would force the government to stop deporting her Africans. She was so naive. Even if she got her hands on the missing legal opinion, Regev's people would produce a dozen others that said exactly the opposite, and Dr. Yigal Shemesh would find himself out of a job. The government wanted them deported. No piece of paper was going to prevent that from happening.

HIS cell phone rang. Inbar. He decided not to take the call. He wasn't ready to tell her what happened. Not yet. Even if she didn't get hysterical when he explained that he'd gotten smashed and wound up outside his ex-girlfriend's house, she'd be horrified by the thought that his bruises wouldn't clear up in time for the wedding and his nose would be swollen in all the pictures. It wouldn't matter how hard he tried to assure her it would be fine by then. It was better to wait until she got back and deal with her face-to-face. Ever since they set a date, every second of her time had been spent planning the event. Everything had to be perfect, and expensive, of course. She went on and on about appetizers, Swarovski crystal, table settings, flower arrangements, play lists, and all sorts of other items. Half the time he had no idea what she was talking about, and he wasn't particularly interested in finding out.

Yariv finished checking his e-mail and idly surfed the news on the Internet to calm his nerves. Everything will work out in the end. You always land on your feet, he told himself in an effort to lift his spirits. Some people were born lucky, and you're one of them. He could say he wasn't there, that she made it all up because she was distraught with grief over the death of her African lover. Who was she anyway? Nothing but an anonymous volunteer in an organization no one had ever heard of. He could count on Regev to have a field day with the "bleeding heart leftist" who had turned her back on her country and its "fine lads."

Yariv was scrolling down to an article about a new spray that claimed to enhance virility when he stopped suddenly and began scrolling back up the page. His head started pounding again, harder than ever. He recognized the building in the photograph under the headline, "Woman in Her 30s Found Dead in Her Tel Aviv Apartment."

Chapter 12

BOAZ Yavin was sitting in the living room rocking Sagie in his arms, praying for him to fall asleep quickly. "Your turn," Irit had said, poking him in the ribs with her elbow when the baby woke up for the umpteenth time.

He looked at his watch. Two thirty in the morning. He was exhausted. The past few nights he'd hardly gotten any sleep. "His teeth are coming in. He'll sleep better soon," Irit had assured him as she shoved him out of bed. Despite his crankiness, he kept his thoughts to himself and refrained from reminding her what she'd said when they were debating whether to have another child. "The third kid takes care of itself," she'd insisted.

The room was lit only by the flickering blue light of the television. Yawning, Boaz turned his attention to the repeat broadcast of the evening news as he continued stroking Sagie's head. Suddenly, his hand froze.

He recognized the face of the woman filling the screen. It was the girl who'd screamed at him near the old bus station just a few days ago, before Faro's thugs dragged her away.

It was cold in the house, but he found himself sweating. His eyes were glued to the TV, which now showed cops and paramedics outside an apartment building. He turned up the volume just a bit, not wanting to wake Irit. He kept hearing the word "murder," and it was making his head spin.

He'd called Itzik to tell him about the girl and was told to get out of there fast. He was glad to cut his visit short. He hated the place. With any luck, after this incident they wouldn't make him do the rounds there anymore. It didn't happen that way. Itzik was furious, but a lot of money changed hands on those "rounds," and he had no intention of canceling them because of some interfering woman.

On the screen, a young policewoman was talking. "At this point, we're looking into every possibility, following every lead," she said somberly.

Did it have anything to do with what happened at the old bus station? Sagie started whimpering again. Boaz rocked him distractedly, keeping his eyes on the TV in an effort to learn as much about the murder as he could.

He had no one to blame but himself and his own greed. He was working at an accounting firm when they caught him using privileged information to play the stock market. That was right after Shira was born, and he and Irit were having a hard time making ends meet. It was in the firm's interest to keep it quiet. They agreed not to go to the police if he returned the money. All of a sudden he had a huge debt, two kids, and no job. He was too ashamed to tell Irit. His whole world had collapsed; he was a broken man.

But then, in his darkest moment, someone came to his rescue, just like in a fairy tale. A week after he lost his job, Itzik, one of the firm's clients, proposed that he work for him privately. He was impressed by the way Boaz handled his account, he claimed, and he didn't want to lose him just because he had left his previous place of employment.

Thrilled, Boaz thanked his lucky stars and accepted the offer immediately. At first, everything was great. Itzik gave him a lot of work, referred clients to him, and his new business was off to a running start. Before he knew it, he was making ten times his former salary. It took him several months to realize that Itzik was just a front, that he actually worked for Shimon Faro, the notorious syndicate boss. He still cursed himself every day for not pulling out as soon as he learned the truth. His greed had gotten the better of him. He didn't want to give up his fancy office, the nice house in the prestigious suburb of Ramat Hasharon, his new status. And he had another incentive to toe the line as well: Itzik had made it very clear that his financial debts would be the least of his worries if he ever decided to walk away or pull one of the tricks he'd played in his previous job. The syndicate knew all along why he had left the firm.

Instead of washing his hands of Faro's business, he'd gotten in even deeper and been given more and more responsibilities. He didn't have a record, so for all intents and purposes he was squeaky clean. Why not use him?

Faro set up a private banking system for Africans without papers who couldn't use regular banks. In addition to handling the books for the boss's other businesses, Boaz now served as a traveling "teller" for this so-called bank. Once a week, sometimes twice, he had to do the rounds at the old bus station, collecting deposits and doling out cash. His contact was a man Faro called the "General." It was the worst day of the week for Boaz. He tried not to think about the other things Faro was involved in, and he knew better than to ask. It was obvious to him that he was just a small cog in a much larger machine.

When the government started talking about sending the Africans back where they came from, Boaz felt a glimmer of hope. He drank in MK Regev's impassioned speeches and wished him luck. No clients, no bank, he thought. He and Faro could part company as friends. But it didn't take him long to realize it wasn't going to happen. There would always be a bank because there would always be Africans. And if it wasn't Africans, it would be someone else. Why? Because money made the world go round. All those people left their homes because they needed money, and they found work here because it was good for the economy. Israel needed migrants to wash dishes in its restaurants, to clean the streets, to pick strawberries—all the dirty work no Israeli was willing to do. Developed economies needed slave laborers, and there were plenty on offer in Third World countries. So Boaz was stuck with Faro. There would always be illegal aliens in the country, and as long as there were, there would be a bank like Faro's.

Sagie had fallen asleep on Boaz's shoulder. He gazed at his son dolefully. He was so beautiful, so pure, so innocent.

The woman's face was showing on the screen again. Boaz felt her eyes staring at him accusingly. Did the abrupt end she put to his rounds that day cost her her life? Was that the price she had to pay? Was that the price he would have to pay?

Chapter 13

ITAI stared into the darkness. He'd been lying in bed for the past three hours, tossing and turning, unable to fall asleep.

After finally listening to Michal's message, he tried over and over again to reach her at home, but all he got was a busy signal. As soon as he got back to Tel Aviv, he went straight to her apartment, but by the time he arrived it was too late. The building was surrounded by patrol cars and TV crews. There was no doubt in his mind what had happened or who was responsible.

In spite, or maybe because of, his emotional state, he elbowed his way over to a group of policemen standing at the entrance to the building and demanded to speak with the officer in charge. He waited a long time until a tall bearded cop came over and introduced himself as Yaron. Itai told him everything he knew.

IT all started with Hagos. Shortly before he was taken away, he let slip something about the "Banker." It wasn't unusual for asylum seekers to share their troubles, fears, and hardships with the aid workers. Some of those conversations touched on very intimate topics. Still, Itai had learned that certain subjects remained off-limits and it was best not to pry into them. To this day, for example, he had no idea if, where, and with whom the men who came to them for help slept at night. And while the money they didn't have was a popular topic of conversation, they preferred not to talk about the money they did have.

Michal had pressed Hagos for information about his life. He didn't want to say too much, didn't want to make waves, but she didn't let up. She felt it was her duty to put up a fight against Israelis who took advantage of asylum seekers. Knowing she couldn't get at the Bedouins, she declared war on the "Banker." "It's because of what they did to us in the Holocaust," she once told Itai with characteristic ardor. "Every country closed its doors to the Jews. Israel was established by refugees. I'll never get how people who grew up in this country can exploit other refugees. Is that so hard to understand?" When Hagos was picked up and subsequently deported, Michal convinced herself that it was because he knew too much and had told her too much about the "Banker." Itai thought she was being paranoid.

Michal wouldn't let it go. She said OMA had to make the fight against the gangsters a priority. Naturally, he objected. He was as disgusted as she was by what they were doing, but he knew very well that a tiny organization like theirs couldn't go up against the syndicate. Michal's idea was absurd, and it would jeopardize everything they'd built. The battle they had over it was more acrimonious than any of their previous arguments. For the first time since she started working at OMA, he said if she didn't like it, she could leave.

Michal was taken aback by his belligerence. Atypically, she didn't insist on having the last word, just said quietly, "At least think about it." The next morning she walked into his office and told him she'd decided he was right. She'd report what she knew about the "Banker" to the police and let them handle it.

ITAI threw off the blanket and got out of bed. He had a headache. Michal had lied to him. Just like she'd gone behind his back and filed the complaint against Yariv Ninio, she'd continued to poke her nose into the "Banker's" affairs. Her message said they hadn't succeeded in scaring her, that they didn't know who they were dealing with. But in the end she was the one who didn't know who she was dealing with. And now he'd never know, either.

Why had he screened her calls? She needed his help and he ignored her. He was tormented by the thought of what might have been if he'd just answered his phone.

He reached out for his cell phone and it made him even more

depressed. Gabriel still hadn't called. It was late, but he tried his number again. No answer this time, either. He wanted to be the one to tell him, to comfort him. He'd be there for him. Itai knew how close Gabriel and Michal were. It worried him that he couldn't reach him. Where was he?

Chapter 14

KOBI Etkin looked at Yariv with mixed emotions. His friend was weeping bitterly. In his six years as a lawyer, Kobi had sat opposite hundreds of tearful clients. He usually felt sorry for them. They came to him when they were weak, helpless, and frightened, and he was their only hope.

Kobi had no delusions. He knew very well that some of his clients had committed horrible crimes. He was no different from any other law-abiding citizen. If he saw these people on the news or read about them in the paper, he'd want them to die a painful death. But as an attorney, it was his job to defend them. And it was hard to hate someone whose life was hanging in the balance and they were begging for your help. The defense attorney's schizophrenia, he'd once heard a colleague call it.

He'd known Yariv since law school. Now and again they met for lunch or drinks in the evening. Kobi's office on King Saul Street was just a short walk from the State Attorney's Office.

Yariv's decision to work for the State Attorney for not much more than minimum wage had taken Kobi by surprise. He'd always pictured him in a large law firm where the money was. But Yariv explained that he planned to use the job as a stepping-stone. After a few years in the public sector, he'd have the experience, and, more important, the connections, that would give him a leg up when he went into private practice.

He had to admit that he'd felt a touch of satisfaction when Yariv told him about last night. They'd had dozens of arguments over the years about the role of the defense attorney. Kobi had a hard time putting up with his friend's contempt. "How can you defend such scum?" he said repeatedly. It infuriated him that Yariv, a lawyer himself, pretended not to understand that the day you got rid of defense attorneys was the day you closed the courthouse and turned out the lights. But he forced himself not to gloat. Yariv looked too miserable and lost for him to enjoy this moment of triumph.

If he was already being honest, Kobi also had to admit that he felt a bit uncomfortable about the whole thing. He saw that Yariv was drinking too much last night and he didn't say anything. And he wasn't overly sympathetic when Yariv kept whining about Michal Poleg and the complaint she filed against him. It was an inconvenience, but it wasn't the end of the world. The ethics committee wouldn't sanction him or take away his license. And no one was going to launch an investigation into whether or not he ever saw the Foreign Ministry document. Still, Kobi would probably have given his friend his full attention if it hadn't been for the pretty girl sitting at the next table who kept making eye contact with him. At a certain point, he got up and went over to talk to her. Left alone at the table, Yariv went on drinking. When Kobi sensed that the girl was ready to take things to the next level, he went back and asked Yariv if he was okay getting home on his own. His friend didn't object. That was around two in the morning. Now Kobi was feeling a little guilty. He didn't think it would be a problem; Yariv lived close by. But on the other hand, if he hadn't been so taken by that girl (in the end he didn't even get lucky), Yariv wouldn't be sitting opposite him feeling like his whole life was in shatters.

"I couldn't have killed her," Yariv said, sniffling and wincing in pain. "Who is she anyway? What is she to me? Nothing, that's what. And anyway, I'm no murderer. I've never been violent. I've never raised a hand to anyone, and certainly not a woman. There's no way I killed her."

Kobi kept silent. After six years in the profession, he knew that anybody was capable of murder. Everyone had a breaking point. Sometimes it was only a matter of bad timing or bad luck. And whatever Yariv said, Kobi knew he had a temper. He'd seen him blow up and lose control. He also knew that Yariv hadn't stopped ranting against Michal from the moment he caught sight of her outside the bar.

"You believe I can't remember anything, don't you? I swear on my life, Kobi, I don't remember a thing. I know I knocked on her door and she told me to go away, but that's it. After that it's all a blank."

Kobi nodded. It didn't matter what he believed or didn't believe. As a defense attorney, he represented his client and served as his mouthpiece. This wasn't the first time a client told him he didn't remember what happened. People say that, hoping that if they claim they don't remember, somehow it will all just go away. Others really can't remember. Yariv was plastered, and the beating he'd taken was severe enough to leave him with a broken nose and bruises on his face, so maybe it also gave him a concussion. Given those circumstances, it was quite possible he didn't remember anything.

"I'm going to the police and I want you to come with me," Yariv said, breaking the silence in the room.

The profession Kobi had chosen was full of contradictions. On the face of it, he should encourage Yariv to go to the cops and give them any information that could further the investigation. But Yariv didn't want his help as a friend; he needed him to act as his lawyer.

"Why?" he asked, clearing his throat.

Yariv gazed at him, puzzled.

"Let's consider what you know," Kobi said. "The girl is dead, and you don't know if you killed her or not. All you remember is that you knocked on her door, and . . ."

"And that's exactly what I'll say," Yariv cut in.

"So then they'll start to investigate, and you can't tell where it will lead. They might reach the conclusion that you had nothing to do with the murder. But they might not. There's also a third possibility—they won't know for sure whether you did it or not, but in the absence of any other suspects, they'll decide that the fastest way to put the case to bed is to charge you with homicide. And then they'll convince themselves, and your friends in the State Attorney's Office, that you're guilty."

Yariv stared at him in shock. Kobi could see how shaken he was by his use of the word "guilty." If they'd had this conversation a week ago, it would have sounded ludicrous. Now it didn't seem beyond the realm of possibility.

"All I'm saying," Kobi went on, "is that for the time being, you don't really know anything. Maybe you did it and maybe you didn't. Odds are you had nothing to do with her death. Like you said, you're not the violent type. But if you go to the police, that 'maybe' could easily become a 'yes.' Assuming nobody saw you, there's no reason for you to risk sticking your head in a noose at this point. Even if they find your fingerprints or DNA there, they won't know they're yours. You've never been arrested, so you're not in their files. There's no way for them to know who they belong to. In my opinion, going to the cops now would be a mistake."

Yariv remained silent.

"That is, unless you *are* guilty. In that case, go. Confess and get it off your chest. Tell them what happened and hope for the best. If they find out later that you did it, they won't be willing to reduce the charges to manslaughter."

Pure terror showed on Yariv's face.

"I say wait until you know more. There's no need to rush into anything. Maybe someone else killed her and the cops will make an arrest. Who knows?" Kobi was working hard to convince his friend, to give him a good reason to sit tight.

"How long am I supposed to wait?" Yariv sounded frustrated.

"We both know there's a criminal prosecutor assigned to every investigation from the very beginning. The cops have to tell them what's going on, consult with them, get their consent for all sorts of procedures. They have to make sure they'll be able to use all the evidence they turn up. That could . . ." Kobi didn't have to go on. He wouldn't be saying this to a regular client, but Yariv was his friend. And he was also a prosecutor himself.

Yariv nodded. He understood very well what Kobi was trying to say. Working in the State Attorney's Office gave him a distinct advantage. He had access to information that other people didn't have.

The two men sat opposite each other in silence.

"I said things about her in the bar," Yariv said finally. "Maybe someone heard me talking."

"I don't think you have to worry about that," Kobi said dismissively.

"And my face is swollen. People have been asking me about it, you know. I told them I fell off my bike. I wasn't thinking. I don't even have a bike. I told you, someone stole it . . . What if the cops find out I was roughed up? That I don't have a bike? It won't look good."

"How are they going to find out? Why should anyone be interested?" Kobi's tone was scornful but firm. "No one's going to remember what you said. I'm sure it went in one ear and out the other. If they ask, say it was a rent-a-bike. Trust me, you have nothing to worry about. Nobody's going to care."

Yariv leaned closer and put his hand on Kobi's arm. "You can be my alibi. If they ask, you can say there's no way I could have done it, that you were with me . . . I mean . . . ," he said hesitantly.

Kobi didn't respond. He'd already said too much. And he had no intention of lying to the police.

"This is driving me nuts, Kobi. You have to tell me you believe I didn't ki . . . kill her, that it's not possible . . . ," Yariv said, his voice breaking.

Kobi remained silent.

Chapter 15

ANAT passed her fingers through her hair nervously as the medical examiner, Dr. Yiftach Sassoon, described Michal Poleg in his usual flat, clinical manner: build, age, height, weight, hair, teeth, clothing. Meeting with the pathologist was one of the worst parts of her job. It wasn't the sight of the corpse or even the smell that got to her. By now she'd been to enough crime scenes to see corpses in every possible condition and state of decomposition. Another body didn't faze her.

What was hard for her to take was the autopsy room itself. Unlike what she'd imagined before the visit to the Abu Kabir Institute of Forensic Medicine during her training, it was nothing like a sterile operating room. The stainless-steel table and sink, the white tiles, and the array of knives and other instruments reminded her more of an industrial kitchen. It was always hard for her to see the body laid out in this setting. A crime scene was chaotic, with people coming and going. The body of the victim was just another piece of evidence. But here there was only the corpse spread out on the table in a quiet room, looking so alone, exposed, and vulnerable. The presence of death was unnervingly tangible.

Anat lowered her eyes as the autopsy team began removing Michal's clothes. She seemed even smaller than at the crime scene, almost childlike.

Anat had already questioned the family. She got the impression that Michal was quite a character. She wasn't afraid to speak her mind, to go against the rest of the family, or to pay the price. She didn't have a cell phone (she hated gadgets) or a driver's license (she couldn't bear the thought of accidentally taking a life). She didn't eat meat, fish, honey, or eggs, and there were times when she would only eat fruit that fell from the tree. She didn't have a job, except for the volunteer work she did for OMA and an organization for victims of sexual abuse. She lived frugally on the small inheritance from her grandmother. According to her brother, Michal felt it was only right that the money left by her grandmother, a Holocaust survivor and once a refugee herself, should be used to help other refugees. He was incensed by her attitude.

"Trauma to the abdomen," Dr. Sassoon stated, interrupting her thoughts. He pointed to a bruise below the right rib cage.

"Somebody punched her," he said before Anat had a chance to ask.

About fifty hours had gone by since the call came in. At some point during that time Anat had gone back to her apartment on Bloch Street where she'd showered, changed clothes, and allowed herself about three hours of uninterrupted sleep. She'd spent the past two nights in her office at district headquarters, napping periodically on the floor on an old army mattress.

She watched as Dr. Sassoon made an incision in the body and began peeling back the tissue. She felt sorry for Michal lying there, helpless, while strangers mauled her and stripped her of her clothes and her flesh.

Meanwhile, Anat had nothing to go on. Except for Shmuel Gonen, no one else had seen an African man fleeing the building. They'd combed the area for cameras. There was one in the grocery store at the end of the block, but it hadn't picked up anything useful.

They found prints belonging to a number of different people in the apartment, but none of them were in their database. Whoever murdered Michal Poleg had never been arrested. The blood on the outside of the door didn't belong to Michal, but the person who left it there didn't leave any inside the apartment, and there was no blood trail.

The pathologist turned the body over.

"Ah, here it is," Dr. Sassoon said in a tone of satisfaction.

"What?"

"She was struck hard on the back of the neck. That's what killed her."

"A direct blow?" Anat asked in surprise. She'd assumed Michal had been strangled. She'd seen the marks on her neck.

"It's hard to be certain," Dr. Sassoon answered, raising his eyes
to her, "but it looks more like a blow with a blunt object than a
bruise sustained in a fall."

"And what about the marks on her neck, the scratches on her
face, the black eye, the bruise on the abdomen?"

"I'd say she got those a day, maybe a day and a half, earlier."

Anat looked at Michal's face. What happened to her in the last
days of her life? Was there a connection between the beating and the
murder? It didn't seem likely that someone would beat her up and
then kill her a day later. Maybe if she had a husband or a boyfriend,
but as far as she knew, Michal wasn't in a romantic relationship at
the time of her death.

Yaron had told her what he learned from her boss, Itai Fisher.
In Yaron's opinion, all the talk about the "Banker" being out to get
her was paranoid nonsense that wouldn't lead anywhere. Just wild
speculation. Anat wasn't convinced yet. At this stage in the investigation, they couldn't ignore any lead.

Her cell phone rang. She switched it off. David was demanding
constant reports even though, or maybe because, he was in Austria,
acting like a guardian angel sitting on her shoulder with a cigarette
in his hand. Yochai, the District Commander, was also on the phone
to her every couple of hours to satisfy himself that she had things
under control until David got back. They were driving her crazy,
wasting her time instead of letting her get on with the job.

"Can you estimate time of death?" she asked as her phone rang
again. She'd planned to let Sassoon finish the autopsy in peace, but
the persistence of her callers made it clear that wouldn't be possible.

Sassoon scratched his head as he checked his notes.

"Sometime between one and three in the morning," he said.

"You sure?" He was full of surprises. The events described by
Shmuel Gonen had taken place around noon.

"Absolutely."

Anat pulled out her phone and saw a message from Yaron: "We
got a lead on the African."

Chapter 16

GABRIEL was curled up in a fetal position. He was cold and wet and his teeth were chattering. Dawn was still a few hours away. Until the sun came up, the temperature would keep falling and it would get even colder. Other people were lying on the grass around him, struggling to keep dry.

He'd taken Arami's advice and come back to Levinsky Park. For most of the day, he'd sat on the grass in a quiet corner, trying not to attract attention, to fade into the background. New people showed up here every day. He was surrounded by unfamiliar faces. The newcomers wandered around in a daze, frightened and bewildered. He was the same way when he first arrived. It was easy to merge with them and make himself invisible.

He was still haunted by the sight of Michal lying dead on the red carpet, her face even paler than usual. When he didn't see the image of Michal in his head, he heard the sound of Liddie screaming, calling out to him, pleading for her life. It was driving him insane.

He spoke to no one, just sat by himself, consumed by his thoughts and his torments, shivering from the cold and terrified. He had no idea what was happening in the world outside the park. How was Itai reacting to his disappearance? Was anyone looking for him? Had the police identified him? Had Michal's body been buried? He wanted to go to the funeral so he could tell her how grateful he was, so he could say good-bye.

Gabriel shut his eyes, trying to force himself to fall asleep. He was very tired, but he couldn't get any rest. He was too wound up. Drawing gave him some release. When he sketched, he was totally absorbed in what he was doing. It calmed him, allowed him to forget for a moment.

All of a sudden he sensed a flurry of activity around him. Gabriel opened his eyes. People were getting up. The police were in the park.

Up until yesterday afternoon, he hadn't been afraid of the police. He was Eritrean born and bred. People like him were protected in Israel; they couldn't be deported. Hagos had lived with his family in Ethiopia for several years, so the Israelis decided he was Ethiopian. But Gabriel had never left Eritrea. In fact, until he set out on the journey with Liddie, he'd never even left his village. But things had changed. Michal's neighbor must have told the police that he killed her.

He counted three policemen. They were searching the park, shining their flashlights in people's faces. They would find him. They'd take him away and hang him, just like Arami said. And then the men who were holding Liddie wouldn't get their money and she would die, too.

Should he run? The tall police officer walking in his direction was still about five yards away. Gabriel was quick on his feet. He could make a run for it. But what if the park was surrounded? How would he get away?

The tall policeman crouched over a man sleeping nearby, blinding him with his flashlight. As the man raised his arm to shield his eyes from the light, the policeman grabbed him by the sleeve and pulled him upright. Then he let him go and the man fell to the ground.

Gabriel was shaking. There was no longer any doubt in his mind. They were looking for him. He wanted to flee, but his feet wouldn't budge. He was paralyzed by fear.

The rain started coming down heavily just as the tall policeman shone his flashlight on the man beside him. Gabriel's heart was racing. They'd never believe he had nothing to do with Michal's death. They'd say he fled and tried to hide because he was guilty.

It was Gabriel's turn. He couldn't breathe. The light hurt his eyes. He pulled his shoulder up close to his face in an attempt to hide the scar. Maybe the policeman wouldn't see it in the dark. Please, God, he prayed, don't let him see it. It will be the end of me. The end of Liddie.

The raindrops falling from the sky merged with his tears.

Chapter 17

"**WELL,** Nachmias, did you get him?" The DC asked when she walked into his office to give him her morning report. She'd been here yesterday, too, but then she was in a hurry to get to Abu Kabir for the autopsy so they'd only talked for five minutes. That was the first time she'd ever met with him one-on-one. Before that, David had always been present and the DC had barely glanced in her direction. Now she was feeling the pressure of flying solo.

"Not yet," she confessed. "But we're getting close."

Yochai licked his upper lip in silence. Part of the tension she was feeling stemmed from the fact that it was hard for her to read him. Was licking his lip a sign of irritation or displeasure, or just an urgent need for lip balm? She could read David like a book, but it had taken her a while. By now she knew what worried him, what annoyed him, and, most important, what made him go in a certain direction.

Anat debated whether to raise the subject of the medical examiner's report. She'd e-mailed Yochai the main conclusions yesterday and called his secretary to make sure he'd gotten it. He hadn't replied.

"Have you been to her place of work, that aid organization? Did you find out who she had dealings with?"

"She was very devoted to the people she worked with," Anat answered, sensing the need to defend Michal and her principles. "We got a list of the people she was close to. One of them has a scar on his face that fits Gonen's description. We're focusing our attention on him."

She decided there was no need to explain the difficulties they were facing. The DC was well aware of them, and if she spelled them out it would just sound like she was making excuses. The biggest problem was the suspect's lack of any roots or history in Israel. People like the African man they were searching for didn't have family in the country who they could lean on to get them to reveal his whereabouts. There were no friends he grew up with, no one who went to school with him or served in the same army unit, no address or employment records. Moreover, all Africans looked alike to Israelis, so it was very hard to get an identification. Even the sketch they'd made with the help of Gonen didn't do much good. The man in the sketch looked like all the other Africans around the old bus station, except for the scar on his face.

The refugees, illegal aliens, asylum seekers—or whatever you chose to call them depending on your politics—were hard for law enforcement, or anyone else for that matter, to get their hands on. "A black hole that's getting bigger, in every sense of the word," the district intelligence officer, Gilad, had described the situation.

"What about the community leaders? Have you spoken to them?" Yochai asked, breaking into her thoughts. "It's in their interest to cooperate with us. They want to demonstrate that they're law-abiding people. Especially now with all the clashes with the Israelis in the neighborhood. We're protecting their butts."

"Yes, I spoke to everyone I could find. They promised to help," Anat answered. "The thing is there's a good chance the guy we're looking for is Eritrean, so there's no community to speak of. The Eritreans keep to themselves. They're not as organized as the Sudanese."

Yochai grimaced.

"We showed the sketch around the old bus station, asked people if they recognized him, told them to contact us if they see him. We offered a reward for information. A few tips came in from people who claimed to have seen him. We sent a squad out to Levinsky Park last night on the basis of one anonymous tip, but no luck yet."

"Okay, keep the pressure on. You can always find informants in places like that where there's no strong community and money is hard to come by. Eventually someone will see him and rat him out," the DC said, turning his attention to his computer screen to signal the end of the meeting.

"If I may, Yochai," Anat said, not yet ready to leave. "There are a few more things I'd like to run by you."

"Go on." He raised his eyes to her with obvious reluctance, passing his tongue over his upper lip again.

Anat took a deep breath. It was clear to her that it was no accident she hadn't heard back from him yesterday.

"The theory that the African killed her," she began, "is based entirely on Shmuel Gonen's statement. But there are problems with that. He admitted he wasn't on good terms with Michal, but he forgot to mention that she filed two harassment complaints against him in the past year. In addition, the medical examiner's report rules out the African he saw as the perp. I'm sure you noticed that."

Yochai gazed at her in silence with an expression she couldn't read.

"Besides," she went on quickly, knowing the time he was willing to allot to her was running out, "nobody else saw an African fleeing the building. We checked the whole area for cameras, questioned the neighbors. We didn't turn up any other evidence that he was there. And that's not a neighborhood where the presence of an African man would go unnoticed."

"So what are you saying, Nachmias? Gonen made it up? Maybe he killed her himself because of the complaints?" Yochai's tone was disdainful.

"No, that's not what I'm saying. I don't think he assaulted Michal and I don't think he made up the story. He doesn't give the impression of being clever or cold-blooded enough for that. I believe he saw an African man leaving her apartment, but what he was doing there I don't know. I think we have to check other possibilities, not just concentrate on that one guy. We might be looking under the streetlight." Anat sat up straighter, trying to project confidence and professionalism.

"Okay, let's say you're right. What else have you got?" The DC's lack of patience was apparent.

"First of all, there's her family. There wasn't a lot of love lost between them. The grandmother left everything to Michal, including the apartment on Stricker Street. The family contested the will. Her younger brother told me how furious they were when the will was read. They claimed in court that Michal exerted undue influence on the grandmother. According to her brother, the son-in-law was the ringleader. He's the one who convinced the family to take it to court. Michal didn't leave a will, so now her family gets its hands on the apartment."

Yochai gestured for her to continue. Clearly, he wasn't buying the story about the family.

"There's also the matter of the blood on the outside of the door . . ."

"Which could belong to our guy. We won't know until we catch him," Yochai cut in.

"True, but in any case it's odd that it wasn't found anywhere else."

Yochai's scowl persuaded her to move on. He was right. The blood would only figure into it when they had a suspect.

"We can't forget the message she left on Itai Fisher's phone. She said she was assaulted, that she found out something. Fisher says she got on the wrong side of a crime syndicate. In my opinion, it's definitely worth checking into. The poor woman went through hell the last week of her life."

"Yaron told me it was all nonsense. There's no evidence," Yochai interrupted.

"I know, but . . . ," Anat went on, filing away for future use the information that Yaron had gone to the DC behind her back.

"But what? Where do you want to go with this? What's your theory, Nachmias?" Yochai didn't even try to disguise his irritation.

"I don't have one yet," she replied, stressing the final word. "And I don't think I need one at this early stage. We have to keep gathering evidence, not eliminate any options at this point. The African is one possibility, but in my opinion . . ."

"I heard your opinion." Yochai cut her off abruptly, looking back down at his computer. "I'll make a deal with you. First find the African and then we'll talk about other options."

"I'm not saying that finding him isn't a priority. I told you, we're getting closer. I'm just asking not to devote all our resources to him. Let me . . ." Anat didn't want to leave the meeting empty-handed.

"You're not trying hard enough, Nachmias," Yochai declared. "I want results, not speculations. The African first, then we'll talk about whatever you want, if there's still anything to talk about. The time you're wasting here would be better spent working the case."

Chapter 18

ITAI'S voice was shaking. He'd rewritten his eulogy over and over again last night, typing and deleting, struggling to come to terms with the fact that he was writing it for her.

He cleared his throat. There were a lot of people there. His mother, who ranked funerals by the number of mourners, would call it a "respectable turnout." The sun was shining after a string of rainy days and the sky was a clear blue. He was pleased to see several Africans in the crowd. He looked for Gabriel among them but didn't spot him.

Itai suddenly caught sight of Yaron, the tall bearded cop who had questioned him. Were they any closer to finding Michal's murderer, he wondered. He knew the information he'd given them was sketchy. He'd said the same thing to Michal when she outlined for him what she intended to tell the police about the "Banker." Just like in the complaint she filed against Yariv Ninio with the Bar Association, she produced a litany of allegations but not a shred of evidence. He suspected the police wouldn't do anything about it, but he didn't want to say so. He knew that if he convinced her there was no point in going to the cops, she'd revert to her original plan and take a more direct approach. But things had changed. Now the police could no longer ignore him, ignore her. If only Michal didn't have to die to make them listen.

At two o'clock in the morning, he'd tossed out the final version of the eulogy. Michal deserved more than a speech filled with clichés about a caring woman who wasn't afraid to swim against the tide, who lived by her principles and was prepared to pay the price.

"I want to tell you a story about a man who was saved and the woman who saved him," Itai began.

There were a lot of stories he could tell, but in the end he'd decided to talk about Mahadir Alfadel. Itai was in the office with Michal that night when a cabdriver knocked on the door around eight thirty and said he had a "package" for them from Soroka Hospital. They went downstairs and were shocked to see a man in hospital pajamas sitting on the curb. His left arm and leg were paralyzed, and in his right hand he was holding a bag of urine attached to a catheter. Before they had a chance to get any details, the cabdriver waved good-bye and took off. A crumpled piece of paper was sticking out of one of the man's pockets—his discharge form. It turned out he was an asylum seeker from northern Sudan who had been shot by Egyptian soldiers close to the Israeli border. He'd managed to make it across the border and was picked up by an army unit and transferred to the hospital in Beersheba. Since asylum seekers were only entitled to emergency treatment, the man's condition was stabilized and he was discharged. There was no one to talk to at Soroka at this hour of the night, and no one left to answer the phone in any government office, either. What were they going to do with him? OMA didn't have the budget or the facilities to house asylum seekers in need of medical care. They were a tiny organization struggling to keep their head above water. Michal didn't hesitate for a moment. She took Mahadir home with her, and for the next few weeks she took care of him—gave him food, clothing, and shelter, and made sure he got the medical attention he required. During that time, she got to know him. After all, in Michal's eyes, everyone was first and foremost a human being, not just another refugee, another story, another problem. At first, the "package" hardly uttered a word, still in shock from the trauma he had undergone. But in time he opened up, and she learned he was a lawyer who had gotten his degree in England and then returned to Sudan to help his people. As soon as he got back to his homeland, he was targeted by the government. Fearing for his life, he fled, making his way to Egypt and from there to Israel.

Out of the corner of his eye, Itai saw one of the cops talking on his cell phone. He looked away, indignant. The cops are vulgar brutes, he thought to himself.

Clearing his throat again, he went on to recount the conversation he'd had with Mahadir that very morning. The lawyer had called him from London with a request: "When you go to the cemetery today, say thank you for me one last time to the woman who saved my life."

He had planned to say more, to speak about Michal's unique personality, her militant pacifism, her refusal to learn to drive because she was afraid of hurting someone by accident, how unthinkable it was that a woman like her could be the victim of a violent act, but he was too choked with emotion. He handed the microphone back to Michal's father.

Silence fell over the graveside.

ON his way out of the cemetery, Itai passed the huddle of cops. He noticed that one was a short, slender woman with an attractive face. She reminded him of Michal, maybe because they were both so petite. "You spoke very well," the policewoman said with the hint of a smile as he walked by.

"Thank you," he mumbled, hesitantly returning the smile. Michal's family had stood there frozen throughout his eulogy. He couldn't tell what they were thinking.

Then Itai recognized the unmistakable voice of Yaron, standing next to the policewoman. He snapped out of his reverie. "We'll be in touch very soon, Fisher," the tall cop said. There was nothing subtle about the threatening tenor of his words.

Chapter 19

ANAT scanned the crowd at the funeral. The cops liked to say that the criminal might not always return to the scene of the crime, but a murderer always shows up at the cemetery to be sure the victim is dead. She estimated the number of people at around two hundred. Unfortunately, she didn't have her mother's skill at funeral profiling. She could always tell you exactly how many were there, who had come and who hadn't bothered to turn up, and the most pertinent fact of all: whose absence was scandalous.

The sunshine was deceptive. Anat was cold, and she needed to pee.

Michal's father recited the prayer for the dead tonelessly. As she told Yochai, there wasn't much love lost in Michal's family. Her parents had taken the news of their daughter's murder stoically. When Anat told them that Michal had been beaten up a few days earlier, her mother said it didn't surprise her. "Michal liked to get under people's skin," was how she put it. That was one of the reasons Anat was glad to learn that her parents' attempt to challenge the validity of the grandmother's will had been thrown out of court. She was shocked by the way this supposedly "normative" family treated her like a black sheep. But there was another reason, too. Anat knew that Michal had spent most of her life fighting big battles she was destined to lose. She was glad that she'd been able to win at least one of them.

She was dutifully following Yochai's orders and concentrating all the team's efforts on finding the migrant. David told her to do the same thing, although he agreed with her that the theory that he was the murderer was full of holes. In their last phone conversation, David had made it very plain that MK Ehud Regev was putting a lot of pressure on the brass to find the "black brute." Regev's sources on the force had leaked to him the information that the neighbor had seen an African man kill Michal. If they pursued other leads at this moment in time, it would only lend credence to Regev's claim that the police weren't doing enough to solve the problem, that they were going easy on the migrants in order to ensure quiet on the ground. "Do whatever you have to to find him. We'll reassess the situation when I get back," he'd instructed her just before he left for the airport. "We'll get the right guy in the end, whether Regev likes it or not. And don't let Yochai get to you. He wants the same thing we do, but he's got the brass on his back. He's taking a lot of heat. Keep looking for the African. When I get back I'll talk to Yochai about expanding the investigation."

Anat was pretty sure the man they were looking for was the kid called Gabriel. When she questioned the OMA workers about the people Michal was in close contact with, his name came up again and again. That also fit with the letter "G" at the bottom of the portrait on Michal's wall.

They got Gabriel's address and place of employment from OMA, but when they checked them out, they were told that he'd vanished. No one knew where he'd gone. His boss, Amir, reported that Gabriel had asked to leave work early the day Michal's body was discovered. According to his coworkers, he'd gotten a phone call just before he left. Anat tried to find out what the call was about and why he'd left so suddenly, but nobody seemed to know. Amir also confirmed that Gabriel had a scar on his left cheek. She didn't mention the scar to the OMA workers because she didn't want them to know that Gabriel was the target of their investigation. If they knew he was a suspect, they'd close ranks and refuse to answer any more questions. Everyone she spoke to at the aid organization described Gabriel as a likable, gentle boy with the soul of an artist. They were all very fond of him. Anat didn't want to set off any alarm bells that might prompt someone to warn him or help him hide from the authorities. People were always suspicious of the police. Regev claimed the cops had an interest in abetting the migrants; the aid workers were convinced of the exact opposite.

She also read the Immigration Police records on Gabriel. Like every other African infiltrator caught by the Israeli army (in fact, once they were across the border, they actually sat there and waited for the soldiers to come), he'd been taken to the detention camp at Ketziot Prison for questioning, and a hearing had been conducted to determine whether or not he was eligible for deportation. Gabriel claimed to come from Eritrea. He said his mother had urged him to leave the country to avoid conscription into the army, and he'd taken his sister with him because she was at risk of being raped and tortured. His sister had been abducted by their Bedouin guides in Sinai, and he hadn't seen her since.

Gabriel was granted a temporary work visa and had to register with the Interior Ministry every three months. The law required asylum seekers to provide a current address and report any change of address. In actuality, few migrants complied with that regulation, and from what Anat understood, no one ever bothered to enforce it.

In Yaron's opinion, the fact that Gabriel fled the scene and went into hiding was proof enough that he killed Michal. Anat didn't agree. People like Gabriel fled at any sign of trouble, whether they were guilty or not. It was just force of habit.

If, in fact, Gabriel was responsible for Michal's death, Anat presumed it was the result of a lovers' quarrel. That was merely her gut feeling for the time being, based mainly on his portrait of Michal. He'd not only made her look much prettier than she was, but he'd drawn her face with a softness and serenity that didn't jibe with what they'd learned about her. Gabriel saw something in Michal that no one else did, something Anat thought could only come from an intimate relationship.

"THAT'S her boss, Itai Fisher," Yaron said, interrupting her thoughts.

Fisher was a tall, solid man with long hair, big hands, and large, expressive eyes. His voice broke as he spoke about Michal, but his words were articulate despite his obvious emotion. He was wearing jeans and a white shirt that was a bit small on him, like an elementary school kid dressed for a Memorial Day ceremony.

Anat's mother thought she'd never go out with a cop because they were barely literate. She couldn't be more wrong. Almost all the people she worked with had been to college, and most of them had a master's degree, thanks in part to the boost in salary that came with it. The reason she'd never fallen for a cop was that police work attracted macho types, and she didn't go for he-men. She'd never be one of the boys, either. On the few occasions when they let her in and she kidded with her colleagues, the conversation inevitably ended with the line, "If you weren't a lady, I'd have an answer for that."

Anat's phone vibrated while Fisher was talking. She ignored it. It would be rude to answer it in the middle of a funeral, and anyway, she was listening very closely to the story he was telling.

"Yochai wants to talk to you. He says it's urgent," Yaron told her. He had no qualms about answering his phone.

"Turn that thing off," she snapped. Everything was urgent with Yochai.

Yaron threw her a nasty look. Like many of the cops in the district, he didn't trust her. She was a woman, and a young one at that, and they didn't believe she was in it for the long haul. Fully aware of their attitude, Anat pulled rank as seldom as possible.

She continued to scan the crowd, trying to judge their response to Fisher's moving words. When he passed her on his way out, she couldn't resist complimenting him on his eulogy.

From the interviews with the OMA workers, they knew that Gabriel was close to Itai as well as Michal. Consequently, at this stage they'd decided not to question Fisher about Gabriel to be sure he didn't interfere with the investigation. They'd also discovered that Gabriel was a bone of contention between Itai and Michal, who argued about him like parents fighting over their child's future. They seemed to fight a lot, but always over issues that came up at work.

All their colleagues agreed that the arguments were never personal; they stemmed only from their deep commitment to the people who asked for their help. The general feeling was that Itai usually gave in. In the words of one of the girls who clearly had a crush on him, "He's such a kind person."

Anat didn't want to draw any hasty conclusions. It was still too early in the investigation. Nevertheless, there was something to be said for Yaron's dismissal of Fisher's theory about what happened to Michal. Anat had read the report of Michal's accusations against the "Banker." She didn't have any hard evidence, just speculations and hearsay from people she refused to name, supposedly to protect them. You couldn't build a case on rumors and the presence of some Israelis in suits around the old bus station. Besides, Anat was pretty sure Michal knew her killer, but by her own account, she had no idea who the "Banker" was or who he was working for.

Fisher reacted to her compliment with a perplexed look, which she found quite attractive.

As soon as she left the cemetery, Anat returned Yochai's call. She'd harbored a vague hope that the scar-faced African kid had turned up, but she was disappointed.

"David broke his leg in Austria," the DC announced with no preamble.

"What? How? Is he okay?"

"Major Crimes doesn't want the case, so we're stuck with it," Yochai went on, ignoring her questions. "Can you handle it?"

"Yes," she said instinctively.

Silence. Had she answered too quickly? She could see him sitting at his desk amid the piles of paper, licking his lip.

"All right, then. It's yours. Don't let me down, Nachmias. And keep me informed." Yochai hung up.

Anat smiled inwardly. Michal Poleg was her first homicide.

Chapter 20

YARIV lay awake in bed. Inbar was sleeping peacefully beside him. Her rhythmic breathing irritated him. He hadn't been able to sleep like that in days.

Inbar had no idea what he was going through. She was so naive. She thought he was nervous about the wedding and kept trying to reassure him, saying it was only natural. He'd told her the bruises came from banging into the closet door. He couldn't use the bicycle excuse with her because she knew his bike had been stolen and he hated rent-a-bikes. She accepted his story without reservation and didn't ask any questions. There were no raised eyebrows, no cross-examinations, no sarcastic remarks about his clumsiness. As he'd expected, her main concern was whether or not the marks would disappear in time for the wedding. "I want them to take photos in both black-and-white and color," she'd explained, continuing to nag him with details that only aggravated him even more.

He had to pull himself together and keep his nerves in check. Every little thing set him off. He was bickering with everyone. Yesterday he'd even lost it in court, virtually yelling at Judge Barak. Luckily, she didn't make a big deal out of it, just declared a ten-minute recess to give him time to cool off.

Michal's funeral was on the evening news. He knew he ought to be saddened by her death, but all he felt was anger. He was angry at her for filing a complaint against him and then getting herself murdered, angry at Aloni for making him take garbage illegal alien cases, angry at Regev for urging him to stick with them, angry at the whole pile of shit he was in.

He felt a small spark of optimism when he listened to Regev's latest public tirade. The politician accused the migrants of murdering Michal, implying that the same fate was in store for anyone who had anything to do with them. Maybe he knows something I don't, Yariv allowed himself to speculate. But that hope died as quickly as it hatched. He knew Regev too well. Blaming the migrants was just a knee-jerk reaction for him.

Inbar changed position in her sleep, throwing an arm over his chest. He flinched and moved farther away. The secret that lay between them was making him feel contempt for her. They were supposed to meet with a photographer yesterday, but he canceled at the last minute. He'd deliberately waited till the last minute. He couldn't talk to photographers now. He knew she was disappointed, but she held her peace. Her silence aroused his contempt as well. Couldn't she see that he was falling apart?

Throwing off the blanket, Yariv got out of bed. Outside, the rain was coming down hard. It was freezing cold, but he was sweating. On his way past the kitchen he saw the time on the microwave oven: 2:46 a.m.

He'd been calling Kobi several times a day. He had to talk to someone, and Kobi was the only one he could be open with. His friend knew the whole story, and their conversations were confidential. Yariv realized he was starting to get on Kobi's nerves—he could hear it in his voice—but he couldn't stop. He needed to hear him say that he had nothing to worry about, that the cops weren't going to knock on his door any minute.

Yariv paced back and forth in the apartment, just like he did every night. Yesterday he read an article on the Internet about how the mind worked. It seemed the brain could protect itself by blocking out painful memories. They were simply erased. Maybe that's what was going on with him. Maybe he couldn't remember what happened that night because he killed her.

Chapter 21

ITAI was walking down one of the narrow streets in the Shapiro district adjacent to the old bus station. A group of teenagers were gathered on the sidewalk, smoking and talking loudly. Children were riding their bikes in the street. Two toddlers dressed in rags were playing on the curb. An old man was pawing through a trash can looking for plastic bottles he could redeem for a few agorot.

Itai climbed the stairs of a dilapidated building, making his way through the garbage strewn everywhere. The whole place reeked of urine. At least the cold weather had sent the cockroaches into hiding.

Drug dealers used to live here. The line of junkies waiting to score used to reach down the stairs and out the front door. The cops cleared them out, and the asylum seekers moved in. There were only a few Israelis left, those who were too poor to move, who were left behind and forgotten like always.

Itai knocked on one of the doors. Like all the other doors in the building, it bore a sign with a number, but it wasn't the apartment number. It was the rent. Every now and then the landlord would show up, cross out the number, and replace it with a higher one. Several local rabbis had forbidden their congregants to lease apartments to migrants and the ban was having an impact. Rents were going up.

Why didn't they understand that as long as there was no comprehensive solution to the problem, it was in their best interest not to make life any harder for the asylum seekers? When people have their backs to the wall, something's going to explode, and you can expect a lot of casualties—to say nothing of the blow such behavior dealt to the basic values of Israeli society. It was a heavy price to pay.

Water dripped on Itai's head from laundry thrown haphazardly over an improvised clothesline on the landing above.

He missed Michal. Their incessant arguments had caused him to regard her mainly as a thorn in his side. But now that she was gone, he realized how much help she had been to him, how much he had relied on her, how often he had sought her advice.

"Enough with those Africans already," his mother shouted at him over the phone yesterday. "You're driving your father and me crazy. What did we do to make you obsess over them?" Itai said good-bye and hung up.

He'd gotten an earful from Ronny, too. He told his friend to ask his wife to explain to Ayelet that he couldn't take her out for the time being, not her or anyone else. "Asshole," Ronny sputtered. "I don't know how you did it, but she likes you. You need to get out there and have some fun, get laid. You still remember how to do it, don't you?" He told Ronny he'd think about it, but he knew he wouldn't. "Just wait. We've got reserve duty in a couple of months and I'll be on your back night and day until you to understand how fucked up you are," Ronny promised.

"IT'S Itai Fisher from OMA," he called through the door when no one responded to his knock. A few months ago, Gabriel had overcome his embarrassment and agreed to show him where he lived.

The door was opened by a young woman wrapped in a woolen shawl. Itai vaguely remembered her face. He was hit by a wave of cigarette smoke mixed with the smell of frying and strong spices.

"I'm looking for Gabriel," he said, retreating a few steps.

The woman gazed at him with hollow eyes and said nothing.

"Does he still live here?"

"I need medicine," the woman said, coughing.

"Come to the office with me and I'll see how we can help you," he replied with a warm smile.

"There's no food," she went on. "No warm clothes."

Itai stood there in silence. She was using a common tactic of asylum seekers. They made you feel guilty in order to get what they wanted, whether it was money, food, medicine, or help with the authorities. It worked very well on Michal, for one. He was more immune. As an Israeli, he already had enough things to feel guilty about, and the condition of the asylum seekers wasn't one of them. We aren't responsible for the situation in Africa, he reminded himself. They came into our homes as uninvited guests, trespassers. But now that they're here, we owe it to them, and to ourselves, to treat them as humanely as possible. Guilt has nothing to do with it. Israel has no reason to feel guilty.

"Does Gabriel still live here?" he repeated.

"The children are hungry," she said, gesturing behind her with her head and coughing again.

When Itai first started working at OMA, it infuriated him that on the rare occasions when he asked asylum seekers for something, they demanded something in return and almost never said "thank you" when you gave it to them. Meanwhile, he'd learned to keep his emotions in check, to maintain his distance. He'd come to understand that the weak need to manipulate others in order to survive. You couldn't judge a hungry person by the same standards as someone who had plenty to eat. Whether he liked these people or not, he helped them because they needed his help. And that gave him satisfaction. "You do whatever has to be done," he remembered his German grandmother saying. Unlike her daughter-in-law, she never complained.

He took a fifty-shekel note from his wallet and handed it to the woman.

"Gabriel left," she said, as the bill quickly disappeared into the folds of her dress.

"Do you know where he went?"

"Nobody knows. One day he just left. The police came here looking for him."

"Why?" Itai asked, his body tensing.

The woman didn't reply.

"Why? Why were the police looking for Gabriel?"

"They said he murdered an Israeli woman."

Itai couldn't breathe. He thought the cops were going after the "Banker," but it turned out it was Gabriel they were hunting. What a fool he'd been. Why didn't he realize it sooner?

Chapter 22

WHEN Yariv learned that Galit Lavie was the prosecutor assigned to Michal's murder, he nearly gave up on the attempt to find out if the cops were on to him. Galit was known for her keen instincts and unbending integrity. It goes without saying that he couldn't stand her, and she didn't give the impression of being overly fond of him, either.

The gag order on the case made him even more irritable. He was constantly fighting with Inbar, mainly over the wedding plans and all the money she was spending.

Despite his qualms, he strolled casually by Galit's office and stuck his head in. She wasn't there. Her intern, Zohar, told him she'd left early. Yariv realized he'd stumbled on a golden opportunity. He didn't usually show much interest in the interns, but this one could be useful. One glance at Zohar with her dyed blond hair, manicured nails, and low-cut blouse told him she was on the prowl. He started talking about his single friends who were dying for a "serious relationship." Her eyes lit up immediately. There was no doubt in his mind that she'd tell him everything he needed to know.

It wasn't long before Zohar had revealed that the cops were looking for an African migrant with a scar on his face. Michal Poleg's neighbor saw him do it. The investigation was being led by the lady cop Yariv had seen on TV, Anat Nachmias. They hadn't gotten anywhere yet. The migrant was still in the wind.

Yariv felt a huge sense of relief. It was one of her Africans, that's all. Michal was killed by one of the black guys she was so bewitched by.

He wasn't guilty of anything. He didn't kill her. How could he even entertain such a thought? He wasn't a violent man. It was ridiculous to think he could be a murderer. What a relief!

Now he only needed to find out what Aloni wanted from him. He'd be meeting with him soon. Maybe he should talk to Regev first, just to give himself added insurance? He'd gotten a very flattering e-mail from him yesterday after his case ended with the deportation of another illegal.

Things were finally falling into place. In two months he'd be married, Regev had his back, and his whole life was ahead of him. All that was missing was for Nachmias to find the black guy.

Chapter 23

GABRIEL hurried to the alley behind the computer store where he had arranged to meet Arami. Everyone he passed seemed to look at him suspiciously, as if they could tell he was on the run. It was the same here as back home in Eritrea: the police were everywhere, spying on you, sniffing around, shadowing you. They probably had a thousand eyes and ears reporting anything unusual, scouting for the man with the scar on his face.

The last time he'd escaped by the skin of his teeth. Someone called out to the policeman in the park, distracting his attention. He released his grip on Gabriel without ever taking a good look at him. Otherwise, he'd be in prison now. He had to leave Levinsky Park. He couldn't go home and he couldn't go to the restaurant. No place was safe anymore.

Gabriel didn't speak to anyone but Arami. He couldn't trust anybody else. There were bad people around, people whose heads were messed up by what they saw in Africa or what happened to them in Sinai. Gabriel had also seen horrible things and been through hell and back, but he didn't let it change him or make him forget what he'd learned at home. His parents had taught him to be a good person. But there were a lot of people here who weren't like him. They no longer had a conscience or any scruples. Hunger didn't help, either. Nor did alcohol.

Itai kept calling, but Gabriel didn't answer. He was too scared and too ashamed. The shame got worse as the hours passed. Yesterday he left the little park he'd moved to and went to an Internet café where he finally made contact with his uncle in Spain. He told him he needed money to ransom Liddie, that if he didn't have twenty-five thousand shekels in four days, they'd kill her. His uncle had been living in Barcelona for ten years. He had a good job working as a gardener for the city. Tears fell from Gabriel's eyes when he recounted how he heard Liddie screaming and coughing. His uncle promised to send him around ten thousand shekels. That's all he had.

Tomorrow or the next day his uncle would let him know where he could pick up the money. He was going to give it to someone in Spain who knew someone in Israel. That was the only way for them to transfer money. If he was lucky, in the end Gabriel might get eighty-five hundred shekels after everyone in the chain took their cut. He had thirty-six hundred of his own that he'd managed to save, and Arami had promised to give him another two thousand. Altogether, he'd have about fourteen thousand one hundred. Where would he get the rest?

Gabriel walked quickly, keeping his head down. It was best not to make eye contact with anybody.

A noisy group of Eritrean boys his age were coming toward him. He moved aside, hoping to avoid them.

"Hey, where d'ya think you're goin'?" one of them demanded, blocking his path. He was a head taller and twice as wide as Gabriel, and he reeked of alcohol.

"Nowhere, excuse me," Gabriel said quietly, trying to get out of his way.

"I asked you a question." The young man grabbed his arm, pinning him in place.

"Please, I'm late for work," Gabriel implored, raising his head.

Their eyes met for a split second. Realizing his mistake, Gabriel immediately looked down at the ground again. But it was too late. He could tell the boy knew who he was, that he'd recognized him. He'd seen it in his eyes.

Alarm bells were ringing wildly in Gabriel's head. He had to move fast. He managed to free himself from the boy's grasp and started running.

"He's the guy they're looking for, the guy who murdered the Israeli. Grab him," he heard the troublemaker shout to his friends.

Gabriel kept running. He had no idea where he was going, but he had to get away.

"Stop!" The running footsteps behind him were drawing closer.

A passerby tried to intercept him, but he managed to evade him. He was running as fast as he could. He couldn't get caught. Not now. He needed every minute of the few days he had left to free Liddie. He had to get off the main street. If he stuck to the back alleys, he might be able to escape.

At the first chance he got, Gabriel turned right into a narrow alley. Children were jumping on a tattered mattress in the middle of the street. He veered around them and then around a group of women arguing in raised voices. A man sitting next to a drum of burning coals followed him with his eyes.

Gabriel was gasping for breath, but he couldn't stop. He had to keep running. Liddie's life depended on it. He looked behind him. Two of the Eritrean boys were still chasing him.

He turned into another alley, and then another. A garbage truck was blocking the end of the street. Gabriel leaped over a pile of garbage and squeezed past the cans, ignoring the curses flung at him by the sanitation workers.

He twisted his head around again. He'd put more distance between himself and his pursuers. He might just make it, he thought, turning into another alley and finding himself in front of a concrete wall. Gabriel stood there panting. He was dripping with sweat. It was the end of the line for him. He was trapped.

Out of the corner of his eye, Gabriel saw an old man with a cane entering the building on the corner. Maybe he still had a chance. He raced over and slipped inside before the old man could close the door behind him.

The room was large and bright, filled with rows of wooden chairs. At the far end was a small platform and on it a table covered in a white cloth. The odor of floor polish hung in the air.

They were all alone, just he and the old man, surrounded by silence. The room made Gabriel's head spin. It took him a while to get his bearings. It was as if he had stumbled on an oasis in the middle of the desert. It was so different from everything around it, so pure and clean. A thrill went through him when he realized where he was. He hadn't been in a church since his father was killed several years ago. He couldn't stand to hear the voice of another preacher, to see someone else standing where his father should be.

He looked around for a cross or a statue of Christ. There weren't any. It wasn't the kind of church he was familiar with. Instead of the figures of Christ he expected to see, there were only Jewish symbols.

Gabriel looked at the old man. His cane was on the floor and his hands were raised in the air. "No money, no money," he kept repeating. Gabriel stared at him in dismay, not knowing how to respond. He'd never seen an Israeli look so terrified. This one was wearing a hat. Michal once told him the Orthodox Jews were the worst, that he had to keep away from them. Itai said that was nonsense; there were good ones and bad ones and she shouldn't generalize. As usual, Michal insisted she was right. It was the Orthodox Jews who forbade renting apartments to migrants, she shouted at Itai, and they were the ones behind the smear campaign. Besides, the Minister of the Interior was Orthodox.

The old man with his hands raised didn't look frightening at all. On the contrary. Gabriel's heart was moved by his defenselessness. He wanted to reassure him, but he didn't know how.

"Okay, okay," he said with a smile. The old man didn't move. Gabriel did the only thing he could think of. Crossing himself, he genuflected toward the altar.

Stunned, the man dropped his arms. They were standing there side by side in silence when they were startled by loud knocking on the door. Someone called out in Hebrew. The old man gestured for Gabriel to follow him. As he led him into a side room, they heard the front door open, followed by the thud of heavy footsteps.

Chapter 24

WHEN he left the women's shelter, Itai decided to make his way back to OMA on foot. He needed time to clear his head. He dealt with hardship and human distress on a daily basis, but no one he encountered was more wretched than the women in the shelter. Crammed into a tiny apartment, they slept side by side on filthy mattresses on the floor, surrounded by battered toys, broken strollers, and charred pots. The rooms stank of unwashed bodies.

Some of the women were pregnant; others had recently given birth. They all shared the same story: they had been brutally raped by their Bedouin guides in Sinai.

The OMA office was a noisy place, filled with the sounds of chatter, shouting, weeping, and occasional laughter. But in the shelter there was only silent despair. It seeped into the walls and mixed with the stench. The women sat on their beds not speaking, absorbed in their own thoughts. They regarded what happened to them as punishment. Convinced they were to blame, they were ashamed to tell their story and afraid of the outside world. They wanted only to be left alone, to forget, and, if they could, to rid themselves of the poison growing in their body. Periodically the silence was broken by a crying baby, a baby whose mother hadn't found a way to abort it in time, a baby nobody wanted.

Dahlia, the social worker, and her small team of aides did their best to get the women back on their feet, teaching them to sew, knit, and perform simple tasks that would enable them to support themselves. As soon as they felt a woman could fend for herself, she was asked to leave in order to make room for one of the many others who needed a bed. OMA did what it could to help the women after they moved out of the shelter.

Even though Itai visited the shelter regularly, the experience invariably left him shaken. He always needed time to pull himself to-gether afterward. But today he was unnerved by something entirely different than usual.

Dahlia had pulled him outside into the back alley, still wet from the rain, and told him that a few days ago the women had witnessed a confrontation between Michal and three Israeli men, one dressed in a suit and tie, right outside their window. Michal was yelling at the man in the suit, accusing him of being a thief, taking advantage of the refugees, stealing their money. The other two men pounced on her, grabbed her by the arms, and dragged her away.

This was the first Itai had heard of it. Dahlia said she urged the women to report the incident, but as only to be expected, they refused to talk to the police. They didn't trust anyone, especially policemen. In fact, not surprisingly, they didn't trust men in general.

Ever since Itai had learned that Gabriel was a suspect in Michal's murder, he'd been racking his brain trying to think of a way to convince the cops that the idea was absurd, that they ought to be looking in a different direction. He knew it wouldn't do any good to tell them Gabriel wasn't capable of such a thing. He needed something more solid.

The incident Dahlia described might persuade them to take Michal's allegations more seriously. It was no longer simply a matter of what she thought she saw and what she thought it meant. Now he could also tell them what they actually did to her. She'd lied to Itai. She hadn't left it to the cops to deal with the "Banker"; she'd confronted him and his goons herself. According to the women in the shelter, they assaulted her in the street. They were probably the ones who roughed her up near her home as well. They were professional criminals, and there was a lot of money involved. They wouldn't let a little girl with a big mouth interfere in their business. She must have gotten too close, so they decided to make the problem go away. They squashed her like a bug. He had to go to the police. They wouldn't be able to ignore him anymore. They'd have no choice but to go after the "Banker."

Chapter 25

MICHAL Poleg's murder was a headache for Shimon Faro. It was just the sort of thing that could do him in. In the end, men like him were brought down by something stupid like this, not by anything major.

For a year now he'd been investing a lot of effort in his private banking system at the old bus station. He alone could take credit for the idea, the planning, and the execution, and he took a lot of pride in what he'd accomplished. The business was already raking in millions. If the blacks kept coming, he could easily double or triple his earnings. He had to admit that he was frustrated by the need to keep it all under the radar. He imagined himself giving interviews to the financial press about how he identified an opportunity and made brave decisions, and now it was paying off. He could see himself sitting in a café like any respectable businessman, a tape recorder on the table and an ambitious journalist opposite him with a notebook and a look of awe on his face. "I did it all with my own two hands," he'd say to the fawning reporter. "I wasn't born with a silver spoon in my mouth." But Faro knew better than to entertain such thoughts. The only time men like him gave interviews was when they had a noose around their neck. Besides, the suits in the financial circles in Tel Aviv would never accept him as a legitimate businessman.

Still, no one else had seen the economic potential of the Africans as soon as they started to fill the streets around the old bus station. Who doesn't want a bank where they can keep their savings, transfer funds, and borrow money? It was a basic human need, just like gambling and hookers. If he didn't provide these services, someone else would. Migrants who tried to go through legal channels were buried in red tape and had to pay exorbitant fees. And when Interior Ministry inspectors started staking out the banks near the bus station and picking up illegals, Faro's revenues soared. He had his people spread the word: there was another bank they could use where there was no red tape and no inspectors, and it charged next to nothing. He even composed a little jingle in his head, something catchy in the style of the songs the army entertainment troupes used to sing. He loved those old songs.

Faro had originally gotten into the banking game because of the Bedouins in Sinai. They had a good thing going. They negotiated a price to take the Africans to Israel, and then halfway there they demanded more and held them hostage until they paid up. Where did they get the money? They called their relatives in Israel or Europe or wherever and said they had to send it. That worked fine as far as it went, but there was one hitch: getting the money to the Bedouins wasn't easy. That's where Faro came in. His organization had proven itself very adept at collecting and transferring funds. And they were already working hand in hand with the Bedouins in the drug-smuggling business.

After Faro got the system up and running, he expanded his banking activities in new directions. Today, if an African wanted to send money home to his family, he used Faro's bank. Faro had tried to do something similar with the Asians a few years ago, looking to set up an unofficial channel through which the foreign workers from the Philippines, Nepal, China, and the rest of the Far East could send money back home. That enterprise had failed miserably and cost him a bundle. But where he couldn't pull it off with the slant-eyes, he'd scored big with the Africans. First of all, unlike the Asians, the Africans only moved in one direction. There was nobody in Israel who was going back to Sudan or Eritrea and could act as a private courier. Also, the Asians could send their money to some major city and tell their family to go and collect it. But the families of the Africans lived in refugee camps or some godforsaken village in the middle of nowhere, and that's where the money had to go. And number three, the Asians had entered the country legally. They had passports and they could purchase money orders at the post office. Most of the Africans didn't have papers. They needed someone like Faro who could move cash around, didn't demand to see any documents, and charged what he felt was a fair fee for his services.

Faro got the job done. He knew people all over Africa. He'd been selling army surplus on the continent for years. He bought outdated munitions from the Defense Ministry, ostensibly for sale to some friendly country (although even the ministry knew that wasn't where they were going to end up), and auctioned them off to the highest bidder. The ministry didn't ask, and he didn't tell. The army wasn't using the stuff anyway. As long as he didn't try to get his hands on new technology, nobody cared. Yes, one way or another, the blacks were a very nice source of income.

Faro's bank was also making a hefty profit from savings accounts. Since most of the migrants couldn't open an account in an official Israeli bank, even if they wanted to go through all the hassle, they walked around with their cash in their pocket—sometimes with everything they owned on their back as well. They ran the constant risk of being robbed by other migrants. That's where Faro came in. He offered them a place to deposit the money. Admittedly, it was a while before that idea took off. The Africans were reluctant to give their money to anyone, especially Israelis. His people had to explain that if they didn't hand over the cash willingly, they'd have to take it from them by force. But even if his customers initially agreed out of fear, they soon learned that what they deposited in Faro's bank they got back, minus a reasonable commission, of course. When it came right down to it, he was doing the cops a favor.

Today the bank was a well-oiled machine. The Africans used it to transfer funds, keep their money safe, and take out loans when they got laid off and had to support themselves until they found another job, or when they needed cash to ransom relatives being held hostage in Sinai. They might not be happy about the arrangement, but what other option did they have?

If only those stupid blacks didn't spend their money as soon as they got it, if only they gave a little more thought to the long term, Faro could increase his earnings tenfold. But there was nothing he could do about that. It was a problem of mentality and the fucked-up way they were brought up.

Government policy was also playing into his hands. In fact, he originally got the idea for the savings accounts when he read about the Templars in the nineteenth century. Those German bastards made a killing from pilgrims. They set up posts along the route to the Holy Land and told the pilgrims the place wasn't safe. Leave your money with us, they said, and we'll give it back to you on your way home. The ones who went home got their money back, but what about all those who stayed in the Holy Land? It was the same with the Africans. When one of his customers was deported, the money in his account went straight into Faro's pocket.

It hadn't been easy to set up the machinery. He had to find migrants to use as go-betweens. His people didn't work with end users. It was always best to keep a healthy distance, and besides, there were issues of communication and trust to be considered. It was rough going at first, but as soon as the "General" hooked up with him and became a major player in the operation, things went much more smoothly. The "General" was what they called a "strategic asset." Faro was lucky to have him. He recruited new customers and rode herd on the go-betweens. He was very effective, and very ambitious.

For things to go without a hitch, there were also palms that needed to be greased in the ranks of the Immigration Police so he could be sure the right people got deported. Nowadays, when a cop picked up a migrant and told him, "I say you're from Ethiopia, not Eritrea, so wave good-bye to Israel," there was a good chance he was working for Faro.

He still hoped to have someone from the State Attorney's Office in his pocket. That would be sweet. Controlling the State's objections, trading on who got deported and who didn't—it could take his business to the next level and dramatically increase his earnings. He hadn't managed to pull it off yet, but he was a patient man. He already had beat cops and immigration cops at his beck and call, and he'd ferret out a prosecutor, too. It was only a matter of time.

He heard that Michal Poleg had gone to the Economic Crime Unit with information about the man she called the "Banker," but that didn't worry him. His contacts told him nothing would come of it. It even tickled him that she gave Boaz such a respectable title.

Faro was more upset by the fact that the Poleg woman had confronted Boaz in the street. That sort of public scene wasn't good for business. He sent Ilya and Noam to scare her off, but they got carried away and roughed her up. He didn't like that. He didn't approve of gratuitous violence, particularly when it came to women. But it wasn't the end of the world. He'd decided to let it slide.

But now that cunt had gone and gotten herself killed. As far as he knew, it wasn't the work of anyone in his organization. Faro kept a very close eye on his people ever since that incident with David Meshulam, may he rest in peace, who'd gone behind his back and almost killed the lady ADA.

Still, even if none of his men were involved, it was no reason to be complacent. You could never tell where a police investigation might lead. And there were plenty of cops who'd be very pleased to pin the murder on him. He didn't need that kind of bother now.

A little bird had told him the cops were looking for some scar-faced African. At least that was good news. Faro had ordered Itzik to use all of their connections to find the African and get him to confess to the cops. He told him to pay for the information if he had to, and he was willing to pay the guy, too, so he'd have something to send home to his family.

The last thing he needed now was complications. He had to keep a low profile so he could continue to expand his business in peace. He had rivals who envied his success and wanted a piece of the pie. Even the fucking terrorist organizations recognized the potential of the migrants. Muslims from Sudan donated part of their salary to Hamas agents in Israel, who sent it to the West Bank to buy weapons to kill Israelis with. Hamas also had agents in Sudan who could pass money to the families of the migrants. They actually offered the same service Faro offered, but while he did it to make a profit, they did it to finance terror.

Faro didn't want Boaz Yavin behind bars. He was planning to send him to Argentina next week. A big arms deal was going down. Michal Poleg's murder had come at a very bad time.

He had to get a move on. He had to locate the African with the scar and turn him in as soon as possible. The "General" needed to make it his first priority, and he'd better deliver. Faro had a business to run, goddammit!

Chapter 26

ARAMI was waiting for Gabriel in an alley near his apartment. He'd missed their meeting yesterday when those boys started chasing him. He only managed to escape with the help of the old man, who let him out of the Jewish church through the back door. After that, he was too scared to go back to where he was supposed to meet Arami. He'd gotten away from them once, but he might not be so lucky the next time.

"The police are hunting for you. They're going around telling people to look for a man with a scar on his cheek," Arami had warned him last night on the phone after he told him what happened. So Gabriel's suspicions had been right. He broke out in a cold sweat. The words "the police are hunting for you" took him back to another time and another life in the country he'd fled. He'd crossed thousands of miles to find a better life, and here he was, right back where he started from.

"I'm sorry, Gabriel," Arami said somberly after they embraced. "I tried, but I can't get you the money I promised."

Gabriel gazed at his friend in despair. He'd been counting on him. Where would he get what he needed? Time was running out. He wouldn't be able to pay. Meanwhile, Liddie was suffering. She sounded very sick on the phone.

"Listen, Gabriel," Arami said, interrupting his dark thoughts. "Something happened yesterday that might solve at least one of your problems."

"What? What happened?" Gabriel asked expectantly. He desperately needed good news, something that would help him figure out what to do.

"Someone stopped me outside the OMA office and asked about you. I don't know who he was, but he looked important. He said he was looking for you."

"Why? What did he want?" Gabriel asked fearfully.

"He said he wanted to give you money for Liddie . . ."

Gabriel kept his eyes fixed on Arami, waiting to hear the catch.

"But there's one condition."

"Just tell me what it is. I'll do anything to save Liddie."

"You have to go to the police and say that you killed Michal."

Chapter 27

YARIV was at the computer, preparing his response to Michal's complaint to the Bar Association. The past few days had been a roller-coaster ride. Sometimes he was up, convinced he was safe because the cops were directing all their efforts at finding the African. But at other times he was down. Like yesterday, when Galit Lavie marched into his office and took him to task for pumping her intern for information. Under any other circumstances, he would have answered her in kind for her patronizing tone. But he panicked and just apologized profusely, chalked it up to curiosity, and kept repeating how sorry he was.

He hoped that would be the end of it, but he couldn't be sure. What if she told the cops? They could decide to shift the focus of their investigation. He called Kobi again and his friend told him he had nothing to worry about. Galit liked to think she was better than everyone else, and never missed an opportunity to tell them so. In Kobi's opinion, Galit wouldn't do anything about it, and even if she did, what difference did it make? The cops were looking for a black illegal, not a white attorney. Besides, Kobi said with a knowing laugh, when did the police start second-guessing themselves?

YARIV reread the complaint for the hundredth time. Michal claimed that Hagos's death was the direct result of Yariv Ninio's actions and his insistence that the deportees were not in any danger.

Now that Michal was dead, nobody was showing any particular interest in her complaint. It was highly unlikely that the Bar Association would exchange information with the Foreign Ministry. And there were very few people in the ministry itself who even knew of the existence of any legal opinion written by Dr. Yigal Shemesh regarding the fate of the deportees. Yariv still had to submit a response for the record, but with Michal out of the picture, they'd file the whole thing away and forget about it. Why bother with lengthy explanations?

"The undersigned has no knowledge of the legal opinion referred to in the complaint. The alleged facts presented are solely figments of the complainant's imagination. No such document has ever come to my attention," Yariv typed, watching the words take shape on the screen. That was the best way to go about it, he thought—deny everything. If he never saw the document and didn't know of its existence, then he didn't do anything wrong.

Chapter 28

GABRIEL was standing in an alcove across from the familiar building. He'd picked the darkest, most isolated spot he could find from which to keep watch. Another light went out. It was time.

He checked to make sure there was no one around. This was a busy street during the day, filled with people and cars going in and out of the many body shops in the area. But at night it was deserted. Gabriel stepped out of his hiding place and quickly crossed the road. He couldn't allow himself time to think. He had to do it now. It was the only way to save Liddie. What kind of future could he make for himself in this country anyway? The Israelis didn't want him here. Every day, more Eritreans arrived, and it was getting harder and harder to find work. He couldn't leave, either. Where would he go? No country wanted him, and returning to Eritrea meant certain death.

Gabriel was frightened and apprehensive, but he also felt a deep sense of shame. What would his father say if he knew what he was about to do?

He climbed the stairs to the second floor. He didn't hear any sounds, but what if he wasn't alone? In order for his plan to work, he had to be alone.

Gabriel stood in front of the closed door and knocked.

"Who's there," he heard the familiar voice call out. "Who is it?"

Chapter 29

ANAT hadn't been planning to question Itai Fisher herself, but fifteen minutes before he was scheduled to arrive, they got a tip that the scar-faced African had been spotted near the old bus station. Yaron, acting as her second in command for the time being, was so eager to rush over there and haul the guy in himself that she didn't argue with him. With the investigation treading water, she knew her team needed action. Nothing improved cops' morale faster than telling them to put on their vests, briefing them for an operation, and letting them race through the city with lights flashing and sirens screaming. She'd learned that sometimes it was best if she kept out of the way. Most cops believed policewomen should stick to searching female suspects and interviewing rape victims. They were useless, even a nuisance, when it came to things like breaking up brawls or making an arrest where the use of force was required. Anat tried to absent herself from such incidents so as not to interfere with their male bonding. The fact that it was freezing outside made the decision even easier. And it would give her a chance to think in peace.

Michal Poleg's body was found five days ago, and there'd been no sign of Gabriel until now. This morning, when she went to deliver the daily report Yochai demanded, he made it abundantly clear that he wasn't happy with the way she was handling the case. "I want results, not theories," he said with a tone of condescension. At least this time he didn't lick his lip. Anat restrained herself, and instead of turning their meeting into a confrontation, she outlined what they'd done thus far and asked as sweetly as possible if there was anything he thought they'd missed. Naturally, he had no answer for her.

Fisher called the station just as she was leaving the DC's office, claiming it was urgent that he speak to the lead detective on the case.

Yaron had questioned him the first time around, so she wanted him to be the one to talk to Fisher now. But meanwhile, the tip had come in and Yaron had gone off to play cops and robbers.

"YOU said it was urgent," Anat began, getting straight to the point. "What's up?" People respond differently to being interviewed by a police officer. Itai Fisher was nervous. And trying to hide it was making him even more nervous.

He passed his hand through his hair. It was long, not a common sight among men his age. Anat had been on enough dates with guys over thirty to know that for a fact.

"I just wanted to know how the investigation is going," he said, fidgeting uncomfortably in his seat.

"That's what you call urgent?" Anat asked, deliberately feeding his uneasiness.

"Michal was very devoted to her work. We worked side by side for a long time. It's only natural . . . you came to the office the other day . . . I was out . . . I thought," he stammered.

Anat kept silent. Silence made people anxious, so they kept talking.

"I understand you're looking for Gabriel."

Anat nodded, not speaking.

"Can I ask why? What makes you think he's your prime suspect?" Itai's tone was becoming more assertive. He crossed his hands on his chest.

She could say it was none of his business, that she was asking the questions, not him. But instead she merely remained silent.

"Gabriel didn't kill Michal. She was helping him. She was good to him. What reason would he have to kill her? I guess it's easy to pin it on the African. Ehud Regev's demagoguery works on cops, too, right?" Itai's puny attempt to go on the attack seemed to encourage him. His voice was steadier and more confident.

Anat's cell phone beeped. Yaron. They'd located the target. "Good luck," she texted back quickly.

"So who killed her?" she asked. The text from Yaron had eased her mind. Finally. They'd been chasing a ghost. The guy had vanished into thin air. People say it's hard to disappear in Israel, that Israelis are too nosy. You can move to another city, switch jobs, but it won't work. Your new neighbors will want to know where you went to school, what you did in the army, who you're seeing, how come you're not married, what friends you have in common. But it was different with migrants.

Anat was stunned by the places she'd seen in the course of this investigation. In the middle of Tel Aviv, just under the surface, there was another country with its own foods, smells, colors, and customs. It was like she was entering a foreign land governed by a secret code she didn't understand. She'd been struggling to make sense of it all, to read the faces of the migrants and interpret what they said. But she didn't have the necessary tools.

More than anything else, her forays into this territory left her feeling depressed. She had pity for the Africans living in such abject poverty, as well as for the Israelis who still resided in those neighborhoods, the people who'd been left behind. With twenty or thirty migrants occupying the apartments all around them, they were afraid to leave their homes.

As a detective, she had to be able to read people, to unearth their motives, their concerns, their ambitions. But the deeper she delved into the world of the migrants, the more she realized how convoluted the issues were. The soldiers at the border were forbidden to help them cross into Israel so as not to encourage others to follow. On the other side of the border, the Bedouins were out for their blood. And it wasn't long before terrorists took advantage of the situation and started insinuating themselves into the groups of Africans trying to steal across the border. Then, if you made it easy for those who snuck into the country to get a work permit, there were fewer jobs for disadvantaged Israelis, but if you didn't, you had hundreds of hungry people loitering in the streets—a crime wave waiting to happen. There was no easy way out of this maze. People thought there was a quick fix even for complicated problems, but she knew from her experience on the force that there was no such thing. Sometimes there was no kind of fix at all.

"I told that detective, Yaron, who did it . . . Michal did more than just go to the police. She took pictures of those people, screamed at them in front of witnesses, confronted them in the street. They dragged her away. They're violent people. They must have been the ones who beat her up outside her house. Why aren't you going after them?" Itai asked. Civilians always had theories. They come up with a simple answer and they're sure it never occurred to the police. But a good cop knows better than to start with a theory. First you have to get as much information as you can. And the answer is rarely simple.

Anat's phone beeped again. Yaron. "One minute," she read.

"Am I keeping you?" Itai asked, annoyed.

"Not at all. We're well aware of everything you said. We read Michal's testimony. We take all the information we get very seriously."

Itai gave her a skeptical look.

To prove she wasn't just trying to mollify him, Anat pulled a file from the shelf behind her. Leafing through it until she found the report of Michal's allegations, she spun the binder around for him to see.

"Do you know the name of the man she photographed?" Itai shook his head.

"Do you have any evidence that they assaulted her outside her home?" she went on, closing the file and pushing it aside. The fact that the incident had taken place the day before she was killed still gnawed at Anat, even though she didn't believe it was directly connected to her death. Michal knew her murderer. She opened the door to him. But both her own allegations and Itai's testimony indicated that she had no idea who the "Banker" was.

Once again her phone beeped. Anat looked at the screen and her heart sank. "Wrong guy. Sorry," the message read.

"Sure?" she texted, deeply disappointed.

"Forty, scar on right cheek, not our guy," Yaron texted back.

"INSPECTOR Nachmias, you've got to listen to me. Gabriel didn't do it," Itai insisted, breaking the silence. He sounded desperate. "Forget the stereotypes and the rhetoric. Being African doesn't make him a murderer. Neither does running and hiding. Asylum seekers come from countries where people are persecuted and tortured by the government. Cooperating with the police isn't part of their world. And you've got to understand, they don't know our language or our norms. Israelis frighten them. They see a police officer and automatically they think of torture and deportation. You have to understand the cultural context."

Anat found Itai's self-righteous tone abrasive. "We're not dealing with stereotypes here, Mr. Fisher. Just facts and evidence. You may be convinced that Gabriel didn't kill Michal, but I don't know whether he did or not. All I *do* know is that someone saw him outside her apartment on the day she was murdered. So we're looking for him. As soon as we find him, he'll be able to tell us exactly what he was doing there. I'd be grateful for any help you can give us. Otherwise . . ." Anat stood up.

"All I'm asking is that you don't assume he's guilty. Just listen to him when you question him. Really listen. He's not like the suspects you're used to interrogating. You have to understand his circumstances. People like him are preyed on. They're coerced, threatened. They live in a constant state of fear. You have to read between the lines, see the big picture. Even if they confess, it doesn't mean they're guilty." Itai remained seated.

"I can assure you, we know how to do our job," Anat said, making no effort to hide her impatience. "Now, if you don't mind . . ."

Anat stopped in mid-sentence and stared at Fisher, who was still sitting there looking at her. He was telling her something, but she'd been so preoccupied by the futile chase that she hadn't been listening.

"You know where he is, don't you?" She returned to her chair and trained her eyes on him.

Itai nodded. "Yes, Inspector. I know where he is. He told me the whole story."

Chapter 30

ITAI was alone in the room. He'd told Nachmias how Gabriel had shown up at the office last night, what he said, and where she could find him. The policewoman had become very agitated. "Wait here," she ordered, hurrying out of the room.

Although Itai had been searching everywhere for Gabriel, he was taken by surprise when the young man knocked on the OMA door late in the evening. Itai was dismayed by the look on his face. He seemed extremely tense and flustered.

"Gabriel, where have you been? I've been very worried about you. I've been trying to get in touch with you for days."

Gabriel avoided his eyes. "I did something terrible, Itai. Please, please, don't be mad at me," he said, his voice trembling. Then he burst into tears.

Itai stared at him, petrified.

"What are you trying to tell me?" he asked. His own voice was unsteady as well.

Gabriel just kept on sobbing.

"Is it because the cops are looking for you?" Itai asked hesitantly.

Silence.

"Is it about Michal?"

Gabriel raised his eyes. They were red and swollen from crying.

"Yes . . . it was me . . . I . . . I killed her," he mumbled, covering his face with his hands.

The bare statement made Itai flinch. He'd been hoping Gabriel would tell him he had fled from the police because he was being accused of a crime he didn't commit.

"Don't say that, Gabriel. Why would you say such a thing?" Itai refused to believe it. He knew how close Michal and Gabriel were.

Gabriel didn't respond. He just stood there in silence looking lost and miserable.

"What happened? Tell me what happened. Why did you do it?" Itai pleaded.

"I would like you to come to the police with me."

"No, not until you tell me why," Itai said angrily. Of the host of emotions that were overwhelming him, it was the anger that came out.

He waited, helpless and confused, as Gabriel went on sobbing. A lot of asylum seekers had sat opposite him in tears. He'd learned to distinguish between those who did it for effect and those who were genuinely wretched. Gabriel clearly belonged to the latter category.

"I thought you liked her. She helped you. So why . . ." He couldn't get his head around it.

"I did like her. She was like a big sister to me," Gabriel whimpered.

"So what happened?"

Gabriel remained silent.

"Did you want money from her? Did you have feelings for her but she rejected you?" Itai asked, trying the first explanations that occurred to him.

"No, no, of course not."

"Gabriel, I want you to look me in the eye and tell me you killed Michal." The whole situation seemed unimaginable. It didn't make any sense. Why would Gabriel hurt Michal?

The African kept his eyes lowered.

"I'll go to the police with you, but first you have to look me in the eye and tell me you did it," Itai insisted.

ITAI got up and opened the door of the detective's office. He was tired of waiting. The eagerness Nachmias had displayed when he told her about Gabriel was not to his liking.

The more questions he asked, the more he became convinced that there was something odd about Gabriel's confession. He didn't know any details of the murder and didn't offer any explanation for killing her. As a rule, people don't confess to a crime for no reason, and guilty people don't usually turn themselves in voluntarily. But the asylum seekers lived in a different reality. Theirs was a world of despair, hunger, insecurity, and very often extortion, and those pressures made them behave in a way that didn't always seem logical. Besides, Itai knew Gabriel, and he knew he wasn't a murderer.

When he asked Gabriel if someone was forcing him to say he killed Michal, if someone was putting pressure on him, the young man's whole body tensed up. Itai's instincts told him he was on the right track. But no matter how hard he tried to get him to talk, Gabriel refused to say any more.

Itai had no doubt it was a done deal as far as the cops were concerned. They wouldn't read between the lines the way he did. They'd accept Gabriel's confession at face value and be thrilled that it fell into their lap. After all, a confession is the "king of evidence," the ultimate proof of guilt. Itai had studied law. He knew that confessions aren't admissible in court in Jewish law. But the criminal courts in Israel aren't governed by religious precepts. On the contrary, in the country's secular legal system, if you confess it means you're guilty. Even if Gabriel was an Israeli citizen, a confession would be enough to convict him.

The end was a foregone conclusion. Gabriel would be convicted of a crime he didn't commit, and the real murderer would continue to walk free.

THE hallway was empty. Itai had asked to be present when they questioned Gabriel to make sure he was treated properly, but Nachmias refused. She promised they'd be gentle with him, that they wouldn't hurt a hair on his head. Itai wondered if he'd given in too easily. Maybe he should have been more assertive. He could have refused to tell them where Gabriel was until they agreed to the terms of his arrest. But it was too late to second-guess himself. He had no experience to draw on. Even during the short time he'd actually worked as a lawyer, he'd steered clear of criminal law.

Itai closed the door and started pacing the office restlessly. He wanted to help Gabriel and he wanted to bring Michal's real killer to justice. Maybe he could make up in some small way for ignoring her cry for help. But to do that, he had to take concrete action.

He didn't even remember what the "Banker" looked like. Michal had shown him the pictures she took, but a lot had happened since then. Itai glanced at the door. He had to get another look at her pictures. He couldn't just wait here without doing anything. The best way to help Gabriel was to point the cops in the right direction.

The thought of what he was planning made his blood run cold, but he couldn't agonize over it. He had to move fast. He didn't have much time. Nachmias would be back any minute. Along with the gratitude she'd displayed when he handed her Gabriel on a silver platter, he'd also seen the accusing look in her eyes. And what if they didn't find him in the park where he said he'd be? He should have brought Gabriel with him. The young man wanted to come. In fact, that's why he went to Itai in the first place, so they could go together. But Itai convinced him to let him talk to the detective alone first, even though he knew he had little chance of getting her to see things his way.

Itai pulled the file toward him. What would he say if the detective walked in? What excuse could he offer?

Quickly, he leafed through the documents searching for the report. He believed in playing by the rules. Michal called it cowardice, but he preferred to think of it as being prudent and realistic. If only she could see him now!

Itai paged through the whole file, but he didn't find what he was looking for. He started again from the beginning. It had to be there; Nachmias had shown it to him. He found it on his second attempt and breathed a sigh of relief. Three pictures of the "Banker" were at-tached to the report of her allegations against him.

He pulled out his cell phone and aimed the camera at the photo-graphs with trembling hands. He pressed the shutter button twice, just to be on the safe side, and then slid the file back across the desk.

Shaken by his own defiance of the rules, Itai returned to his chair. He was sitting down when the door opened. Inspector Nach-mias was back.

Chapter 31

A shiver went down Gabriel's spine when he heard the sirens approaching. He was all alone in the world, and his stomach ached from hunger. Once he'd had big dreams. He wanted to be a famous artist, to bring honor to his family. He wanted to fall in love, get married, and have children. Life was very bad in Eritrea. He'd hoped it would be better in Israel. But it was bad here, too. And now it was going to be even worse.

He'd gone to see Itai at the OMA office last night even though he didn't want to. He wanted Arami to go to the police with him, but his friend advised him to ask Itai to accompany him. That way, Gabriel could say he didn't know English, and then the police would have to call an interpreter. Arami would make sure to be nearby. But they wouldn't let him in if they realized the two men knew each other.

"You'll be fine," Arami told Gabriel before they parted. "This way you'll have two friends with you, me and Itai. If you don't know what to say, I'll help you. Just be careful not to let them see you understand what they're saying. Play dumb. They don't think we have a brain in our heads anyway. I'll see you there, at the police station."

The Israeli had promised to give him twenty thousand shekels if he turned himself in and said he killed Michal. What if he didn't keep his promise? He wanted to get the money first, but Arami said the man would never agree.

Arami didn't know who the Israeli was or why he wanted Gabriel to confess to the murder. The most likely explanation was that he killed Michal himself or worked for the person who did. Gabriel was tormented by the thought that the man who murdered his friend would never be punished, and he would be helping him get away with it. But what choice did he have? There was no other option. If he didn't do it, Liddie would die and the police would eventually arrest him anyway. And as for that Israeli man, who knows what he'd do?

Michal is dead and nothing will bring her back, Arami said. But Liddie is alive. He could still save her. Besides, even if he went to the police and told them the truth, they wouldn't believe him. In their eyes, all Africans were bad, uninvited guests who were overrunning their home and taking advantage of them. Justice didn't matter. Truth didn't, either. Israelis only care about themselves, Arami said, and they're consumed by racism and hatred. If he was going to go to the police, he might as well get something out of it.

Last night he'd knelt in prayer, begging Christ for forgiveness. It was only the second time he'd prayed since his father was killed by the soldiers. The first time was in the desert, with Liddie, when he was sure they were about to die. Then it had been mainly for her sake. He was furious with Christ for taking the life of a good man like his father. But last night he felt compelled to pray, and the words came pouring out.

Itai offered him a bed in his apartment, but Gabriel refused. It was even harder to face him than he'd feared. He was afraid that if he didn't leave soon, he'd break down and tell him the truth. He hated lying to Itai.

Arami said the police wouldn't ask a lot of questions. They thought all Africans were criminals. If one of them came and said he was guilty, it would just prove their point. Gabriel hoped Arami was right. His whole plan depended on the police believing him.

In the end, they decided that Gabriel would spend the night in the OMA office. In the morning, he'd go to the little park on the corner of Hachmei Israel and Neveh Sha'anan Streets and wait there while Itai spoke to the police. He didn't get any sleep. He was terrified of what was ahead for him. Men who had been held in Israeli prisons said conditions weren't that bad. There were showers and regular meals, and the guards didn't beat you. But none of those men were accused of murder. The Israelis might not be so nice to murderers. And maybe they'd want to take revenge on an African who killed one of their own. Or maybe they'd deport him like they deported Hagos. They sent Hagos to Ethiopia and the Ethiopians sent him back to Eritrea and he was killed there. The same thing could happen to him.

THREE patrol cars squealed to a halt at the entrance to the park. The deafening sirens were making Gabriel dizzy. His mouth was dry. He'd been in such a hurry to leave the OMA office in the morning that he hadn't even had a drink of water first. He wasn't a big eater, but since Michal's death he'd hardly been able to keep anything down.

Police officers jumped out of the cars and started running in his direction. Someone was barking orders through a microphone, but he couldn't understand what he was saying. There was so much noise. The cop in the lead pulled out his gun.

THE soldiers in Eritrea burst into the house when the family was having supper. They grabbed his father and dragged him outside. His mother was screaming. He and Liddie were crying. Outside in the yard, they shot their father in the head. Gabriel was only eight years old at the time, but the image of his father lying dead on the ground in a pool of blood was burned into his memory forever. When he left home, his mother told him that was the moment she decided to send her children away the first chance she got. There was no future for them in Eritrea.

THE policemen were running toward him, shouting words he didn't understand. They all had their guns out now, aimed at him. All of a sudden Gabriel felt ice cold. The blood drained from his head and he fell to the ground.

Chapter 32

ANAT was sitting in her office preparing for her confrontation with the suspect. In the past half hour, both the District Commander and the Region Commander had called to congratulate her. News of Gabriel's arrest had apparently reached the highest levels, even leaking to political circles, with people like MK Regev calling the RC to offer their congratulations.

The message Anat received from her superiors was crystal clear, but she said nothing besides thanking them politely. It was only when the district press officer asked her to try to put the investigation to bed within two hours so he could get it on the evening news at eight that she really lost it.

This wasn't going to be a simple matter. You're always at a disadvantage when a suspect doesn't know the language and you have to use an interpreter. You lose the spontaneity of the responses, and you can't control the momentum of the interrogation. Moreover, she'd never questioned an Eritrean before, and that had her worried. The tactics she used on Israelis might not work with him. You can break Israelis by telling them that if they don't talk you're going to have to interrogate their families, that their arrest will bring shame on themselves and their loved ones. But Gabriel's family was thousands of miles away. She didn't know what buttons to push. Should she show him a picture of Michal Poleg and remind him how well she treated him, or would that just make him clam up? The triggers were different in every culture. Gilad, the district intel officer, told her to threaten to deprive him of his liberty. These people had to work, he said. Their families depended on the money they sent home.

"Stop worrying, Nachmias, everything will be fine," Yaron said, slapping her on the back before he left to pick up Gabriel in the park. He offered to conduct the interrogation himself. He was known in the district as the go-to guy when they needed a confession. The way he hammered at a suspect, they almost always broke in the end. Anat thanked him for the offer but turned it down. It was her case.

THE door opened and Yaron poked his head in. "He's all yours, Nachmias," he said. Anat got the distinct impression that it was an effort for him to refrain from adding, "Don't screw up."

"Is the interpreter here?"

"Yes. Joshua wasn't available, but we got lucky. Arami was nearby."

"Excellent," Anat said with a broad smile.

She stood up and adjusted her blouse. She'd decided to wear her uniform for effect. She took a deep breath. It was time to go get a confession.

Chapter 33

THE door opened, startling Gabriel out of his chair. A short skinny policewoman came in, followed by the tall bearded officer who'd run toward him in the park pointing his gun at him. Gabriel had fainted from fright. The policeman threw water on him and slapped his face until he came to.

With his hands and feet cuffed, they led him into a small room that contained nothing but a table and four plastic chairs. Gabriel checked the walls for bloodstains but didn't see any. He felt a little better. A policeman gave him a glass of tea with a lot of sugar and gestured for him to drink it down. When he didn't move fast enough, the policeman shouted at him in Hebrew he didn't understand.

The policewoman smiled at him and said, "Shalom." He didn't respond. Some of the women soldiers in Eritrea were more sadistic than the men.

Gabriel stifled a sigh of relief when the door opened again and Arami walked into the room. He was so glad to see him, it was hard to keep from jumping up and throwing his arms around him. Arami had warned him that the police wouldn't let him stay if they suspected they knew each other. He said they should both be very careful, but even so, Arami gave him a tiny smile. The small gesture encouraged Gabriel and made him feel that he wasn't alone. Arami sat down beside him and patted his knee below the table where the policemen couldn't see.

Speaking in English, the policewoman asked his name, Arami translated the question, and Gabriel replied. Then she asked him where he came from, where his family was, how he got to Israel, where he worked, where he lived. She wrote all the answers down on a pad in front of her.

The questions stopped abruptly and the detective started talking about the rights granted by Israeli law to a person in his situation. Gabriel didn't understand everything she said, but he didn't really care. Even the policewoman didn't seem to care if he understood or not. She was obviously reciting pat phrases. Arami took the opportunity to tell him not to worry, he would look out for his interests. The Israeli was going to give him the money tomorrow.

The policewoman asked if he wanted an attorney. Gabriel shook his head. Alarmed, he realized he'd answered before Arami translated the question, but the detective didn't seem to notice the slip.

Arami said he thought he was very brave and he hoped his sons would grow up to be as loyal to his family as he was. Gabriel's eyes filled with tears.

Then the policewoman stopped talking and her face became very severe.

"Itai Fisher said you told him you're responsible for Michal Poleg's death," she said after a long pause.

Arami translated.

Gabriel sat in silence. His heart was pounding.

She asked if that was right, and Arami translated again.

Gabriel took a deep breath. It was the moment of truth. Itai said that once he confessed there was no turning back. He wouldn't be able to retract what he said. Gabriel thought about Liddie and the money he needed. He was doing this for her. He had to be strong.

Arami nodded encouragingly. He was doing the right thing. He didn't have any choice.

Gabriel nodded and lowered his eyes.

"You have to say it," the policewoman instructed.

Raising his eyes, Gabriel stated quietly, "Michal died because of me."

Arami translated.

The policewoman didn't move a muscle. She continued to stare at him with a grave expression on her face. The tall policeman smiled and then quickly tried to hide it.

"You killed her?"

Arami translated and Gabriel nodded.

"Say it out loud," the policeman ordered.

Gabriel waited for Arami to translate and then said in a trembling voice, "I killed Michal."

The two officers sat opposite him in silence. The policeman no longer tried to disguise his pleasure. Grinning, he stretched and placed his hands on his head. But the policewoman continued to pin him with her eyes. "Why?" she suddenly fired at him.

That was the question Gabriel was afraid of. He kept silent and only bowed his head again, hoping she would let it go, that she would move on. But she didn't. She repeated the question and Arami translated.

Did Itai tell them he didn't do it? Did he know he only said he did it because he needed the money?

"Help me, Arami. Tell me what to say," he begged.

Chapter 34

"**WHAT** are you two talking about?" Anat snapped.

The exchange between Arami and Gabriel was making her uneasy. She didn't like having to go through an interpreter to question her suspect. She wanted to control the interrogation, but that clearly wasn't the case here. Her question had been simple and direct. It shouldn't take so long to translate.

"He asked me to repeat the question," Arami answered.

"So do it," Yaron barked impatiently.

Arami lowered his eyes submissively and said a few words. The suspect replied.

"It was an accident," Arami said softly.

"What does he mean 'accident'?" Anat asked, trying to catch Gabriel's eye. Something was gnawing at her. If she didn't know better, she might think he understood everything she was saying.

Arami translated the question and Gabriel replied. She waited for the interpreter to translate the answer, but he went on talking with the suspect.

Anat struggled to understand what they were talking about from their expressions and gestures, but it was a futile effort. She tried counting the words to see if the length of the translation was similar to the length of her question, but it was hard for her to tell where one word ended and another began in their guttural language.

She was losing control of the situation and she couldn't afford to let that happen, particularly not at this crucial stage in the interrogation.

"Stop that!" Yaron yelled, slamming his hand down on the table.

His raised voice and the resounding bang brought an abrupt end to the exchange between the two men. They both looked at him apprehensively.

"Please translate precisely what he said," Anat instructed gently. She had no other choice. She needed Arami. If she could keep things calm, she had a better chance of regaining control. From the corner of her eye she saw the angry expression on Yaron's face.

Chapter 35

GABRIEL remained silent.

"What does he mean 'accident'?" the policewoman repeated, looking straight at him. He could tell from her tone that she didn't believe him. Itai didn't believe him, either. Itai wanted him to say that he wasn't responsible for what happened to Michal, that it wasn't true, that Gabriel was still the same person he had taken under his wing, the same person he believed in, not some murdering monster. The policewoman wanted him to say that it wasn't an accident, that he did it on purpose.

"Tell them you had an argument and you didn't mean to do it. She gave you money and she wanted you to pay her back but you didn't have it," Arami coached him.

Gabriel nodded.

"What are you saying?" the policewoman interrupted again.

"I explained the question to him," Arami said innocently.

"Then please tell him to answer it."

Gabriel was about to repeat what Arami told him to say, but the policewoman didn't give him a chance.

"You had an intimate relationship with Michal, didn't you?" she said, her eyes boring into him. "She wouldn't have sex with you anymore. That's why you killed her?"

"No. Never!" he burst out, not thinking.

She set a trap for him and he fell right into it.

The policewoman said something to the policeman in Hebrew. She looked furious. The tall policeman leapt out of his chair, grabbed Arami, and pulled him up.

"Be strong, Gabriel," Arami said. "I'll help you, I swear! I'll get

Liddie out. Don't let them break you. They're no better than us, and we're stronger than they are. Don't forget that."

"Let me know as soon as Liddie is free," Gabriel begged before the policeman threw Arami out of the room.

"Don't worry, Gabriel, everything will be all right!"

The door closed behind Arami. Gabriel was all alone now.

Chapter 36

WHEN it was made clear to Itai that he would not be allowed in the interrogation room, he realized there was no point in his sticking around. He considered acting as Gabriel's lawyer but dismissed the idea immediately. He might have a law degree, but he'd never practiced criminal law. It would be reckless and irresponsible on his part to represent him. Instead, he'd make sure the public defender's office appointed an attorney for him as quickly as possible. Still, he was feeling very guilty as he stepped out into the street, as if he was abandoning Gabriel.

There was a lot of work waiting for him at OMA, but he didn't feel like going back to the office. He had to do something constructive, not just sit behind a desk. It was already dark out. He'd spent the whole day in the police station. He was cold and hungry. He'd been in such a rush this morning that he'd forgotten his jacket. Itai went into a nearby fast-food place and ordered hummus.

Taking out his cell phone, he stared at one of Michal's photos of the "Banker." He was standing in front of a restaurant, but it wasn't clear if he'd come out of it or was just passing by. Itai didn't recognize the place. He zoomed in on the picture until he could make out a sign with the name of the street on the corner of the building. Although he couldn't read the name, he could see it was short. There weren't many streets around the old bus station that had restaurants. If Itai had to guess, he'd say it was Fein Street. He wiped his mouth with a napkin and got up from the table.

It didn't take him long to find the restaurant with the sign on the corner of the building. It was suppertime, and the place was full. There was little chance he'd be able to speak to any of the customers in private.

Yesterday he'd debated whether to ask the asylum seekers in

the office if they knew someone called the "Banker" but decided against it. OMA was a place of refuge. The people who came to them needed help, comfort, and a sense of security. He didn't want to make them nervous by asking questions. Michal's murder was traumatic enough. OMA had to remain off-limits.

The busy restaurant lifted his spirits. Aid workers only saw the distress of the asylum seekers. The life they described was a long tale of woe, tragedy after tragedy. Itai was glad to see there were places where they could chill out, enjoy themselves, forget their troubles for a while.

He inhaled the odor of berbere, the reddish-orange spice the Eritreans used in their cooking. The sharp smell issued from all their restaurants, even managing to overpower the pervasive stench of garbage outside.

This establishment was no different from the others in the area: a small, poorly lit space that was formerly a storefront. Black plastic tables and chairs were scattered haphazardly around the room. At the far end was a bar with a cheap string of Christmas lights above it. The walls were adorned with an Eritrean flag and colorful tapestries showing scenes of African village life.

The clientele was exclusively male. The men sat side by side, sometimes two to a chair, touching shoulders and eating with their fingers from a large tin tray in the center of the table. The tray was covered with injera, a spongy flat bread with a mousy gray color and a slightly sour taste, over which was a beef stew called zigni, a dark red chicken stew called dorho, or shiro, an orange vegetarian dish made of chickpea flour cooked with tomatoes and seasoned with onions and garlic.

Itai scanned the restaurant, looking for a free table. The waiter, who was most likely also the owner, pointed to a small table in the corner with a single chair beside it. Itai walked toward it, aware that every eye in the restaurant was on him. Such places are rarely visited by Israelis, but when they do come, they are welcomed graciously.

Itai searched for a familiar face, someone he knew from OMA, but he didn't recognize anyone. When he was seated, the waiter presented him with a menu written only in Tigrinya. "Just tea," he ordered apologetically in English. He'd tried Eritrean food a few times, but he wasn't fond of the cuisine. While the purple, red, and orange colors were a feast for the eyes, the flavors were either too hot or too bland for his taste. He remembered that Michal had once admitted, reluctantly, that she didn't like it, either. It was unusual for her to make such a confession. She was an all-or-nothing type of person: if she liked something, she gave it her unconditional love. It was the same with the things she hated. It was hard for her to say a bad word about the asylum seekers, whom she insisted on calling "refugees." He recalled how he couldn't keep from laughing at the sheepish expression on her face when she admitted she didn't like their food. Naturally, she didn't understand what he found so funny.

The men at a nearby table were in the midst of a lively discussion punctuated by laughter. Itai tried to make out what they were talking about, but he couldn't follow the conversation. He knew even fewer words in Tigrinya than Michal. From time to time, someone glanced over at him and he smiled back politely.

When the waiter arrived with his tea, Itai showed him the picture on his phone. "Excuse me, but do you happen to know this man?" he asked. The waiter took the phone, looked at the photograph, and then back at him. "Do you know this man?" Itai repeated. The waiter shook his head and quickly returned the phone. "He lost something and I want to give it back to him," Itai lied. "Sorry, not know him," the waiter said, walking away.

Even though the restaurant was already full, more and more men kept streaming in, cramming themselves around the crowded tables and rubbing shoulders, the customary Eritrean expression of friendship and affection. Itai noticed that some didn't take a seat but instead continued on to what appeared to be a back room. He couldn't see inside from where he was sitting.

A young man at an adjacent table smiled at Itai, who seized the opportunity to show him the photograph. The man took the phone accommodatingly, but as soon as he saw the picture he shrugged his shoulders. "Not know him, sorry," he said. "Can you ask your friends? I really want to talk to him," Itai said.

There were six other men at the table. Itai watched their faces as they passed the phone from hand to hand, whispering among themselves. Two of the men looked in his direction, but they lowered their eyes when he looked back. "Sorry, sir, nobody know him," the young man said, returning the phone and twisting his chair around slightly so that his back was to Itai. He'd spent enough time with asylum seekers to know that the small gesture was a sign of dismissal.

Itai glanced at the television hanging over the entrance. An African entertainer he'd never seen before was singing into a microphone, but his voice was drowned out by the noise in the restaurant. The door opened and three more men walked in. Instantly, all eyes turned to them and the noise level dropped dramatically. The three men, one carrying a black leather bag, crossed the room quickly and disappeared behind the bar. The diners immediately resumed their conversations.

Itai sat there a few minutes longer. Something was going on in the back. Could it be the illegal banking activity Michal was on to? If he wanted to convince the cops to look into it, he had to bring them something concrete. He might be able to persuade them if he could snap a picture of what they were doing back there.

Another man walked in and hurried toward the back. This was his chance. Itai stood up and followed the man as he made his way between the crowded tables. Passing behind the bar, he found himself in a dark stuffy hallway. Itai's heart was pounding. He turned his head, but no one seemed to notice what he was doing. The man turned right into another hallway. Cigarette smoke hung heavily in the air, making Itai gag. At the end of the corridor, he pulled out his phone and pressed the camera button. The man knocked on a white door. A few seconds later, the door opened and he disappeared inside.

Itai pressed his ear to the door. He could hear raised voices. He stood there debating with himself whether to knock on the door, but before he could come to a decision, it opened again and the body of a tall African filled the doorway. Itai was six foot one, but the man was a head taller and twice as broad.

"Toilet?" Itai spluttered, uttering the first thing that came to him.

The big man shook his head and gestured for him to leave.

"What's in there?" Itai asked, standing his ground.

"Go away," the man ordered, giving him a shove. He very nearly lost his balance.

"Let me in."

The man shoved him again, harder this time. Itai fell backward. He saw the waiter behind them, watching.

"What are you trying to hide?" He picked himself up and pointed his phone at the man in the doorway.

Itai's heart stopped even before he felt the pain of the sucker punch to his stomach. He could hardly breathe. He dropped to his knees. The phone went flying.

Chapter 37

ANAT watched Shmuel Gonen as he made his way to her office. His eagerness aroused her suspicions. No more than half an hour had elapsed since she'd called and asked him to come in for a lineup, and he was already here, unmistakably ready and willing to do his part. Anat didn't like overly eager witnesses. They were always a headache in the end.

According to regular police procedure, a suspect is taken to the scene and asked to give a detailed account of what happened there. The reenactment is recorded and placed into evidence. Only after that is a lineup conducted. But this time Anat's bosses had told her to switch the order. The police force suffered from a lack of public confidence, and they didn't want to miss a chance to improve their image. Gabriel admitting that "Michal died because of me" and "I killed Michal" would be leaked to the media and repeated time and again. They had to get the lineup out of the way as quickly as possible to pave the way for their moment of triumph.

When they finished questioning Gabriel, Yochai descended from his lofty chamber to congratulate Anat. "I always knew I could count on you," he said, shaking her hand. She played her part impeccably, thanking him dutifully. She would have been more pleased by his compliments if she hadn't gotten a call from David five minutes before the DC walked into her office. David told her Yochai had called him yesterday and leaned on him to get his ass back to Israel.

Anat herself hadn't yet decided how she felt about the interview with Gabriel. In her opinion, he looked more frightened than guilty. But no one else had any qualms. "He confessed, we didn't drag it out of him, we didn't threaten him, we didn't keep at him for hours. What else do you want, Nachmias?" Yaron said, adding, "That's why you're still single. Nothing satisfies you.

"Seriously, Nachmias," he went on, wiping the smile off his face when he saw the expression she shot at him, "we don't have any evidence that contradicts what he said. There's nothing that suggests he didn't do it. Not a single thing."

Anat envied his self-assurance, the confidence not to second-guess himself. With Yaron there was no "do this, do that," "he did it, he didn't do it." For him, there were no two ways about it: Gabriel was guilty. Things always seemed more complicated to Anat.

She kicked herself for not picking up immediately on the fact that Gabriel spoke English. She should have asked Itai Fisher or, at the very least, not simply assumed he didn't. She got the sense he understood what she was saying at the very beginning of the interview, but she chalked it up to her lack of experience with Africans. Then when she asked him if he wanted an attorney, he shook his head without waiting for the translation. She noticed it but decided to ignore it. Still not certain she was reading him correctly, she didn't want to bear down on him too hard at that early stage in the interrogation.

Anat was also pissed off at Yaron for not making sure the two Africans didn't know each other. She'd told him to check, and he came back saying there was no reason they couldn't use Arami. That kind of mistake could easily affect the admissibility of the confession. She had to keep a closer eye on Yaron. In an effort to remedy the situation, she'd asked Gabriel the same questions a second time and was relieved to get the same answers without Arami in the room.

Gabriel claimed that he didn't mean to kill Michal. It was an accident. Anat managed to get him to admit halfheartedly that they'd fought over money, but he couldn't say how much he owed her. And he continued to insist that it happened in the morning, when Anat knew for certain that Michal was killed during the night. Bottom line: on two critical points, the how and the why, Gabriel's explanations were less than persuasive.

Anat couldn't forget what Itai Fisher said, that Gabriel might not be telling the truth, that someone might be threatening him or squeezing him for money. And maybe he was covering for somebody else. But who? Unlike Itai, Anat was convinced that Michal knew her killer. Was it someone Gabriel knew, too? Was the man coercing him somehow? What was he holding over him?

THEY usually had a hard time finding the right number of decoys for a lineup, people whose appearance was close enough to that of the suspect and who were willing to take the job. For Gabriel's lineup, all it took was one call to a foreign labor contractor and they had fifteen candidates. Six even had a scar on their face. Israelis turned their nose up at the pittance they were paid for the service, but it sounded very appealing to Africans. Now they just had to wait for the public defender to show up.

Shmuel Gonen was standing next to Anat, looking very tense. "I hope I don't get a heart attack when I see him. He nearly killed me, that black punk, like he killed Michal."

Anat tried to calm his nerves, assuring him he had nothing to worry about, that the police would protect him. She watched him closely when the men were revealed. He passed his eyes rapidly from one to the other. Too rapidly, in her opinion. It was always hard to ID a person of a different race. She'd explained that to Gonen before the lineup.

"Number four," he declared after only a few seconds.

"Are you certain?" Anat asked.

"It's number four. I'm positive. I'll never forget him," Gonen answered confidently.

"Take another look."

"No need. Number four." Gonen made no effort to hide his irritation.

Anat remained silent. Gabriel was number seven.

Chapter 38

LIDDIE lay on her thin mattress. Although her eyes were closed, she was wide awake. The room was dark, with no more than a narrow ribbon of light filtering in through the small crack between the door and the floor. The heavy smell of sweat and semen in the air seeped into her skin, the mattress, and the flimsy sheet that was her only blanket.

Her body ached. She had been sick for two weeks, coughing constantly. The hacking cough came from deep down, sending waves of pain through her whole body. She pulled the stinking sheet tighter around her in an effort to keep warm. Her teeth were chattering and she was trembling from the cold.

The room she was in was tiny. She'd been imprisoned here, the sole occupant of this cell, for two months. In all that time she hadn't seen the world outside, hadn't heard the sound of cars or the noise of the city. They hadn't let her out even once.

The only items in the room were the mattress, a small sink, and a bucket that functioned as a toilet and a receptacle for the condoms the men left behind. Ahmed insisted they use condoms and that she wash herself in the sink every night. He didn't want to damage the merchandise.

Lately, he'd stopped bringing the men to her. They were put off by her coughing, he told her angrily. He worked her hard before she got sick, usually sending in two or three men at once. The record was six. They were all Africans. Some lay down on top of her and rammed themselves into her; others wanted her to put her mouth on them down there. It was like an assembly line; the men came one after the other, rubbing against her, invading her body, spilling their seed on her.

The first time was in Sinai when Rafik forced himself on her.

Liddie wept, screamed, begged him to take pity on her. She was only seventeen, and still a virgin. Rafik slammed the barrel of his rifle into her stomach and punched her in the face. He held a finger up to his lips, signaling her to remain silent, and then moved it across his throat to warn her what would happen if she didn't obey. That was the last time she let anyone see her cry. She still wept when no one was around, but that soon stopped as well. Even when Rafik brought the other Bedouins to her, she didn't let out a sound.

Liddie wasn't the only girl here. There were others like her elsewhere in the apartment. She could hear them screaming, hear Ahmed shouting at them, hear the footsteps of the men entering their rooms. Sometimes, late at night, she could hear them sobbing.

Three times a day the door opened and Ahmed flung food inside: a pita bread, a tomato, a cucumber. Every now and then she got rice or chickpeas. Sometimes, when Ahmed was in a particularly good mood, he was more generous. Once or twice he even brought her meat.

Other than that, the door only opened to let in clients. She never looked at their faces, just stared off into space, biting down on her lip when they hurt her. Periodically, Ahmed gave her the signal that meant the client was paying extra and she was expected to groan.

At first Liddie tried to hide her face from the clients. She didn't want to be recognized by a man from her village or somebody she had met on the way here in the refugee camp in Sudan, in Egypt, or in Sinai. There had been many stages on the long journey to Israel. She didn't want anyone to know what she was doing now, what had become of her. People talk. Gossip travels fast and slips easily across borders. The rumor could reach her mother or Gabriel. She couldn't bear the shame.

Ahmed beat her when he realized what she was doing. He charged more for her because of her pretty face. How dare she hide it!

A while ago, maybe a month, maybe more, one of the clients recognized her. There was no point in denying who she was. His name was Fotsom and he was also from Eritrea. He had been in the truck that took them from Sudan to Egypt. For several days they had been packed together on the floor of the truck covered in sacks, praying not to be discovered by the police at one of the checkpoints they crossed. To pass the time, they told each other about the villages they had left behind and tried to imagine what they would find in their new home, what their life would be like there.

Liddie whispered in his ear, begging him to go to the women's shelter on Neveh Sha'anan Street and tell Dahlia, the social worker, where she was, or at least tell her she hadn't simply left without saying good-bye. But he could only tell Dahlia. He mustn't speak to Gabriel. Her brother mustn't know that she was in Israel or find out anything about the fate that had befallen her.

Ahmed had caught them talking and pulled Fotsom off her, shouting that if he didn't want a bullet in the head, he'd better not tell anyone anything. He had connections, Ahmed yelled. Wherever Fotsom went, he'd find him. Then Liddie heard a thud followed by a groan of pain.

A few days ago, the door opened and Ahmed came in and started beating her. He punched her in the stomach, slapped her face, pounded her all over. Liddie had no idea why. What had she done?

"I'm fed up with you," he thundered. "This isn't a hotel. You lie here like a fat cow, eating and coughing all the time. The clients don't want you. They're scared of catching something."

Ahmed grabbed her by the throat and sat down on top of her, pinning her to the floor.

"I hear you've got a brother in Israel," he said, pressing down harder on her throat. "Call him and tell him to come get you. I've had it with you. Your brother has money. If he pays up, he can have you. Got it?"

Liddie didn't respond. She wanted nothing more than to escape

Ahmed's prison, but she was too ashamed to tell Gabriel and she didn't know what was waiting for her outside.

"If you want your brother to come, you have to beg. Understand? Otherwise he'll leave you here. He doesn't need the shame of having a whore for a sister," Ahmed said, slapping her across the face. "You do what I say and he'll come get you. Understand?"

Liddie nodded. He slapped her again. Blood streamed from her nose.

She was so excited to hear Gabriel's voice. She wanted to tell him how sorry she was for everything that had happened, how much she missed him. But she was afraid she'd never see her brother again if she didn't do exactly what Ahmed said.

So Liddie obeyed her jailer. Since then, she'd been waiting, but nothing had happened.

She coughed, hastily covering her mouth. Ahmed said he'd kill her if he heard her coughing again.

It was still raining outside. Liddie lay in the cold room, shivering.

Chapter 39

ANAT climbed the stairs of 122 Stricker Street. Gabriel, his hands and feet shackled, stumbled ahead of her, supported by Yaron. Behind her was Nimrod with his recording equipment, breathing heavily. He'd asked her out a few months ago when they went to record a suspect's reenactment of some other murder. He was twenty years older than she and a hundred pounds heavier, but she'd almost taken him up on the offer just to see her mother's face. Wasn't she always telling Anat that "looks aren't everything"?

At the bottom of the stairs she could hear Amit Giladi, the crime reporter, talking loudly on his cell phone. He was waiting for them downstairs when they arrived, claiming to have permission from the district press officer.

She informed him that there was no way he was coming upstairs with them. Anat was unhappy in general with the practice of allowing reporters to be present at the reenactment of a crime. But this time her natural aversion to the press was accompanied by uneasiness: she couldn't be sure how this would play out or what Gabriel would say.

"Don't do anything stupid, Nachmias," Giladi said, trying to reach the press officer to prove he had his permission to be there. "My sources tell me you're on the way up. You can use someone like me on your side. Nobody gets anywhere these days without good press and a public relations campaign. A smart woman like you doesn't need me to tell her that."

Anat was pleased to see that the press officer was unavailable. She took advantage of the fact to order her team to start making their way upstairs.

"You're making a mistake," Yaron whispered on the way up. "Why not let him come? Everyone else does."

She looked at Gabriel. He was shaking so badly that he kept tripping over his feet. The last thing she needed now was a media frenzy.

"I want calm and quiet," she said firmly. After the way he screwed up with Arami, she'd been keeping Yaron on a short leash.

EARLIER that morning, Anat had joined up with Michal's family at the cemetery when they made the traditional visit to the graveside at the end of the shivah, the weeklong mourning period. They were all there: her parents, sister, brother, and brother-in-law. Anat felt uncomfortable intruding on the intimacy of the occasion. The family was made equally uncomfortable by her presence. They stopped talking as soon as she approached.

Michal's father recited kaddish briskly, as if he wanted to get this over with as quickly as possible. The rest of the family stood in silence, staring at the fresh grave. When he finished the prayer, Michal's mother wiped her eyes, hidden behind large dark glasses.

In the past week, Anat had checked the alibi of each of the family members. The parents were in their apartment in the posh north Tel Aviv neighborhood of Ramat Aviv. Shai, Michal's younger brother, was with his girlfriend. Dana, her older sister, was at home with her children, and her husband, Shlomi, was in Belgium on a business trip.

They were about to leave when Shai said softly, "I think we should put on the headstone the verse, 'Whoever saves one life in Israel, saves the world entire.'"

"In Israel? What, she was helping out Jews?" Michal's father spat.

"What difference does it make? It's the principle. Michal was a good-hearted person who helped other people," her brother answered.

"It makes a big difference. If she helped Jews this wouldn't have happened. She'd still be alive," his brother-in-law said.

"Shlomi, please," Michal's mother broke in. "This is a family discussion."

"And I'm not family?" Shlomi said, offended. "I'm only family when it comes to money? Wasn't I family when you came crying to me that your daughter was throwing away your inheritance?"

"Enough," Michal's father barked, nodding toward Anat.

Instantly, they all fell silent and looked away.

Anat let out a deep sigh. She was forced to agree with Yochai. The family might be dysfunctional, but there was zero chance that any of them had committed the murder. Besides, Michal had opened the door to her killer late at night. If she were Michal, she wouldn't let any of these people into her apartment at any hour of the day or night.

ANAT stood outside Michal's door with Gabriel and Yaron. As soon as Nimrod caught his breath, she ordered him to start recording. She'd decided to let Yaron run the show; he'd worked more homicides than she had.

She wasn't too bothered by the lineup. If Gabriel had been an Israeli, Shmuel Gonen's inability to identify him would have carried more weight. It wasn't so dramatic in this case. It was only natural for him to have trouble picking out the right African. Nevertheless, it reinforced her feeling that Gonen's testimony was biased, that as far as he was concerned, any African would do. She wondered if she hadn't been too quick to dismiss Gonen as a suspect.

For the record, Yaron noted the location, the time, and the people present. Everything that was said or done from that moment on would be documented. Once charges were filed, Gabriel's attorney would have access to the videotape.

Yaron asked Gabriel to describe what happened, step by step. Neutral questions were allowed, as long as they didn't lead the suspect.

Gabriel remained silent, looking around in bewilderment.

"Let me get you started," Yaron said with obvious impatience. "You're standing here. Did you knock on the door? Ring the bell?"

He was speaking very slowly, stressing each word as if the person he was talking to was backward.

"The door was open," Gabriel said, his voice barely audible.

Yaron and Anat exchanged glances. She gestured for him to go on. Gabriel's answer came as a surprise, but at least he was talking. Anat's greatest fear had been that he wouldn't utter a word or that what he said wouldn't fit with the evidence.

"You went in. Where was she?"

Gabriel pointed to the living room.

"Show me exactly where she was," Yaron instructed, urging him forward.

Gabriel walked to the spot where they had found Michal's body. Anat went and stood where he indicated.

"What happened next?"

Gabriel bowed his head, not answering.

"What did she say to you? What did you say to her? What happened?" Yaron fired at him. Anat motioned for him to slow down.

Silence.

"How was she standing?" Anat asked. "Was she facing you or did she have her back to you?"

"Come on . . . answer the question," Yaron chided.

Silence.

"I understand this is hard for you, Gabriel," Anat said. "It's only natural. Just take a deep breath and tell us what happened. That's all we want. We just need to know how it happened. Tell us and we'll be done here. I promise."

Gabriel continued to stare at the floor.

Yaron scratched his head. Anat recognized the signal. She knew what was coming.

"I think there's a problem with the recording equipment. I have to turn it off for a minute," Nimrod said with perfect timing.

Yaron grabbed Gabriel by the shoulder, forced his head up, and pulled the African toward him. "Listen up, you idiot. Your act isn't going to work with us," he said belligerently. Anat debated whether or not to intervene. She decided to wait. Yaron hadn't crossed the line yet.

"I don't envy you if you don't tell us exactly what happened, how you killed her. We won't be so nice to you anymore. We'll start treating you like they did where you came from. We might even send you back there and let your friends take care of you," Yaron threatened.

"Enough, Yaron," Anat said quietly, stepping between them and positioning herself next to Gabriel. They had to be quick. The time was indicated at the beginning of the recording. Every minute the camera wasn't running increased the chances that Gabriel's reenactment of the crime would be declared inadmissible.

"Nachmias, I've got the press officer on the line. He'll tell you I have his permission to be here," Anat heard Giladi's voice behind her.

"Get him out of here," she ordered Nimrod, who rushed to block the reporter's entry, using his large belly to push him out of the apartment.

"Get off me, you fat slob," Anat could hear from behind the closed door. "Nachmias, you're making a big mistake. You don't want me as an enemy. You hear me?"

Ignoring the shouts from the hallway, Anat looked back at Gabriel. "Just tell me what happened," she said gently.

"Did you strangle Michal?" Maybe she could get him to start talking if she suggested something he could deny, she thought.

Gabriel turned his eyes to her but remained silent.

"Did you strangle her?" she repeated. "If you didn't, that's fine. Just say so."

"Yes, I strangled her," Gabriel answered softly.

Anat exchanged another look with Yaron. The whole thing was about to blow up in their faces. Back at the station, Yaron had suggested that they have what he called a "preliminary talk" with Gabriel to prepare him before they took him to the scene. Anat had rejected that proposal out of hand.

"Let's start over at the beginning," she said, taking a deep breath.

"Let me handle this," Yaron said, almost shoving her aside in his frustration.

"Listen and listen good," he said, pushing his face into Gabriel's and grabbing his shirt. "Stop lying. We're going to turn the camera on again and you're going to tell us how you had an argument with Michal and how you got angry . . ."

"Stop it, Yaron," Anat commanded.

"And you hit her with a beer bottle. She fell and hit her head. Got it?" Yaron went on, totally ignoring Anat.

"Stop right now! What do you think you're doing? Are you out of your mind?" Anat spluttered, raising her voice.

Gabriel remained silent.

"Got it?" Yaron repeated, undeterred.

Gabriel nodded.

"How's the camera, Nimrod?" Yaron asked over his shoulder.

"Leave it off," Anat ordered. "We're not doing this now."

Everyone turned to stare at her.

"The suspect is agitated. He can't give an effective account of the crime." Her heart was racing but she managed to keep her voice steady. She had to get back to the station and think this through.

"Don't be naive, Anat. This is how it works. You're just making trouble for yourself. Let it go," Yaron said insolently.

"Watch it, Yaron," she answered. "I'm in charge here, and I say we're leaving."

"WHAT'S going on? You finished already?" Giladi asked as they passed him in the hallway. Anat headed hastily for the stairs, not replying.

"The press officer promised I could see it," the reporter insisted, following after her. "If you don't believe me, I'll get him on the line again."

"There's nothing to see," Anat said, turning around angrily.

"Why not?"

"Nothing," Anat said, hurrying down the stairs.

Chapter 40

SHIMON Faro was so enraged that he couldn't keep from screaming at Itzik and Boaz, who stood in front of the boss with their heads bowed. Faro didn't often raise his voice. In his experience, it was more effective to leave people guessing if or when he was going to charge at them.

He was under a lot of stress these days. The Argentinean deal was keeping him up at night. He'd been brokering weapons sales for years, but never anything of this magnitude. And it wasn't only the volume that he was losing sleep over, it was the destination as well. He sold arms to Nigeria, Ethiopia, Namibia, but never before to Sudan, a country boycotted by the whole of the Western world. There were bans on such transactions from here to Timbuktu.

He'd never have gotten involved in the first place if it hadn't been for the promise of a direct supply of drugs from Egypt under cover of the refugees streaming into Israel. He made good money from the refugees, just like he did from call girls and gambling, but drugs were still his major meal ticket. Ever since the shit with David Meshulam, may he rest in peace, deliveries from Lebanon had been almost totally cut off. There was no room for a vacuum in the world Faro lived in. If he didn't provide what people wanted, someone else would. He couldn't afford to let that happen.

He had to face facts. His back was to the wall. Even so, he wouldn't go so far as to sell arms to Iran or Syria, and he kept clear of sophisticated technology. But Sudan was a different story. Army surplus. Blacks killing blacks. No big deal.

Boaz was supposed to go to Argentina to handle the details. As usual, there were two parts to this transaction, the legal side and the rest of it. In order for the deal to go through, the legal elements had to be impeccable, with all the necessary signatures on all the necessary documents.

Then Itzik comes and tells him that Michal Poleg took pictures of Boaz near the old bus station and now the cops have them, and some clown by the name of Itai Fisher, a friend of the dearly departed, is going around and showing them to everyone. He even had the gall to visit one of Faro's enterprises, but the guys on his payroll beat him up and kicked him out.

"You're suddenly a male model?" Faro screamed at Boaz, who kept his silence. "You didn't see she was taking pictures? Don't you have eyes in your head?"

Boaz mumbled something incomprehensible.

"And what about you?" Faro went on, turning his attention to Itzik. "Forget Boaz, he doesn't know his ass from his elbow. But you? Why didn't you stop her? How did you let a cunt like her, barely five feet tall, set you up? For the life of me, I can't understand it."

Itzik, too, held his peace. They both knew better than to talk back to Faro.

The boss wasn't through. "And how the hell did the cops get their hands on the pictures without you knowing about it?"

"Shimon, I'm telling you, you've got nothing to worry about. Nobody read the report and nobody's gonna read it. Not now, for sure," Itzik said, his voice trembling. "I swear, the African went to the cops and told them he did it. Nobody's ever gonna piss in the direction of that report anymore."

"We've got that Fisher kook on our back now," Faro went on, slamming his fist on the desk. "What are we supposed to do about him? Take him out?"

Itzik was about to say that didn't sound like a bad idea, but he changed his mind as soon as he saw the look Faro threw at him. You don't waste anyone unless it's absolutely necessary, the boss always said.

The problem was that he had morons working for him. He had

plenty of candidates to choose from if he needed to use force. But when it came to brains? Who could he call on? How could he run a business when he was surrounded by retards? No business could grow when one person had to do all the thinking.

Boaz wasn't a total imbecile. But he was a fucking idiot to let her take those pictures. If he could, he'd throw him out on his ass, but then who would he replace him with? He didn't have enough quality people, that was his problem.

At least that nut job only took pictures of Boaz, not the "General." Otherwise, they'd have a bigger problem on their hands.

Boaz glanced at his watch discreetly, but not discreetly enough that Faro didn't notice the slight movement of his wrist. The little shit must be over the moon, Faro thought. He knew how much Boaz hated the trips he was forced to make to the old bus station, how much he prayed to be released from that responsibility. Maybe he needed a little reminder of why he was here and what Faro had done for him. If he hadn't had a private talk with the owners of the accounting firm, Boaz would be in prison now.

"Am I boring you, Mr. Yavin? Is there somewhere you have to be? Am I keeping you?" Faro asked, piercing Boaz with his eyes.

"No . . . no, of course not . . . I . . . ," Boaz muttered.

"I've had enough of you two. Get out of here, both of you," Faro said angrily.

It would be a mistake to keep Boaz around now. The smart move would be to put as much distance between them as possible, tell him to go to another country and stay there. Even that might not be enough. But where would that leave him? He needed the deal in Argentina. He didn't have any choice. He had to send Boaz. Anyone who ran a business will tell you that you sometimes have to take risks.

Chapter 41

"I have to talk to you," Anat said firmly, walking unannounced into Yochai's office. She had to explain what she'd done and why before he heard about it from someone else. She and Yaron had barely exchanged a word on the way back to the station. She was furious with him. Blatantly putting words in the suspect's mouth was crossing every red line in the book.

She told Yaron to escort Gabriel to the interrogation room and informed him she was going to talk to Yochai. "It's your funeral, Nachmias. Use your head. It isn't all about you. You're part of the system. You've got to understand how it works," Yaron replied calmly as he led Gabriel away.

"Make it snappy," Yochai said, getting out of his chair. "I've got a meeting with the Chief. But I want a report. How did it go at the scene? I promised the Chief it would all be tied up in a pretty bow today."

Anat kept silent. She was eager to explain, but she didn't want to have to do it in shorthand when she didn't have his full attention.

"Speak up. We'll have to walk and talk," Yochai said, leaving the office.

Anat followed after him. "It was a disaster. The suspect didn't open his mouth. Yaron tried to get him to open up, but he pressed too hard, started putting words in his mouth. The African just clammed up even tighter. I had to stop the recording before the whole case fell apart."

"You did what?" Yochai spluttered, stopping in his tracks and staring at her. Startled by his vehemence, Anat took a step backward. They were standing at the door to the squad room, which was buzzing with cops.

"Let's talk later," she said softly. The last thing she wanted was a public scene.

"No! We'll do it now!" Yochai was nearly screaming. "I want to hear it now!"

"What choice did I have? Yaron . . . ," Anat began.

"What is it with you, honey?" Yochai cut in. "Did you lose the plot? Is it that time of the month?"

Stunned, Anat could only stare back at him, speechless. Out of the corner of her eye she could see the cops in the squad room watching. She felt her face go red.

"What do you think we do here? Play with ourselves? You had a suspect who confessed of his own free will, nobody coerced him, and you . . . you . . . you fucked it all up. You just shit on everything. Do you even understand what you did?" he raged, waving a finger in front of her face.

Anat's legs were shaking. Obviously, she hadn't expected Yochai to be pleased by the way things played out. She herself was deeply disappointed at their failure to get Gabriel to reenact the crime. But she hadn't anticipated being yelled at in front of everyone, being publicly humiliated.

"And for what? For who?"

"Calm down, Yochai. Let's talk calmly," Anat whispered, her face burning. "There are problems with the case that have nothing to do with the reenactment. We have to rethink everything. I don't think Gabriel did it." No matter how hard she tried, she couldn't keep her voice steady. She'd never seen Yochai like this. And she'd never felt so demeaned. It shouldn't surprise her. Racism and sexism always went hand in hand.

"So why did he confess?" Yochai shouted, his face red. "Explain it to me!"

Anat cleared her throat and forced herself to get the words out. "There are a lot of reasons why people confess. You know that as well as I do," she said. All eyes in the room were turned to her. She knew all these cops. She worked with them. How could she go on working with them after this?

"Listen up, baby," Yochai cut in again. The vein in his forehead looked about to burst. "I've been on the job for over thirty years. I don't need some young filly with a law degree, a little girl who probably became a cop just to annoy her parents, to teach me anything. You had a textbook confession. The guy comes of his own free will, sits himself down in front of you, and without you saying anything or pressuring him in any way, he says, 'I killed her.' So explain it to me, goddammit, what's your problem?"

Yochai turned and started walking away. Anat hurried after him. At least they wouldn't have an audience anymore.

"Why? Can you tell me why?" he demanded, stopping suddenly and turning around. "I could understand if the guy had a team of hot-shot lawyers looking to trip us up. But all we've got is a confession, and there's not a shred of evidence to refute it. And in front of the press, too? You're unbelievable, that's all I can say, unbelievable."

"I didn't let the reporter inside," Anat hastened to explain.

"Thank God for that." But the information didn't seem to appease him in the slightest.

Anat took a deep breath. "I suggest we continue this conversation later," she said in a quiet voice. "We have to consider how to proceed from here." She didn't see any point in running down the corridor behind him while he went on chewing her out.

"That's the first sensible thing I've heard out of your mouth," he said acerbically as he turned and walked away.

Chapter 42

YARIV bit into the pita bread, savoring the taste of the crisp falafel balls inside. The bright sun and clear blue sky added to his light mood.

It turned out he'd been worried about his meeting with Aloni in his office for no reason. His boss had called him in to inform him that he was raising his job status to "permanent." Of course, he made the announcement with a sour face and undisguised distaste. It was obvious that the order had come down from up above, from as high as you can get.

"Let me give you some advice, Ninio," Aloni said before dismissing him. "Politicians can't be trusted. They come and go. As a state attorney, your loyalty should be only to the law, not to anything or anyone else."

Yariv looked at him impassively. What did Aloni know? He belonged to a different generation. He still didn't get that the world had changed, that it didn't play by the same rules anymore.

As soon as he got back to his office, Yariv called to thank Regev.

"You've got a great future ahead of you, Ninio," his patron said. Yariv lapped up every word. And to think that only a few days ago he'd been walking around in a daze because of that business with Michal, trying desperately to figure out if he killed her or not. He almost went to the police. Lucky he didn't.

He still couldn't remember anything about that night, but it didn't matter anymore. He didn't do it. That Eritrean did. Yariv was ecstatic when he heard about the confession.

He leaned back in his chair, feeling contented. He thought about Inbar, the way she smelled, how soft her skin was. They hadn't had sex in a long time. He was sick of jerking off in front of some porn site on the computer. He needed to fuck her. Maybe tonight. They'd both feel better afterward.

Tomorrow he had to argue against another petition filed by another illegal. Another sob story. Another time he'd say, "However much we might regret it, the law requires deportation." Another case he'd undoubtedly win.

The change in his status came at just the right moment. It gave him immunity, enabled him to make demands. The first would be a transfer out of the illegal alien division. He was sick of it. The problem was how to convince Regev. He had to find someone with white skin for Regev to turn his sights on. There were plenty to choose from. He remembered how enraged the politician was when Michal and her cohorts demonstrated across the street from his house. He said they were lynching him in the press, ruining his reputation. Michal in particular made his blood boil. She'd organized the demonstration and stayed behind long after the others had left, even came back a few times on her own. Another target like her would be just the right thing for Regev.

Yariv switched on his computer. The latest news flashed on the screen. His heart skipped a beat when he saw the headline: "No Reenactment of Michal Poleg's Murder." He bit down hard on his lip, drawing blood.

Chapter 43

ANAT was furious. How could Yochai speak to her like that? He wouldn't dare use that tone with her if she were a man. In an instant he'd destroyed everything she'd worked so hard to achieve. He'd humiliated her in front of everybody.

She was also furious with herself. She didn't regret pulling the plug on the reenactment. It was the right decision. She was well aware that a lot of cops would disagree. Plenty of them would do the same as Yaron: ignore what they considered senseless regulations in order to bring a criminal to justice. But Anat didn't believe in bending the rules. In her opinion, you had to follow procedure, even if it wasn't perfect and you didn't always like where it led you. As she saw it, the regulations were in place for a reason; without them, the whole system would collapse.

So she wasn't kicking herself for her decision, but for how she behaved afterward. She knew Yochai would be upset. She should have handled him better, should have prepared for the meeting. Yaron warned her, but she didn't listen; she was in too much of a hurry to talk to the boss. What was the rush?

Anat was furious with herself for crumbling, for not standing her ground. Yochai was right: Gabriel confessed of his own free will. She couldn't ignore that. People didn't generally incriminate themselves without reason, certainly not when they were looking at life in prison. But Gabriel seemed too eager to put his head in the noose. And he didn't have a clue about how Michal was murdered. He was happy to go along with any version of the crime he was offered. He even nodded when she asked him if he strangled her. How could she accept his confession and declare the case closed when there were so many unanswered questions? A confession might be considered the "king of evidence," but royalty wasn't what it used to be.

She needed to learn from this experience. The next time she walked into Yochai's office, she wouldn't whine about other cops getting in her way. She'd present him with concrete facts, new avenues of investigation.

To do that, she had to start over from the beginning, interrogate everyone who had a beef with Michal, "leave no stone unturned," as TV cops liked to say. For instance, Shmuel Gonen said he heard shouting outside her apartment on the night of the murder. She didn't give that enough attention, didn't ask any questions. At the time, she just assumed it was the African they were looking for.

She could still fix her mistakes. Every investigation hit a rough patch from time to time. That's all this was, a hiccup. The only thing that mattered was the final outcome. She just had to believe in herself. She could do it. She knew she was a good cop.

Anat turned to the computer. Mindless computer games always calmed her nerves. She'd play for a few minutes and then reassess the situation, she thought, moving the mouse to bring the screen back to life.

A headline came up on the screen. Her heart stopped as she scrolled down. "The police have announced that a second attempt to get the suspect to reenact the crime will be carried out in the coming days by the head of the Special Investigations Unit, Chief Inspector David Carmon, who is returning from a seminar in Austria," she read. Anat bit down hard on her lip until it hurt.

Chapter 44

GABRIEL was waiting. The tall policeman had shoved him back into the interrogation room and left him there. No one had come in since. Had they forgotten about him? After what happened in Michal's apartment, maybe they figured out that he didn't kill her. He froze when they took him back there. He could feel her presence. He expected her to come out of the other room any minute with a smile on her face. The picture he drew of her was gone. Who took it? He remembered the day he did it. "I went to the hairdresser's specially, so make me look pretty," she said, laughing. The way she was always bustling around, he didn't think she'd be able to sit still for more than five minutes. But she surprised him and posed for two hours straight without moving.

Back in her house, the good memories mixed with the bad one from the last time he'd been there. It was hard for him to talk, and anyway he didn't know how to answer the questions they asked him. And he couldn't bring himself to say it out loud, to say that he killed her. He knew he had to do it, but he couldn't. He liked her and he looked up to her too much.

When the policewoman went and stood in the exact place where he'd seen Michal's body, he had to fight to hold back the tears. She even looked a little like Michal—the same height, the same kind face. He had to remind himself that she wasn't on his side. And he didn't want to cry in front of her.

Gabriel knew he had to be strong. He had to make them believe him. Otherwise, the Israeli wouldn't pay Arami, and Arami wouldn't be able to pay Liddie's ransom. If Michal were here, she'd tell him to do it.

He looked at the door. He didn't notice if the tall policeman locked it when he left. He could try to escape and look for another, a better, way to save Liddie. He stood up, sliding his shackled feet slowly across the floor. But even if the door wasn't locked, how far could he get chained up like this? And where would he go if he got away?

Gabriel took a deep breath before pressing down on the handle. If the door opened, it would be a sign from God.

The door swung open abruptly, hitting Gabriel in the head. He fell backward.

"Where do you think you're going?" the tall policeman asked, towering over him. Before Gabriel could respond, he was grabbed by the shirt, heaved into the air, and thrown down on the table. He tried to sit up, but the policeman was too quick. With his large hand, he pressed him to the table.

"Trying to escape, you motherfucking asshole?"

Gabriel shook his head. His back hurt.

The policeman pulled him up and slammed him into a chair.

"Listen up," he shouted, sticking his face in Gabriel's. "The commander is coming, and you're going to tell him exactly what you did. You tell him how you asked Michal Poleg for money and she didn't want to give it to you so you got mad. You took a beer bottle and hit her on the back of the head. She fell and broke the table. When you saw she was dead, you ran. Nobody saw you. The next morning you remembered the bottle and you were afraid we'd find your fingerprints on it. You went back for it and Michal's neighbor saw you, so you ran again. You threw the bottle in a Dumpster."

Gabriel listened in silence. God had sent him a sign. It wasn't the sign he was expecting, but that didn't matter. "God moves in mysterious ways," his father always said. He'd been given a second chance to describe how he killed Michal. If he got it right, the Israeli would pay Arami and Liddie would be safe.

"Got it?" the tall policeman asked, his tone threatening.

Gabriel nodded.

"Repeat what I said. I want to hear you say it."

Gabriel repeated the story, not missing any details. He could feel the blood spilling from his lower lip as he spoke.

The tall policeman patted him on the back. "Well done. Maybe you're not such an asshole after all," he said, before leaving again.

Alone, Gabriel brought his hand to his face, gently wiping away the blood.

The door opened and the tall policeman came back in with another officer. He was short, dumpy, and bald.

The tall one moved closer to Gabriel, making him flinch. But this time he didn't put a hand on him, merely straightened the table and arranged the chairs around it.

The short one stood and watched, licking his lip.

Chapter 45

LIDDIE lay, bound and blindfolded, on the floor of the car. A few minutes ago, Ahmed had suddenly burst into the room and tied her hands behind her back. "Move it, cunt," he'd snarled, grabbing her and dragging her roughly out the door.

Nothing changed after the call to Gabriel. She continued to lie on the mattress in her cell, the thin sheet wrapped around her. From time to time, the door opened and Ahmed tossed some food on the floor. Except for that, she was all alone. Her cough was getting worse. She called out to Gabriel in the dark, begging him to rescue her. And she prayed. She knew that if he didn't come soon, she would die in this room.

She didn't ask where they were taking her. She remembered only too well the last time she was moved without warning. That was in Sinai. Rafik got rid of her when he discovered she was pregnant. "Yalla, get out of here. The Jews can have you," he'd grumbled, taking her to the border and ordering her to start running.

She was fired on by Egyptian soldiers, but she kept running. This was her chance to escape—from Rafik, from the daily violations of her body, from the beatings she took from her captor and his cohorts, from the constant abuse. She knew about Israel from church. It was the land of milk and honey, the Holy Land, the place where Christ was born. She ran for the border as fast as she could. She had to get away from Rafik and reach the Promised Land. Liddie had no idea where Gabriel was, but she believed with all her heart that he was already there, waiting for her.

She was picked up by Israeli soldiers who took her to the detention camp along with the other refugees who snuck across the border. For the first time since she'd left home, she was given a hot meal, a real bed to sleep in, and a chance to shower. A doctor examined her. Then they questioned her, wanting to know where she came from, why she left, how she got here, why she chose to come to Israel. Two weeks later they handed her a bus ticket to Tel Aviv and the address of a shelter for women in her condition.

That's where she met Dahlia, her guardian angel. She also met a lot of other girls like her, all of them carrying a baby they didn't want. Some arrived too late to do anything about it. She was one of the lucky ones. Dahlia arranged for an abortion, but she had to lie about how far along she was. She heard from the other girls that the Israelis wouldn't do it if she'd been pregnant for more than a few weeks.

Dahlia comforted her, telling her time and again that she had nothing to be ashamed of. What Rafik did wasn't her fault. Almost all the African refugees ran into someone like Rafik on the way to Israel.

Dahlia promised that everything would be fine now, and Liddie was starting to believe her. She didn't know that Rafik had sold her to a pimp in Israel, to Ahmed. He was just waiting for the Israeli doctors to get rid of the baby. As soon as she was fit for work, Ahmed snatched her from the shelter. Rafik had lied when he pointed her in the direction of the border. He wasn't letting her go, he was delivering her to her new owner.

Now Ahmed was fed up with her, too. She was no use to him sick. Where were they taking her? She knew Gabriel would do what he could to help her. But the ransom Ahmed was demanding was too high. How would her brother get that kind of money?

The car slowed to a stop.

Liddie's mother had pleaded with them to leave. "There's no future for you here," she said over and over, urging her children to flee. Her poor mother. She had no idea where she was sending them.

Ahmed opened the door and tugged at her dress. "Yalla, yalla," he barked, pulling her out of the car. She prayed every day for God to release her from Ahmed's prison cell. Now that it was finally happening, she was frightened. What was waiting for her outside?

She landed painfully on a hard surface. "Move," Ahmed said, punctuating his order with a kick. Liddie cringed, readying herself for the next blow. There was a lot of noise. Where was she?

The second blow never came. She heard Ahmed walk away, but she continued to lie there without moving, shivering from the cold. She could hear voices nearby. Traffic in the street. Horns honking. She thought she heard the car drive away. If she could only get the blindfold off her eyes she could see where she was, but her hands were tied behind her.

"Here, let me help you," a man said in Tigrinya.

Liddie tried to pull away from the voice. She could sense more people around her. What did Ahmed do with her? Where did he take her? Who did he sell her to this time?

Abruptly, the blindfold was removed. Liddie saw four men standing over her. They were going to rape her. Ahmed had tossed her like a wounded animal into a pack of hungry wolves. She looked at them in terror. No, not again.

A hand reached out to her and she flinched. Her teeth were chattering. The cold night air penetrated down to her bones. Liddie looked around for Gabriel, but she didn't see him.

"Gabriel?" she shouted. "Where are you?" He didn't appear.

"It's okay, Liddie. I'm Arami, Gabriel's friend." A man she'd never seen before reached out and touched her face. Ahmed had known her name, too. He'd waited for the Israelis to take out the baby, waited for her to get better, and then he'd come for her and made her one of his whores. She wasn't going to go through that hell again. This time she'd fight back. She didn't care if they killed her. Her life wasn't worth living anyway.

"Liddie." She could feel his breath on her cheek.

"No," she screamed, and bit down hard on his hand.

Chapter 46

ANAT rang the bell of Apartment 3 at 122 Stricker Street. No one had spoken to her since the item appeared on the Internet news site. Even David hadn't called. As far as Anat was concerned, until she was officially notified otherwise, she was still the acting chief of the Special Investigations Unit and would continue to work the case as she saw fit.

A dog barked on the other side of the door. The last time she'd seen Shmuel Gonen was at the lineup, when he failed to ID their suspect.

Mrs. Gonen cracked the door open.

"Shmuel's resting," she said with a sour expression.

"I just need a minute," Anat promised, reaching out to pet the mastiff that was rubbing up against her leg.

"You said he got it wrong at the lineup. He took it very hard," Dvora Gonen said accusingly, blocking Anat's entry.

"I'm very sorry," Anat said gently, although she didn't feel she had anything to apologize for. "It happens. People make mistakes. It's fine. No one's blaming him. It wasn't some kind of test."

"That's exactly what I told him, Inspector Nachmias. But he really wanted to help the police, to feel useful. You don't understand what that means to people like us," Mrs. Gonen scolded. She stepped into the hall and closed the door behind her, making it clear that as long as she had anything to say about it, Anat wasn't coming in.

"I do understand, but I have a few more questions to ask him. It's important," Anat said with as much empathy as she could muster. She found Dvora Gonen's protectiveness a little ridiculous.

"I think you've asked enough questions," Mrs. Gonen answered, not conceding an inch. "What else do you need? Shmuel told you what he saw. Why do you have to talk to him again?"

Anat remained silent.

"Is this how you spend the taxpayers' money?" the old lady said in a loud whisper. She doesn't want to make a scene for the neighbors, Anat thought, struggling to keep a straight face. "You've got enough. Throw the African in prison and move on to something else. There's no reason to keep harassing law-abiding citizens. That politician, what's his name, Regev. He's right. You should be making sure they get what they deserve instead of protecting them."

"Your husband told me he heard shouting the night Michal was killed. I just want to ask him about it," Anat said quietly. It's hard to go on attacking somebody if they don't fight back. That was one of the first lessons she learned when she was working as a patrol officer.

"That's absurd," Dvora said, waving her hand dismissively. "Shmuel doesn't hear anything at night."

"Excuse me?"

"He sleeps like a log," Mrs. Gonen went on. Leaning in closer, she whispered, "You should hear him snore."

"But he told me that the night of the murder, he heard . . ."

"It was me. I heard it," Dvora cut in.

"What exactly did you hear?" Anat hadn't even questioned Mrs. Gonen. They'd focused all their attention on her husband. He was the one who said he'd seen Gabriel. They'd canvassed the neighbors, but no one had thought to ask Mrs. Gonen. She was playing bridge when Shmuel ran into Gabriel.

"Shouting . . . someone was calling her name . . . yelling obscenities at her." She was no longer whispering.

"Was it a man or a woman?"

"A man, definitely a man." There was a trace of condescension in her voice. "Women don't shout like that in the middle of the night. And they don't use that kind of language, either."

"Did you recognize the voice? Did you see who was shouting? Do you know who it was?" Anat fired at her.

Dvora Gonen shook her head.

"What happened after that? Did you hear anyone else? Did you see anything?"

"No. The noise was so loud I couldn't hear the television. I had to turn up the volume. It's none of my business what goes on in other people's homes."

Anat gave her a skeptical look.

"There was a good movie on, I didn't want . . ." For the first time, Anat sensed a hint of embarrassment in her voice.

Anat stared at her in silence. Something she said was niggling at her. What was it? All of a sudden it came to her.

"You said he was shouting obscenities at her?"

Mrs. Gonen nodded.

"In Hebrew?" She had to be sure she wasn't wrong.

"Of course. I'm old, but I'm not deaf."

Chapter 47

MORE and more people were crowding around Liddie. She looked up at them in fear. What did they want from her? What were they going to do to her?

She was afraid the man she bit would hit her. She could see the pain on his face. But he didn't raise a hand to her. He didn't even shout at her or curse her. He just told everyone else to move back.

No one obeyed.

The man bent down to her. "I'm Arami, Gabriel's friend," he repeated.

A chill went down her spine at the sound of her brother's name.

"Where's Gabriel?" she asked, her voice breaking.

"He's not here. He asked me to take care of you," the man said in a gentle voice.

No! It was a trap. Ahmed had spoken to her nicely at first, too. When he came up to her outside Dahlia's shelter, he invited her to go for a ride in his car. He said he'd show her the city. She refused. That's when he grabbed her and dragged her to the car.

Liddie tried to stand up, but everything was spinning around her. The man held out a piece of paper.

"This is a letter from Gabriel. He asked me to give it to you. It explains everything," he said, urging her to take it.

Liddie shifted her eyes uncertainly from the man to the paper in his hand. He's trying to entice me, she thought. Alarm bells were ringing wildly in her head.

"It says here he wants you to stay with me until he gets back. I'm a friend of his."

Liddie shook her head vehemently. She's wasn't going anywhere and she wouldn't agree to take anything from him. She'd learned her lesson. She made another attempt to stand up and fell back down again.

"Take this, it's water," the man said, holding out a bottle.

She didn't want to give in, but the temptation was too strong. Her throat was so dry. She took the bottle from his hand. While she drank thirstily, he kept asking the other people to go away, to give them some privacy.

"Thank you," Liddie said, returning the bottle.

The man smiled. She couldn't remember the last time anyone had smiled at her.

"Come with me, Liddie. I'll take care of you," he said, reaching his hand out again. The look in his eyes seemed sincere.

"No!" Liddie screamed. Whatever happened, she wouldn't let him touch her. She didn't want anyone to touch her ever again.

The man said nothing. Most of the crowd had dispersed, losing interest in the little drama. If he was planning to grab her, he could have done it already.

Liddie pushed herself up. Her legs were shaking. She wasn't sure they would support her, but she had to force herself to walk on her own if she wanted to get away from him.

People moved aside, letting her pass. Even the man who called himself Arami didn't try to stop her.

Liddie looked around, desperately trying to figure out where she was. During her time at the shelter, Dahlia had taken her for a walk a few times. Other than that, she'd hadn't been outside.

"Where are you going?" the man asked, following at a safe distance.

She ignored him, concentrating only on putting one foot in front of the other, struggling not to fall, not knowing where she was going. The light hurt her eyes and the noise of the people and cars was painful to her ears. She'd been locked in a cell for months. Now she was in the middle of a bustling city. She was terrified.

"At least tell me where you're going so I can let your brother know," the man pleaded.

Liddie turned to look at him. He didn't seem like a bad person.

And as long as she was out in the street with other people around, she felt safe. Was he telling the truth? Did Gabriel really send him?

Before she had time to regret her decision, Liddie blurted out the address of the shelter.

"You're going to Dahlia's place? You know Dahlia?" he asked in surprise.

Liddie nodded.

Chapter 48

ANAT jumped out of the car and ran into the building. The rain was coming down hard. She'd been in such a rush, she'd forgotten her umbrella. What she'd learned from Dvora Gonen had given her a renewed sense of urgency. Her gut feeling was right. Maybe now she could prove it.

They'd only done the most basic tests on the blood found on the outside of the door, checking for no more than blood type. It was time to dig deeper.

Anat had decided to go to Abu Kabir and talk to Grisha in person. They'd sat next to each other in a seminar a couple of months ago. She'd hardly been able to concentrate on the speakers because Grisha was constantly whispering in her ear, mostly making cynical comments that had her in stitches the whole time. At the end of the seminar, he invited her to come see what he described as the "state-of-the-art labs" at Abu Kabir. His heavy Russian accent made her smile. "You won't believe it, zero cool, just like *CSI* on TV," he said with a serious expression in response to her skeptical look. Anat was meaning to go, but she kept putting it off, like everything else that wasn't directly connected with the case she was working on at the moment.

When she walked in, Grisha was leaning over a microscope that looked exactly like the ones they used to have in the biology lab in high school. She knew what kind of pressure they were under here. The lab Grisha ran was the only one in the country that was responsible for identifying victims, body parts, and bones. It was also the only one that conducted DNA tests in major felony cases. "That's why the government gives me such a large staff," Grisha had told her, explaining that it consisted entirely of himself and two assistants.

"Hey, Inspector Nachmias. How nice of you to drop by. We've

missed you," Grisha said when he caught sight of her standing next to him.

"I came to see what's new in the world of science," Anat said in an attempt to butter him up. She sensed the words had come out wrong.

"Of course you did. That's why you all come here. Everybody knows cops are science lovers." As always, Grisha maintained a poker face, but Anat already knew him well enough to tell when he was teasing.

She wanted to come up with a clever retort, but she couldn't think of anything. The same thing happened to her when she went on a date. She tried to be funny and witty, but in the end she came out with some lame remark that earned her a forced smile at best.

"And as part of your interest in science, you said to yourself, Grisha might do a little DNA test for me. Am I right?" Apparently he'd decided to make it easier for her.

"You can read me like a book," Anat said, smiling. She needed answers, and she needed them fast, before David got back and she was kicked off the case.

"It's something urgent that can't wait, right?" Grisha went on. Anat nodded.

"You're all the same," he said with a deep sigh. "It's always rush, rush, rush with you people. But money for Grisha to hire another assistant, that you don't have."

Anat remained silent. If she'd learned anything in the short time she'd known Grisha, it was that there was no stopping him when he started grousing.

"Go on, get it out. I heard you're on an important case. I bet the brass are breathing down your neck. It's not easy when you're a lady cop," he said, adding, "or a new immigrant."

"Is it true DNA can tell you if a person is Caucasian or not?" Anat asked, although she knew the answer. She'd give Grisha the opportunity to explain it to her. She might not be witty, but she'd been on enough dates to know that men like women who make them feel smart. Especially men with an inferiority complex.

"DNA can tell you everything, Inspector Nachmias. There's an allele that's present in ninety-nine-point-nine percent of Caucasians and almost never in Asians or Africans."

"So you can find out if the person whose blood was found at the scene is white or black?" Anat asked with wide eyes and an innocent look on her face.

"Absolutely. That's why they pay me the big bucks. Six thousand shekels a month," Grisha grumbled. Still, Anat could see she'd succeeded in stroking his ego.

Dvora Gonen said that the man banging on Michal's door was swearing in Hebrew. Normally, she'd report that information to Yochai immediately, but in view of the circumstances, she'd decided not to risk it until she had proof. Witnesses are unreliable. They can change their story. When Anat went to Yochai, she wanted something more solid than the statement of a peevish old lady. She wanted irrefutable scientific evidence.

"How fast can you do the test?" Anat asked with a pleading look in her eyes. "I really need it, Grisha. As soon as possible," she said softly when she got no answer.

If the results confirmed her suspicions, Michal Poleg's killer might not be an African migrant. He might be a white Israeli. And not any Israeli, but a man Michal knew and had no qualms about letting into her apartment late at night.

Chapter 49

"I thought you quit smoking," Itai said to Dahlia. They were standing outside the shelter. It still hurt where the gorilla at the restaurant had punched him, especially when he made any sharp movement. There's no telling what would have happened to him if the waiter hadn't dragged him outside. He told the staff at OMA that he'd run his bike into the curb and taken a fall. His mother, who had never understood his fondness for bikes, snatched at the opportunity to launch another attack. "Who's going to want you now?" she said, raising her arms to the heavens and letting out a deep sigh. "You earn a miserable salary, and you've got a limp. You'll be the death of me one day."

Dahlia and Itai were taking advantage of the break in the rain to get some fresh air. There were parts of the city where people delighted in the smell of the air after the rain, but here it still stunk of garbage.

Dahlia had called him a couple of hours after Liddie showed up on her doorstep. She didn't stop asking about Gabriel. Itai had told Dahlia about Gabriel the last time he was here, and Dahlia had put two and two together.

She shrugged her shoulders in despair. "Every day there's something new and I tell myself this is as bad as it gets. There can't be anything more appalling than this. And the next day I see something worse," she said, exhaling smoke.

A half-naked baby crawled out of the shelter toward them, her hands dirty from the unwashed floor. Dahlia tossed away her cigarette and picked up the infant. The baby smiled at her and then turned her head to smile at Itai. He made a face and she laughed.

"Poor thing. What that girl must have been through," Dahlia said, bouncing the baby in her arms. The tiny bundle was leaving black stains on her clothes.

"Did she say anything?" Itai asked as he continued to make funny faces at the baby. He'd come as soon as he got Dahlia's call, but by the time he arrived, Liddie was already asleep.

Dahlia shook her head. "She just kept asking for Gabriel."

"Does she know where they were keeping her?"

"No. She was blindfolded both times, when they took her away and when they dumped her in the street."

The two aid workers fell silent, watching the baby who was holding on tight to Dahlia.

Gabriel had spoken to Itai about his sister. As far as he knew, the Bedouins killed her in Sinai. Her suddenly turning up like this was no accident. Her jailers wouldn't let her go without a reason. Someone had paid them, and that someone had to be Gabriel. But he couldn't have raised the money on his own. He must have gotten it from somebody else. Who? Itai might be tempted to accept the cops' theory that Gabriel killed Michal for the money, if he didn't know for a fact that she didn't have it to give him. All the work she did was on a volunteer basis. He himself had lent her money a few times when she was strapped for cash.

"How did she get here?" he asked Dahlia.

"The guy who helped deliver a baby in the detention camp brought her. The one who proved to the soldiers that not all Africans just came down off the trees." Dahlia was still bouncing the baby, who had started crying. "You know him. He was a friend of Hagos, the interpreter that got deported."

"Arami?"

"That's the one," Dahlia said nodding as she began singing to the baby.

Itai wasn't surprised to hear that Arami had helped Liddie. He'd expect nothing less of him.

Itai had been to see Gabriel several times since his arrest, using his attorney's credentials to get in. But his visits had only fed his frustration. He tried again and again to convince Gabriel to tell him the truth, to reveal the names of the people who forced him to take the rap for Michal's murder, but to no avail. Gabriel sat across from him in silence, staring at the floor, refusing to look him in the eye.

Each time he saw him, Gabriel repeated the same question: had he spoken with Arami. Itai kept asking what he meant, but he didn't get an answer. He didn't get an answer from Arami either when he asked him why Gabriel was so interested in what they had to say to each other.

But now everything was clear. He had to talk to Arami as soon as possible. He finally had a lead. If Arami knew where to pick up Liddie, he might also know who Gabriel got the money from and who he gave it to. There was no longer any doubt in Itai's mind. Gabriel took money from someone to confess to a crime he didn't commit in order to rescue his sister. And the person who paid him was also the person who killed Michal. What's more, whoever that man was, Itai was convinced he had some connection to the "Banker."

Chapter 50

YARIV was totally absorbed in preparing for a hearing tomorrow in district court. When his mind was on his work, everything else faded into the background. There was no greater rush than arming himself for a legal battle and looking forward to another win.

A knock on the door forced him to raise his eyes from the stack of papers on his desk. Galit Lavie was standing in the doorway. Beside her was a petite woman who looked vaguely familiar.

"Let me introduce you. This is Inspector Anat Nachmias, the acting head of Special Investigations. She's the lead detective on the Michal Poleg case," Lavie said as she walked in.

Now Yariv remembered where he'd seen her before. He gazed at the two women in surprise. He hadn't been expecting this visit.

"I know you have an interest in the case," Lavie said with a fake smile. "Anat was just filling me in. I thought you might like to talk to her." Yariv cursed her under his breath. Oh, how he hated that woman.

"Actually, there are a couple of questions I'd like to ask you. Can you spare me a few minutes?"

Slender, with a head of unrestrained curls, Nachmias looked to be around his age, maybe a little younger. Yariv knew from the days when he was working criminal cases that the ladies who appeared the most innocent were sometimes the most lethal.

"What do you need?" he asked, keeping his expression as neutral as possible.

"I understand you were in a relationship with Michal," the detective began.

Yariv remained silent, not taking the bait. If he wanted to make it safely through the ambush Lavie had laid for him, he had to stay calm. Kobi had predicted the cops would get to him sooner or later.

"I'll leave you to it," Lavie said, turning to go. This time there was no disguising the malice in her smile. How dare she set a trap for him? He should have known she wouldn't turn a blind eye when she found out he'd pumped her intern for information. Now she was getting even.

"May I?" Nachmias asked, pointing to a chair.

"To tell the truth, I'm very busy. I've got a hearing tomorrow. Maybe some other time?"

"I only need a couple of minutes. I promise I won't take up too much of your time," she said, sitting down without waiting for an invitation.

Yariv looked at her in silence. Her allegedly spontaneous visit was making him nervous. Why was she here? Did they know something? If I were a suspect, they'd bring me in, he said to himself in an effort to calm his nerves. The arrest of an assistant state attorney would make a great photo op. The cops wouldn't want to pass up such an opportunity. He knew how it worked.

"About Michal Poleg. I understand you knew her."

"Yes, a long time ago . . . We were together for a while. It didn't work out. We both knew it was time to call it quits," Yariv said, clearing his throat.

"I'm getting married in two months," he went on quickly, wanting to make it clear he wasn't still carrying a torch for Michal.

"Congratulations," Nachmias said with a warm smile.

He'd had another fight with Inbar last night. In the end he'd shouted that he was sick of "her" wedding and stormed out, slamming the door behind him.

"I understand she recently filed a complaint against you," Nachmias went on.

Yariv felt his face turn red. But he was ready.

He sat up straighter in his chair and started reeling off the response he'd worked out with Kobi: ideological differences, opposite ends of the political spectrum, groundless complaint, full backing of the State Attorney.

Nachmias didn't seem convinced. "She made very harsh allegations. Concealing the legal opinion of the Foreign Ministry. That's a very serious . . ."

"Stop right there! I never saw the legal opinion she claimed I concealed, and I find your insinuations offensive." Yariv had to make an effort to keep his voice steady.

The detective remained silent.

"It's all in my response to the Bar Association. That legal opinion, if it exists at all, never crossed my desk." Yariv had been in a rush to submit his response, positive it would put an end to the whole affair. It would be filed away and forgotten, together with Michal's complaint. That was a mistake. He should have squared it with Regev first, told him what he planned to say. After all, he showed the position paper to Regev as soon as he got it, and it was the politician who suggested he make it disappear. Now he had to be sure they got their stories straight.

Nachmias gave him a skeptical look that was very unsettling. Did she know something he didn't? He had to project confidence, to show her he was in control, that she wasn't getting to him.

"Inspector Nachmias," he said, following Kobi's notes and looking straight at her, "if you're asking if there was anything personal between me and Michal Poleg after all this time, the answer is no. We were in a relationship a few years ago. It ended. I moved on. So did she."

"Nevertheless, you went to Galit's intern to find out about the case," she said evenly. It was clear that nothing he'd said had made any impression on her.

"I'm not sure I understand where you're going with this. And I don't like what you're implying," Yariv answered, raising his voice.

"I'd just like to know why you were so interested in our investigation, that's all," Nachmias said in the serene tone that grated on his nerves.

"Like I told Ms. Lavie, I shouldn't have spoken to her intern. It was mere curiosity, that's all. I'm sorry. But since we were close once, I wanted . . . well, you can understand." Yariv hated having to apologize to the cop.

They sat across from each other in silence. It seemed to Yariv that she was waiting for him to say something, but he didn't know what.

"As for the complaint, it was rubbish," he said, breaking the silence. "I didn't give it the time of day. Unfortunately, people are always filing bullshit complaints against us."

Nachmias still didn't respond.

"You're a cop, you know that. People like to complain. They get the idea they're being persecuted," Yariv went on, trying to engage her with a smile.

"Have any complaints been filed against you before?" the detective asked, not returning the smile.

"You have to understand. Complaints against attorneys are almost always dismissed. It happens all the time." Yariv realized she had put him on the defensive.

"We're not talking about other complaints," she reminded him.

"You're right, Inspector Nachmias. We're talking about one ridiculous complaint I didn't lose any sleep over," he retorted.

Yariv smiled to himself. That took the wind out of her sails. He debated whether to deliver one of Regev's pet monologues about "enemies of the state" and "Israelis filled with self-hatred" but decided against it. She didn't need him to spell it out for her.

"When was the last time you saw Michal?" Nachmias fired at him.

Yariv had an answer ready. "Let me see, I'm trying to remember . . . I'm not sure. We lived in the same neighborhood. We ran into each other in the supermarket from time to time, on the street. It's a small world, you know. . . . It must have been a few weeks ago, maybe a few months. . . . I can't be sure," Yariv said just as he'd practiced, including the hesitations. Only the guilty have a clear memory of every detail, Kobi had reminded him when he coached him.

"Were you in her apartment recently?" the detective asked, her face totally expressionless.

"No," Yariv answered quickly. She was getting too close. "I really don't understand why you're asking me these questions." Kobi had advised him to remain on the offensive. "I'm willing to do whatever I can to help, but with all due respect, you can't just come in here and . . ."

"Where were you the night Michal was killed?" Nachmias cut in, leaning closer.

"I was in a bar with a friend." Yariv made an effort to sound unconcerned by the question.

Nachmias pulled out a pad and pen, signaling that she wanted more details.

"My fiancée was in Eilat, so I went out for a drink with a friend, Kobi Etkin. . . . You might know him," he went on as the detective took notes.

"The defense attorney?" she asked, raising her head from her pad.

Yariv nodded.

"When did you leave the bar?"

"I don't know . . . twelve thirty, something like that," he said reluctantly.

"Where did you go after that?"

"I went home. Alone."

Nachmias wrote something down before looking back up at him.

"I'm sorry, Inspector Nachmias, but I'm really . . . I have to be in court tomorrow. I think we're done here," Yariv said, attempting to put a swagger in his voice.

"Yes, of course," the detective said, rising.

Yariv walked her out, anxious to make sure she left.

"I see you hurt yourself," Nachmias said in the doorway, nodding toward the fading bruises under his eyes.

"Yes, I fell off my bike," Yariv responded with another answer he had prepared in advance.

"When?"

"On the way to work . . . it was a stupid accident."

"I hope it goes away by the wedding," Nachmias said.

Chapter 51

ITAI looked out at the commotion beyond his office door, hoping it would die down soon. Every few minutes he checked his watch. He'd left Dahlia convinced he knew why Michal was murdered and who was responsible. Even more important, he was sure he knew how to find her killer.

He was waiting impatiently for a chance to talk with Arami. As it turned out, he didn't have to wait long.

"I need your help, Itai," Arami said, walking into his office. "I need you to tell Gabriel that his sister, Liddie, is safe and sound. Everything's fine. I tried to tell him myself but they wouldn't let me in."

Itai considered feigning surprise in the hope of getting more out of Arami, but he realized it wouldn't work.

"I know. Dahlia told me you brought her to the shelter." He got up and went to stand next to Arami. "Actually, I wanted to talk to you about it."

ARAMI sat across from Itai with a look of innocence on his face. He claimed that Gabriel paid for Liddie's release, but he didn't know who he gave the money to or how much he paid him. Gabriel arranged it all himself before turning himself in, including the time and place of Liddie's release. He asked Arami to take care of Liddie for him, and that's what he did. That's all he knew.

There was no doubt in Itai's mind that Arami was lying. When he first started working for OMA, Itai was hurt every time the enormous efforts he invested in helping an asylum seeker were rewarded with fairy tales. Over time, he learned to take it in stride, or at least not to take it personally. The people he was charged with aiding weren't angels, and yes, sometimes they lied.

But this time was different. Itai was infuriated with Arami. It wasn't only because they'd known each other a long time and he paid his salary, or because Arami was a grown man with a wife and kids who should know better. He was infuriated with him because of what was hanging in the balance. He expected more of him.

"Did you see the man who left her in the street?" Itai wasn't going to let Arami off the hook so easily.

"Someone pulled her out of the car and drove away," Arami said with a shrug.

"And you don't know who it was?"

"No. Gabriel told me where to go and when to be there, and I did what he said."

"Where did Gabriel get the money?" Itai was starting to lose his temper.

Arami looked away. "People in the community are always lending each other money. Gabriel was very well liked. I gave him a little, too, what I could," he said finally.

Itai knew the asylum seekers helped each other out, but it was just petty cash. They fought a daily battle for survival and sent the little they had left back home to their families. They wouldn't be able to come up with the kind of money Gabriel needed to ransom his sister. They were probably talking tens of thousands of shekels. And most of the others in the community were being threatened and squeezed for money themselves.

"Why did Gabriel say he killed Michal?" Itai was hoping to break through the wall of silence that Arami had thrown up, but the interpreter only shrugged his shoulders again. "Do you believe he killed her?" he persisted.

Silence.

"Help me out here, Arami. We're talking about Gabriel and Michal. Does it make sense to you that he killed her?" Itai asked, hoping to elicit an emotional reaction.

Arami just sat there with a blank look in his eyes.

"There's a restaurant on Fein Street. I think there's some kind of illegal activity going on there. Maybe Michal was on to them," he said, trying a different approach in an attempt to get a response from Arami.

Arami remained silent.

"I went there myself. I tried to find out what was going on," Itai continued. "All I got for my trouble was a beating."

"You ought to be more careful, Itai," Arami said, getting up.

"Talk to me, Arami. Tell me what you know," Itai begged. "I think the people in that restaurant, or whoever they work for, I think they killed Michal because she was poking her nose in their business."

"I'm sorry," Arami said, turning and walking out of the office.

ITAI had been desperate to get Arami to talk. He'd even entertained the fantasy that he'd go with him to that detective, Anat Nachmias, and Arami would tell her what he knew. Maybe then the cops would finally understand that they had the wrong man, that they had to look elsewhere to find Michal's killer.

Gabriel was lying in order to save his sister. Arami knew more than he was saying, but he wouldn't break his promise to Gabriel and divulge his secret, certainly not to Itai. He learned a long time ago that it didn't matter how much he went to bat for them, the asylum seekers would never really trust him. They'd been through hell to get here. They'd been cheated, abused, betrayed. After that, it was hard for them to trust anybody except one of their own. In their eyes, he'd always be a white man. That was one of the things Michal found so frustrating. She couldn't come to terms with it.

Watching Arami exit his office without answering his questions, Itai was equally frustrated. If Arami didn't talk, Gabriel would be convicted of manslaughter, maybe even murder, and Michal's real killer would never be caught.

He had to go outside his comfort zone, he thought to himself, passing his hand gently over his painful ribs. He'd tried his usual sober approach, but it hadn't worked. He had to start screaming at the top of his lungs so everyone would know what he'd found out.

A plan began taking shape in Itai's mind. Ironically, he was considering exactly the kind of action Michal was always pushing for.

Chapter 52

GABRIEL kept his eyes focused on the lawyer's lips, which were moving rapidly. It was the third or fourth time they'd met. It was always the same. The lawyer rattled on and he sat in silence.

The lawyer was angry with him, and he said so repeatedly. He wanted Gabriel to tell him what happened when he went to Michal's house. "I can't go to court with nothing. I'll make a fool of myself. You're being charged with murder. I don't want to look like a clown. Do you understand?" he said again and again, waving an accusing finger in Gabriel's face.

Gabriel didn't pay much attention to what the lawyer was saying about the Israeli justice system. The only thing that mattered to him was that Liddie was safe. Arami promised to let him know the moment she was released, but several days had gone by and he hadn't heard from him. That made him nervous. It made him suspicious of Arami. It made him wonder if he hadn't sacrificed himself for nothing. But then Itai came yesterday and told him that Liddie had been released, and Gabriel was sorry for all the bad thoughts he had had. Itai said Arami tried to visit him a few times but they wouldn't let him in.

Knowing that Liddie was safe filled Gabriel with joy. What he was doing had a reason and a purpose. He wanted to hear more and more about his sister, how she was, where she'd been all this time, what they did to her. From the window in his cell he could see it was raining. Was she warm enough? Did she have the right clothes? Why did he hear coughing on the phone? Itai didn't say much. He kept pressuring him to talk. If Gabriel told him what happened, he'd tell him about Liddie, he said. He couldn't do it. Itai already knew too much.

The lawyer treated him as if he were backward. He spoke slowly in a loud voice, emphasizing each word. He kept asking him if he understood. That had always been a sign for Gabriel. He was wary of Israelis who talked to him like the lawyer did. That's why he trusted Michal and Itai. They spoke to him like he was an adult, a real person. The little policewoman spoke to him like that, too.

Gabriel wanted Itai to represent him, but he said he couldn't, that he didn't have experience in criminal cases. Gabriel didn't care. Anybody was better than the lawyer he had now.

Prison wasn't easy for him. Having a bed to himself and regular meals wasn't enough. He felt stifled. He had no room to move around.

Eritrea was all open spaces. Sometimes he went days without seeing another human being. He had all the fresh air and sunshine he could ever want. Gabriel missed the wide expanses of his home, the sense of freedom, the feeling of being surrounded by the majesty of nature and being able to breathe it all in. In Tel Aviv there were buildings everywhere, high towers that reached the sky and made him dizzy. There was no quiet, no privacy, only smoke, people, and cars everywhere he went. Too many people, too many cars.

Everything was smaller in prison. Closed off. He sat in a corner of his cell, not moving, drawing pictures in his head because they wouldn't give him paper and pencils. His feet longed to run like they used to; his lungs yearned for fresh air. But his feet had nowhere to go and all he breathed in was the stench and congestion.

They were eight in the cell. The others were all Israelis. Most of the time they ignored him, except when they cursed him or ordered him around like a slave. The tall smelly one with the tattoo on his head beat him up once. He kicked him, punched him in the face. The others didn't interfere. He'd learned from Rafik in Sinai that it was best not to react, not to show him that it hurt. In the end, he'd stop. It wasn't much fun to kick an inanimate object. The tall smelly one stopped, too.

The lawyer said he wanted to help him; he could get him out if he talked. Gabriel didn't believe him, and he wouldn't say anything even if he did. The Israeli man gave Arami the money on condition that Gabriel took the blame for what happened to Michal. Before they told Arami to leave, his friend made him swear to uphold his side of the bargain. "If you tell the truth he'll kill Liddie and have us both deported, like Hagos. He's a very powerful man, I can tell," Arami said.

Gabriel had to stay strong. He couldn't give in. His fate had been decided and he had to accept it.

FOR a change, the lawyer looked happy today. He even smiled at Gabriel. The detective who interrogated him was off the case, he said. He'd met with her second in command, who was in charge now, and he said the State Attorney was open to cutting a deal.

The lawyer thought it was good news. They could use it to their advantage. "Something we can work with. Do you understand? Trust me, Gabriel," he said with obvious self-satisfaction, "this is what I do. They'll offer twenty-five years and I'll counter with fifteen. In the end we'll agree on twenty. If you're a good boy, you'll be out in thirteen. Do you understand?"

Too many numbers. It was confusing.

"So what do you say?" the lawyer asked, leaning in, raising his voice, and emphasizing each word. "Should I say yes? I need your consent. I don't want to pressure you. Do you understand? It's a good deal. Thirteen years, fifteen at most, and you're out. Do you understand? You'll be able to start over."

Chapter 53

ANAT was sitting in her office poring over the documents on her desk. The first time she'd read Michal's complaint against Yariv Ninio a few days ago, she hadn't given it much weight. The phrasing was overwrought and histrionic, and the allegations sounded over-the-top, like the claim that by concealing the Foreign Ministry's legal opinion from the court, Ninio "was signing the refugees' death warrant." But the real problem wasn't the style, it was the content. Michal didn't have a shred of evidence to back up her claims. It was obvious to Anat that she'd never seen the alleged document she contended could have saved Hagos from deportation and subsequent death.

Still, what she'd learned from Dvora Gonen was causing Anat to reconsider her theory of the crime. Yariv Ninio wasn't the ideal candidate for the role of murderer. The motive was weak, no more than what seemed like a hysterical complaint to the Bar Association. But there was no denying that he was a white man with whom Michal was closely acquainted and he had a grudge against her. Anat had learned from experience not to judge a motive from her own perspective. She had to see it through the suspect's eyes. Something that seemed trivial to her could mean the world to somebody else. It could even be a motive for murder. She'd worked a case where a man killed his wife because of an argument over who was going to take out the garbage.

Anat aligned the papers neatly, put them through the hole punch, and filed them in a fresh binder.

She hadn't been planning to question Ninio. She'd gone to the State Attorney's Office to have a word with Galit Lavie, to let her know that it wasn't a slam dunk yet, that she shouldn't be in a rush to file charges against Gabriel. She didn't say much, just that there were still some questions that needed answers, but she was sure Lavie got the message.

If any of Anat's colleagues found out that she'd spoken to Lavie, they'd brand her a traitor. In theory, the police worked hand in hand with the prosecution, but reality was very different. There was a lot of tension between them. Lavie had a reputation for being nobody's fool. Anat hoped she could trust her.

During their conversation, Anat happened to mention Michal's complaint. She could see that it was the first the prosecutor had heard of it. When she pressed Lavie to tell her why she seemed so troubled by the information, she learned of Ninio's attempt to find out about the progress of the case from her intern. That set off another alarm in Anat's head. She decided to risk questioning him even though she hadn't prepared for the interview.

Now she was glad she'd followed her gut instinct. Ninio had confirmed her suspicions. She could tell he was putting on an act, making a supreme effort to appear unconcerned. Some of his answers even sounded rehearsed, as if he'd been expecting to be questioned by the cops. And the way he panicked when she noticed his bruises strengthened her conviction that he was worth a closer look.

Anat's first call when she got back to the station was to the Bar Association. Within half an hour, Ninio's official response to Michal's complaint was on her computer. The words "police investigation" could work wonders. People were willing to divulge a great deal to a police officer, even more than they had to, or ought to. In contrast to Michal Poleg, Anat wasn't met with silence or indifference.

She'd expected a long statement in convoluted legalese, but the document was short and simply phrased. Ninio denied Michal's allegations one by one and claimed to know nothing of any legal opinion composed by the Foreign Ministry.

Anat was disappointed. It looked as if Ninio was telling the truth: the complaint was little more than a nuisance, nothing to get upset about. Nevertheless, she decided to look deeper. If she wanted to develop a solid theory of the case, she had to tie off all the loose ends. The result of her call to the Bar Association wasn't enough for her to cross Yariv Ninio off the list of possible suspects.

Her next call was to the Foreign Ministry. She had to go through ten different people before finally reaching Dr. Yigal Shemesh on the African desk. It turned out Michal had been to see him. She went to his office to bawl him out for the Foreign Ministry's official stance on refugees, which held that deportation did not put them in harm's way. Dr. Shemesh admitted to Anat that he did indeed write the legal opinion Michal referred to in her complaint. So it wasn't a figment of her imagination. Still, he swore he never showed it to Michal or even acknowledged its existence in so many words, although he confessed he might have alluded to it indirectly.

"I've gotten into enough trouble over it already," he said. The bitterness in his voice was unmistakable.

Anat found out that several months ago Dr. Shemesh had written a position paper arguing that the lives of migrants deported to Ethiopia were in danger. "All I did was repeat what the British Foreign Office has said, what you can find in UN reports. It was nothing new, certainly nothing revolutionary. Everybody knows it," he said apologetically.

He told her he sent copies to the Ministry of the Interior and the Ministry of Justice. At Anat's request, he e-mailed her a copy as well.

Despite Dr. Shemesh's efforts to minimize its importance, Anat immediately recognized the significance of his position paper. For the past few nights she'd been reading up on what people liked to call the "refugee problem." From the court transcripts she read, she could see that the main battles were fought over the issue of a migrant's citizenship. Eritreans and Sudanese couldn't be deported. They were protected because of the situation in their countries and the risks they would be facing if they returned. In contrast, Ethiopians were subject to deportation.

Anat learned that Ethiopia and Eritrea weren't strangers to each other. They didn't merely share a border, either. It was only in 1993 that Eritrea declared its independence from Ethiopia after a thirty-year war. Consequently, some of the Eritreans in Israel used to be Ethiopian citizens, and they speak the language. The Ministry of the Interior took advantage of this fact, labeling them Ethiopian in order to deport them.

Dr. Shemesh's position paper could potentially seal up this crack in the legal wall by spelling out the threat to Eritrean migrants who were deported to Ethiopia. The paper could actually save a lot of lives. As Dr. Shemesh told Anat, everything in it had been published before by various bodies around the world. But this was the first legal opinion written in Hebrew on the official stationery of the Israeli Foreign Ministry, and that's what made it so important. The good doctor understood that himself.

The document had a further significance. If it was presented in court, it would put an end to the string of victories credited to Yariv Ninio, the golden boy of the Interior Ministry and people like Ehud Regev, who built their careers on stoking the flames of hate against Africans.

Anat's next task was to trace the document itself. She had to prove that Ninio had received it, despite his insistence to the contrary.

It took her less time than she anticipated to locate the right person in the Justice Ministry. Chen Shabtai in the International Affairs Department confirmed that she had, in fact, received it from the Foreign Ministry. "It's just a position paper," she said, trying to downplay its importance.

"What did you do with it?" Anat asked.

"I passed it on to the relevant party." Anat could almost hear Shabtai shrug her shoulders.

"Would that happen to be Yariv Ninio in the State Attorney's Office?"

After a pause, the government official stammered that she wasn't sure she should answer that question.

"This is a murder investigation," Anat said sharply in a threatening tone. "You can tell me now or you can come to the station for a formal interview."

"Yes, he's the one I sent it to," Shabtai said. Any qualms she might have had about passing on this information were suddenly gone. It was the oldest trick in the book. It worked with everyone, even legal advisers.

"Are you certain he received it?"

"Yes."

"How can you be sure?"

"I've got his reply right here. He e-mailed back 'thank you.'"

ANAT leaned back in her chair. David's flight was getting in this afternoon and he'd be taking over the case. She had worked with him long enough to know he'd put it to bed in a day or two. He'd send it to the prosecution with the firm recommendation that charges be filed against Gabriel for the murder of Michal Poleg.

He'd be wrong. But as things stood at the moment, no one would listen to her. Ever since she stopped the reenactment in the middle, she'd been a pariah around the station. Nobody spoke to her, nobody made eye contact. Before he got on the plane, David sent her a text message: "Don't worry. I've got your back. Keep your head down."

Again she read Dr. Shemesh's legal opinion and the e-mail she'd received from the Justice Ministry. Michal was shooting in the dark. She filed a complaint with the Bar Association not knowing if there was any evidence to back it up. But Yariv Ninio knew. Despite his adamant denial, he received the document and he concealed it. And he lied to the Bar Association about it. There was no doubt in Anat's mind that he understood its significance and the implications it could have for his career.

This was a major development. But it wasn't enough. She needed more. At least now she knew where to look.

Chapter 54

ITAI stared at the computer impatiently, waiting for the news site to refresh and the items on the screen to change. The journalist had sent a text message half an hour ago notifying him that the story would appear in a few minutes. But he still didn't see it. The sluggishness of the computer was making him even more jittery. He was sick of having to put up with outdated equipment, fed up that nothing worked the way it was supposed to.

He'd debated with himself a long time before calling Amit Giladi. Itai kept as far away from the media as possible. He'd been burned once, and that was enough to last a lifetime. It was back when he was new at OMA. In an effort to get the Ministry of the Interior to cancel the deportation order issued for Sue, a young woman from Thailand who put out a small news sheet for the local community, he spoke to a reporter, hoping to get public opinion on his side. The reporter asked him to describe Sue. Naturally, he painted a glowing picture of her: she was charming, intelligent, attractive. The subhead over the story in the paper the next day hinted snidely at a direct link between his desire to help the woman and his fondness for Thai masseuses. It didn't matter that there was no evidence of such a connection in the article itself, the damage was done. And not just to Sue, who was deported soon afterward. Itai's own reputation was also tarnished, along with the cause he was trying to promote. Not to mention his mother's reaction. As soon as she saw the paper, she purchased cemetery plots for herself and his dad, claiming they wouldn't live long with the shame of it all. He joked that she could make it easier for herself if they moved closer to the cemetery. "You're laughing now, but you'll cry later," she said, ending the conversation with one of her pet platitudes.

But now he had to take action. A woman he was close to had

been murdered, and a fine young man was in jail. He couldn't explain why he was so protective of Gabriel, but the fact was that he felt a special responsibility for him, almost like a father, or at least an older brother. It wasn't merely his gentleness and modesty or the ease of communicating with him thanks to his knowledge of English. It was more than that. Gabriel's artistic talent gave Itai hope that he could make a better life for himself. Itai's job was to help provide asylum seekers with the bare necessities. Beyond that, he had few expectations. He didn't see a future for them in Israel, where they'd never be a real part of society. Virtually all of them would go on living the way they did now. But Gabriel was different. His talent could be his ticket out. Itai yearned for that, not only for Gabriel's sake but for his own sake as well. He badly craved a success story. Maybe that's why Gabriel's arrest affected him so personally.

Itai chose Giladi because he knew from his articles that he'd been present at the reenactment. And when he Googled his name, what he found made him think the reporter wasn't in anyone's pocket and wasn't easily intimidated.

He was sure Giladi would jump on the story. It had everything going for it: a man wrongly accused; a brother sacrificing himself for his sister; a girl abducted, tortured, and raped in Sinai and then brought to Israel as a sex slave; cops turning a blind eye to the truth in their rush to close the case; a gangland killer and extortionist still walking free.

To his surprise, the reporter was skeptical. "The guy confessed, so where's the story?" he asked when Itai called.

Finally, he got Giladi to agree to meet with him. Once they were face-to-face, Itai could see that he was breaking through the reporter's initial lack of enthusiasm. Giladi took copious notes and seemed particularly interested in the account of how Arami had found Liddie in the street, the condition she was in, and the traumatic experiences she had undergone.

"I want to talk to Liddie and Arami," Giladi said. "The interview with Gabriel will have to wait since he's in custody for the time being."

Itai explained that it was impossible to speak to the asylum seekers themselves. Arami was too vulnerable, to say nothing of Liddie. Neither of them would ever consent to talk to a reporter. They came from a dictatorship where the first law of survival was to keep a low profile. Even if Itai could convince them that things were different in Israel, they'd be afraid that going public would make them a target of the Immigration Police, who would find a way to make them pay. The fact that asylum seekers were invisible to most Israelis was in the best interest of both sides: Israelis didn't want to know, and asylum seekers didn't want to draw attention to themselves. That was their worst fear.

"At least give me some pictures. I need something," Giladi insisted.

Itai couldn't agree to that, either. He didn't have any pictures, and even if he did he wouldn't turn them over to the reporter without their consent.

"It's too bad they're migrants," Giladi said before he left. "If they were Israelis, this would be a real scoop."

ITAI checked the time at the bottom of the screen. He'd been waiting forty minutes, but nothing had happened. Annoyed, he pushed his chair back and stood up. He realized he'd moved too fast again. His ribs still hurt. He kept having to remind himself to avoid abrupt movements. He thought of Michal and the way she must have felt after they roughed her up. She called to tell him about it but he was screening her calls. Why did he have to do that? He was haunted by the question "what if."

He didn't like to make a nuisance of himself, but he had to know. "What's going on?" he texted Giladi. The reply came less than ten seconds later: "Check the site."

Itai waited anxiously for his ancient computer to refresh. He had to scroll down to find it. The item wasn't given the prominence he'd hoped for, but at least it was there.

The headline was disappointing: "Civil Rights Lawyer Accuses Police of Mishandling Migrant Case." Itai wasn't naive. He knew the title "civil rights lawyer" was distasteful to most Israelis and cast doubt on his reliability.

It got worse. The item itself was laconic, dry, and very short. People relate to a human-interest story, something they can identify with. This was nothing like that. Michal was described briefly as a "single woman, 32, from Tel Aviv who volunteered at an aid organization." Itai had spent half an hour explaining to Giladi who Michal was, how devoted she was to her work, how much empathy she had for people in trouble, and how much they loved her for it. And this was all he had to say about her? Single woman, 32?

Itai skipped to the end. According to the police, it said, "there is no basis for the allegations." The brusque official response made it clear to Itai that the hope he had pinned on the power of the press was unwarranted. The item wouldn't change anything. Giladi had told him as much. The Israeli public was indifferent to the problems Itai encountered on a daily basis.

Despite the relative insignificance of the item, he noticed that it had already drawn quite a few responses. Every one of them, without exception, was negative. They demanded the immediate deportation of all asylum seekers and their friends and relatives, and they didn't spare Itai, either, suggesting a variety of ways he should be put to death as befitting a traitor. Well, at least they'd read the article.

Maybe he was jumping to conclusions. Something positive might still come of it. If it went viral, the cops would be forced to look deeper into the story.

Itai scrolled back up to the beginning, intending to read the article more closely. The computer had finally finished downloading the pictures that accompanied the text. His heart stopped. He saw the faces of Gabriel and Arami, with their names in the captions. Their

names also appeared in the body of the item. Itai hadn't noticed that
the first time around when he was just scanning it quickly.

How could Giladi do that to him? Itai had made it a condition
that no names be used, and the reporter had promised. He must
have gotten the photos from the cops. The one of Gabriel was obviously a mug shot, and Arami's probably came from his employee
file. Itai looked at the faces. They seemed to be looking back at him
accusingly.

He closed his eyes. There was a bitter taste in his mouth. He
should never have spoken to the reporter. Whatever happened next,
it wouldn't be good.

Chapter 55

AN old lady emerged from the bushes, startling Anat. She jumped back in alarm. "Can I help you, officer?" the woman asked.

Anat couldn't understand where the woman had come from or how she knew she was a cop. She wasn't in uniform.

Instead of sitting in her office being shunned by her colleagues, she had decided to talk to Dvora and Shmuel Gonen once more. She planned to ask them if any of Michal's visitors were white men, and if they knew their names. Someone besides Yariv Ninio could have had a grudge against her. The interview didn't yield any new information. "The black ones, that's all she had eyes for," Shmuel said bitterly. His wife nodded in confirmation. They'd never seen anyone answering Ninio's description. Shmuel, who had previously claimed to know everything about everybody, was now making himself out to be clueless. Anat counted at least three times that he declared, "I've told you everything I know. I have nothing to add." When he left the room to go to the bathroom, Dvora parroted the same statement.

On the way back to the station, Anat had made a short detour. She wanted to check the distance from Michal's apartment to Ninio's.

"Sarah Glazer," the old lady said, reaching out her hand. "I live on the third floor. Forty years I've lived here. I was feeding the cats in the yard," she added, gesturing with her head in the direction she'd come from. "Poor little things. Especially in the winter. Nobody cares. What's going to become of them when I'm gone? I don't even want to think about it. I saw the blue light on your car from upstairs before I came down. Are you looking for someone? Is somebody lost? Maybe I can help," Mrs. Glazer went on. She obviously wasn't going away.

"Inspector Nachmias. We're looking into the theft of bicycles in the neighborhood," she said quickly before the woman could launch another monologue at her. It was the blue flasher she'd placed on the dashboard to warn off parking inspectors that had given her away. Never mind. The neighborhood gossip can be a valuable tool in an investigation, if you manage to filter out the white noise. Ninio said he fell off his bike on the way to work, but Anat hadn't seen a bicycle in the stairwell of his house, or a bicycle chain, either.

"Well, it's about time, isn't it? Do you know how many bicycles have been stolen around here? And let me tell you, Inspector Nachmias, that's not the only thing you should investigate. You should also do something about the people who leave their bicycles in the hallway. I don't like to gossip, but some people simply have no consideration. Do you know how many times I've asked them to move their bicycles?"

"Can you tell me which of your neighbors have bicycles? Which of them had their bikes stolen?" Anat asked, ignoring the "hallway criminals" for the time being.

"That's a hard question to answer. I have to think. After all, it's been forty years."

"Just concentrate on the last few weeks," Anat said, forcing herself not to smile.

"There's the lady on the first floor, Julia Rosenthal. She's had a bike for years. It's so old, even the thieves don't want it. She doesn't even bother to lock it up. Then there's . . . Of course, the lawyer. His bicycle was stolen a few months back."

"Yariv Ninio?" Anat asked, wanting to be sure.

"That's right. He was very upset about it. He stopped me on the stairs several times and asked me if I saw anything."

"And did you?" Anat was buying time until she decided what direction to lead her in.

"Why would I? I have my own problems to worry about. At my age, you know, it isn't easy," Mrs. Glazer answered with feigned innocence.

"Did he buy a new bike?"

Mrs. Glazer shook her head.

"I understand he's getting married soon," Anat said matter-of-factly, hoping to draw her out on the subject of his relationship with his fiancée. She might get some insight into the kind of person he was.

"Really? I had no idea." It was very clear from her tone that this wasn't the first Mrs. Glazer had heard of the wedding.

"You didn't get an invitation?" Maybe that would light a fire under her. It usually worked.

"I wasn't expecting an invitation. They don't have to invite me if they don't want to. Of course, it's just common courtesy. You live across the hall from someone, don't you give them an invitation?"

Anat nodded emphatically.

"With him, I'm not surprised. He thinks he's some kind of hotshot. Barely says 'shalom' when he passes me on the stairs. But I expected more from his girlfriend. She's so sweet. Always smiling, always polite. But it's their decision. I don't go where I'm not wanted."

"When's the wedding? Maybe they haven't sent the invitations out yet?" Anat suddenly felt the need to console the lonely old woman. "If you ask me, I'm not sure there's going to be a wedding." Mrs. Glazer leaned closer as if she were about to share a secret. Her words took Anat by surprise. Ninio had made a point of telling her he was getting married soon. In fact, he repeated it several times.

"At my age, you can sense these things," Mrs. Glazer said with a trace of pride in her voice.

"Why do you think there won't be a wedding?"

Mrs. Glazer shook her head. "I'm not uttering another word. I don't want them to say later it came from me," she said, placing her hand on her heart.

"Anything you tell me is confidential," Anat said, keeping as straight a face as possible. Her mother played the same game. She always declared dramatically that she wasn't going to utter another word "so they can't say later," and then delivered a long monologue that didn't miss out on a single detail of what she wasn't going to utter.

"They've both been down in the dumps lately. And they're always fighting and yelling at each other. Him especially. Before our wedding, me and Sefi, may he rest in peace, we were skipping in the streets. You're not married?" she asked accusingly, looking at Anat's bare ring finger.

Anat chose not to respond.

"You kids aren't in a hurry these days, are you? You think you have all the time in the world, and then by the time you're ready, nobody wants you. Take my advice, Inspector, some things are best done when you're still young and pretty."

"Do you know what they fight about?" Anat asked in an effort to get the conversation back on some kind of track. Any minute now the woman would try to set her up with her wonderful grandson.

"It all started when she went away for a few days," Mrs. Glazer went on, happy to continue gossiping about her neighbors across the hall.

"What happened?"

"If you want my opinion, when she got back she found out he cheated on her," the old lady whispered. There was a look of pure pleasure on her wrinkled face.

"You think so?" Anat said, urging her on.

"Are you sure this has to do with the stolen bicycles?" Mrs. Glazer asked suspiciously.

"It's all connected," Anat assured her.

"Well, his whole face was swollen. A man comes home drunk in the middle of the night with bruises on his face. Where was he? With his mistress, that's where."

Anat nodded. Mrs. Glazer had a dubious theory about the connection between a sore face and a mistress. But mistress or not, it didn't matter. Yariv Ninio had lied to her again.

Chapter 56

ITAI was going over the books when the three men walked in. They caught his attention immediately. Asylum seekers who came to OMA for the first time were hesitant, confused, frightened. They'd just arrived in Tel Aviv after being released from the detention camp down south and had nothing but the clothes on their backs. They came to ask for help.

But these men were dressed in custom-made worsted suits designed to keep them warm in the chilly weather. They strode briskly and confidently across the room, ignoring the curious looks of the people crowding the office.

Itai had been trying in vain to get Arami on the phone ever since yesterday when the item appeared on the news site. The interpreter didn't show up for work today. He'd never missed a day before and was invariably punctual. Itai wanted to apologize, to assure him that he wouldn't let anything bad happen to him, that he would take personal responsibility for his safety.

"Itai Fisher?" one of the men asked in a polished British accent. He looked to be in his forties. The other two took up positions behind him.

"That's right. And you are?" Itai replied, standing up to greet his visitors. His job involved recruiting donors and applying to philanthropic organizations for grants. He allowed himself to hope these gentlemen represented such an organization.

The stranger smiled and reached out his hand. Itai caught a glimpse of the gold watch on his wrist.

"I'm pleased to make your acquaintance. My name is Tapsmariam Apoworki, and I have the honor of being deputy consul general of Eritrea in Israel," he said smoothly.

The introduction wiped the smile off Itai's face. He knew that Eritrea was a brutal tyranny with no freedom of speech, movement,

or religion, and no free press. It was a place where every male was conscripted into the army for life and the citizens were routinely terrorized
by the government. In fact, Eritrea led the world in the number of refugees who fled the country in search of a safe haven, whether in Israel
or elsewhere. Tens of thousands, maybe even hundreds of thousands,
of Eritreans were in refugee camps in Africa. Hagos had told him a
lot about life in Eritrea. He said it was important that Itai know, even
if he couldn't fully understand. No one who was born in a democ-
racy like Israel was capable of understanding what it meant to live in
constant fear for your life, he claimed. There was a consensus among
human rights organizations that the Eritrean regime was one of the
most repressive in the world. In Itai's opinion, the very fact that Israel
maintained diplomatic relations with such a regime was scandalous.

"What can I do for you?" Itai's tone left no doubt as to his distaste
for his visitors. He wasn't a zealot and he shied away from slogans,
but he couldn't help thinking that these men served Satan. How
could he imagine for a second that they were potential donors? Their
expensive clothes, silk ties, gold watches, pricey cologne—they were
all the marks of the corrupt mercenary regime they represented, a
regime that flagrantly stole from its citizens.

"We're looking for Mr. Arami Ligas. I understand he works here,
that you are in contact with him. We thought you might be able to
help us," the deputy consul general replied with the same practiced
veneer of refinement.

"What do you want with Arami?"

"We just want to talk to him."

"What about?" Itai shot back.

The diplomat didn't answer. His silence angered Itai, but it also
frightened him.

"Mr. Ligas is a citizen of Eritrea. We would like to talk to him.
We were unaware that he was in Israel, that is, until yesterday when
we saw the item on the Internet," Apoworki said finally.

"I'm going to have to ask you to leave," Itai interrupted. The
men were making him very nervous. "You aren't welcome here. The

people who come here are victims of your government. I have no intention of helping you in any way."

"There's no need to get upset, Mr. Fisher."

"Please leave." Itai was unimpressed by Apoworki's cordiality, gentlemanly manners, or excellent English.

"Don't worry, Mr. Fisher, we're going. We don't want to keep you from your work. If you happen to see Mr. Ligas, please let him know we'd like to speak with him." The deputy consul general held out a vellum business card with gilt embossed lettering. "We'd be happy to speak with you, too, Mr. Fisher, if you'd like to pay us a visit."

"I have nothing to say to you," Itai barked. He was so furious, he was shaking. Israel had deported Hagos on false pretenses. But it wasn't responsible for his death. His blood was on the hands of the regime these men represented.

"I'm sorry to hear that. Where our country is concerned, it's not all . . . how should I put it? Black and white."

Itai slumped back down onto his chair. He'd never imagined that talking to the reporter would lead to Arami's persecution by one of the most ruthless governments in the world. Arami had been a human rights activist in Eritrea and was forced to flee for his life. Itai had placed him in danger again. Maybe Gabriel, too.

Chapter 57

ANAT lay awake in bed, papers strewn all over the covers. For the past few nights she hadn't been able to sleep. She listened to the monotonous patter of the rain on the window. Her eyes hurt from reading in the dim light of her bedside lamp.

Yariv Ninio had lied to her and to the Bar Association. What else was he guilty of? She knew only too well that despite everything she had discovered thus far, she still didn't have a smoking gun, especially not when everyone else was convinced the murderer was already in custody. She needed more. And she needed more time to get it.

David had called half an hour ago and said he wanted to see her in his office in the morning. "We have a lot to discuss," he said laconically. He seemed to be in a good enough mood. At least she didn't pick up on any recrimination or anger in his voice.

Who would listen to her? All she had was a theory based solely on the statements of two women well past their seventieth birthday.

The cell phone on her nightstand rang, startling her. Anat reached out for it.

Grisha.

"Your murderer's white," he said with no preamble.

Chapter 58

ITAI decided to try Arami one more time before turning out the light and attempting to get some sleep. He'd called his number over and over again since the visit of the three "dark angels."

"Where have you been? I've been worried about you," he exclaimed with huge relief as soon as he heard Arami's voice.

"You don't act like you're worried about me. Why did you do it? I trusted you," Arami cut in.

"I'm sorry . . . the reporter . . . he promised," Itai stuttered.

Silence.

"I've been looking for you. I want to apologize. And also . . . something happened today." Itai took a deep breath before telling Arami about the men from the consulate.

Arami remained silent.

"Arami, are you all right?" The lack of response was unnerving.

"Why did you do it, Itai? Do you have the slightest idea what it means?" Arami asked finally in an agitated voice.

"I'm so sorry . . . if there's anything . . ." How could he get it so wrong? His job was to help people, not make things worse for them.

"It's probably a good idea for you to stay away from OMA for a while," Itai said, the guilt eating at him. "If they see you're not here, maybe they'll stop looking."

"I can't do that. People need me. And I need the money for my family."

"We'll manage," Itai said reassuringly, although he had no idea what they'd do without an interpreter. Since Hagos's deportation, Arami was the only one they had. "It's just for a little while. Naturally, we'll continue to pay your salary."

More silence.

"Is there anything I can do to help?" he asked again.

"You've done enough already," Arami retorted, disconnecting.

Chapter 59

ANAT took a deep breath before entering David's office. "I think you did the right thing," he said as soon as she sat down, disarming her immediately. He was sitting at an angle, his right leg, in a cast, resting on a footstool. Not surprisingly, he had a cigarette in his hand.

Anat made an effort not to display her huge relief. She was thrilled to hear he agreed with her. His opinion meant a lot to her. Besides, she was sick of being treated like a pariah.

"You were right, but you weren't smart," David added, bursting her bubble. Anat's disappointment showed on her face. She should have expected it. The carrot and the stick. That was his management style, as well as the way he conducted interrogations.

"You know what your problem is?" he asked. It seemed to Anat that there was more than a trace of empathy in his voice. She hoped she wasn't imagining it.

"I'm sure you're going to tell me."

"You're an outstanding detective. Intelligent, thorough, one of the best I've ever worked with. But you don't understand politics."

"What's that supposed to mean? I don't suck up to the right people?"

"It means you don't understand how the system works and what it demands from you." Despite his harsh remarks, David's voice remained calm. "You never stop a reenactment in the middle. Especially not when there's a reporter standing outside. And especially not when the suspect is the only one you've got."

"What was I supposed to do? Let Yaron put words in his mouth?" Anat protested.

"Come on, Nachmias. You've got to understand. A homicide makes everyone itchy. Particularly the bosses. The whole world is breathing down their necks: the RC, the Chief, the minister, the press, the victim's family. And in a case like this, you've also got politicians like Regev in the mix trying to milk it for all it's worth. The only way to get them off your back is to trot out a suspect. As soon as you have somebody in custody, everything quiets down. No more pressure. Then you can start investigating. You got it backward. You kicked up a storm instead of calming the waters. You tried to force them to admit the only suspect you had wasn't the killer. No wonder they got their backs up."

"So what happens now?" Anat asked. She didn't have the patience for a lecture on the workings of the system.

"Nothing. I spoke to Yochai. He's willing to overlook it this time. Your first homicide—there were bound to be hiccups," David answered, blowing smoke in her face.

"I meant what happens to Gabriel?"

"He's going to jail." David crushed the cigarette out.

"But he didn't do it. He didn't kill her," Anat fired back.

"That's not what he says. It's not what his lawyer says, either. I'm betting he'll cop a plea very soon." David lit another cigarette. She wondered how he made it through a whole flight without smoking.

"And the reenactment was perfect. Gabriel confirmed every little detail," Anat said, not hiding her sarcasm.

"The reenactment will do just fine. Like I told you, the little show you put on made the brass even more determined to hold on to the only suspect we've got."

"So you're saying it's my fault he's going to prison? With all due respect, David, that's bullshit," Anat said angrily.

"That's not what I said, and you know it. Gabriel is going to prison because he confessed," David answered, keeping his voice steady. He clearly had no intention of getting into a shouting match with her.

"But what you meant was I should have held on to Gabriel as the prime suspect and gone on investigating. I might have gotten a lead on someone else and things would be different now."

"Not necessarily. We've still got a confession. The guy turned himself in. But you get the point. If you had your doubts about Gabriel, you should have handed him over to Yaron and conducted your own investigation under the radar. That's how it works. You have to offer up an alternative. You can't leave them empty-handed," David said with a smile.

"I guess great minds think alike," Anat said, returning the smile. "I've got one."

David's eyes opened wide.

"Like I told Yochai, you've got a good head on your shoulders, Nachmias. Okay, let's hear it." He leaned back into the cloud of smoke.

Anat poured out what she'd learned, excited to finally have someone who was willing to listen. She told him about Yariv Ninio's odd behavior when she questioned him in his office, the legal opinion he concealed, the lie he told her about how he got the bruises on his face, and, most important, the results of the blood test she had Grisha perform.

David listened in silence. A few times he leaned forward and scribbled a note to himself.

"Not enough, Nachmias," he pronounced when she was done. "Forget it. You're not bringing Ninio in for questioning."

Anat's heart sank. "Weren't you listening? I don't get it. Why not?" Her disappointment was evident.

"A million reasons. One, you're too late. The case has already been turned over to the prosecution. Two, if you want to swap out a migrant for an ASA, you're going to need much more than you've got. Three, nothing you told me about Ninio proves he's our murderer. It's just speculation."

"So let's bring him in and find out. We can fingerprint him, get his DNA, compare it with the evidence from the scene," Anat cut in.

"No way, Nachmias. I told you, let it go," David said, raising his voice for the first time.

"He lied to me about almost everything. He got the position paper from the Foreign Ministry. He didn't get the bruises from falling off his bike. And when we compare his DNA with the blood we found at the scene, we'll be able to prove that he lied about not seeing Michal for months. He was there the night of the murder."

"Do I have to remind you the blood was on the outside of the door, not in the apartment?"

"I know, but it's a start," Anat said, undeterred. "We have to see where the investigation takes us. There were unidentified prints in the apartment. I'm willing to bet they're his."

David remained silent.

"Why did he lie about the legal opinion, about falling off his bike?"

David shook his head.

"I told you, let it go. Do you know what it means to interview an assistant state attorney under caution? You need the consent of the Attorney General and the State Attorney. You're not going to get it on the basis of what you have. Especially not when they know that someone else confessed and his lawyer is trying to cut a deal."

"We both know how much confessions are worth."

"Okay, so explain to me why he confessed. Did you coerce him? Did you twist his arm?" David started to get up before remembering his broken leg.

Guessing what he was after, Anat went to the drawer at the far end of the desk and took out a fresh pack of cigarettes.

"A million reasons," she said, quoting her boss. "One, because there was a search on for him. We touched base with all our informants, promised to pay for information. He couldn't take the pressure."

David waved his hand dismissively.

"Two, because someone paid him to confess." Anat could hear Itai Fisher's voice echoing in her head.

"Who? Ninio? That's your theory? Yariv Ninio killed Michal Poleg and then paid some random migrant to take the rap for him?"

Anat didn't respond. She didn't have an answer yet. David's question had been nagging at her ever since she started looking in Ninio's direction. There had to be some connection between Ninio and Gabriel. Someone could have brought them together. Maybe they met through Michal, or at Hagos's trial. She might not have an answer yet, but give her time and she'd find it.

"Don't eat yourself up over this, Anat. We've got a confession. The suspect has legal counsel. Let it go and we can move on to the next case," David said gently.

"They can't convict on a confession without corroborating evidence. What evidence have we got?" Anat wasn't ready to give up.

"Gonen's testimony."

"He identified the wrong man in the lineup."

"Then the reenactment," David said. He was losing patience.

"The one I conducted or your scripted one?"

"Okay, that's enough. I've already explained. We're just going around in circles." David crushed out the cigarette with excessive force. "It's the prosecution's problem now. As far as we're concerned, the case is closed."

Chapter 60

ITAI was surprised to see the name that came up on the screen of his cell phone. After their last conversation, he wasn't expecting to hear from Arami anytime soon.

"I'm leaving the country," Arami announced as soon as Itai answered. "I got a travel document from your Interior Ministry."

Itai was impressed. A travel document was the refugees' wet dream. Not only did it enable them to leave Israel, but it allowed them back in as well. They were issued very sparingly, to say the least. It goes without saying that a lot of people would be very happy to see the asylum seekers find someplace else to live. The problem was that no other country would let them in without an official guarantee that they could return to Israel if they wanted to, and the government was naturally reluctant to give such a guarantee. It preferred to send the message that Israel was like a prison: once you were in, you couldn't get out. The idea was to make asylum seekers think twice before coming here to begin with.

"Well done, Arami. I'm proud of you. You achieved the impossible," Itai said as he congratulated him.

"Don't think it was easy," Arami said, answering the question Itai had refrained from asking. "The fact that the Eritrean consulate was on my heels, thanks to you, worked in my favor."

Itai didn't know what kind of reaction Arami was expecting. Should he apologize yet again for talking to the reporter, or should he say he was glad he could be of help?

"I need my paycheck now. I can't wait for the end of the month," Arami said, interrupting Itai's inner debate.

"Of course. I'll take care of it. It'll take a few days . . . you know how it is." Itai regularly denied requests for an advance. He was always teetering on the edge of the abyss in terms of cash flow. But these were extraordinary circumstances.

"You people are good at making promises—you, the police, the restaurant owner. I need the money now. I can't wait around for it."

"Let me see what I can do. I'll call as soon as I've got it, I swear," Itai said apologetically. Arami was right. He couldn't afford to waste any time. He had to leave immediately.

Silence.

"Where are you planning to go?"

"France. I've got a brother-in-law there. Then I'll try to get my family out. Your little item on the Internet put them in danger, too. It won't be easy, but I think I've got a chance. The French don't regard every African as a threat to their existence as a nation."

"If there's anything else I can do," Itai said, wondering if it was the proper time to voice his own request.

Silence.

"Listen, Arami," he said softly. "I need you to do me a favor. I know I don't have the right to ask for anything, but it's not for me, it's for Gabriel. Before you go, please tell me who paid Gabriel to say he killed Michal."

Silence.

"It's our last chance. We won't get another one. Gabriel is going to go to prison for a long time if you don't help him," Itai went on in an effort to persuade him.

"Please. You know it's the right thing to do," he implored when he got no response.

"Is he African? Israeli?"

"Have you spoken to Gabriel? Do you have his consent?" Arami finally said.

"I spoke to him, but that's not the point. He's confused, frightened," Itai said, trying to steer the conversation away from Gabriel.

"Why do you always think you know what's best for us? Gabriel made his decision. He knows what he's doing. Why do you have to interfere? What do you really know about him, about his reasons? Stop treating us like children. We don't need your help or your protection. Start showing us some respect. What do you say, Itai, do you think you can do that?"

"I understand what you're saying, but I think these are special circumstances . . ."

"Good-bye Itai. Just get me the money you owe me. I need it," Arami cut in before disconnecting.

Itai clenched his jaw. Arami was Gabriel's only hope. Without him, he had nothing.

Chapter 61

ANAT was sitting at her desk trying to decide on her next move. She was debating with herself how to continue the investigation without disobeying David's direct order when Yariv Ninio himself burst into her office.

"Listen up, you," he barked, standing over her and waving a finger in her face.

Anat gazed at him in shock.

"This harassment is going to stop. I'm putting an end to it right here, right now. Who do you think you are?" Ninio shouted. "Yes, I know all about it. How you poked your nose around outside my house, your big 'bicycle theft investigation.' It's all documented and on its way to Internal Affairs."

Anat wondered why his neighbor had blabbed. Had Ninio finally seen the error of his ways and invited her to the wedding? Mrs. Glazer would now have something new to kvetch about to her friends. "Who needs it?" she'd say. "But of course I have to go. They insisted. It wouldn't be right not to go."

"Since my bike got stolen, I've been using rent-a-bikes, Ms. fifth-rate detective," Ninio yelled, slamming his hands down on the desk. "That's the bike I fell off, okay? You can stop asking your idiotic questions now."

Anat remained silent, even when he threatened to go to her superiors and end her short career before it ever got started. Even when he accused her of harboring a sick love for Africans and hatred for her fellow Israelis. All the while, her eyes were fixed on his hands.

People never learn. They keep making the same mistakes over and over again. The cops count on that. It helps them solve crimes.

Ever since her talk with David, Anat had been racking her brain trying to think of a way to set a trap for Ninio. Although she was sorely tempted to ignore David's order to leave the lawyer alone and move on, she was reluctant to openly disobey him. And naturally, she couldn't do anything that might be construed as illegal.

Ninio had solved all her problems. His arrogance was his undoing. Hubris—she'd seen it time and time again. The only thing left for her to do was to make sure she was right. Then let them try to deny her a warrant for his arrest.

Chapter 62

YARIV left in a rage. His confrontation with Nachmias was bizarre and disturbing. He'd been hoping for an apology, had been prepared for a shouting match, but all he got was silence. She didn't utter a word the whole time, didn't respond in any way to the barrage of threats and accusations he threw at her.

"Don't you have anything to say for yourself?" he'd fired off at the end.

"Duly noted," Anat answered calmly.

"What?" Yariv was taken aback by her incongruous reply.

"Duly noted," she repeated, "everything you said."

"What do you mean 'duly noted'? You don't get it, do you? I told you, if you don't stop harassing me I'll make sure you're kicked off the force. They won't even let you be a traffic cop."

"Good luck," she said with a pleasant smile.

Yariv was left speechless by her show of indifference. Turning on his heels, he marched demonstratively out the door. He'd interpreted her silence as an indication that she couldn't think of any way to justify her actions, but now he wasn't so sure.

It all began when he got home last night. For a change, he was in a good mood. Kobi had run into the lawyer representing the illegal accused of Michal's murder, and he referred in passing to the plea bargain he was working on. It was nearly a done deal, he said. His client had consented to the terms and he was waiting for the prosecution to draw up the papers. "All's well that ends well," Kobi concluded, after reporting the conversation to Yariv. Yariv could barely contain his excitement. He felt the tension drain from his body for the first time since Nachmias had showed up in his office unexpectedly. He called Regev right away to inform him that the cops had questioned him about Michal's complaint. Regev's first response was to ask nervously if he'd mentioned his name, but Yariv assured him he hadn't. Regaining his normal composure, he advised Yariv to keep a low profile and wait it out. He was sure the whole thing would blow over soon. After all, the woman behind the complaint was dead. Now Yariv just had to hope nothing went wrong.

"Inbar, I'm home," he called out cheerfully when he came in. He'd been wound up tight the past few weeks and had been taking it out on her. She was consumed by the wedding arrangements, obsessing over insignificant details, when he had a cloud hanging over his head that threatened to change his life forever. It was too much for him to deal with. Once she asked for his advice deciding where to put his aunt Bella and uncle Ephraim and he completely lost it. He couldn't care less where his mother's cousin sat. "Do what you want with them," he flared, getting up and going into the bedroom. He heard her crying in the living room and slammed the door shut.

HE found Inbar in the bathroom, smoking a cigarette. She was clearly upset. It turned out she'd gone to invite Sarah Glazer to the wedding. They hadn't been planning to invite the nosy old lady from across the hall. Why should they? It was enough that they had to deal with Inbar's grandmother with her wheelchair and Filipina caregiver. He didn't want any more old people there to put a damper on the evening. Yariv thought the subject was closed, but he should have realized that Inbar didn't have a backbone. She needed everyone to like her. Unable to bear the old lady's resentful looks each time they passed in the hall, she'd gone to bring her an invitation.

Mrs. Glazer was delighted to get it. They chatted for a while, and she told Inbar how she'd met a policewoman downstairs who asked all sorts of questions about stolen bicycles, his in particular. Irate, Yariv marched across the hall to talk to their neighbor. She told him that the cop's name was Anat Nachmias. He'd suspected as much.

The fact that Nachmias was slinking around behind his back asking questions, even interviewing his neighbors, made Yariv's blood boil. He was incensed that she didn't believe him, that she was checking out his story about falling off his bike as if he were a common criminal.

STILL seething, Yariv stormed out of the police station, jumped back into Inbar's car, and sped off. Now he was stuck in a traffic jam caused by a stoplight that had been shorted out by the rain. He punched the steering wheel angrily and honked at the driver in front of him. The asshole kept letting other cars cut in.

He'd had big plans for his confrontation with Nachmias. He intended to cut her down to size, put the fear of God in her. And he tried his best. He yelled and screamed and threatened to ruin her. He even used one of Regev's tactics and accused her of having a dirty penchant for Africans and being a traitor to her nation. But she just sat there calmly, refusing to rise to the bait.

Yariv leaned on the horn, warning off a car that was trying to cut in front of him. In the end she'd turned the tables on him. It was her silence that got to him. Now he was the one running scared.

Chapter 63

THE call from Argentina put a big smile on Shimon Faro's face. Boaz reported that everything was going very well. There was no cause for concern. You have to know when to take risks in business, Faro thought, and he was very glad he'd taken this one.

I moved forward in conditions of uncertainty, keeping a steady hand on the wheel, he said to himself, phrasing how he would describe his actions in the interview he'd never give. Yesterday, the Israeli company he'd set up had sold its consignment of weapons to an Argentinean enterprise, just as it was obligated to do by the Defense Ministry tender it had won. All the documents had been properly signed and were on their way back to Israel.

What the Defense Ministry didn't know was that the Argentinean company had no intention of honoring its obligations. The surplus armaments weren't going to the Argentinean military, but to a Peruvian firm, which, in turn, would sell them to Sudan. If any allegations were directed against Faro, he'd simply claim that he had no control over the Argentineans. To his dismay, he, too, was an innocent victim of their duplicity.

That wouldn't be entirely true, of course. The Argentinean company would indeed be violating the terms of their contract, but it wasn't accurate to say that he had no control over them. He had an agent there, a company director appointed by a Brazilian firm. Entirely by chance, his name happened to be Boaz Yavin.

The good news just kept coming. This time it was Itzik. Faro was still upset with him for allowing that aid worker to take a picture of Boaz.

Itzik informed him that with the help of the "General," they'd be able to get their hooks into an assistant state attorney. Faro's dream was finally about to come true. He had plenty of government officials and cops in his pocket, but no prosecutor. The ASA in question represented the state in petitions filed by African migrants. He could be his golden goose.

"He did what? Is he crazy?" Faro asked when Itzik told him how the "General" had caught the prosecutor in his net. Faro was disappointed. He thought the "General" was smarter than that, more careful. At the very least, he hadn't expected him to keep that sort of information from him for so long.

"The only thing that matters is that he delivered in the end," Itzik said, trying to smooth his boss's ruffled feathers. The "General" was in charge of recruiting customers for Faro's bank. He took a lot of weight off Itzik's shoulders.

Faro was still angry, but he decided to let it go. The "General" might make a mess, but at least he cleaned up after himself, which was more than he could say for some of the birdbrains who worked for him. The question was what to do now. You couldn't rush these things. You had to take your time, not gobble down the fish as soon as you caught it.

Ninio was a bad boy. The worse they were, the more scared they were, and the easier it was to manipulate them. When they set their sights on Boaz, Itzik told him he had two options: work for them or go to jail. Boaz wasn't eager to work for Faro, but he was even less eager to go to jail. And look how it paid off for both sides. Nowadays the accountant was closing million-dollar deals and had a beautiful home in Ramat Hasharon. He had nothing to complain about.

Finding good professional people wasn't easy. That's why Faro always treated them well. After he got over his initial shock and natural resistance, Ninio would see how much he had to gain from cooperating with Faro.

But he had to move cautiously. An ASA was no patsy, not just another clerk in the Interior Ministry or another corrupt politician. It would be a shame to miss this opportunity because of some stupid mistake. On the other hand, he had to make it clear to Ninio as soon as possible that they knew everything. And in view of that fact, the prosecutor now had a new employer and new priorities, and he'd better get used to it.

He decided the best course of action was to have Shuki Borochov talk to him. Shuki was a lawyer, but Faro liked him anyway. They'd been working hand in hand for years. When it came right down to it, there was no one more suited for recruiting people in the legal profession than Shuki.

Chapter 64

"CAN I help you?" Yariv said sullenly to the well-dressed man who was waiting for him outside his office. Still worked up about his encounter with Nachmias, he wasn't in the mood to talk to anyone.

"Shuki Borochov. Pleased to meet you," the man said with a pleasant smile, extending his hand.

Yariv took it reluctantly, intending to give it a perfunctory shake, but Borochov didn't let go.

"I'm an attorney myself. I happened to be in the building and I wanted to meet you in person before I left," he said, striding into Ninio's office without waiting for an invitation.

"I'm sorry, but it'll have to be some other time. I'm very busy." Yariv stood his ground in the hallway. Ordinarily, he'd give the man a few minutes of his time. It was enough to see his suit to know he didn't work for the State Attorney's Office, and most likely he didn't represent illegals, either. Yariv needed contacts in the private sector, especially the kind of prosperous attorneys this one appeared to be. But today he just didn't have the energy. He wanted to be alone with his thoughts.

"Of course, of course. I'm sure a prosecutor like yourself is very busy," Borochov answered, still smiling. "I won't keep you. I merely want to compliment you on the fine job you're doing."

The vote of confidence improved Yariv's mood slightly, but it wasn't enough to drown out the echo of his outburst at the police station. It was still resounding in his head and making it hard for him to carry on a normal conversation. He walked into his office and gestured to his guest to take a seat. Borochov lowered himself into a chair, the smile still glued on his face.

"Aloni and I were just talking about you," Borochov said. "I read some of your cases. I could see from the way you phrased your arguments that they were the product of a brilliant legal mind. If I'm not mistaken, you haven't lost a single case."

"Are you involved with illegal aliens?" Yariv asked suspiciously. Since when did lawyers start applauding each other? He hadn't gotten compliments like this from another attorney in his entire career, no matter how much he deserved them.

"No, no, not at all. Just interested. It's a fascinating legal issue." Borochov rested his hands on his large belly. From the looks of it, he wasn't planning on leaving anytime soon.

Yariv desperately needed to be alone for a while, but he had the feeling that it would be a mistake to show his visitor the door. The man was apparently on good terms with Aloni, he didn't represent illegals, and his clothes were expensive. It wasn't worth it to Yariv to pass up an opportunity like this because of a nobody like Anat Nachmias. He had to pull himself together.

"I view it as a calling. I see myself as the dam holding back the tide, you know what I mean? If I fail, we'll be flooded," Yariv said facilely, spouting the formulas that were music to Regev's ears.

"It's so good to find an idealist in our profession. It's a rare pleasure," Borochov replied, smoothing his tie. Yariv could hear the rustle of the silk.

"I imagine it's not an easy matter to deal with," Borochov went on.

Yariv didn't answer. He'd learned to be wary when he spoke about illegals. You could never tell where the other person stood on the issue. More often than not he'd deliver his credo only to be rewarded with a sanctimonious lecture about human rights, compassion, and all the other crap. The opposite happened as well. He'd say something about the migrants' rights and get a tirade about ticking bombs, catastrophic results, and the Jewish character of Israel. The zealots on both sides tried his patience.

"The human rights groups," Borochov said, leaning closer, "I'm guessing you're not a fan."

"The courts don't make my job any easier, either," Yariv said, deciding to play it safe. Lawyers were always bitching about the legal system.

Laughing, Borochov played along. "I always say if we're nice to them now, it will just be crueler for them later when we're forced to put a stop to it. I'm sure you get my drift."

Yariv nodded. His guest was paraphrasing one of Regev's favorite arguments.

"Maybe after the recent incident, the bleeding hearts will finally come to their senses. I understand the woman who was murdered was one of them," Borochov said calmly. "That's what happens. If you go to sleep with dogs . . . how does it go?"

"You wake up with fleas," Yariv completed automatically. The reference to Michal made him uneasy.

"I represent a large financial organization that employs Africans now and again, so I'm very familiar with the problems that can arise," Borochov continued.

"What's the name of your organization?" Yariv asked, glad for the change of subject.

"It doesn't matter. Monotonous work. Just fiddling with numbers all day. I'd be happier if I were doing something important, like you."

Yariv nodded, smiling in response to the flattery. For the first time, the grin on his face wasn't forced.

"Now that I think about it, we might be able to be of help to each other," Borochov said, clapping his hands in delight. It seemed to Yariv that his enthusiasm was excessive.

"Help? How?"

"That's my motto in life, Yariv. Can I call you Yariv? When people work together, they can achieve much more. Ask anyone who has made a success of himself. He'll tell you the same thing. Don't you agree?"

"I'm a civil servant, Mr. Borochov. I don't think I can help you. You understand," Yariv said warily.

Most prosecutors would kick Borochov out for even suggesting such a thing. Yariv would probably have done the same if it weren't for the fact that his first conversation with Regev had gone down a very similar track. If he'd slammed the door in the politician's face, he would have missed out on one of his most important connections.

"Shuki, please. Call me Shuki. And I didn't mean to imply that you can help us, heaven forbid. I meant we can help you," Borochov said amiably, smoothing his tie again.

"How can you help me?" Yariv was still suspicious.

"We can help you be even more successful, reach your full potential. When you win, we all win."

Yariv remained silent. Borochov wanted something from him, but he couldn't figure out what.

"There are shortsighted people who go around saying things . . . you know what I'm talking about, don't you?" Borochov had lowered his voice to a whisper.

"Shortsighted people? What exactly do they say?" Yariv asked, trying to give the impression that he was in control of the conversation, although he had no idea what Borochov was driving at.

"It's not important. Just talk. Not worth concerning yourself over," Borochov said with a knowing smile.

What the hell was he getting at?

"I'm really very busy," Yariv said, standing up. If he had something to say, let him say it. His time was too precious to waste playing games.

Borochov rose and held out his hand.

"They say the girl who was murdered was making trouble for you," he said as they shook hands.

Yariv pulled his hand back quickly.

"She filed a complaint against you with the Bar Association." Borochov wagged a finger at Yariv as if he were a naughty child.

"Oh, that? That was nonsense. I certainly wouldn't call it trouble."

"Of course not. Like you say, it's nonsense. I'm on the Bar Association Review Board, and I have to tell you, Yariv, I was very upset by what she said about you. I can imagine how mad it must have made you." Borochov gave Yariv a piercing look.

"Not really. It was nothing to get worked up about," Yariv said, forcing himself to smile.

"A woman scorned. That's how I'd characterize it. It was obvious from the complaint that she was still in love with you. She was trying to get back at you. She heard you were getting married," Borochov said quietly.

Yariv stared at him in surprise. How did he know about his former relationship with Michal? There wasn't a word about it in the complaint. And how come he knew about his impending wedding?

"Well, I'll be going, Yariv. I wouldn't want to keep you," Borochov said, patting him on the back.

Yariv nodded, glad that this incomprehensible conversation was finally over. Borochov walked to the door. He reached out for the handle and then stopped and turned around again.

"Let me leave you with one piece of advice, my friend," he said with a grave expression on his face. "Watch out for yourself. There are bad people out there who want to hurt you, who don't want to see you succeed."

"What are you talking about?" Yariv spluttered. The man was making him very nervous.

"Don't worry, I'm on your side. I've got your back, I'll look out for you," Borochov said, fixing Yariv with his eyes. His smile was gone.

"Look out for me? How?"

"Sometimes people make mistakes, especially when they're drunk and not in control. You know how it is. You have too much to drink and you lose your head. Particularly if you're mad at someone. Then somebody else has to clean up the mess so your career isn't ruined because of one silly mistake. That's why you need friends like me. Don't worry, Ninio. Like I said, my motto is cooperation. People work together, they help each other out, and everything's fine, everyone's happy." Aside from his lips, not a single muscle moved in Borochov's face.

"I still don't know what you're talking about," Yariv said. His mouth was dry.

"I think you do, Ninio. I think you know exactly what I'm talking about."

Chapter 65

IT was only when Itai caught a glimpse of himself in the mirror that he realized he'd unthinkingly smoothed back his hair. He wondered why. Where did he think he was going?

Bringing Nachmias along suddenly seemed like a bad idea, but he had only himself to blame. He'd been pressuring Dahlia for days to allow him to take Liddie to see Gabriel, but to no avail. Dahlia insisted that Liddie was too fragile, both mentally and physically. She wasn't ready to face Gabriel yet. Even Liddie herself didn't appear eager to visit her brother, although she never said so explicitly. When she first arrived in Israel she didn't seek him out, either. Then she was too ashamed of what had happened to her in Sinai. Now, in addition to the shame, she had to cope with her sense of guilt. Actually seeing her brother behind bars, surrounded by felons and prison guards, would merely add to her distress.

Itai didn't give up. He'd tried using the media, tried to convince Arami to talk, but nothing had worked. And now that Arami had left for France, he was out of ammunition, as well as ideas. He didn't have much time until a plea bargain was signed and they'd pass the point of no return. Liddie was his last hope. If Gabriel could see his sister, he'd understand how much she needed him, and then maybe he'd change his mind and recant his confession. That was the plan, at least. Itai finally succeeded in breaking down Dahlia's resistance ("I can't take any more badgering. I didn't know you could be such a nag!" were her precise words), who, in turn, managed to persuade Liddie. But she would only agree to visit her brother if Itai went with her.

The three of them—Liddie, Dahlia, and Itai—had gone to the jail the day before yesterday. Itai had called ahead to be sure there wouldn't be any problems, and had even borrowed his mother's car for the occasion. They made the ride to the Hadarim Detention Center in silence. Liddie sat hunched up in the back, shivering slightly, although he turned the heat up to the maximum. Dahlia sat beside her, cradling her in her arms, stroking and reassuring her.

It never entered his mind that they wouldn't be allowed in. He knew Dahlia would have to wait outside, but he didn't have the slightest doubt that they'd let Liddie see her brother. He'd been told on the phone that detainees were permitted visits with members of their immediate family. But it turned out that this regulation had certain provisos. The guard at the gate demanded proof that Liddie was in fact Gabriel's sister, and since Liddie didn't have any papers, she couldn't produce such proof.

Itai's attempts at persuasion didn't make the slightest impression, nor did flashing his attorney's credentials and threatening to file a complaint against the guard. "No one gets in without ID. What part of that don't you understand?" she asked hostilely.

Defeated, Itai called Gabriel's lawyer, Yossi Knoller, who refused to get involved. How did he know that she was his sister? Attorneys could get themselves in serious trouble by trying to sneak people into the detention center who weren't supposed to be there, he said. He didn't want any part of it. The case was enough of a headache already.

It was only when they got back to Tel Aviv that Itai thought of Nachmias. She was the main reason Gabriel was in custody in the first place, but Itai couldn't forget the sensitivity she'd displayed at Michal's funeral. Even Gabriel said she was kind to him, at least compared to the other cops. Besides, he didn't have a better idea.

"It's not right, not letting his sister in to see him," Nachmias said when he told her the story. "Take her back there tomorrow. I'll make sure there's an entry permit waiting at the gate."

Itai expected Nachmias to take advantage of the opportunity to make some sarcastic remark about the Internet item, which quoted him accusing the police of being insensitive and incompetent. To his

surprise, she didn't mention it. He wondered whether she was showing restraint or simply didn't attribute any importance to it.

Alone in the OMA office that night, it suddenly occurred to him
to ask her to accompany them. If Nachmias witnessed the meeting
between Liddie and her brother, it might convince her that Gabriel
wasn't a murderer. What did he have to lose? And he had to admit
that he didn't want to be alone with Liddie. It was only too obvious that men frightened her, and he couldn't blame her. He didn't
feel comfortable imposing his presence on her. But Dahlia couldn't
make it tomorrow, and he hadn't been able to find another woman
to take her place.

Nachmias surprised him again by agreeing immediately. He was
so encouraged by her response that he suggested they pick Liddie up
together. They could meet at the shelter. It was such a sad place. It
got to everyone. For his plan to work, he needed the detective to be
sympathetic, to understand the circumstances.

Itai started giving her directions to the shelter, but he soon realized that he was making a mess of it. "Forget it. I'll pick you up at
the police station," he said, admitting defeat. Navigation wasn't his
strong suit.

ITAI figured it was for the best. They'd be alone in the car on the way
to the shelter, and that would give him another chance to explain to
Nachmias why Gabriel couldn't have killed Michal. Maybe he could
finally convince her the cops were making a big mistake. But for some
strange reason, when the time came he was flustered and seemed incapable of forming coherent sentences.

When Nachmias climbed into the car, she appeared less like a
cop and more like an ordinary woman his age. Actually, a very attractive woman his age.

"I didn't want the uniform to frighten her," she explained when
she saw him looking at her clothes.

Itai nodded. He'd been so preoccupied trying to come up with a plan and making the arrangements that he'd forgotten something so basic. He was pleased that his instincts about Nachmias were right. She was a sensitive and perceptive woman.

"I guess we have to thank your mother for the ride," she said, breaking the silence in the car.

"You're a real Sherlock Holmes, Nachmias," he said. Itai had intended it as a joke, but even he could hear the cynical tone in his voice. "How did you work that out? The color?"

"Elementary, my dear Watson," Nachmias answered, laughing. Itai was glad to see she hadn't taken offense.

"Actually, it's not the color of the car that gave it away, but the color of the lipstick. It's not your shade," Nachmias said, pointing to the cosmetics scattered around the gearshift. "The driver's license stuck on the sunshade was another clue."

Itai laughed sheepishly.

"If we're already talking about your mother, can you turn the radio to a station that plays something besides the news?"

"To be honest, that's me," Itai admitted apologetically.

"You're a news freak?"

"I think it's called a masochist, no?"

"Things aren't always that bad," Nachmias said.

"In my business, they're usually very bad," Itai answered, his tone becoming serious.

"You're right. As far as that goes, I imagine we have a lot in common." Nachmias was interrupted by a text message. Itai glanced in her direction while she read it. She had a dimple in her cheek that he hadn't noticed before.

"Good news?" he asked when he saw her smile.

"Yes, very good. Something I've been waiting to hear for a long time."

Chapter 66

GABRIEL had vowed to be strong, not to break down. Itai had warned him that Liddie hadn't recovered from the brutal treatment she'd been subjected to, but he hadn't imagined it would be so hard to keep his vow. He barely recognized his sister. Her face was bruised and she was hunched over and walked with a limp. She seemed to have aged ten years since he'd last seen her. The most upsetting part was her constant coughing. She reminded him of those people in the refugee camp in Sudan, the ones everyone kept their distance from, the ones they knew would be dead soon.

What happened to his little sister? What did they do to her? Gabriel's heart was breaking.

Their father called his baby girl "princess," and the name stuck. After he was killed, she became Gabriel's responsibility. With no one else to provide for the family, their mother had to work. She couldn't look after little Liddie. Gabriel took her with him wherever he went. Even to school. He carried her on his back for miles, told her stories, sang to her. She was only two years old, but she was already learning to read and write. "Your princess is very clever," the teacher, Mr. Jackson, used to say whenever he saw their mother, and she'd grin from ear to ear. Gabriel remembered his mother's smile very well. He hardly ever saw it again after their father was gone.

He loved his sister, and he was proud of how smart and beautiful she was. When his mother told him to leave and take Liddie with him, he raised no objections.

Gabriel missed Liddie's bubbling laughter. He'd been picturing the first moment of their reunion for a long time. She'd laugh, and he'd laugh along with her, and everything that had happened when they were apart would be forgotten.

The broken woman in front of him bore little resemblance to the laughing girl he remembered. He should have fought harder for her in Sinai. He shouldn't have been so weak. Maybe if he'd stood up to them, they would have left her alone. What would their mother say if she saw Liddie now? She'd say he hadn't kept his promise, that he hadn't protected his little sister.

Despite his determination to stay strong, Gabriel couldn't stop the tears that streamed from his eyes when he saw her. Without a word, he went and hugged her to him. His tears fell on her hair. Liddie sobbed in his arms. Gabriel could feel how thin and fragile she was. He wouldn't normally embrace his sister, especially not when people were watching, but he didn't care. He ignored Itai and the police-woman. He had to show Liddie that she could count on him from now on, that he would keep her safe and never leave her again.

"Do you remember," he whispered in her ear, "when the driver suddenly ordered us out of the truck on the way here?" Gabriel re-leased his grip and looked into Liddie's eyes. It was shortly after they crossed the border into Egypt. The man told them to get out, and when they hesitated, he forced them out of the truck and drove away. They were left standing in the middle of the desert without any food or water. Just the two of them. All alone.

Liddie nodded through her tears.

"Do you remember how we thought it was the end? That we'd never get out of there alive?" he went on.

"You said we would be all right, that God would save us," Liddie whispered.

"And He did, Liddie, He did. He answered our prayers." Gabriel was glad to see that Liddie was responding, sharing the memory with him.

"He'll save us again," he said, gazing into her wet eyes. "You'll see. You have to be strong and God will save us."

"He told me," Liddie replied, nodding her head toward Itai who was standing next to the policewoman, "that you killed somebody to rescue me."

Gabriel remained silent. He looked over at the two Israelis. The policewoman's eyes were trained on him expectantly. He lowered his gaze.

"You're not a murderer, Gabriel," Liddie said, grasping his hand. "You couldn't hurt anyone. I don't want you to say you killed somebody because of me."

"It's okay, Liddie. Everything will be fine," Gabriel said in an effort to comfort her.

"I don't want you to do it, Gabriel. I don't want you to die in prison because of me. Tell them the truth and they'll let you go," Liddie begged.

He knew he ought to tell her that he killed Michal. That way, she could go on with her life without feeling guilty. But even though he knew it was the right thing to do, he couldn't say the words.

"There are bad people in the world, Liddie," he whispered in her ear so Itai and the policewoman couldn't hear.

"Don't be afraid, Gabriel." Liddie's voice was steadier. "There are good people, too, and they're looking out for me. If we have to, we can run away again, like last time. Just you and me."

Gabriel didn't respond.

"Do you remember, when we were in the desert I thought no one was going to pick us up and we'd die there like animals. And then a truck stopped?"

He nodded.

"He took us to Cairo. And he didn't even ask for money, remember?" Liddie went on.

Gabriel smiled at his sister. Ali was one of the few good people they met on the way.

"It happened just like you said, Gabriel. Exactly like you said." Liddie stroked his face gently. "I need you. I can't make it on my own. I'm frightened all the time. I'm scared they're going to come for me again one day." Liddie lowered her eyes.

Once more Gabriel's eyes welled up with tears. If he told the truth, he'd be putting his sister in danger. Arami had warned him not to break their agreement. The man who gave him the money was very powerful, he said. If Gabriel didn't do what he promised, Liddie would pay the price. Arami, too.

"We can't give in to them," Liddie said, raising her eyes to her brother. For a moment it seemed as if she were the older one. "Tell these people that you didn't do it. Please, Gabriel, you can trust them. They'll protect us."

He couldn't take back his confession now, could he? But Liddie might not survive on her own while he was wasting away in prison. He would be sacrificing himself for nothing. He didn't know what to do.

Chapter 67

YARIV took the stairs two at a time. He was so worked up, he couldn't wait for the elevator. Suddenly, all the pieces had fallen into place. He raced out of the building, hardly noticing the rain that was coming down heavily.

Borochov's parting words had made his blood run cold. They left no doubt that Borochov knew everything. He may not have come right out with it, but his meaning was crystal clear. He knew Yariv went to see Michal that night. And he seemed to think he killed her. Or maybe he knew it for a fact.

Yariv wanted payback. "Is he in?" he barked at the secretary.

She gave him a puzzled look, not responding. He was panting and drenched from the rain.

"Is he in?" he repeated testily.

The secretary nodded.

He ran past her, not stopping when she called after him to wait.

"You fucking bastard, you sold me out!" he yelled as he burst into the office and slammed the door behind him.

Alarmed, Kobi jumped up.

"What? What are you talking about? What happened?" he stammered, watching Yariv hurtle himself across the room toward him.

"I'm never going to forget this. You ruined me, you ruined my life," Yariv hollered, lunging at Kobi.

Losing his footing, Kobi fell back onto his chair. Yariv stood over him, his fists clenched. The only way Borochov could have found out was if Kobi told him. There was no other way for him to know. Yariv had Googled him as soon as he left his office and was astounded to learn that the chubby attorney in the fancy suit and silk tie, the man who looked like everybody's favorite uncle, was the "chief gangland mediator," closely associated with the heads of several crime families. Kobi was a defense attorney. He represented criminals for a living. You didn't have to be a genius to put two and two together.

"Have you lost your mind? What're you doing? Look at yourself! What's wrong with you, man?" Kobi said, trying to get up. Yariv pushed him back down.

"Should I call the police, Kobi?" he heard the secretary ask from the doorway.

"No, there's no need," Kobi replied, standing up. "Let's just all take a deep breath."

Yariv took a few steps back. The secretary's question had unnerved him. He was so full of rage that he hadn't given a thought to the potential consequences of his attack on Kobi.

"Sit down, Yariv. Tell me what happened." Kobi was taking charge now. "Close the door on your way out," he instructed his secretary.

The secretary left, but Yariv was too wound up to sit down. The two men stood facing each other. Yariv's heart was pounding. He was dripping wet.

"You blabbed about my being in Michal's apartment," he shot at Kobi, feeling the fury rising again.

"What do you mean? No way." Kobi sounded simultaneously bewildered and offended.

Yariv was about to lunge at him a second time. The man didn't even have the guts to admit it. He was lying to his face, and here he'd thought he was his friend. But before he could raise a hand, Kobi moved aside, causing Yariv to lose his balance.

"Don't lie to me. I know," he said, struggling to right himself. The humiliation of almost falling flat on his face fed the flame of his rage.

"You don't know anything, because I didn't say anything to anyone. Instead of screaming like a banshee, why don't you calm down and tell me what happened," Kobi said, moving farther away.

"Don't play games with me and don't tell me to calm down. I know what you did. I had a visit today from your friend, Shuki Borochov." Yariv virtually spit the name out.

"Borochov? Shuki Borochov was in your office?" Kobi asked. Despite his agitation, Yariv didn't miss the expression of incredulity on Kobi's face.

The door opened and the secretary peered in again.

"Is everything all right?" she asked.

"Yes, everything's fine, isn't it Yariv?" Yariv nodded. The last thing he wanted was to get the cops involved. "Thank you, Ora."

The secretary left, and Kobi poured water from the pitcher behind him into two plastic cups. "In the movies, this would be scotch, right?" he said, attempting to lighten the atmosphere. Yariv gave him an icy look. He wasn't in the mood to kid around.

"Come on, sit down and tell me the whole story," Kobi said cajolingly, holding out a cup to Yariv. "Please sit down, Yariv. If you calm down, maybe I can help."

Reluctantly, Yariv took a seat and began telling Kobi about Borochov's visit. He still didn't know if Kobi was lying or not, but he told him anyway. He was desperately in need of someone to talk to.

Kobi sat opposite him in silence. His silence was ominous.

"I have to agree with you. They know you went to her house and they know exactly what happened there," he said finally. Those were the very words Yariv didn't want to hear. Deep down, he'd been hoping that Kobi would offer a different explanation for Borochov's surprise visit, something that would convince him he was wrong.

"Who's 'they'?" he asked in a trembling voice.

"Who knows? Borochov has ties to all the crime bosses: Assulin, Faro, the Debachs, Rosenfeld, all of them," Kobi answered quietly.

"How do they know?"

Kobi shrugged his shoulders. Seeing the skeptical look on Yariv's face, he said, "It wasn't me. If you don't believe me, you can believe this: I'm way below Borochov on the food chain. Even if I wanted to talk to him, I doubt he'd give me the time of day. I do business with sardines, not sharks."

"What do they want?" Yariv envisioned a huge shark bearing down on him with its terrifying teeth exposed.

"You. That's how they operate. That's how they get people to work for them. They find a sore spot and apply pressure."

"Why? What can I do for them?" Yariv asked. A shiver went down his spine.

"I guess they need an attorney," Kobi replied, stating the obvious.

In a strange way, Yariv found the explanation comforting.

"Look, maybe it's not so bad," Kobi said after a pause. "I ran into Yossi Knoller in the courthouse again. You remember him, he's representing the migrant they're holding for Michal's murder. He told me they're about to sign the plea bargain."

"How does that help me with the bad guys?"

"It might help," Kobi said pensively. "As soon as they close the deal, Borochov and whoever he's working for won't have anything to hold over you. Once the African is convicted they lose their power, and with the guy copping a plea, there's every reason to believe that's what's going to happen."

"So what are you saying? What am I supposed to do now?" Yariv was having trouble following Kobi's line of thinking. He couldn't get the picture of the shark out of his head.

"Sit still. Don't answer the phone, even if Borochov calls. And pray the African doesn't change his story."

Chapter 68

THE joy Itai felt when Gabriel finally opened up was quickly replaced by frustration. Were they too late? Would Nachmias believe him? Was there anything they could do now after Gabriel's lawyer had already notified the prosecution that he was willing to cut a deal?

Most of all, Itai was frustrated with himself. He shouldn't have waited so long before insisting that Dahlia let him take Liddie to see her brother. His plan had worked. As he'd hoped, in a few short minutes, Liddie had succeeded in doing what he himself had failed at time and time again.

Itai kept his eyes pinned on Nachmias the whole time Gabriel was talking, trying to read her reaction from her face. She was listening intently, but her expression didn't change. Gabriel admitted he had lied, that he didn't kill Michal. He would never hurt her. He liked her very much and he had a lot of respect for her, he said, the tears welling up in his eyes yet again. Liddie was sitting next to him, stroking his hand, unwilling to let go. He related how he had gotten a call from Liddie's captors demanding ransom for her release, how he'd gone to Michal's apartment to ask for her help. Michal was dead when he got there. Her neighbor showed up with his dog, and Gabriel fled. Arami told him a powerful Israeli man would pay him to go to the police and say he killed Michal. He did it to save his sister.

"Arami? The interpreter?" Nachmias asked, the surprise apparent in her voice.

Gabriel nodded.

Itai cut in, saying that Arami had been issued a travel document and was already in France. Consternation showed on the faces of both Gabriel and Nachmias.

That was another reason for Itai's frustration with himself. He should never have let Arami leave the country without revealing what he knew. He should have pressed harder. He should have convinced him that despite his promise to Gabriel, he had to be the responsible adult. By now it was probably too late. When Arami got on the plane, they lost their only lead to Michal's killer.

Just yesterday, Itai had been very glad Arami was gone. He arrived at the OMA office in the morning to find a man in a black suit waiting for him. He recognized him as one of the two men who had been there before with the Eritrean diplomat. "We wish to make a donation to your organization," the man said in the same courteous manner that had characterized the deputy consul general. "We hear you took two more women into your shelter yesterday."

Itai couldn't restrain himself. "How do you know that?" he snapped.

"We know a lot of things," the man said enigmatically.

Itai asked him to leave. No matter how desperately they needed money, he wasn't about to take a penny from the Eritrean consulate. Before he left, the man repeated the invitation to pay them a visit, saying he might learn "some very interesting things" if he did.

NACHMIAS rose and began pacing the small room. Itai watched her tensely. So far, she'd kept her opinion to herself. The last time they'd met, she'd listened patiently to everything he had to say and then dismissed it out of hand. He hoped that this time would be different. She had witnessed for herself the exchange between Gabriel and his sister. She could see it wasn't an act.

"Do you know Yariv Ninio?" Nachmias asked Gabriel, sitting down again.

"The attorney?" Itai asked, bewildered. What did Yariv Ninio have to do with anything?

She nodded.

"No," Gabriel said in a quiet voice.

"He knew Michal. They used to be a couple. You don't know him?"

Gabriel shook his head.

"It's very important that you tell us the whole truth," Itai urged, even though he had no idea where Nachmias was going with her questions. "Like I told you, we'll help you, we'll protect you. But you have to tell us the truth."

"I don't know him," Gabriel repeated.

"Do you know if Arami knew him?"

Again Gabriel shook his head.

"Okay. I heard everything I need to know," Nachmias said, getting up. "Now I've got work to do."

"What do you mean?" Itai had to be sure the visit to the detention center had produced the outcome he was hoping for.

"It means I believe him," Nachmias said.

Chapter 69

ANAT was relishing the look of growing stupefaction on David's face as she delivered the lab results. The fingerprints Yariv Ninio had left in her office when he came to bawl her out were a perfect match to the ones found on Michal's door. What's more, according to the CSI techs, the location and condition of the prints indicated that they were recent. Ninio wouldn't be able to claim they were left there from the time he and Michal were together.

"You're telling me he let you print him?" David was having trouble taking it in.

"He came to my office and gave me a set of prints of his own free will," Anat answered.

"Just like that?"

"He even spread out his fingers to make it easier for the lab techs," she said laughing, demonstrating how Ninio had slammed his hands on her desk.

Her performance elicited a guffaw from David.

"I hope you told the migrant to keep his mouth shut and warned Fisher not to call a press conference," David said, training his eyes on her.

"They don't know anything about Ninio," she assured him. "You can trust me, David. You only have to tell me once and I get it. For the time being, the information is safe with me. Until we pull Ninio in and he confesses to killing Michal Poleg, Gabriel stays where he is and nobody knows he recanted. Just like you said, I'm leaving the brass with a suspect in custody, so everyone's happy."

"What about the plea bargain?"

"They'll stall for a few days. Gabriel's lawyer won't have a clue what's causing the holdup."

David lit another cigarette, took a deep drag, and blew the smoke in her face. "So your theory is that Yariv Ninio killed Michal Poleg because her complaint to the Bar Association revealed that he'd concealed information from the court?"

"That's right," Anat said, coughing. She'd gotten the lab results on the way to the detention center and had been planning to run straight to David as soon as she got back to the station. But after what happened at the jail, she felt she needed time to pull herself together. Although she'd done her best to remain detached, to focus on the facts and not get caught up in the emotion, the meeting between Gabriel and Liddie had struck a chord deep inside her. She herself was an only child, which explained why her mother was always on her back. And then there was the shiver that ran through her every time Itai leaned over and whispered in her ear, trying his best to translate what was being said. What was that all about?

"You still haven't explained why the African confessed if Ninio's the killer. You said he didn't know Ninio, so what's the connection?" David asked, enveloping her in another cloud of smoke. She knew from experience she'd have to wash her hair when she got home.

"I've got a theory, but I want to hold off until I hear what the counselor has to say after we pull him in. Okay?" This time she managed to get the whole sentence out without coughing. She'd been searching for a connection between Gabriel and Ninio, and she thought she'd finally found it: Arami. They weren't the only ones who used him as an interpreter. He worked in the courthouse, too. He and Ninio could have met there.

"Could you give me a little hint, Nachmias? You do realize we're about to arrest an assistant state attorney? If it turns out to be bullshit, they'll hang us both out to dry."

"It's so unlikely, it has to be true," Anat said with a smile.

"I've got a real Sherlock Holmes on my hands, don't I?" David said, crushing out the cigarette.

Anat was about to say that someone had already called her that today, but she decided to keep it to herself.

Chapter 70

YARIV immediately recognized the number that came up on the screen of his cell phone. Before leaving his office, Shuki Borochov had handed him his card and promised to be in touch "very soon." Since then, Yariv's heart had stopped every time the phone rang. He was hoping to have more time to think before he called, but it had barely been six hours and Borochov was already making contact.

Yariv stared at the phone in terror. It was ten at night. What did they want with him at this hour? Kobi told him not to answer, to wait for the plea bargain to be finalized. But he still wasn't sure he could trust Kobi.

"Riv? Why don't you answer your phone?" he heard Inbar call from the next room. Yariv muted the phone hurriedly. The last thing he needed was for Inbar to start asking questions.

"Who was it?" she asked, coming into the living room.

He didn't reply. He didn't have the patience to deal with her. Especially not now.

"What's the matter, Riv? Why don't you answer me?" She was standing over him.

He got up from the couch, ignoring her.

"What's going on?" she asked, placing a gentle hand on his shoulder.

Yariv shrugged her off. The phone in his hand vibrated. Out of the corner of his eye he could see that it was the same number and a shudder went through him.

"Talk to me, Yariv," Inbar persisted. "What's going on with you? Ever since I got back from Eilat you've been acting like I did something wrong. Are you mad at me?"

Infuriated, Yariv turned to face her, about to shout that every-

thing wasn't about her, that she should quit thinking that the whole
world revolved around her and leave him alone, that he was sick of
her nagging. The ringing of the landline nipped his tirade in the
bud. The shrill sound was deafening. It reverberated in his bones.

"Don't answer it," he yelled as Inbar headed for the phone.

"What?" Puzzled, she turned to look at him.

"Don't answer it and don't ask any questions," he ordered, his
heart pounding.

"Why not? It might be the DJ from Navit's wedding," Inbar said,
turning and continuing in the direction of the phone.

Yariv raced across the room and grabbed her arm.

"I said don't answer it," he screamed.

"What do you think you're doing? Take your hands off me! Do
you know how long I've been waiting for him to call? Do you know
how busy he is? How hard it is to get hold of him? Do you even care?
You act like the wedding has nothing to do with you." Undeterred,
Inbar went for the phone again.

"He can call back tomorrow. You can call him tomorrow. I don't
give a fuck. Inbar, are you listening to me? Don't answer the phone.
Just do what I say for a change. I'm sick and tired of arguing all the
time," Yariv shouted, grabbing her arm a second time.

"It's my house, too, mister! You can't tell me what to do," Inbar
retorted, struggling to free herself from his grip.

Her resistance made him even more livid. He shoved her against
the wall and stood in front of her.

"You're not going anywhere, get it?" he said, blocking her path.

The telephone stopped ringing.

They stood face-to-face, both breathing heavily.

"What happened to you? I don't understand it," Inbar moaned.
In tears, she went into the bedroom and closed the door behind her.

Yariv knew he should go after her and apologize, but his cell
phone started vibrating again. Number withheld, the screen read.

He could hear Inbar crying in the other room. Then her cell

phone rang. Yariv ran for the bedroom, hoping to stop her in time, but when he opened the door she was already holding the phone to her ear.

"Who's calling, please?" she said, trying to disguise the fact that she'd been crying.

Yariv gestured wildly with his hands: don't give me the phone, say I'm not here.

"Yariv isn't here," she said in a trembling voice and disconnected. The landline began ringing again.

"Riv, what's going on? What's the matter?" Inbar asked through her tears. Her sobbing was more than he could stand.

"Who was it?" he asked, ignoring her question. The sound of the phone in the living room was deafening.

"He didn't say. Talk to me. Tell me what's going on?"

Yariv marched out of the bedroom. He'd had enough. He couldn't take the ringing anymore. It was driving him mad, messing with his head. He pulled the phone out of the wall and the house fell silent. He stood there in the middle of the living room, gasping for air.

"I won't do this anymore, Yariv. I demand an answer. You can't just ignore me!" Inbar pleaded tearfully beside him.

Someone knocked sharply on the door and they both jumped. Yariv held a finger to his lips, signaling her to be quiet. The banging continued. Inbar collapsed onto the couch, covering her face and weeping bitterly.

Now the loud knocking was joined by the sound of the doorbell. They'd come for him.

The phone in his hand was vibrating. Whoever was outside kept pounding on the door and leaning on the bell.

He was a goner. People like that weren't happy if you didn't jump when they called. He should have gone to the cops instead of listening to Kobi. At least he'd still be alive tomorrow.

Yariv wiped the sweat from his brow. What was he supposed

to do now? Their apartment was on the third floor. There was no escape. He was trapped.

"Police! Open up!" he heard on the other side of the door.

"Police?" Inbar looked at him in fright.

His cell phone started vibrating again. Yariv dropped it like a hot coal. Inbar's phone also started ringing.

"Stop it!" he shouted, clutching his head in his hands. "I can't take any more!"

"Ninio, open the door. We know you're in there." He knew that voice. It belonged to the detective, Inspector Nachmias.

Chapter 71

ANAT barely recognized Ninio, and not just because he was dressed in a T-shirt and sweat pants instead of the usual suit. It was the haunted look in his eyes, the mixture of confusion and fear on his face.

"They're trying to kill me," he said in a shaky voice as he gestured for her to come in.

A warrant for Yariv Ninio's arrest had been issued half an hour ago. David wanted to wait until four in the morning to haul him in. As a rule, you get the best results if you drag someone out of bed and interrogate them when they're exhausted and dazed.

But Anat objected. She didn't want to give Ninio the chance to claim later that he was coerced into confessing. They would conduct the interview by the book. For the same reason, she didn't send Yaron out alone to pick him up. This time they'd do things her way from start to finish.

"They don't stop calling," Yariv said in a panic.

Behind him she could see a girl, presumably his fiancée, weeping quietly on the couch. Anat noticed her blue nail polish and the all-too-obvious nose job, and wondered why Mrs. Glazer hadn't mentioned them. The distracting thought faded as quickly as it came.

"Who's 'they'?" she asked calmly. Following normal procedure, they'd called to make sure he was home before making the arrest. When he didn't answer his cell phone, they'd called the landline and then his fiancée's mobile. When they got back to the station, she'd have Yaron get a printout of all the calls to and from Ninio's phone. She wanted to find out who he'd spoken to and who he was so afraid of.

"Borochov, his people. Isn't that why you're here?" Yariv asked, scanning the faces of the cops in the room.

Anat remained silent, waiting for him to keep talking.

Ninio gave her a puzzled look and stepped back. Not a muscle moved in her face. As David always said, the interrogation begins from the moment of the arrest.

"Borochov, Borochov. I know it's him," Yariv shouted.

Anat kept silent.

"Wait a minute. What are you doing here?" Yariv asked, focusing on Anat.

"Why do you think we're here?" she asked.

"I don't know, Detective. Maybe to apologize?" Ninio had reverted to his habitual tone of voice.

"What's going on, Riv?" the girl cut in.

"It's nothing, Inbar. They're just leaving. Inspector Nachmias came to offer her apologies," Yariv answered coolly, not turning his head.

Anat debated whether to ask him to tell her more about the calls and who this Borochov was but decided against it. She'd missed her chance. Yariv Ninio was his old self again. She'd have plenty of time to interrogate him later.

"We're bringing you in for questioning," she said matter-of-factly.

"What do you mean? Questioning about what?" The panic had crept back into his voice.

"You'll find out at the station." Anat had no intention of giving him time to prepare for the interview.

"Tell me right now or I refuse to go with you. I'm an attorney, or did you happen to forget that? The tricks you use with petty criminals won't work on me," Yariv snapped derisively.

Anat decided not to respond. No reason to get ahead of herself. Two hours from now he'd be no different than any other suspect. When push came to shove, everybody behaved the same way in an interrogation.

"Well, Nachmias, I'm waiting," Yariv said. Despite his patronizing manner, he couldn't manage to hide the fact that he was clearly feeling the pressure.

"It's up to you, Counselor," Anat said serenely. "You can come with us of your own free will, or we'll arrest you right here and now. What's it going to be?"

Yariv didn't answer.

"Well, Ninio, I'm waiting," Anat said, unable to restrain herself.

"I'll come, I'll come," Yariv said, taking a step toward her in an attempt at intimidation. "But don't think your conduct here isn't going to cost you."

Chapter 72

YARIV crushed a cup in his fist. They'd already kept him waiting for half an hour. He got up and started pacing the interrogation room, totally bare except for a table, three chairs, and a small stack of plastic cups. He knew he wasn't really alone. Every move he made was being monitored by hidden cameras.

What were they waiting for? Why was he here?

On the way to the station, it occurred to him that Borochov might have been calling to warn him. He'd been wrong to listen to Kobi. He should have answered the phone and heard what Borochov had to say. He'd assumed the fleshy lawyer had put Nachmias on to him, but apparently he'd been wrong about that, too. She had no idea what he was talking about.

That left him with the question of what the cops wanted with him. It couldn't have anything to do with Michal's murder. The case had already been turned over to the prosecution and they were about to reach a plea bargain agreement. He knew how it worked. The minute the cops signed off on an investigation, that was the end of it. There was nothing they liked better than to declare a case closed.

So what was it? The stupid position paper? Had the cops looked into Michal's complaint and found out that he'd kept it from the court? If that's what it was, he had nothing to worry about. There were plenty of ways he could justify not disclosing Shemesh's legal opinion. Even more to the point, Regev would look out for him. Once he got his claws into Nachmias, she wouldn't even be able to get a job as a crossing guard.

Yariv sat down and leaned back in his chair. He was feeling much better. He wondered if he should ask to consult with a lawyer. That would be the smart thing to do, the golden rule every attorney learned the first day in law school. But why bother? The more he thought about it, the more positive he became that they'd hauled him in to question him about the legal opinion. Demanding to speak to a lawyer would arouse suspicion and make him look guilty. No, it was better to deal with it on his own.

His thoughts were interrupted by Nachmias, who walked in with a tall, bearded cop. The man introduced himself as Detective Yaron Waldman. Yariv had to take care not to look nervous. If they had anything solid to go on, he'd be under arrest. But Nachmias said they came to bring him in for questioning, not to arrest him, and that was significant. It meant they were on a fishing expedition; they didn't have probable cause for an arrest warrant. They must have forgotten he knew a thing or two about the criminal justice system.

"Do you want to consult with a lawyer before we begin?" Nachmias asked, taking the seat directly across from him.

"I *am* a lawyer, baby," Yariv answered, his voice dripping with contempt, "and the first thing I want to know is why I'm here."

"So you understand what it means when I tell you that you're being interviewed under caution?"

"I hope *you* understand what it means," he retorted.

"You lied to me, Mr. Ninio," Nachmias said, looking him straight in the eye.

"Pardon me, I didn't know we were married. You're holding me because I hurt your feelings?" Yariv looked over at Waldman, wanting to share the joke with the other man in the room, but the cop's face remained expressionless.

"The Justice Ministry sent you Dr. Yigal Shemesh's legal opinion," Anat went on, leaning closer.

Yariv made no attempt to hide his grin. He was right. They'd hauled him in because of the idiotic legal opinion. If he'd answered the phone, Borochov would have warned him this was about to happen.

"I suggest you wipe the smile off your face," Waldman barked.

"And I suggest," Yariv snapped back, "that the two of you say you're sorry and call me a cab. Even if I received the opinion, and I'm not saying I did, so what? If you did your homework, you'd know I was under no obligation to make use of it. There are opposing opinions, too, you know. Just because some bleeding heart who doesn't give a shit about the country decided to write it, it doesn't necessarily mean anything. I used my discretion as an attorney, and I had the necessary authorization."

"From who?" Nachmias cut in.

"I don't have to answer that, Detective. With all due respect to you and the show you're putting on for my benefit, it's none of your business. We're talking about internal decisions of the State Attorney's Office. That's a few hundred levels above your pay grade." Yariv's voice was steady.

"The legal opinion could have a dramatic impact on a lot of people. It might prevent their deportation. It might even save their lives. Michal claimed that the man she worked with, Hagos, was deported and subsequently murdered because you concealed it. The opinion would also bring an end to the string of legal victories you're so proud of. So don't tell me it doesn't mean anything," Nachmias chided.

Yariv was irritated by her self-righteous tone.

"Too bad you're not listening. Or maybe you don't get it. Let me spell it out for you again, in words even you can understand: there are other legal opinions. They say the exact opposite. Is that clear, or do I have to repeat it a third time?" Yariv asked sarcastically, his voice rising.

Nachmias remained silent.

Good! He had her on the ropes.

"Get this into your head," he went on with renewed confidence. "Hagos was deported because he was from Ethiopia. I'm not the one who said so, the Ministry of the Interior said so. As soon as that determination was made, nothing could stand in the way of his deportation. Nothing! Not me, not the court, and not Michal Poleg, who was probably fucking him. So I suggest you calm down and stop poking your nose in things you don't understand."

The detectives remained silent, keeping their eyes on Yariv. Everything they say about the cops is right, he thought. They're a bunch of clowns.

"I've had enough of this," he said, standing up.

"Sit down!" Waldman rose threateningly from his seat.

"We're not done yet, Mr. Ninio. Please sit down," Nachmias said quietly.

Yariv hesitated for a moment before obeying.

"You've got five minutes," he said sharply to Nachmias. She nodded.

"When did you last see Michal Poleg?" she asked, scribbling something on the pad in front of her.

Yariv didn't reply. Why were they asking him about Michal?

"You said you hadn't seen her for months," she prodded.

"I don't know if it was months. We might have run into each other in the street . . . in the supermarket . . . I don't remember," Yariv muttered. "What difference does it make?"

"You haven't been in her apartment recently?" Nachmias persisted. Her detached tone of voice was making Yariv nervous.

"No, of course not. I told you, we broke up a long time ago. I'm getting married soon. We were together for a while and then we ended it," he answered irritably.

Nachmias remained silent.

"I presume we're finished here," Yariv said, clapping his hands together and starting to rise.

"You see, Counselor, that's my problem. You keep lying to me." Nachmias leaned across the desk, propping her head on her hands.

"What? What are you talking about? I demand an immediate apology!" Yariv said belligerently, despite the agitation this new line of questioning had sparked.

"Do you want to rethink your answer and tell me when you were last in Michal's apartment?"

"I already told you . . ." Yariv's confidence was slipping away.

"What did you tell me?" Nachmias asked, maintaining her exasperating calm.

"It was months ago. . . . Why are you asking me these questions?" Yariv felt his heart sink.

"We found your fingerprints," Nachmias said matter-of-factly, leaning back in her chair.

"What?"

"You're lying to me, Mr. Ninio. You were in Michal's apartment the night she was murdered." Nachmias leaned forward again.

"I didn't . . . what are you talking about? Are you out of your mind?" Yariv wiped his forehead. He hadn't noticed how hot the room was.

"So how do you explain the fact that your fingerprints were there?" the detective said sharply, raising her voice for the first time.

Yariv didn't answer. What was going on here? How did they identify his fingerprints? Kobi assured him that any prints he might have left in the room would never lead back to him. Since he'd never been arrested, his prints weren't on file. That's why he felt confident claiming he hadn't been there in months. What went wrong? How did they find out? Did he leave something behind in the apartment? Did something fall out of his pocket?

"So you found my prints, so what?" he said, making an effort to sound as unconcerned as he had a few minutes ago. "They're probably still there from when we were going out. Didn't that occur to you?"

"Wrong answer, Mr. Ninio," Waldman jeered. "No way they're that old. Our lab says they're recent, very recent."

Yariv was speechless.

"Yariv Ninio, you're under arrest for the murder of Michal Poleg," Nachmias declared.

"What? You can't do that . . . I didn't . . . Have you gone completely insane? Why are you doing this?"

"You lying bastard, you killed her!" Waldman yelled. "What did you think, that we wouldn't find out? That we're idiots. That we'd let you get away with it because you're an ASA?"

Suddenly it all made sense. He'd been a fool. Instead of keeping his conversation with Borochov to himself, he'd gone and told Kobi. They'd been watching him. When he didn't answer the phone, they got mad and sold him out. That's how the cops knew. Borochov wouldn't have called the cops himself. He must have gotten someone else to do the dirty work for him.

"Tell me, Ninio, how did you kill her?" Nachmias asked.

He'd handled the whole thing wrong. Now he was done for. They knew everything. Maybe even things he didn't know himself.

Chapter 73

ANAT watched in silence as Ninio broke down in tears. She signaled for Yaron to get him some water. She needed him to get a grip on himself and describe how he murdered Michal Poleg.

"I didn't kill Michal," Ninio said, raising his eyes to her the moment the door closed behind Yaron.

She examined him closely. She was disappointed that he was sticking to his story, but then she hadn't expected him to break so soon.

"The fingerprints? It's a setup. Someone's out to get me. They must have planted my prints in her apartment." Anat could hear the desperation in his voice.

She remained silent. She couldn't count the number of times a suspect claimed he'd been framed. Once she got him in the interrogation room, Ninio was no different from anyone else. This was just one of the stages they all went through before they confessed.

"I was set up. There are people out there who don't like what I do, self-loathing Israelis who see me as the enemy," Ninio went on, trying to make eye contact with her.

"You've got to believe me. I'm telling you the truth."

"It's a shame you're going down this road, Ninio, a real shame."

"When you showed up at my door, I thought you were there to protect me." He was breathing heavily. "I thought he sent someone to kill me. I told you . . ."

"Who?"

"Borochov. Shuki Borochov." Yariv's voice was trembling.

"Borochov? What's he to you?" Anat asked, puzzled. She was finding it hard to maintain her poker face. She knew the name Shuki Borochov very well. And she knew Ninio would have to be a fool to accuse him of framing him for murder. Is he stupid or is he telling the truth, a little voice in her head demanded.

Anat listened to Ninio's story without interrupting. He told her how Borochov had paid a visit to his office and hinted that they knew things about Michal's murder and if he didn't cooperate and do what they wanted, they'd retaliate by framing him for the crime.

"What things did they know about the murder?" Anat asked when he stopped talking.

Ninio shrugged.

"Maybe they know the truth, that you killed her? People like Borochov don't make idle threats."

"I didn't kill her," Ninio insisted. "I told you, it's a setup."

"You weren't in her apartment the night of the murder?"

Ninio shook his head.

"You've got to protect me. The mob wants to get its hooks into someone in the State Attorney's Office. They're trying to manipulate the legal system. You and I are on the same side here. What happened to me could happen to you, too."

Anat looked straight at the camera concealed in the wall of the interrogation room and offered a little smile of thanks to David. It was his idea to proceed one step at a time, not to hit Ninio with all the evidence at once. The blood on Michal's door was an uncommon type, and it was the same as his: A-. They'd gotten that information from his army file yesterday, and it was only then that the State Attorney had given his okay for the arrest warrant. "I almost believe you, Ninio," she said, knowing that she was about to take a wrecking ball to the house of cards he'd constructed.

"I'm telling you the truth. You've got to believe me," he stammered.

She'd misjudged the ASA. He was shrewder than she thought. As soon as she got his confession, she'd question him about Borochov. She had to admit this little diversion was a cleverly crafted strategy.

"Believe that your prints were planted at the scene?" she asked with undisguised skepticism.

Ninio nodded.

"You see, that's where I've got a problem. It just doesn't make sense." Anat kept her voice calm, accenting each word.

"Why not? It's the simplest thing in the world. . . . You see it on television all the time. . . . You don't have to be a genius. . . ."

"Because it wasn't just your prints we found. We also found your blood at the scene," Anat cut in. "Can you explain that to me, Mr. Ninio, how your blood made its way to Michal's apartment? Did Borochov plant that there, too?"

Chapter 74

YARIV stared at Nachmias in despair. It had completely slipped his mind. He'd been focusing on the fingerprints and completely forgotten about the bruises he had when he got home that night. It's not surprising his blood was found at Michal's apartment. He'd dug his own grave, ratted out Borochov for no good reason.

He gulped down the water the cop had brought him. The two detectives gazed at him icily. He'd been too cocky. He shouldn't have underestimated them.

It was time to demand to speak to a lawyer. Meanwhile, he was just making things worse for himself. But if he stopped the interview and then told them later what really happened, they'd never believe him. They'd assume he was just parroting what his lawyer told him to say, that it was just another fairy tale.

He had to gain their trust. No more games. He needed to tell them everything he knew, or at least everything he thought he knew.

They were right—he was in Michal's apartment that night. But he didn't kill her. If he had, he was sure he'd remember. But everything was still a blank.

Chapter 75

FARO topped up Borochov's glass with more of his favorite scotch. Any time one of his people went abroad, they knew enough to bring a bottle back for the boss. "The quiche is delicious," the attorney said, stuffing another forkful into his mouth. Faro knew he'd prefer a thick steak to the eggplant and mozzarella in front of him, but since he'd gone vegetarian, nobody touched meat in his presence.

Borochov had been working for him for more than twenty years, but Faro still didn't know what attracted a man like him to their world. He himself had been born into abject poverty, grown up in squalid surroundings where crime was the only way to survive. But Borochov came from money. And his father was a district court judge. The question gnawed at Faro for the first few years of their collaboration. If he didn't understand what drove the men who worked for him, he couldn't rely on their loyalty. Borochov claimed his secret life gave him a rush, but Faro had a different theory. In his opinion, the attorney was getting back at the people who had blocked his father's appointment to the Supreme Court. But whatever his motivation, it was no longer an issue. Faro had put him to the test more times than he could count, and Borochov had always proved himself trustworthy.

Itzik's son, Ethan, poked his head in to ask if they'd like some cabbage ravioli. Itzik had come to him several years back, crushed by a tragedy in his family: his son wanted to be a chef. Ethan now owned one of the most popular restaurants in Tel Aviv, thanks in no small part to Faro.

Faro usually met with Borochov in his office, but that would be unwise at the moment. With the cops sniffing around, they couldn't risk being seen together. The private room in Ethan's restaurant was an excellent alternative.

"What happened to Ninio, it's too bad," Faro said, gesturing to Ethan to bring them more quiche.

"He would have been a useful acquisition," Borochov agreed. "And he was the ideal candidate, the kind who's driven by ambition, who's only looking out for himself. He doesn't give a damn about the migrants."

"Well, we wanted to give him a leg up, but it didn't pan out," Faro said, taking a sip of scotch.

"As soon as I heard, I called to warn him he was about to be arrested, but the fool didn't pick up." Borochov was chewing contentedly on tuna tartare made from fish flown in specially from Japan.

"Do you think he'll have the sense not to tell them about your little visit?" Faro wiped his mouth delicately.

"I wouldn't count on it. In my opinion, he's already singing like a canary."

"You know what that means. They're going to bring you in for questioning, maybe even under caution." The two men burst out laughing.

Over the years, Borochov had been subjected to dozens of police interviews. It was the same each time. He sat there complacently, claiming attorney-client privilege. The cops couldn't do anything about it. It gave Faro such a kick, he'd even considered sending the birdbrains who worked for him to law school so they could all claim privilege. He might even start his own law firm. There were so many new colleges in the country offering a law degree these days that the idea wasn't as ludicrous as it sounded.

"What do you think they'll do now, file charges against the African or the attorney?"

"Galit Lavie has the case, so it's hard to say," Borochov answered. Almost simultaneously, they each uttered a juicy curse at the mention of the prosecutor's name. Since David Meshulam's bungled attempt to get rid of her, the woman's career had soared.

"By the way, what's happening with your 'General'?" Borochov asked while Ethan served the main course. "In view of recent events, don't you think it's time to take him out of the picture?"

Faro focused on the vegetarian spaghetti carbonara and purple squid in front of him. He didn't like his companion's cavalier attitude. Taking a life was not something to be treated lightly. Maybe he should order Borochov to ice somebody for him. He'd sing a different tune if he had to stand there and watch the light go out in a man's eyes.

Besides, even if the "General" lied to him about Ninio, and he probably did, he'd have to overlook it. It was hard to find quality people with his kind of ambition. He had no intention of losing an asset as valuable as the "General."

Chapter 76

ANAT stared at the computer screen, watching Ninio pace back and forth in the interrogation room. He seemed calmer, no longer in the throes of a panic attack.

"What's the matter, Nachmias? Why the long face?" Yaron's question bugged her.

Without answering, she looked over at David, who was already on his fifth cigarette. The boss understood.

Frustrated by Ninio's account of the events of that night, Anat had gone on the attack, telling him straight out that she didn't believe him. She should have kept her cool and waited for him to dig his own grave. There was no going back now. Ninio had asked for a lawyer and she was obliged to stop the interrogation. She'd tried the usual tactics: "What do you need a lawyer for? He'll just make it harder for you"; "If you tell the truth now, we can help you"; even, "You're an attorney. Why do you have to pay someone else to do what you can do yourself?" It didn't work. Ninio just kept shouting frantically, "Lawyer, lawyer." There was nothing they could do about it.

"What is it? Tell me, Nachmias?" Yaron insisted. "The story of a setup, is that what's worrying you? It's bullshit. You said it yourself, we found his blood at the scene. He didn't even bother to deny it. And the whole 'I don't remember' thing? Come on, don't tell me you're buying into it. How many times have you heard a suspect claim they don't remember what happened. It's the oldest scam in the book."

Anat didn't reward Yaron with an answer. She'd also thought Ninio was playing games with her, but now she wasn't so sure.

"Remember the trial of that tycoon last week? The one who ran over the two kids? He claimed he didn't remember anything, but it didn't do him any good. The judge said he was lying and sentenced him to ten years behind bars. It won't be any different with Ninio, believe me," Yaron went on.

"Besides," he added, "you're the one with the law degree, right? It makes no difference if he was drunk or sober when he killed her. What is it your legal friends always say? When he decided to drink, he knowingly took the risk of losing control, so he has to accept the consequences. Ninio has no one to blame but himself. He might get the charges reduced to manslaughter, but he's still going away for a long time. Am I right or am I right?"

"The problem," David said, lighting another cigarette, "is that his story jibes with the evidence. Yeah, we found his prints and his blood, but only on the outside of the door. There's nothing to show he was in her apartment. In terms of the forensics, his story fits. He went there, banged on the door hard enough to hurt his hand, and left without going inside."

"At the very least, it's enough for reasonable doubt," Anat said.

"So that's it? We throw in the towel? Are you fucking crazy?" Yaron yelled.

"No, we don't throw in the towel. We think," David chastised, blowing smoke in Yaron's direction.

"I know he's guilty," Anat said. "He's toying with us. But everybody's got a weakness. We just have to find it."

"Maybe we should bring Borochov in and hear what he's got to say," Yaron suggested.

"A waste of our time, trust me," David said, shaking his head. "We know the guy. He'll claim he never went to see Ninio, and even if he did, Ninio misunderstood what he said, and it doesn't matter anyway because it's all privileged. We won't get anything out of Borochov. We've tried it before, but the son-of-a-bitch doesn't break a sweat." David turned to Anat. "Any ideas, Nachmias?"

"Give me five minutes alone with the bastard and he'll spill his guts," Yaron cut in.

"Pipe down, Yaron. I thought we were past that by now," David said angrily.

"He gave us Borochov. Let's explain to him what would happen if we decided to leak that little tidbit," Yaron went on, ignoring David's rebuke. "He wouldn't last a night out on the street, or even in Abu Kabir. Borochov's clients would get their hands on him and crush his balls. We tell him that and you'll see how fast we get a confession."

"He's an ASA. He'll be under protection," Anat said.

"He doesn't know that."

"We're not there yet," David interrupted, ending the argument. "I'm still waiting for ideas from you, Nachmias. Now would be a good time, before the brass has our hide."

Anat cleared her throat. "Gabriel said that Arami told him the Israeli who gave him the money was a powerful man . . ."

"You thought it was Ninio," David broke in.

"Well, that's one possibility." Ninio admitted seeing Arami in the courtroom, but he adamantly denied ever having any personal contact with him.

"What's the other?" David asked.

"That Ninio got drunk and killed Michal, and somehow the bad guys Borochov represents found out about it and they were trying to blackmail him."

"And paying Gabriel to confess was the help Borochov promised him?"

Anat nodded.

"How did they find out?"

Anat shrugged. "We know Michal was threatened, and soon after that she was assaulted. They might be the ones responsible. She turned up something about their activities around the old bus station, some kind of illegal transactions, and they wanted to shut her up." Anat suddenly realized that the theory she was proposing came, at least in part, from Itai Fisher. "Maybe they were keeping an eye on her, watching her house to see who she was in contact with, and they saw Ninio there. If we can find exactly who 'they' are, we might get our answer."

"You think they were that uptight about a babe your size?" Yaron said dismissively.

Anat was about to say something vulgar, but she restrained herself. "She was a very determined young lady. She believed in what she was doing."

"Maybe they killed her themselves," David suggested.

"I considered that, but it doesn't fit the evidence," Anat replied. "She knew her killer. She opened the door for him. Besides, the mob operates quietly. They don't bang on doors, they don't make a racket in the middle of the night."

"So you're saying we've got the murderer, but we don't have any witnesses. We need to get a lead on them, and we won't get it from Borochov," David summed up.

Anat nodded.

Ninio was shouting again. "Get my lawyer. I want him here now!" They couldn't delay much longer. In less than twenty-four hours they'd have to go before a judge and ask to have his remand extended. It wasn't going to be as easy as it was with Gabriel. The migrant was represented by a public defender who didn't even bother to object. Ninio's lawyer would put up a fight.

"We have to follow the money," Anat said.

David nodded. "I agree. We'll start with Arami. He's the one who got the money from the Israeli. If we can identify him, we'll be a step closer to nailing the perp."

"Okay, let's bring Arami in and find out what he knows. What are we waiting for?" Yaron leapt out of his chair, ready for action.

"He was issued a travel document. He left the country a few days ago," Anat admitted reluctantly.

"Where is he now?" David asked.

"France."

Yaron exhaled irritably.

"Do you know how to reach him?" David gave Yaron a withering look and took a deep drag on his cigarette.

"There's someone who might know."

"Your boyfriend?" Yaron asked.

"Who?" Anat felt herself blush, but she wasn't sure why.

"What's his name—Itai Fisher. The one whose eulogy you found so moving, you couldn't take your eyes off him. Don't think we didn't notice, Nachmias."

"Yes, Itai Fisher," Anat said, her face turning a deeper shade of red.

Chapter 77

GABRIEL gazed out through the bars on the window at the night sky. The moon was making a brief appearance through a break in the heavy clouds. Outside, the world went about its business as usual, but his life had ground to a halt.

The policewoman had come this morning and asked him to videotape a message to Arami. Gabriel released him from his promise and begged him to reveal everything he knew. When he asked the detective if they'd let him out now, she said he would have to be patient for a little while. But he didn't have any more patience, not since he'd seen Liddie. He couldn't wait. He needed to know what his sister was doing at this very moment. How was she getting along without him? Was she still coughing? Was she in danger? He was sick with worry that the men who had abducted her would come back for her again. Before she left, he promised they'd be together soon. He knew that waiting was as hard for her as it was for him.

Seeing her had changed him. He'd resigned himself to a life behind bars, but his little sister had given him renewed hope and strength. He was no longer willing to let other people decide his fate.

His lawyer came later and told him he'd tried to finalize the deal with the prosecution but it was apparently off the table. They weren't returning his calls. "Is that good or bad?" Gabriel asked. "Bad, very bad," the lawyer said. Then he got up and left.

The policewoman promised to protect them, not to let anyone hurt Liddie or him. They wouldn't abandon the people who helped them find Michal's murderer, she assured him.

Could he trust Israelis?

Hagos would have said he could; Arami would have said he couldn't. But now he was on his own, without Hagos or Arami to advise him. He wondered what Michal would have said. She'd probably say there are some you can trust and some you can't. He wanted to believe that Itai and the policewoman belonged to the first type. He'd been thinking about Michal a lot lately. It was a shame she never got to meet Liddie. They would have liked each other. And Michal could have helped Liddie overcome the terrible things they did to her. He knew she volunteered at the shelter for women like his sister. Maybe what he was doing would help them catch her killer. He'd like that.

A black cloud covered the moon and the world outside grew darker. Soon the rain would come.

Chapter 78

THE longer the meeting went on, the worse Anat's headache got. At the end of the day, it was all in the hands of bureaucrats and paper pushers. She never imagined she'd have to get her head around so many international conventions and laws with incomprehensible names just to go to France and ask Arami a few simple questions. She discovered that she couldn't pursue an investigation abroad without official approval from Interpol and the justice ministries of Israel and France, as well as the French police.

Yochai had spoken to the Israeli police liaison in France, a high-ranking officer on the verge of retirement, hoping to get him to move things along over there. The liaison officer, who thought the chapter of his life when he actually did police work was over, offered only a noncommittal response delivered with a distinct lack of enthusiasm. It was obvious he wouldn't be of any help to them.

David also tried to use his connections, calling a French police officer he'd met at the seminar in Austria. When he started explaining the problem of the migrants in Israel and how the murder could ignite an already explosive situation, the Frenchman laughed. "You Israelis are so dramatic," he said good-naturedly. "You always think you invented the wheel. You really should get over yourselves. Do you know how many Africans there are in my country? You're worried about sixty thousand? We've got millions to deal with, and they've been coming here for decades. *Mon cher ami*, what we've forgotten about the problem you haven't even begun to learn." Although he promised to do what he could, they knew they couldn't count on him to be of much use to them, either.

Yochai kept throwing her accusing looks. As far as he was concerned, this whole avenue of investigation was a waste of time. The Michal Poleg case could have ended in a plea bargain a long time ago. They'd reduce the charges and Gabriel would be out in a few years.

He'd expected the interview with Yariv Ninio to be short and simple. But as it turned out, there was nothing short or simple about it.

He was getting a lot of pressure from the prosecution, who wanted to know whom they were supposed to be building a case against, Gabriel or Yariv. Which one of them was the killer? They couldn't keep them both in custody indefinitely. They had to make up their minds. Was it Gabriel or Yariv, or as Yaron put it, "Black or white?"

THE meeting at the Justice Ministry's International Department had been dragging on forever. Listening to all the legal experts debating the issue, Anat remembered why she'd walked away from the profession. There were endless laws, procedures, and documents to wade through. They kept raising problems, but nobody was suggesting solutions.

Getting the green light was just the first step. There would still be a long way to go. First they had to find Arami, and then they had to convince him to give up the name of the man who bought the Africans' silence. Neither of those tasks would be easy. She was meeting with Itai this evening to ask for his help. She'd suggested they get together over coffee, hoping an informal atmosphere would encourage him to cooperate. He agreed without hesitation. Anat was pleased. She was looking forward to talking to him someplace nicer than in her drab depressing office.

She heard Chen Shabtai say, "We have to take it step by step. There are complicated legal issues to work out," and she felt her patience wearing thin. She didn't have time to waste. It was perfectly clear to everyone in the room that in the end she'd get the approval she needed, but the paper pushers were obviously going to take their own sweet time about it. It might not matter so much with other cases, but it did with this one. She had to move fast before the higher-ups pulled the plug on the investigation.

"I have a suggestion that might solve some of the procedural problems," she said. All eyes turned to her. It was the first time she'd spoken up. Until now, David had done the talking for both of them.

"We're discussing legal matters, Inspector Nachmias, so with all due respect . . . ," Shabtai said in an attempt to silence her.

"We don't need Arami to testify in court," Anat went on, ignoring the interruption. "At this stage, we only need him to tell us what he knows. What I propose . . ."

"If you'd been listening to the legal analysis, Inspector Nachmias . . . ," Shabtai cut in again.

"I heard every word. The police from one country can't conduct an investigation in another country without the proper authorization. That's the core of the problem. I get it. But what if the person asking the questions isn't a cop?"

Perplexed, Shabtai leafed through the papers in front of her, looking for the precise wording of the law.

"I already checked. There's nothing to prevent it," Anat stated firmly. "All the relevant laws and conventions relate solely to police investigations. We can send a civilian, someone the witness knows. He'll talk to Arami and try to get him to open up. I'll go to France with him—not as a detective, simply as a companion, a tour guide, as it were. If you think it's necessary, I won't be present when they meet. Then if it turns out the information we obtain is important and we want to use it in court, we can do everything by the book later, go through all the time-consuming procedures you described at length."

"How do we pay the civilian's travel expenses? There's also the question of insurance. We'll have to issue a tender. It's not so simple," Shabtai said. Lawyers don't like simple solutions. They could put them out of business.

"I'm sure all you brilliant legal minds can find a way to solve the technical problems," David said. Leaning on his crutches, he rose. Anat quickly followed suit.

"Well, well, Nachmias, I see you're planning a romantic getaway in Paris," he teased on the way out, poking her in the ribs with his elbow.

"Knock it off," Anat snapped back.

Chapter 79

YARIV pressed the pay phone to his right ear, covering the left with his hand to shut out the noise. They'd put him in isolation to protect him from fellow prisoners who might not be so fond of a state attorney, and supposedly to protect him from himself as well. (Seriously? The thought never even crossed his mind.) The cell was tiny, without so much as a window. Yariv felt as if the walls were closing in on him. He didn't know if it was night or day. His skin was clammy and he reeked of sweat. On top of that was the constant racket. The noise of prisoners, guards, cops penetrated through the walls and hammered at him like Chinese water torture.

He desperately needed quiet so he could think. He had to plan a strategy, orchestrate a win. The noise was driving him crazy. They were doing it deliberately, trying to unsettle him, to eat away at his confidence. He was determined not to let it get to him.

He wasn't allowed visitors, either. He saw his parents and brother in the courthouse when they brought him in for the remand hearing. Half hidden behind the reporters and TV crews voraciously filming and firing questions at him, his family waved and blew him kisses.

Inbar wasn't there.

As he'd anticipated, the hearing was short. The judge extended his remand for five days and sent him back to Abu Kabir. At least she issued a total gag order. There'd be no mention of his arrest in the media. He couldn't bear the thought of the whole world seeing him led into court like a common criminal. When this was all over, he'd be back, stronger than ever. He didn't need humiliating press photos haunting him for the rest of his life.

He would have liked Kobi to represent him, but he couldn't. He'd probably be called as a witness. The attorney his parents hired didn't have a clue. All he talked about was evidence, reasonable doubt, legal precedents, procedures. In the end, he fired him.

Was he the only one who understood what was going on? It was all a conspiracy. The people who were trying to bring down Regev, and maybe Borochov, too, couldn't touch them, so they decided to go after him. The bleeding hearts didn't like what he was doing to the illegals and they wanted him out of the way.

What other explanation was there for the sudden shift in the police investigation? They'd already caught the perp and he'd confessed of his own free will. So what changed? They were probably afraid the African would testify in court that he and Michal were lovers. They didn't want people to find out the truth about all those aid organizations and the symbiosis between them and the cops. The cops were willing to collaborate with anyone, even enemies of the state, as long as they gave them what they wanted—quiet on the ground. Regev could tell them everything they needed to know about Michal. He was all too familiar with her from the demonstrations she organized outside his office. She was a constant thorn in his side.

He wouldn't be surprised if they got him drunk that night on purpose. Maybe he was even drugged.

There was no way Yariv was going quietly. It would all blow up in the cops' faces the minute Regev revealed the truth.

Regev's phone was still ringing, but he didn't pick up. Yariv had finally reached him yesterday, but he didn't get a chance to tell him why he was calling. Regev said he couldn't talk; he was in the Knesset and they were about to vote on a crucial bill.

This time Yariv was determined to make him listen. He needed his help. He'd explain that everything that was happening was part of a malicious scheme to get back at them both for the important work they were doing. He'd tell Regev what he wanted him to do, and if he balked, he'd remind him that he'd had full knowledge of the legal opinion Yariv got from the Foreign Ministry and he'd stashed it away with the politician's blessing. He'd let him know that if he went down, he'd take Regev down with him. He'd say he realized immediately that the position paper was a game changer, but Regev persuaded him to keep it from the court because in his opinion the only good migrant was a dead migrant.

They had a mutual interest here. They had to work together.

But meanwhile, Regev wasn't answering his phone.

Chapter 80

ANAT felt a tingle in her body when she saw him waiting for her in the café. It was very disconcerting. "Hi," she said casually, extending her hand and lowering her eyes for fear he might be able to read her thoughts.

"Hi." His handshake was warm, his smile welcoming.

"Sorry I'm late," she apologized as she sat down. He was wearing a thick black turtleneck sweater that was a little small for him. It looked like it was choking him. In the right clothes, he could really turn heads.

"You've been busy fighting crime?" he asked.

"Bureaucracy more like it."

"That doesn't sound very exciting."

"You should know. You were a lawyer, weren't you? Bureaucracy is their business."

"Guilty as charged," he said with a wide smile that revealed a row of bright white teeth.

"Well, nobody's perfect," Anat replied. She was annoyed with herself. Was that the best she could do? Why did her attempts to sound witty always have to be so forced and heavy-handed? Especially when she was trying to make an impression.

"So what happened? I mean, what made you see the light?" she asked in an effort to redeem herself.

Itai shrugged. "Well, it was fine at the beginning. I interned with a Supreme Court judge and then I got a job with one of those commercial firms everyone's dying to work for. People think the privileged few who work there rub shoulders with the high and mighty."

Anat nodded. She knew exactly what he meant.

"It takes most associates a long time to realize they're nothing more than modern-day slaves, but I knew after a few months it wasn't for me. Making wealthy people wealthier isn't my cup of tea. I was never more miserable than I was the year I worked there."

"Why did you stay?" Anat enjoyed listening to him talk. His voice was rich and deep.

"Guilt and my mother," he said with a chuckle. "Every other day she told me her doctor didn't think her heart could take it if I left. 'But of course it's your choice,' she always added."

Anat laughed. "It's your choice" was one of her mother's favorite phrases.

"In the end they did me a favor and fired me," Itai went on. "The managing partner told me they didn't give a damn that I hated our clients. The problem was that I had less sympathy for them than I had for the other side. The next week I took a job with the Hotline for Refugees and Migrants. I was there a year and a half and then I heard OMA was looking for a new director and I applied for the position."

"What about your mother's doctor? Did they revoke his license?" Anat asked lightly.

"According to my mom, they reached the mutual conclusion that it was a case of divine intervention. God didn't want her to die in peace. He wanted to torment her by making her see my law degree gathering dust on the living-room wall every day."

"The tragic saga of the Jewish mother." Anat laughed.

The waitress arrived and they both ordered draft beer. Anat didn't usually drink, and never when she was working. But she liked Itai. She was hoping the beer would loosen her up a bit. She was having such a good time that she kept putting off the moment when she told him why she'd asked him to meet her here.

She wondered if she would still find him attractive if this were a real date. Dates always made her nervous. She spent the whole time trying to decide if he was the one, if the relationship had a future, where they'd be a month from now. She wasn't doing that now. Who would have believed it—Anat Nachmias was starting to let herself go.

"By the way, I'm also a recovering attorney." Anat decided to keep the conversation going a little while longer before she brought up the subject of Arami and Gabriel.

"Really? You don't look like a lawyer." When he smiled, laugh lines formed engaging parentheses around his eyes, which she now noticed were a stunning shade of green.

"So what happened? How did you go from being a lawyer to a cop?" he asked with what sounded like genuine interest.

"My dad's a lawyer. Ever since I was little, it was pretty clear that I'd follow in his footsteps. When the time came, I wasn't so sure anymore. You and I must be twins who were separated at birth. My parents kept pushing me to get a combined degree in accountancy and law. I finally gave in. I did a specialized program in international tax law, and before you ask, yes, it's just as fascinating as it sounds."

"You didn't want to be a cop when you grew up? You didn't dress up as a cop on Purim?" Itai asked in his warm bass. Anat realized it was one of the few times she didn't feel she had to apologize for her job.

"No, it was pure chance. Mainly because of the army. Of the options they gave me after basic training, attachment to the police force sounded the most attractive. I didn't know a lot about it, but I figured it had to be better than sitting in an office or spending two years making coffee for some colonel. They assigned me to the detective division. I planned to leave when I got out of the army and started college, but they asked me to stay on. I enjoyed what I was doing and the hours were flexible, so I took them up on the offer. The rest is history."

"Do you like your work?"

"There are good days and bad days. What about you?"

"There are good days and bad days," Itai replied, laughing.

"I'm guessing you don't do it for the money," Anat said.

"Well, we don't make huge salaries like you cops."

"It must be hard for you now, with the hate campaign against the migrants."

"That's for sure. It's not easy to do your job when the public is antagonistic."

"Tell me about it," Anat said, and they both burst out laughing.

Chapter 81

ITAI shifted uncomfortably in his seat. The friendly atmosphere was ruined the moment Anat mentioned Gabriel and Arami.

"We want you to e-mail him. Tell him you're coming to France to raise funds and you'd like to get together with him to give him his last paycheck," Anat said, detailing his role in their tactic to locate Arami.

Itai didn't answer. He noticed her use of the plural "we." He didn't like the idea of lying to Arami, and he definitely didn't want to get him in trouble with the cops. What's more, he wasn't pleased that she'd gone behind his back and videotaped a message from Gabriel to Arami without his knowledge.

"We just need him to point us in the right direction, give us some kind of lead. The man's phone number, a description, anything. We'll take it from there."

Itai wanted to trust her. The suggestion that they go to France together took him by surprise. He didn't think the cops would make such an effort, but she said it wasn't uncommon. There was a lot of red tape involved, but it wasn't unusual for them to go abroad to question witnesses. This time they didn't even have far to go. It was France they were talking about, not Australia. Besides, she added, this was a homicide investigation, so it had top priority. If there was any chance that Arami had information that could help them catch the murderer, they had to talk to him.

Anat was very persuasive, but Itai was still hesitant. When he told her where to find Gabriel, she promised his arrest would be handled sensitively. But he found out later from Gabriel that the cops had charged at him in the park with their guns drawn.

"We're not going to get a lead on Michal's killer any other way," Anat said, pressing her case. "And without Arami's statement, I won't be able to convince my bosses to look beyond Gabriel's confession."

Itai didn't like the way Anat was pressuring him. There was

nothing he wanted more than to see justice done, with Gabriel a free man and the real killer caught and made to pay for what he did. Anat knew that. It wasn't fair of her to use it to get him to do what she wanted. When it came right down to it, she was the reason Gabriel was behind bars.

"There's no other option?" he asked.

She shook her head.

"I'm concerned for Arami. It wasn't easy for him to get a travel document. There's no way I'm going to jeopardize it. He doesn't want to come back here."

"He has nothing to worry about. He'll be fine."

"He has plenty to worry about, believe me," Itai snapped, annoyed by her glib response. What did she know about the life of asylum seekers in Israel? About the danger they were in? Arami didn't go to France for the food. He had good reason to get on that plane.

"What, for instance?" Anat wasn't convinced.

"The Eritrean authorities, for one. They're looking for him."

"That's why we need your help," Anat said after a short pause. "If we have to take other steps to find him, it might put him at risk. I'm sure you don't want that."

Itai remained silent. He shouldn't have let himself be drawn into this argument. The police had their own agenda. Despite Anat's smile, he didn't miss the implied threat in her words. The cops would find Arami with or without his help. Like an idiot, he'd just given them another lead. He could kick himself for being so naive, for being lured in by her charming smile and the way she seemed so interested in everything he said. For a while there, he even thought . . . never mind what he thought. She was a detective and she was just using the tactics she'd been trained to use to get someone to cooperate.

"I'll do it, but not for you, and not because you're threatening me," he said coldly, breaking the silence.

"It wasn't meant to be a threat," she said with a shamefaced expression.

"I'm doing it for Michal. And for Gabriel and Arami. That's all."

Chapter 82

BOAZ Yavin strode rapidly up Fein Street. Yesterday's rain had flooded the streets, washing the garbage heaped on the sidewalks into the road. Cold and repulsed by the squalor, he pulled the winter coat Irit had bought him more tightly around him. People followed him with their eyes as he went by. The sullen look on their faces added to his disgust. He hated this place with a passion.

When he was little, his granddad used to take his brother and him on outings to this part of the city. He remembered what it was like then, all the colorful fruit stalls and the toy stores around the bus station. It was all gone now. All that remained were dilapidated buildings, broken streetlights, and overgrown yards. A cloud of soot from countless buses hung in the air, mixing with the acrid smell of urine.

A young man on a bike was hurtling toward him. He moved aside at the last minute, almost tripping over a pile of garbage.

The arms deal in Argentina had gone off without a hitch, thanks largely to his own attention to detail. Even organized crime wasn't profitable without a skilled accountant. He had to talk to Faro and convince him to get somebody else to make the rounds here. He'd paid his dues ten times over. Wasn't it time they left him alone?

Boaz turned and looked back at the white car that had brought him here. The two men inside were watching him with stony faces. Itzik had instructed them to drop him off at a different spot each time. He needed their business to be conducted quietly, with no unnecessary drama. That was rule number one: don't attract attention. The altercation with Michal Poleg was an aberration that couldn't be allowed to happen again.

Boaz had dreamt about her a few days ago. In the dream she was lying dead in the street. It could have been any one of the streets around here. Was that how he'd end up, too? The Poleg woman was single, but he had a family. How would they manage if anything happened to him?

The people who were waiting for him in the back room of the restaurant were scary. He was particularly afraid of the "General," who was always scowling and barked orders at him like he was a soldier under his command. He asked Itzik about him once, who he was, why they called him the "General," but he didn't get an answer.

A lot of money exchanged hands in that room. What if one of them decided to take him out of the equation? Itzik said they wouldn't dare harm him, that they knew Faro would be gunning for them if they did, but that didn't make him feel any better. He'd still be the one lying dead in the street.

Another bike was heading in his direction. He managed to get out of the way in time, clutching the black briefcase tightly as he moved aside to make room for it to pass.

It happened in a split second. Without warning, the rider turned the handlebars to the left and ran straight into him, hitting him hard. Boaz fell to his knees, losing his grip on the briefcase. He reached out for it, but the rider got there first. He kicked Boaz in the face, dropping him to the ground. Before he had time to react, the briefcase was gone and the thief was racing off in the direction he had come from. Shots rang out, the bullets whistling over Boaz's head. He froze. Raising his eyes, he saw the white car tearing down the street toward the rider, the man in the passenger seat firing a handgun through the open window. Panicking, Boaz covered his head with his hands.

The rider turned into an alley and the car squealed to a halt. The shooter jumped out and took off after him on foot. The car sped off.

Boaz remained where he was, curled up on the sidewalk, trying to shield his head from the bullets. After a while, he realized he was alone. They'd abandoned him there. He passed his hand over his face. It came away red with blood.

People were approaching, moving slowly and warily. What was he supposed to do now? Where was he supposed to go?

As the figures closed in around him, he suddenly understood what was happening. They think I've got money. They're going to kill me. It's a lynch mob. Pulling himself up quickly, he started running, not caring where he was going, desperate to save himself.

It wasn't long before Boaz heard sirens in the distance. He was already gasping for air. He was out of shape. If he kept this up, he'd have a heart attack, but he couldn't stop. He didn't want to have to explain to the cops why his face was covered in blood. Terrified, he kept running.

Chapter 83

THE first thing Yariv noticed was that Inbar wasn't wearing her engagement ring. The costly ring he'd bought at a jewelry store near the Diamond Exchange, the ring he'd picked out for her with the help of his mother, the ring Inbar never took off—it wasn't on her finger.

The cops had stopped questioning him. The new lawyer he hired couldn't say if that was good or bad. It was hard to tell. More than likely, it wasn't good. It could very well mean they'd decided they had enough and were working on the indictment. He'd know more in three days' time when they'd have to go before a judge if they wanted to hold him any longer. They'd be forced to reveal at least some of their cards then.

He was led into a private room for the visit with Inbar, "for his protection," the guards claimed. He suspected that it was because the cops wanted to listen in on their conversation.

Yariv reached out to stroke her face. Inbar flinched. He'd told his attorney over and over that he wanted to see her, but this was the first time she'd come. She hadn't even shown up at the courthouse for the initial remand hearing. He'd have to talk to her about that when he got out, but it would have to wait. Right now he needed her by his side, showing the world that she believed in him.

"How've you been, honey?" he asked with a smile.

Inbar didn't answer.

"It's all a bad dream, sweetheart. It'll be over soon, you'll see," he said, making the effort to sound caring and affectionate. He didn't know how long he could keep it up before he exploded.

Silence.

"This will only bring us closer. Our love is stronger than anything they can throw at us. As long as we stick together, nothing can hurt us," he said, tossing off a string of platitudes that almost stuck in his throat.

"Did you kill her," Inbar interrupted, her voice shaking.

"What? Of course not." He was shocked by the question. "How could you even ask such a thing?"

"She was your ex. I was celebrating our engagement with my friends in Eilat and you went to her. And you didn't tell me!" she fired back accusingly.

"It was a mistake . . . I'm sorry . . . I was drunk. I didn't know what I was doing. I missed you and I had too much to drink," Yariv said, struggling to sound apologetic, although he was furious with her. He'd been expecting her to offer comfort and support. He wasn't prepared for an attack.

"So it's my fault?"

"No, of course not. It's nobody's fault. What happened was . . ."

"I thought we didn't keep secrets from each other," she cut in again.

"We don't, I don't . . ."

"Really? What about the call you got that night, the one you said you didn't feel like answering. Who was it?"

"Forget about it, it's complicated. You wouldn't understand," he said, wanting to move on as quickly as possible. He'd had enough of this crap.

"Tell me."

"I already told you, it's complicated," he said dismissively.

"Too complicated for me to understand, right? You always treat me like I'm stupid," she said, getting up. "You know something, Yariv? I'm smart enough to know I don't have a future with you. It's over."

Flustered, Yariv rose. "What are you talking about, Inbar? You can't be serious?"

"I'm sorry. I . . . I can't go on like this." Tears welled in her eyes.

"I told your lawyer this was a bad idea, but he said you kept asking for me, so I came. I'm sorry. I can't do it anymore."

Yariv just stood there, paralyzed. Everyone was abandoning him. Even Regev wasn't answering his calls. He'd sent his lawyer to talk to him, threaten him if necessary. But the two-faced politician alleged that he was unaware of any legal opinion and only knew Yariv in passing. They hadn't spoken more than once or twice when he called to congratulate him for his fine work. "Me? Conceal a legal opinion? Never!" the lawyer exclaimed in an attempt to imitate Regev's response. He even claimed he didn't know Michal Poleg. "There were a few demonstrations, nothing major. I didn't pay much attention," he'd lied shamelessly.

He'd been so naive, such a fool. In retrospect, Yariv realized that they'd only mentioned the legal opinion in conversation. He had nothing in writing to prove that Regev knew anything about it. Whatever he told the police or the press, Regev would simply deny it. Who would people believe—a distinguished Knesset member or an ASA being held on suspicion of murder?

Yariv sank back down onto the plastic chair. "Are you okay?" he heard Inbar ask above him. He waved her away. Let her leave. He didn't need her. If he thought it would do any good, he'd try to persuade her to change her mind, but he knew it was pointless.

"I'm sorry," she said again. Stupid broad. She rapped lightly on the door.

The guard peered in. "Everything all right in here?" he asked.

"Yes. We're done. I'm ready to leave." Yariv heard her footsteps fading into the distance.

Chapter 84

THE phone broke Anat's concentration. She was sitting in her office going through the file again. In order to prepare a list of questions for Itai to ask Arami, she needed to know as much about him as possible. Since Itai wouldn't be interviewing him in any official capacity, Arami might simply refuse to answer. She had to do her homework. They'd only have one chance to get him to talk. If they screwed up, Ninio would walk. His lawyer would argue reasonable doubt on the basis of his supposed lack of memory and the fact that his blood and prints were only found on the outside of the door.

Meanwhile, Arami hadn't responded to Itai's e-mail. Anat was worried. They'd expected the promise of a paycheck to be an irresistible temptation. Were they too late? Had something happened to Arami?

At the moment, she was poring over the report of his interrogation by the immigration authorities when he was first caught crossing the border from Egypt. On her desk was every record of his contact with government officials that she'd managed to get her hands on. Her search had even turned up Hagos's deportation papers.

THE phone was still ringing. Itai.

"Hi," he said when she picked up. She felt a flutter in her stomach.

"Hi," she answered, suddenly finding it hard to speak.

"I got a reply from Arami," Itai stated matter-of-factly. Apparently, he was still upset that she'd leaned on him so hard the last time they met, but there was nothing she could do about it. She was just doing her job. "He ignored my invitation to get together and told me to write him a check and he'd send someone to pick it up."

"That's too bad, but we knew it was a possibility," she said in a needless attempt to console him. She could tell he was relieved.

"Can you forward his e-mail to me?" she asked, following the instructions she'd been given by the IT department. They could trace the IP address and find the server he'd used. With any luck, they'd be able to identify the location the message had been sent from.

"What do you need it for?" Itai asked, his suspicions aroused. "Don't you believe me?"

"No, of course I do. I just have to attach a copy to the requisition form for the trip," she lied.

"Give me your e-mail address." Anat spelled it out for him. "I'm sending it now," Itai informed her.

"So what's the next step?" he asked. Anat felt very guilty about what she was doing. She hated deceit and manipulation as much as Itai. He didn't deserve this, but she didn't have any choice. When it was all over, she'd try to make him understand.

"I have to think about it, talk to my bosses, fill them in," she said evasively before hanging up.

Chapter 85

ITAI paced back and forth in his office. He knew they had to move quickly. The wait was driving him crazy. The police didn't understand the Eritrean regime the way he did. If his slip of the tongue sent the cops to the consulate to ask for their help in locating one of their citizens, they'd never get a chance to talk to Arami. The Eritreans didn't give a damn about procedure and international conventions. They'd go after Arami themselves, and they'd find him and subject him to their own form of interrogation. The French police wouldn't have a clue, and the Israeli police would never hear from him again. He'd simply disappear. That's what happens when you collaborate with a corrupt tyranny that doesn't think twice about murdering its own citizens.

On the other hand, if he wanted to help Arami he might have no other choice than to go to the Eritreans himself. The deputy consul general had hinted that he had valuable information. He had to make sure he got it before the cops did. Unlike them, he knew who he was dealing with.

Itai shut his eyes. Going to the consulate was against everything he believed in. He didn't want any contact with those people whatsoever. If Michal were here, she'd scream her head off. "I can't believe you'd even consider such a thing!" he could hear her thunder. "How can you sell yourself out like that? Don't you understand what you're doing?"

Chapter 86

ALTHOUGH it didn't really come as a surprise, Anat was disappointed when she got the call from the IT department telling her where Arami was. Up until the last minute, she'd been hoping it was just a clerical error, some screwup by the Interior Ministry, the Border Police, the airlines. But it wasn't.

She threw her phone and car keys into her purse, turned off the computer, and stacked the papers strewn across her desk into something resembling a tidy pile. Using the window as a mirror, she did her best to discipline her frizzy hair.

As she walked out the door, she glanced behind her. She wouldn't be back here for a few days. They were very close, but they hadn't pinpointed Arami's location yet.

Her phone rang. Itai. He'd been calling all afternoon. She was reluctant to speak to him. They'd used him to find Arami, and now that the search was almost over, he was of no more value to them.

The phone beeped and she saw he'd sent her a text message: "We have to talk. It's urgent!!!" The three exclamation points were unexpected. She hadn't gotten the impression that Itai was the hysterical type.

Anat was about to call him back when she saw Yaron striding toward her. "Off to Paris, *mon amour*?" he asked with a lascivious grin.

"Beersheba," she answered drily.

Chapter 87

SHIMON Faro paced back and forth in his backyard. Even the sight of his beautiful flowers wasn't enough to calm his nerves. The light rain was another unwelcome irritation.

The whole operation he'd built up with the Africans was collapsing around him. He'd issued orders to do whatever it took to find the punk who'd stolen his money, but meanwhile, they'd come up empty. Half a million shekels had vanished into thin air.

It wasn't the money, it was the principle. It made him look weak. He'd been too complacent lately. Under pressure from Ehud Regev's hate campaign, the Ministry of the Interior had been making life even harder for the migrants, and he'd been raking it in. It was simple: when the government closed off one road, people looked for another one, some other route that would take them where they wanted to go. The way the government was playing into his hands had made him too confident, too smug. He'd lost the paranoia that was an essential feature of any successful businessman.

He'd just informed Boaz that he was relieving him of his banking duties. After what happened near the old bus station, he couldn't risk him being spotted there again. Too many people had seen him. Lucky the guys he sent found him in time and got him out of there. Otherwise, the cops would have picked him up and who knows what would have happened then.

Boaz had done his best to look indifferent, but Faro had seen the hint of a smile on his face. If it weren't for this lousy migraine, he would have given him a piece of his mind. Where was his gratitude, his loyalty? Without Faro, Boaz would be behind bars instead of in a fancy house in Ramat Hasharon. What did he think? That they were done with him? That they'd leave him alone and let him find some other clients? He could think again. He'd learn soon enough.

Faro looked up at the cloudy sky. It matched his foul mood. Who would he get to replace Boaz? It was always the same problem: he didn't have enough quality people.

He rang Itzik again. "Nothing yet. We're still on it." He could hear the apprehension in Itzik's voice. Boaz and the Africans were his responsibility. What was Itzik thinking, getting into a car chase and letting John fire a gun in the middle of the street? Where did he think he was? Chicago? The Wild West? Everyone knew how much Faro hated drama. It was dirty, it wasn't smart, and it wasn't good for business. That's not how you got to the top. Criminal negligence, that's what it was.

Of all the problems he had to deal with, the one that worried him most was the disappearance of the "General." Where the hell was he?

Chapter 88

ARAMI rose quickly when Anat walked into the room. He'd been picked up by local cops in Beersheba, who'd been given strict instructions not to tell him why they were bringing him in.

"What are you doing here, Inspector?" he asked, bewildered.

Yaron appeared behind her. Anat thought she saw a flash of fear cross Arami's face.

"Sit down, please. We just want to talk to you," she said with a smile. Her orders to the arresting officers had been clear: no cuffs, no use of force. He was merely wanted for questioning. The Internet café from which he'd sent the e-mail to Itai had been under surveillance for two days. She'd gotten the call a couple of hours ago: Arami had showed up and they were moving in.

"About what? Did something happen? I'm sorry that you haven't been able to reach me. My wife in Eritrea is very ill. I felt I had to get out of the city. I need time to think, to consider my options," he said apologetically.

Anat had sat down with David and Yaron to plan every detail of the interrogation, but now she wasn't sure they'd made the right decisions. She'd gotten so much new information in the past three days that she didn't know where to start.

"You told Itai Fisher you were issued a travel document, that you were going to France," she began. Itai and David were observing from the next room. It wouldn't surprise her to learn that Yochai was also watching the computer feed in his office in Tel Aviv. Dramatic moments like this were rare in the course of routine police work.

"Yes, well, I just needed to be alone. I've been going through a difficult time."

"So you took a vacation? In Beersheba?" Yaron said sarcastically.

Anat threw him an angry look. Provoking Arami would get them nowhere.

"I'm sorry . . . I've had a lot on my mind lately," he answered, lowering his eyes.

"Tell me," Yaron said, going back to the script they'd prepared, "do you happen to know a man by the name of Imanai Kabri?"

Arami's face froze. He straightened up in his chair as if the mention of the name had alerted an invisible puppet master to tug on his strings and pull him upright. His tentative smile vanished, replaced by a stern expression.

"Do you know him?" Yaron repeated, pushing one of the photos Itai had gotten from the Eritrean consulate across the table. It showed a high-ranking officer in uniform.

"Is that why I'm here?" Arami asked stiffly, crossing his arms over his chest. His expression shifted again. He now looked arrogant and self-assured. "Because of lies they told you at the consulate?"

Both cops remained silent.

"You're out of your mind. You can't be serious. Those people . . . that's why I'm here?" he spat contemptuously.

"No, that's not the reason," Anat said, shaking her head. The change in Arami was startling, even frightening. He had suddenly been transformed into someone else, the person he used to be: General Imanai Kabri of the Eritrean army.

"So what's this all about? Or did you just miss me?" he sneered. It was clear to Anat that he already knew the answer.

"We want you to tell us how you murdered Michal Poleg," she said, looking him straight in the eye.

Chapter 89

ITAI caught his breath. Because of the role he'd played, they'd "ignored regulations" and were allowing him to watch the interrogation from the observation room.

When the deputy consul general first showed him the picture, he didn't understand. The man in the photograph was dressed in a military uniform studded with medals and ribbons. He didn't look familiar.

"Concentrate on the face," the diplomat urged.

Itai didn't recognize him immediately. It took him a while to identify the man behind the uniform.

"Is that Arami?" he asked, his voice trembling.

"General Imanai Kabri," the deputy consul general corrected him.

"Arami is a general? What are you talking about?" Itai was suddenly covered in cold sweat.

Without answering, the man pushed another photograph across the desk.

"I don't believe you. It's not possible. I know Arami." Itai stood up. He was dealing with the representative of a corrupt and ruthless regime that would stop at nothing. They certainly wouldn't hesitate to invent malicious lies if it served their purpose.

The diplomat coolly produced further proof—more pictures and newspaper clippings. Itai was dumbstruck. Arami, or rather Imanai Kabri, was not merely a high-ranking officer; he was the general in charge of recruiting children. Itai knew very well what that meant. He'd heard enough stories from the asylum seekers about soldiers bursting into classrooms and dragging young boys outside. They were conscripted into the army on the spot, without so much as a chance to say good-bye to their families. For the next thirty years they would serve as soldiers or, more precisely, slaves of the ruling junta. There would be no reprieve, no leaves, no contact with their family. Hagos had been a teacher in Eritrea. He'd witnessed such incidents personally and had described them to Itai. He said the soldiers fired on anyone who dared to so much as look at them the wrong way.

As Itai stared at the pictures, the voice of his grandfather echoed in his head. A Holocaust survivor, he'd taught his grandson that wherever there are victims of war crimes, there are war criminals. The deputy consul general was standing over him. "Are you convinced now, Mr. Fisher? Not everything is black and white, is it?" he said imperiously.

Shaken, Itai left the consulate and immediately called Anat.

FROM his seat in the observation room, Itai heard Anat play the recording of Kabri's call to the tip line reporting that he'd seen Gabriel in Levinsky Park. He never had any intention of helping Gabriel. On the contrary, he was setting him up from the very beginning.

Kabri laughed derisively. Where was the man Itai had worked with for so long, the man he'd believed in, trusted, considered a friend?

Chapter 90

ANAT gazed at Kabri in silence, trying to conceal the storm raging inside her. Her suspicions had initially been aroused when she couldn't find his name on any recent flight manifest or Border Police record. The transcript of his interview at the camp where he was detained when he first arrived in Israel convinced her she was on the right track. He reported that the rest of his family was dead, murdered by soldiers. He was the sole survivor. So the stories about his sick wife and the children he'd left behind were total fiction, no more than a barefaced lie. Any lingering doubts evaporated when she asked another interpreter to translate the exchanges that had taken place between Arami and Gabriel in the interrogation room.

"We're waiting," Yaron barked, banging on the table. "Tell us how you killed her."

Kabri smirked, exposing his teeth. A shiver went down Anat's spine. She had been shocked by the information Itai brought back from the consulate. The man across from her wasn't only Michal Poleg's murderer, he was a war criminal who had brazenly been hiding out among his own victims.

"You think you frighten me?" he said haughtily. "You're nothing but rotten parasites. You don't know anything about me. You think if you bang on the table, I'll quiver in fear?"

Yaron started toward him, but Anat held him back. They could put Arami—Kabri—in Michal's apartment. They'd found his fingerprints there. But they were still missing two vital elements: hard evidence that he was responsible for her death, and a motive. The only way to get them was here in the interrogation room. It was up to her to do it.

"We can send you back there, you know," she said, training her eyes on him. "Just so it's clear, if you don't give us what we want, you'll be on a plane before the day is over. A general in the Eritrean army can't claim asylum."

Kabri waved his hand dismissively.

"We're giving you a chance. I suggest you take it," she went on. She was having trouble keeping her voice steady. The suspects she'd interrogated up to now had all been lightweights compared to Kabri.

He didn't answer.

They had no firm forensic evidence. It was all circumstantial. But Anat didn't have the slightest doubt he was the murderer. All the pieces had fallen into place.

"The people at the consulate are eager for us to turn you over to them. It seems they've been looking for you for quite some time," she said, trying a different tack. She had to find the right buttons to push to get a confession out of him.

"Before I say anything, I want to cut a deal," Kabri said calmly.

"I'm listening."

"I tell you what I know and you let me walk out of here and arrange for me to leave your pitiful country without any interference."

Yaron laughed.

"What do you know?" Anat asked, struggling to keep a poker face to hide the hope, and apprehensions, that were flooding her.

"I know about the crime syndicate you're trying to get your hands on. About the man you're after, what do you call him, the 'Banker'?" he said, giving her a self-satisfied smile.

"Let's hear what you have to say and then we'll decide. Start with Michal Poleg's murder."

Kabri laughed.

"You think we're still playing games here, Detective? You're not dealing with meek little Arami anymore. You can't manipulate me so easily. You want information? Fine. But you'll have to pay for it. Before I open my mouth, I want a lawyer and a signed agreement. And go get someone with authority in here. You're out of your depth, Inspector Nachmias."

Chapter 91

ITAI watched as Galit Lavie entered the room and closed the door behind her. Even her promise that Gabriel would be out by tonight and she'd try to arrange for him to be awarded compensation for false arrest weren't enough to temper the bile rising in his throat. He was utterly disgusted by the deal that was about to be concluded between the prosecutor and Kabri's attorney.

"You know her?" Anat asked, touching his shoulder lightly.

"We were in law school together in Jerusalem," Itai replied with a grateful smile. It was good to see a friendly face.

"I don't envy her," Anat said, taking a seat opposite him, "having to cut a deal like this. It turns my stomach."

"They're going to let him go," he said. It was more a statement than a question.

Anat nodded.

"Michal deserved better," Itai said with a sigh, cupping his face in his hands. "She would have found it even more repugnant than we do. She wouldn't have wanted her death to be an excuse to let this scum of the earth walk free."

"You know what? I'm not sure I agree with you." Anat leaned forward and lowered her voice to a whisper. "I think I've come to know Michal a little this past month. She never believed in compromising her principles, no matter what. We're finishing what she started. We're going to get the 'Banker.' A few hours from now, the bastard will be in custody."

"But he's not the one who killed Michal. And you're releasing a war criminal. Can you imagine the international uproar if a country like Hungary let a Nazi criminal go free for any reason whatsoever?"

They sat opposite each other in silence. Itai was still in shock from the revelation of Arami's true identity. And he was consumed by guilt. Michal tried to reach him that Saturday night. She left a message saying she'd uncovered something, that they'd been blind. But he didn't listen. Anat said it was Kabri who informed on Hagos, who told the Immigration Police that Hagos and his family had lived in Ethiopia for a few years. That was enough for the Interior Ministry to decide that he was an Ethiopian national and therefore eligible for deportation. Is that what Michal found out? Did she discover the truth about Arami?

"Galit promised they'd release Gabriel in a few hours," Itai said, breaking the silence.

"I heard. I want to apologize to him, to you, for everything. . . . But you have to understand . . . he turned himself in, he confessed. . . . We couldn't ignore that."

"I know. It's not your fault. The whole issue of the asylum seekers isn't easy. It's not just a matter of what to do about them, how to help them. You also need to understand where they're coming from." For some reason he felt the urge to shield her from the guilt he could hear in her voice.

Anat rewarded him with a grateful smile.

The door opened and Galit Lavie came out.

"It's done," she announced.

Chapter 92

THERE were four of them in the room: Galit and Anat on one side of the table, Kabri and his lawyer on the other.

"We agreed to keep this short and to the point," the lawyer snapped. Galit gave him a dirty look. She was well aware of the need for defense attorneys, but she still found them hard to stomach—particularly when they represented people like Kabri.

"Let me remind you," she said in an authoritative tone, "according to the terms of our agreement, your client is required to answer all questions fully and truthfully. If I'm not convinced that he's holding up his end of the bargain, the deal's off. Is that clear?"

The counselor nodded.

"Are you responsible for the death of Michal Poleg?" Anat decided to open with the most fundamental question.

"Yes," Kabri answered without hesitation. She breathed a silent sigh of relief. Given all the twists and turns in the investigation, she was worried he might deny it.

"How?"

"I hit her on the back of the neck with a beer bottle. She fell and banged her head on the table," Kabri stated with no more emotion than if he were talking about the weather. Anat wondered what Yaron and Yochai in the observation room were thinking. Gabriel had been unable to describe how the murder took place, but Kabri was providing a precise account, including details that had never been released to the public, details only the killer himself could know.

"Why?"

"She found out about my connection with the 'Banker.' She saw us together. She threatened to expose me. She accused me of being responsible for Hagos's deportation."

"Did she know you informed on him?"

"No. It was just a guess."

"Why did you go to the Immigration Police?"

"Hagos latched on to me like a leech. He was getting in the way, making it hard for me to do my job for the bank." He was sitting erect in his seat, as if he were still wearing the uniform with the gold stars on the epaulets that Anat had seen in the pictures Itai showed her.

"What job was that?"

"I brought in new clients. All the migrants passed through OMA. I heard what they needed and offered them a way to get it."

"What about your work for the police?"

"Another source of information," he said cavalierly.

"Do you know Yariv Ninio?" Anat couldn't resist asking.

"I know who he is."

"Were you working together?" she asked, hoping that was one arrest she'd be able to justify. The order for his release had already been signed. Like Gabriel, he would be out before the end of the day.

"No." Anat was ready with her next question when he went on. It was not what she was expecting. "He banged on the door when I was in Michal's apartment. He was drunk. Michal and I were arguing. She wanted me to go to the police and rat out the bank. She tried to get rid of him, but he started forcing his way in. I was standing behind the door. I slammed it into him. He fell down. His face was bleeding. A few minutes later he left."

It all made sense now: the blood and the prints on the outside of the door, the bruises on Ninio's face, maybe even his blurred memory. If the door struck him hard enough, he could have had a concussion. At least that mystery was solved. Kabri was sitting there looking smug, waiting calmly for the next question. "What did you do after you killed her?"

"I was planning to leave the city, lie low for a while. I was about to take off when Gabriel told me he was in Michal's apartment and her neighbor saw him there. It was a golden opportunity. I just had to put you on his tail and then you'd look for him instead of me. I told him to go hide in the park and I called the tip line. But your guys screwed up. So I arranged to meet him in an alley and told some thugs where he'd be. I said the cops were after him and there was a big reward waiting for them if they turned him in. But he got away from them."

"So you decided to pay him to confess to Michal's murder?"

"No, it wouldn't have been worth the money to me. But the bank didn't like it that the cops were swarming the neighborhood. They wanted them out of the way. So I did the math and I figured this way Gabriel would get the money to ransom his sister and the cops would get their killer."

"Were you involved in his sister's abduction?"

"No."

"So you hung Gabriel out to dry and helped his sister?"

"It wasn't personal. I liked Gabriel. I wasn't out to hurt him. But I knew if I helped Liddie, he'd agree to confess. And as long as it served my purposes, I was glad to do it."

Anat got a sour look on her face.

"People like you," Kabri said with a bitter expression in his eyes, "you can't understand people like us. The world we grew up in is a jungle. If you're not on the side of the predators, you get eaten. It's the only way to survive."

Galit gestured for her to move on. There was no reason to listen to his political manifesto.

"Did the bank know you killed Michal?" Anat asked, adopting the term he'd used.

"I was going to tell them, but then Gabriel came along and I decided to keep it to myself. I didn't think they'd be pleased."

"Why not? She was interfering in their business, wasn't she?"

"Not enough to get her killed."

"But you told them later, didn't you?"

"Yes. When my picture appeared on the Internet. It fucked everything up."

"What story did you give them?"

"I said I was in Michal's apartment when Yariv Ninio showed up and murdered her. I knew they'd find a way to use it. Considering the state he was in, I was hoping Ninio wouldn't remember what happened that night. In return for the information, I said I wanted money and a safe place to hide."

"Did you make a lot of money from the bank?" Anat asked, changing direction.

"I worked on commission. It pays better than interpreting for the cops or washing dishes, if that's what you're asking, but not enough to get rich. I figured I needed thirty thousand dollars to get myself out of the country. I already had two-thirds of it."

"Why didn't the bank help you leave after you told them about Ninio?"

"It's almost impossible these days. Ehud Regev has the Interior Ministry running scared. They're not giving out any travel documents."

"Do you have family in Eritrea?"

For the first time, Kabri lowered his eyes. "No. No one," he said, looking back up at her. "I had a wife and three kids. They were killed."

Anat was silent, not knowing how to respond.

"One day they decided I was a traitor and came after me and my family. I was the only one who got out alive," he said quietly.

Anat opened the file in front of her. She sensed herself starting to feel sorry for Kabri, and she didn't like it. He didn't deserve her sympathy.

"Do you know this man?" she asked, pointing to the photograph Michal had taken.

"Boaz Yavin. He lives in Ramat Hasharon."

"Is he the 'Banker'?"

"Yes."

"Who does he work for?"

Kabri again gave her the contemptuous look that made her blood run cold.

"He works for the bank."

Chapter 93

BOAZ had just finished reading *Winnie the Pooh* to Sagie for the third time when the doorbell rang. He wondered who it could be at this hour. Irit was at a Pilates class and the older children were already in bed.

Life was good. After the mugging, Faro had finally taken him off migrant detail. No more Wednesday rounds, no more old bus station, no more stench of garbage and poverty, no more smoke-filled rooms, no more "General," no more Itzik. He still had the cuts and bruises on his face, but they would heal. He told Irit and anyone else who asked that he tripped on a pothole in the street. No one questioned his story. Why should they?

The bell was joined by knocking on the door. A little face peered out from one of the bedrooms.

"Who is it, Daddy?"

"Go back to bed. You have to get up for school tomorrow," he said, going downstairs.

Boaz had just reached the door when a voice shouted, "Police, open up." His blood turned to ice.

Chapter 94

GABRIEL petted Liddie's head. "It's over?" she asked haltingly. "It's really over? You're free for good?"

"Yes, Liddie, I'm free. They let me go." Finding out that Arami had killed Michal shocked him just as much as learning that he'd been a general in the Eritrean army and had been personally responsible for abducting children. It was because of people like him that his mother had urged them to leave Eritrea before it was too late.

They were in Itai's apartment. Their host had gone out to give them some time alone.

Gabriel had never had the slightest suspicion that Arami wasn't a true friend. He was sure that he was doing his best to help him. But Itai said he'd informed on him to the police and sent the boys in the street after him. He'd trusted Arami completely, counted on him to rescue Liddie and take care of her. Now it turned out that he'd sent his sister into the lion's den for a second time. Itai said he shouldn't blame himself, that Arami had pulled the wool over everyone's eyes. At least he kept his part of the bargain with Gabriel. He did look out for Liddie as he promised, even if he was only doing it to protect himself.

Gabriel was very glad the Israelis had caught him. They'd give him what was coming to him, not just for killing Michal but for hurting so many people. Arami thought he could flee to Israel and his past would be forgotten. But now justice would be done. His crimes had caught up with him, following him across thousands of miles to another continent, another country. Gabriel was happy he'd played a small role in that.

"What happens now? What are we going to do?" Liddie asked, raising her eyes to him.

He didn't reply. Itai said they were welcome to stay as long as they liked, but Gabriel knew they couldn't remain here. Itai had done enough. Now he had to stand on his own two feet.

They were holding a memorial service for Michal tomorrow. Itai promised to take him. Gabriel wanted to say good-bye, to thank her for everything she did for him, to apologize for not being able to save her. And he wanted to meet her parents and tell them what a kind and wonderful daughter they had.

Liddie coughed. It was a dry cough that made her thin body shake. He had to take good care of her. He'd failed her last time. He wouldn't let it happen again.

How would they survive? Where would they live? He hadn't slept all night, just lay awake in bed listening to the rain. He had to find someplace warm for Liddie. How would he get the money? Itai said the government might pay him compensation for his arrest, but that would take time. Meanwhile, they had nothing to live on and he didn't even have a job. He'd go to the restaurant tomorrow morning. Maybe Amir would give him back his job as a dishwasher. Amir was a good man. He paid well, and on time.

Gabriel went on stroking Liddie's head. He'd dreamt of this moment for so long, and now that it was here, his heart was heavy. There was no place for them in this country, but where else could they go? There was no place for them anywhere in the world.

Chapter 95

EVEN though Yariv knew that there would be no one there to welcome him, the sight of the empty apartment was like a knife in his heart. He stood in the doorway of his former home, now devoid of furniture, of Inbar, of a future. He couldn't bring himself to go in. His legs shaking, he leaned on the doorpost for support.

Ever since his arrest, he'd been picturing the day of his release. He envisioned himself in front of a bevy of media people, denouncing the police, accusing them of persecuting an innocent man.

But no one was waiting for him outside Abu Kabir except his parents. They drove all the way to his house in silence. "We'll wait here in case you want to come home with us," his father said when they arrived. Irritated, he snarled, "Don't bother. Why should I go home with you? I'm not a kid anymore."

"We'll wait fifteen minutes," his mother said quietly. He climbed out of the car, slamming the door behind him.

His career was over. Kobi informed him that the Bar Association had initiated an action for his disbarment. Although he'd been cleared of any involvement in Michal's murder, the fact that he concealed the legal opinion wasn't going away. Whatever happened, he could never go back to the State Attorney's Office.

Yariv's eyes filled with tears. Where did he go wrong? What did he do to deserve this? He cursed the day he agreed to take on the cases against the illegals. If it weren't for that one stupid decision, his life wouldn't be crashing down around him.

"Would you like to come in?" he heard behind him. It was his nosy neighbor, Sarah Glazer.

"She moved out yesterday. She took everything with her."

Yariv didn't respond.

"Come inside. I'll make you a cup of tea."

"Thank you," he said, surprising himself.

Chapter 96

ITAI fidgeted in the backseat of the patrol car. Abetting in a police raid, even if only indirectly, made him very uncomfortable. On top of that, he was forced to watch Eylon from the Economic Crime Unit brazenly hitting on Anat.

Anat had called him a few hours after he left the police station and asked him to show them the exact location of the restaurant on Fein Street. The higher-ups had decided to move in right away, even before they'd finished interrogating Boaz Yavin. They had the chance for a great photo op—real-time pictures of a crack team busting up an illegal operation—and they didn't want to miss it. But they had to hurry, before the weekend papers were put to bed.

They'd driven by the restaurant almost an hour ago, and then parked a few blocks away. "We'll be able to listen in on what's going on from a safe distance," Anat explained.

"Did you know she studied accounting with my brother," Eylon said, twisting his head around and nodding toward Anat, who was sitting beside him in the front. "She was on the dean's list four years running."

Anat smiled sheepishly.

Turning back to Anat, he said, "You ought to leave Special Investigations and come over to us. You'd be a real star."

Over the radio they could hear the commanding officer issue his final instructions for the raid. Anat adjusted her position, moving closer to Eylon. Their shoulders were touching.

"So what do you say, Anat? You and me? We'd make a great team. Just say the word and I'll arrange for your transfer."

Why don't I have his balls, Itai thought to himself. I wish I could talk to her like that.

"Go!" the officer commanded, silencing Eylon.

They heard the sound of running footsteps and heavy breathing. Itai's thoughts turned to Michal. It was a sad irony that what she'd been trying to achieve in the last days of her life had been made possible by her death: Yariv Ninio could now wave good-bye to the State Attorney's Office and the cops were putting the "Banker" out of business.

Gabriel and Liddie were moving out tomorrow, even though Itai insisted they were welcome to stay. The young man made an effort to sound confident, but Itai could tell that he was nervous about striking out on his own. Instead of trying to change his mind, he decided to do what Michal had always wanted. He'd talk to his uncle at the art school and show him Gabriel's drawings. It might not help, but it certainly couldn't hurt. Sometimes you had to make things happen, not just sit back and wait for them to happen on their own. He'd learned that lesson from Michal, both by her life and by her death.

"We're in. Move to the back room," the commander shouted.

"The moment of truth," Eylon said breathlessly.

Michal was bringing down a crime syndicate. Who would have imagined it was possible? Definitely not me, Itai thought. I never believed in her enough.

"Talk to me. What do you see?" they heard over the radio.

"Nothing. The place has been emptied out. They must have known we were coming. I repeat, nothing here. The room is empty."

Chapter 97

BOAZ Yavin jumped up in relief when Borochov appeared in the doorway. Itzik had given him clear instructions about what to do if the cops ever picked him up. He'd followed them to the letter. As soon as they said they were bringing him in for questioning, he demanded to speak to his lawyer, Shuki Borochov.

Once they got to the station, they tried to persuade him to talk, saying it was in his best interest to cooperate and it would be awhile before the lawyer could get there. But he kept silent. "Never forget, the cops are small change compared to us," Itzik had warned him, and the words resounded in his head like alarm bells.

Boaz thought of Irit and the kids. The cops didn't even give him a chance to say good-bye, refusing to wait until Irit got back from her Pilates class. He had to ask their next-door neighbor, Maya, to watch the children until his wife got home. From the look on Maya's face, he knew she'd be spending the next hour on the phone, spreading the news. He'd never be able to look his neighbors in the eye again.

What did they want from him? The arms deal? The migrants? Who put them on to him?

"Thank you for coming. I'm very grateful," Boaz stammered. Borochov was Faro's personal attorney, and Itzik said he could pull a rabbit out of a hat. Now he'd use his magic to make Boaz's problems disappear. At least, that's what he was hoping for.

"Did you say anything?" Borochov fired at him as he took a seat. The expression on his face didn't give anything away.

"Not a word, I swear," Boaz said, sitting back down.

"Good. Keep it that way." The lawyer's tone was as stiff as his face.

"Are my kids okay? Did you talk to my wife?" Boaz asked anxiously.

"Pay attention, Yavin," Borochov cut in. "You keep your mouth shut. Whatever they ask you, you say, 'On the advice of counsel, I invoke my right to remain silent.' Got it?"

"Yeah, I got it. But do you know why I'm here? What do they have on me?" Borochov's iciness was spooking him. Boaz was no fool. He knew he wasn't the attorney's real client. He'd tell him to do whatever was best for Faro.

"I don't know what they have and I don't care. The only thing that matters is that you keep your mouth shut. Not a word about Faro, arms deals, the 'General,' or anything else."

Boaz's throat was dry and his hands were shaking. They wanted to make a scapegoat out of him.

"Don't worry, I'd never do anything to harm Shimon," he said in a trembling voice. "But you've got to understand. I could be in real trouble. . . . I don't know . . ."

"Take it easy," Borochov said, smoothing his tie. "Let's not blow things out of proportion. It's not that bad. All they can accuse you of is some kind of white-collar crime. Worst-case scenario, you get five to seven inside. Best-case scenario, you pay a fine. It could be much worse, believe me."

Boaz stared at him in shocked silence. Seven years? How would he survive that long in prison?

"Hey, kid, don't look so scared. It's not the end of the world," Borochov said, patting him on the shoulder and smiling for the first time. "Seven years is the most you can get. With time off for good behavior, you'll be out in four. What's four years?"

Boaz remained silent. Unlike Borochov, he failed to see the bright side.

"Be a good boy and Faro will look out for you. Your family will be well taken care of. Faro can be very generous."

Boaz still didn't respond. They were sending him to his grave and they wanted him to be happy about it?

"Are you listening, Yavin? Did you get what I said? It's simple arithmetic. There's nothing to think about. You keep your mouth shut and you're compensated for your trouble. You talk and . . . well, I don't have to tell you what happens then, do I?"

Boaz shook his head. No, Borochov didn't have to spell it out. The message was loud and clear. The only question left to answer was the amount of the compensation he'd be getting. He was going to demand a very high price for his silence.

Chapter 98

FARO put down the phone and breathed a sigh of relief. Borochov had assured him he didn't have to worry about Boaz, he'd taken care of it. Without Yavin's testimony, the cops had nothing.

As soon as Faro got the word that the accountant had been picked up, he shut down the whole banking operation. If the cops came looking, they wouldn't find anything. At most, a few Africans drinking coffee.

The "General" had turned on him, but at least he'd given him time to regroup. He could have ratted on Faro, but he didn't. He only handed them Yavin. Shimon appreciated the consideration. Although their relationship ended on a sour note, the "General" did him a little favor at the last minute. As a reward, his death would be quick. Shimon wouldn't make him suffer.

Yavin's future was less certain. The man liked money, no question about it. But did he like it enough to be able to cope with prison life? Shimon had people inside who'd be keeping an eye on him. If he showed any sign of breaking or having second thoughts, they'd have no choice but to silence him for good.

It was a shame he had to close the bank. He'd built up a thriving business and had been planning to expand it. But in the final analysis, he couldn't complain. He'd be well compensated for his pain and suffering. The customers who'd emptied their accounts in time had gotten their money, less commission, of course. The rest weren't so lucky. The bank was no longer offering its services to the public. If Yavin were available, he'd have him draw up a balance sheet. As a rough estimate, Faro thought the unclaimed funds totaled over twenty million. Not bad.

Faro was curious to see how the government would deal with the wreckage he'd left behind. The migrants now had nowhere safe to keep their money, and a lot of them had lost everything. When the inevitable crime wave struck, the authorities would be very nostalgic for the days of Faro's bank. But the idiots still didn't get it. Without him, things were going to be a lot worse.

Faro was through with the migrants. He'd find another outlet for his business acumen. He already had a few ideas.

Chapter 99

ANAT hurried down the stairs, hoping to leave the frenzy of work behind before they called her back. There was rioting around the old bus station, migrants attacking migrants, Israelis attacking migrants, migrants attacking Israelis, Israelis attacking Israelis. There were incidents of looting, and a few Molotov cocktails had been hurled at the African restaurants. They'd gotten the word that MK Ehud Regev was on his way, which would just add fuel to the fire. In situations like this, they'd need all hands on deck. Reinforcements would be called in from every division.

Before that happened, Anat needed a break. She had to breathe fresh air. Eylon had called and told her that Boaz Yavin wasn't talking. They were hoping he was the loose thread that would help them unravel a whole crime organization, but it turned out that there was a tight knot in that thread and they couldn't undo it.

They were still obliged to release Kabri. He'd kept his part of the bargain and given up the "Banker." It wasn't his fault if they couldn't use Yavin to get to his boss.

Anat got into her car. She'd been going nonstop for the past month. Economic Crimes would handle Yavin; that wasn't her domain. An unfamiliar song was playing on the radio. It was four in the afternoon, still light out. Winter would be over soon. She couldn't remember the last time she'd left work before dark.

She glanced at the people strolling leisurely down Ibn Gvirol Street. The cafés were full. Sometimes it seemed like she was the only one in the city who had a job to go to.

Anat felt deflated. What now? Her mother was right: she buried herself in her work. Here she was, with time on her hands, and she had no one to spend it with.

She hesitated a moment and then grabbed her phone, pressing the number quickly before she got cold feet. Itai picked up on the second ring. The other day in the patrol car, she'd found it hard to resist the urge to take his hand. There was no point in denying it: she'd been attracted to him from the moment she first set eyes on him.

"What's up?" he asked. She could hear the wariness in his voice.

"Nothing . . . I just," she stammered. What was she thinking? To him she was a cop, nothing more. This was very unprofessional of her. "I just thought," she said, taking a deep breath in an effort to slow her racing heart, "I thought now that it's all over . . . you might like . . ."

Silence.

She was lousy at this.

She heard raised voices on the other end. How could she be such a moron? In the middle of the riots—that's when she decided to ask him out.

"I'd be very happy to get together with you," he said, breaking the awkward silence.

Anat felt her face go red.

"Actually," he went on, "I was also thinking . . . I mean . . . you owe me a trip to Paris." It was Itai's turn to stammer.

They set a time and place. Anat smiled to herself. If anything came of this, they'd have to find a better "how did you two meet" story than "we were at a funeral."

She looked at her reflection in the window of the car alongside her. She didn't have anything to wear. Maybe she would use the free time she'd grabbed to look for a dress. It had been a very long time since she'd gone shopping for herself.

Her phone started ringing and the beeper in her bag came to life.

"Nachmias?" It was Amnon, the duty officer. "Male body at 25 Ben Yehudah Street. Possible homicide."

Anat glanced at her reflection again. Her hair was its usual frizzy self.

"On my way," she said.

Acknowledgments

ONE of the most enjoyable stages of writing a book is the research. It gives me a chance to delve into new realms and meet new people. In all my previous books, I had some knowledge of the subject before I began. But I knew nothing at all about the issues dealt with here. The journey I was led on, the people I met, and the things I learned had a strong impact on me, and they continue to resonate with me. I owe a sincere debt of gratitude to all those without whose help this book could not have been written.

To my editor, Noa Menhaim, who was by my side every step of the way. A full partner in the process, she accompanied me on visits to the neighborhoods around the old bus station in south Tel Aviv, offered her support and excellent advice, and, most important, was brutally honest and never cut me any slack. Quite a few of the ideas in this book are hers, and I am pleased to say that because of her, quite a few of my own ideas will never see the light of day. Noa, I thank you from the bottom of my heart.

To my mentor, Amnon Jackont. Although he did not edit this book, his advice and the things he taught me are with me wherever I go.

To Michal Pinchuk, the director of ASSAF, Aid Organization for Refugees and Asylum Seekers in Israel, who was the first to introduce me to the subject. She provided me with fundamental concepts that were a huge help to me. The story Itai tells at the funeral is based on real events related by Orit Rubin of ASSAF at a conference organized by Physicians for Human Rights in collaboration with the Sheba Medical Center at Tel Hashomer and UNHCR, the UN Refugee Agency, in Israel.

To Sharon Harel, assistant protection officer at UNHCR in Israel, who sat down with me several times to share her profound knowledge of the issue. Her valuable insights and balanced approach were a constant inspiration to me. The tour she took me on, the things I saw there, and the asylum seekers I met are carved deeply in my memory.

To Michal Zmiri, the social worker who runs the women's shelter at the old bus station, whose description of herself as "doing God's work" is a gross understatement. To Ilan Lonai, for the riveting tour of the area one rainy Friday afternoon, and the personal stories he shared with me.

To Irit Gabber Shahar, who patiently answered my abundant questions and offered me insights from her experience as a UN worker. I am also grateful to her for taking the time to read an early draft of the book and for her valuable comments.

To all those who are so near, and yet so far from us, who agreed to allow me a glimpse into their harsh lives and tell me their stories. I was astounded and aghast to hear about the ordeals they had been through. To my chagrin, I must admit that it was only after I started researching the subject that I began to notice their presence among us and actually see them in the street.

To attorney Yadin Elam, who deals daily, and with inestimable dedication, with cases many lawyers are unwilling to touch. He is a credit to his profession. The manifesto he outlined for me (including citations of court decisions) clarified the relevant issues and was of great help to me when I sat down to write this book. By the end of our meeting I understood how Itai would behave and, no less important, exactly who Yariv was.

To attorney Erez Melamed, for his legal advice and for referring me to sources of information that proved to be extremely useful.

My research was greatly aided by members of the police force. I found them to be dedicated, professional, and astute. As a citizen of Israel, I am thankful that such people are on the force.

The tour I was taken on by Chief Inspector Aviv Shpentzer of the Levinsky Precinct, in which he explained the issues from the perspective of the police, was one of the most thought-provoking experiences of my life. The commitment and sensitivity with which the police handle the social problems in south Tel Aviv is inspiring.

I wish to thank Chief Superintendent Miri Peled, who agreed to talk to me about her work as a detective. After meeting with her, I knew the hero of this book would be a policewoman.

Finally, I am extremely grateful to Hila Gersi, who spent long hours explaining police procedure and answering a multitude of questions. Our meetings were invariably interesting, informative, and enlightening. It was an honor for me to get to know her.

To the journalist Yaniv Kobovitz from *Haaretz*. The stories he told me during a tour of Lod sparked the urge to look more deeply into the subject.

To my brother-in-law, Nimrod Ram, my CTO, for explaining computers, and to my mother-in-law, Dr. Daniela Ram, my CSO, for explaining genetics (and, of course, for babysitting the kids). And last but not least, to my sister, Einav Shoham, my legal adviser.

To my brother, Shiran Shoham, who read an early draft of the book and offered me his unique perspective.

Thanks also go to Lee Feller, for highly pertinent comments on the first draft of this book.

To Tamar Bialik, who is always my first reader, for her wise comments and for all of our work together.

To the director, Eitan Zur, who watched the book unfold from the beginning, for cues and suggestions, and especially his eagerness to learn more.

To Eilon Ratzkovsky, for his support and encouragement.

To Kinneret Zmora-Bitan, for their unswerving support for so many years (this is my tenth book!), and particularly to Yoram Roz and Eran Zmora for their sage guidance.

To Ziv Lewis, for opening the door to the publication of my books in other languages, for championing my choice of subject, for his commitment and encouragement, and for his instant replies to my e-mails at any hour of the day.

To Riki Danieli, for her perceptive advice throughout the

years. She always helps me understand what I need to do and how to do it.

To Daniel Roz, who is about to hear much more often that "Liad Shoham is looking for you."

And, of course, to Ido Peretz, for his devoted efforts.

To Sara Kitai, for her smooth, deft translations, which leave readers wondering whether my books were originally written in English.

To my parents, Haya and Avi, for their never-ending support.

And last, but actually first, to my children, Rona and Uri, and my wife, Osnat, for all their love.

About the Author

LIAD SHOHAM is Israel's leading crime writer and a practicing attorney with degrees from Jerusalem's Hebrew University and the London School of Economics. All his crime novels have been critically acclaimed bestsellers. He lives in Tel Aviv with his wife and two children.

ML   1-15